# The Earth Bleeds At Night

## Anthology of Horror

AN EERIE RIVER PUBLISHING ANTHOLOGY

# The Earth Bleeds At Night

EDITED BY HOLLEY CORNETTO

Eerie River Publishing
www.EerieRiverPublishing.com
Kitchener, Ontario Canada

Subdivision of Eerie Ventures Ltd.

This book is a work of fiction. Names, characters, places, events, organizations and incidents are either part of the author's imagination or are used fictitiously. Any resemblance to actual persons, living or dead, or actual events is purely coincidental.

Published January 2025
Paperback ISBN: 978-1-998112-42-5
Hardcover ISBN: 978-1-998112-43-2

Editor: Shona Kinsella
Cover Art: Lynne Hansen

Book Formatting by Michelle McLachlin

**EERIE RIVER PUBLISHING**
www. EerieRiverPublishing.com

Jonathan Louis Duckworth

M. Edusa

David-Jack Fletcher

C.M. Forest

Philip Fracassi

Maxwell I. Gold

Laurel Hightower

Patrick Hurley

Ai Jiang

Jenny Kiefer

Joe Koch

Dexter McLeod

Christi Nogle

Christopher O'Halloran

Em Starr

Richard Thomas

SJ Townend

Mark Towse

Ally Wilkes

# Contents

For all those who believe in the power of story, but especially for Michelle
River, for her tireless work to promote indie horror and her friendship.
Without her, this book would not exist.
-Holley


I dedicate this anthology to my children, Eloise and Daxton.
May they one day grasp the profound joy of creation as deeply as I do.
- Michelle

# Dark Abscissions: When the Last Tree Bleeds

by Maxwell I. Gold

In the beginning I remembered how
the trees were endless,
plentiful and strong
like the gods themselves once were

standing without reproach. And there was
no blood, no steel, no false pragmatism
attempting to fell these Great Things;
nor the wild and dark ambition

of a flesh-race forged
in the bowels of their own
insecurity and dastardly innovations,
but the infinity of Trees.

What madness mattered not,
soon after I saw the
smog-faces and silver clouds
roll across the horizon

until at its grotesque pinnacle,
the gray and gloom-gutted maw
of some wicked inevitability
projected shrapnel futures,

and cut up somedays
through the teeth of man-made gods
where soon the trees were
bloody and tired,

scattered across a dying world;
with one thousand twisted
and decayed trunks, nestled beneath
a crown of hunter-green thorns,

they loomed high above
the plastic and pitiful cyber-scraps
which dug remorselessly
into the dirt-bosom of the earth.

Without heed, or care, or consequence
for the wanton despair that
plagued their own civilization. The trees
bled with seed, sap, and crimson-colored syrups

that began to eat away at concrete foundations
whereupon every pathetic structure followed,
brick by brick, bone by bone
beneath a pallid and tattered sky

began the darkest abscission
as I saw the last us swell with rage.
Swallowed inside the broken
and burnt corpse of the Earth,
there was nothing left except cinder and death

In the end I remembered how
the trees were few,
bloody and tired
like a ghostly mythology
whose blood stained the sands of the world, and my soul.

# The Dreaming Box

## Laurel Hightower

I don't know where I go when the music isn't playing.

I don't like that. It bothers me to wake without waking—to simply be here, in the dark, fully conscious but without anything to ground me. Who am I when the dreaming box is closed? Where do I go? Am I resting, peaceful, as the priest wished for me while my coffin was lowered into the earth? I'd like to believe that. I don't want to think about the alternative. That there is no place safe, nowhere I can hide from the suffering he inflicts each night when he comes.

It comes back to me when the tinkling music circles around to the beginning of the song. There may have once been words to accompany it, lyrics to soften the saddening edge of minor chords pulling at my insides, but they're lost in that dark place of no memory. All I have are the notes, the ones that make me think of a jewelry box I had as a little girl. The kind that plays a song when you open its lid, lined in satin as pink and smooth as the fabric in my coffin.  A tiny, plastic ballerina twirls slowly in time to the tune, listing to the left in an endless arabesque. The closing of the lid has done that to her—whenever she is no longer needed, she's silenced by force. Shoved to the side and down to make room for a child's whims.

Dread stirs in my belly. It is no child who controls my dreaming box. It's a man. I remember that now, and memory is no comfort. The image of him is hazy, and I wish it could stay that way, blur the stark reality. It never does. He won't let it. Instead his memory strides through my mind, pulling me from the safety of my grave, violently dispelling the rolling fog that tries to obscure the sharpest jabs of what happened. Of what's still happening.

"Saw your mom today, Tiny Dancer."

His voice comes from behind me and I flinch at the name. Tiny

Dancer? Is that me? I don't know—I can't see myself. I can see nothing beyond the intermittent blinking of colored lights. Darkness broken by shining stars of purple, green, red and blue, the light fractured into beams that call to mind a magic I've all but forgotten. It doesn't penetrate far, and I can't see him, either.

But I feel him.

The prickling rash of his stubble against my thigh. Grimy fingers with ripped and dried cuticles brush roughly across my face and throat. My face pressed into his armpit as he leans over me for the best angle. He's smeared on an overpowering gel deodorant and the chemical representation of pine is all I can smell. His toenails are too long, one of them jagged in the middle where a piece broke off in the flesh of my calf, and the callouses on the sides of his big toes rub my ankles raw. I want to make him happy so I don't say anything about these discomforts, instead pushing them away as best I can and trying to mask my grimaces as a pleasure I don't believe exists.

More than any of that is the weight of him, over my body, and my life.

No, not my life. My death. My belly is crushed, my chest struggling for space to expand and fill the lungs within. My breathing is shallow and everything hurts, but I didn't say no. Did you think I had? Would you respect me more if I fought? But it wasn't like that. It was the only way to feel close to him, so I courted his touch. I craved it, even as it hurt, because the alternative was a disinterest so cold it froze my soul. I'm not the first woman to have sex I didn't want in service of some other need. I won't be the last.

I wonder if that's why I stayed alive so much longer than the others.

"She's pretty broken up," he says in a conversational tone. The music *plinks* discordantly for a note or two, and the unease in my belly grows.

*Mom.* The name calls to mind feelings rather than features. A shielding warmth in winter. A cool hand on my fevered brow. Arms that stayed open to me, no matter what I did or said. Grief for a loss I barely understand blooms in my chest and I feel the dread of whatever comes next. Like a kayaker hearing the rush of a waterfall, powerless to stop their descent over the edge to knowledge I don't want.

"I comforted her as best I could." A phantom touch grazes my shoulder and I shudder. I notice for the first time my skin is bare, goosebumps gathering my flesh painfully tight. My nipples harden and I want to cover myself but I cannot move. Will he misread my physical response to cold and dread as desire? The thought turns my stomach and I wish I could pull my body inward, shield the most tender parts of myself. Still I cannot move, though my limbs are light, nearly weightless.

"She always tells me what a *blessing* I am." There is no consciousness of irony in his tone. He has soaked up the praise and made it part of his persona. Good neighbor. Caring friend. Grieving lover. I grind my teeth and taste blood. Why does he get to see her, when I am trapped here in the darkness of his making? Why does he get to smell her, that light scent of the floral soap she uses, the clinging aroma of the flavored coffee she drinks all day?

*Why is he still alive after what he did?*

I want to scream the words, spit them in his face. Claw at his eyes, stomp on his dick. I want to feel the bulge and burst of testicles beneath my heel, picture coils of vas deferens unwinding through a split of wrinkled flesh. Wrap my hands around his throat and squeeze, steal his breath before he can steal mine. All the things I should have done when it would have made a difference. Now it's too late. I can't make a sound unless he wishes it.

"Goldie's not the same," he says with no real concern for my golden girl. Her name brings more pain, opens a deep pit of knowledge of all that is beyond my reach. I don't want it. I don't want to remember. Loss punches through my chest, makes it hard to breathe. I don't need breath anymore, but that doesn't stop the hurt.

His voice is somewhere else now, still behind me. Always moving in the dark as the blinking lights glow around me. I can't see him, though the light must be growing. My left hand is visible, low at my side, the fingers gracefully splayed. For some reason the sight of those fingers increases my unease, spreading its cold tendrils through my veins.

"She barely gets up from the rug in front of the door, your mom said. Doesn't wag, won't make eye contact. I tried to help. She let me pet her, but she didn't react. She probably won't last much longer, the rate she's going. Skin and bones and fur."

My heart splits in two at the thought of the golden retriever I'd had since she was a puppy. I remember the smell of her head when she'd been in the sun, the feel of her fur through my fingers. The way she'd bowl me over as soon as I came in the door, every time I visited. The weight of her warm body was welcome, and I try to feel only that, instead of him. Fury grips me and hot tears stream down my face. I can't reach to wipe them away, so they gather on my lip and chin.

"It really is a shame, the way none of them are even trying to move on. You've left some pretty big holes, I get that. Your brother... *man.* That dude is full of rage. It just drips out of every pore, every time I see him. He's gonna run into trouble if he doesn't get himself under control. Guys like that are a ticking time bomb."

More grief washes over the ocean of it I'm spinning in. My big brother, Emerson. Laid back, popular. Kind. The voice of reason throughout my teenage angst, sharing the lessons he'd learned a harder way in an attempt to spare me heartache. *Holding onto anger is the same as poisoning yourself.* I couldn't always see it in the moment, the truth of what he said, but always after. If I'd been given the chance, I might have lived up to the potential he saw in me. The thought of him bubbling over with venomous fury breaks my heart. I feel a shift, a pulling in my chest as something tears loose and sags into the dark cavity of my insides. I want to feel that anger. I want to take it from my brother and turn it like a flamethrower on the man who stalks me through the dark, always just out of view. But even my emotions are not my own, and more useless tears gather to drip onto my collarbone.

I can still see my left hand illuminated in the lights as they fade slowly in and out. Raising my gaze to the right, I see my other hand high above my head, the wrist turned lightly, elbow curved to form a half circle. It looks wrong, and as my vision clears bit by bit, I know why. My flesh is loose, purpled more than the blinking lights could explain. Darker near my extremities, the nail beds nearly black, dirt under my broken nails. My thumbs are bent at odd angles, but the pain of my physical body I am spared. It's only my memories that can hurt me now, but it's enough. I'm trapped with them in this box.

I feel pressure as his hands graze my shoulders, attempt to straighten my stance but still my body lists to one side. He sighs and I hear his footsteps keeping pace behind. I want to scream, knowing he's so close, that he can reach out and touch me any time he likes. Does he like to? I don't remember how this dance goes. Has he lost interest in my physical form now that I'm dead?

"I'll never understand people, and not for lack of trying," he says, still in that calm tone. I try to remember if he ever lost his temper, but all I see is the frigid landscape of his face. Blue eyes studying me from behind glasses in a way I found charming at first. He was interested in me, in what I said and thought and felt. Only not in the fashion of a human getting to know another human. Studying was precisely the right word, as he went about crafting his people mask, day after day. Trying first this and then that, observing the results on his little guinea pig.

"It's like they don't even *want* to get better. The holes in their lives—they're only holes because they haven't tried filling them with someone else. I've offered myself, and they take me up on it, but I'm to the side. I'm peripheral because they won't even try sliding me in where you used to be."

He presses himself against me from behind and I close my eyes. "They're just holes," he whispers in my ear. "Anything can fill them."

Holes. My mind goes to my grave, one among many he's filled. The earth must groan against the weight of what he's done, against the way he chooses to fill those *holes*.

My eyelids won't stay closed. The lower ones are heavy, sliding down away from sclera, bringing back the sight of my body. The lights must be brightening still, and now I see my legs stretching out beneath me. They are twined together, pressed close, my feet joined almost as one. At first they look bone white, strangely smooth, but then I see they are clad in tights. I balance on tiptoes, pink pointe shoes laced high up my calves. How I loved shoes like that when I was a little girl. Never co-ordinated enough to be a dancer, I'd given up on ballet early. I wish now I hadn't. Dancers are strong. Limitless as they spin across a dark stage, untouchable in a moving spotlight.

Hands graze down my sides, dried skin scraping me sharply. His grip tightens when his hands reach my hips, but my skin is all wrong. It gives too much, his fingers sinking in close to the bone. It doesn't hurt, at least not right there where it's happening. But the pain in the center of me grows, despair tearing me apart. There is no part of me safe from his touch, from the way he molds my flesh however he wishes.

The memories have returned in full, a flickering reel of idiocy on my part, of cruelty on his. I don't want this knowledge—I want to go back in the box, return to the nothing I inhabit when it's closed.

There is one thing I can't recall, try as I may, and despair is displaced by anger.

My name. What is it? What has he done with my name?

I try to twist, to follow the sound of his voice so I can look him in the face and demand he give it back to me. I'm stuck. Dead enough to be powerless, but not enough to leave this place, this box where he keeps me.

He sighs and a gust of fetid breath stirs the hair around my face. He's losing interest, moving away from me. I can't feel his body back there anymore. He's going to close the box soon, push me back into the void. It was all I wanted moments ago, but now I fight. I want my name back. I want to know it, feel it on my lips, hear the sounds of me echo through my ears. I try to scream but I have no voice: only music, notes I never chose that cover the sound of who I used to be.

Great pressure comes from above and I bend to it, leaning over to the side at an impossible angle. I should stumble and fall, gravity taking over and sending me to the ground, but my feet stay twined together. I'm lying nearly parallel to the ground, the lights around me fading to nothing.

I'm not ready to give up. I push against the weight of that dark, the pressure of his whims, and a sliver of colored light makes it into my prison. If I don't take my name back, no one will speak it, and only his will survive. I will not let that happen.

*Dancers are strong.*

"Kara," he says in an admonitory tone. I remember it well—the way he spoke to me, pushing his judgment into me along with everything else. But that falls away in the sweet echo of my name.

*Kara.* I release my will and the lid comes down, but I will remember. I will know myself and not the version he created, molded and squeezed with uncaring hands.

*Kara.* I whisper it in the confines of my satin-lined dreaming box. It won't always be this way, I promise myself. I will take this broken dream and make it his nightmare.

I will.

# You'll Catch Your Death

## by Dexter McLeod

Leah glanced at Jessica when she started breathing in soft, adorable snores. Jessica was sprawled all akimbo in the passenger seat. She had been napping ever since they had grabbed burgers and shakes back in Dawson Springs. The bangs of Jessica's white-blonde hair were tussled over her face, reminding Leah of Jessica's white lace wedding veil. Her snores alternated in rhythm with the rattle of the air conditioner.

Leah did the driving, as usual, and their second-hand sedan played hide-and-seek with the Cumberland River as they snaked westward down US Route 62. Exit signs came and went like names called in a doctor's office—Princeton, Eddyville, Kuttawa.

Denser patches of verdant summer forests rushed in to replace open farmland as they passed the little lake towns and vacation villages where the Cumberland and Tennessee Rivers met like lovers. As she navigated through the tiny hamlet of Lake City, Leah juggled the map with one hand while keeping the other one on the wheel. Finding her route, she turned north onto a curvy back road which headed inland away from the lakes and up into the Kentucky hill country.

Thunderclouds hovered there as the tree line crept closer to the road, invading the ditches with jutting limbs and tangles of kudzu vines. A peal of distant thunder drew Leah's gaze to the horizon, worrying her that they might not make it to the bed-and-breakfast before the clouds erupted.

As they climbed a hill, a badly dented sign peeked out from a tangle of brush on the roadside. Chipped green reflective paint was pockmarked with what Jessica imagined were the craters from thrown rocks. *Teenagers?* she wondered.

Even a few gunshot holes adorned the lower right side. The official white lettering declared the town of Lederwood was up ahead. Someone had spray-painted the words *Rapture Town* over the village's name in heavy, uneven red streaks, leaving thin rivulets of dried paint running down the height of the sign.

The sign was so well hidden that Leah had only seen a flash of it before it vanished behind them; it was even concealed from sight in the rear-view mirror by a nest of kudzu and ivy. At the hill's crest, a thin gravel path veered off the main road and slithered down into a narrow, wooded valley. The roadside was wider here, and Leah pulled off on the bank.

Leah pretended to cough, her frequent custom for gently waking Jessica.

Jessica stirred begrudgingly, stretching in her seat like a cat before sitting upright and looking down the gravel road.

"Where are we?"

"Running late but almost there. Just left a place called Iuka. We're about to pass by that ghost town you wanted to see. The one from one of your unsolved legend websites."

"Lederwood?"

"Yeah, but there's graffiti on the sign. Someone painted Rapture Town over Lederwood."

Jessica jolted awake and snapped up the map, wrestling it open like a broken accordion. "The locals don't like this place. The town died a long time ago. From photos I've seen, there's almost nothing left but ramshackle houses and graveyards. There were a few attempts to reboot the place, but no one stayed for long. Last attempt was in the 50s, I think. It began as an old settler village in the 1790s. Started off good I suppose. They fed a lot of the local counties."

"Fed? A cattle town?"

"Uh-huh. Close enough to the Cumberland and Ohio Rivers to steamboat out meat and leather. From what I've read, they were a bit *off*, though. Sort of a closed society. A cluster of loosely related families that had immigrated here from Europe via the Carolinas, working their way across Kentucky like a caravan. Some of them moved here and built this place. Houses, the pastures, the slaughterhouse, the tannery. Some settled in a few other spots throughout the rest of western Kentucky."

"What's *off* about that?"

"I found odd stories online about their religion. They claimed they had been told this was their promised land."

"Told? Like, by God? Amish or something?"

"No, not even close. They were obsessed with the rivers here. They had doused the region and claimed there was a convergence of ley lines nearby. Some type of syncretic polytheistic belief system."

"Syncretic?"

Jessica turned the rattling air conditioner down on low. "It's when different religions are blended in a way to make something new. They cobbled together a belief system from lots of different folk traditions. There's a university town nearby—Murray. A local college professor who specializes in folklore wrote a few books about them. He said they were like European cunning folk, but with unrecognizable gods. A lot of folk magic."

"Yeah, I guess that qualifies as *off*."

"They Frankensteined beliefs from Germanic paganism, Scandinavian myths, Renaissance mysticism, Druidism—hell, according to him there was even some stuff from ancient Mesopotamia. They thought everyone had a piece of the truth, and as they travelled, they learned what they could. They thought they were just putting the truth back together again. I wonder if that's what they were trying to do down there in Lederwood. But like you saw, the locals just call it Rapture Town."

"Why?"

Jessica flicked her white-blonde hair out of her eyes, sat the map down, and gestured her upturned, open palms for emphasis, spreading them apart like theater curtains. She gave her best impression of Sophia Petrillo from *The Golden Girls*. "Picture it. Kentucky. 1811. It was the middle of a cold December night. A huge earthquake batters this region. It was so bad it made the Mississippi River flow the wrong way. The backflow was enough to flood an area just south of here in Tennessee and create what is now Reelfoot Lake."

To this, Leah layered on a southern belle accent, invoking Blanche Devereaux. "And Rapture Town?"

"The townsfolk were there that night before the earthquake, and they were gone the next morning. All their stuff was still there—clothes, food, money." Jessica broke with the Sicilian accent, now serious. "The only other thing missing was the cattle. Well, sort of. Nearby townsfolk found piles of untanned leather in the fields, as if the cattle had been squeezed out of their own skin like a burst grape. But no meat. None in the fields, none in the slaughterhouse, none in the tannery. Wherever they went, they took the meat with them."

"Urban legends, unsolved crimes, cults—you really need to stop reading that shit," Leah said, only half joking. She glanced down into Lederwood. She could see Jessica was right. From their perch on the ridgeline, the town—or what was left of it—appeared vacant. The matchstick remnants of fences were barely visible though the overgrown pastures.

What Leah thought might be the frame of the town's old slaughterhouse looked surprisingly sturdy compared to the ruined houses. She wondered if the tannery still stank, as she'd heard the old leatherworking methods of the past century reeked something terrible. Fitting, as the building was little more than a corpse itself.

"Maybe it was for one of their gods," Jessica said.

"What, the cattle meat? Since when do gods need a ribeye?"

"According to that folklore professor, one of their deities was called the Lord of Meat."

"Well, there are probably almost as many burger joints in the US as there are churches. How many billions served?"

A crackle of lightning spiderwebbed through the sky above what remained of the empty, rotting village. The accompanying thunder rattled the windshield just as the first drops began streaking down the glass.

"You still want to see it?"

Jessica glanced down into the town. "Nah, we can drive through tomorrow before we head on to Memphis. We still have a couple of miles till the B&B. Let's try to beat the worst of the rain."

The rope of road writhed through the forest as if laid by a team of professional drunkards. Leah tensed as the rain picked up, making it harder to see despite the best efforts of the windshield wipers. As the downpour hit the sunbaked, summer blacktop, it scalded into a brief steam that swirled into the ditches like fog. The road bucked like a bull as it bent back and forth around the hills.

As they rounded an acute curve, a man appeared on the roadside. He was tall but gaunt, wearing a faded mustard-colored suit. In his bony hand he held a tattered crepe-colored umbrella that was so old and threadbare it tinged pale pink when the lightning backlit him. The talon of his thumb stuck out for hitchhiking, wet in the downpour, and he produced a frenzied grin so absurd Leah wondered what joke he must have told himself to achieve such an expression.

"Oh, the poor man, and in this weather."

"No way," said Leah. "These aren't your stoner days driving around Pittsburgh with your college radio friends." She accelerated.

The man's smile curled even further, and as they neared him, he stepped out into the road.

Tires screeched as Leah braked and swerved to miss him, almost running off the other side of the road. She was jerked back against her seat as the seatbelt snapped taut like a boa constrictor. Leah pumped the gas and corrected the wheel to avoid hitting the ditch, righting the car back into their lane and bursting past the madman and his umbrella.

White-knuckled, Leah risked a glance in the mirror to see the man standing in the road, rain billowing around him. She could see him waving at them before he vanished from sight as they rounded another curve, the *thwap-thwap* of the windshield wipers screaming the whole way.

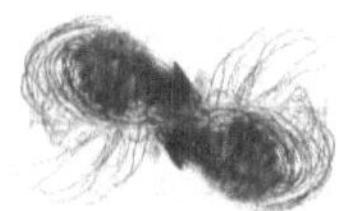

The rain slacked over the next quarter mile, but Leah's grip on the steering wheel did not. The curving road cut deeper into the hills as the elevation changed, and exposed bedrock protruded from the earth along the banks of the road like rotten teeth.

A clearing opened as they approached a narrow one-lane country bridge. A shallow creek wriggled through a crack in the hills beneath the bridge, and Leah slowed to a crawl as they crossed it.

A gaggle of children were playing in the creek. They jumped and splashed as they tossed sticks and rocks into the water. To Leah, they looked like they belonged in an old sepia photograph, as their clothes were antique and faded—muted goldenrods, bleached mustard, pale honey. Each held a faded leather umbrella, though they seemed uninterested in shielding themselves from the downpour. All at once they stopped and faced the bridge, staring at them in unison through the rain.

Leah shot Jessica a glance.

"I love you dear, and I know you wanted a weird, Americana road trip for the honeymoon, but I'm picking the route on our next trip. This place is giving me the creeps."

After another quarter mile, they turned up in a driveway that lassoed around a densely wooded property. A large English Tudor revival house emerged from between the trees as the path spilled into a clearing. Leah parked the car at the foot of the stairs leading up to a covered porch. The windshield wipers creaked to a halt as Leah killed the engine, leaving only the tapping of the rain.

A woman rose from a rocking chair sheltered under the porch and waved at them. She was a short, rotund, grandmotherly figure, and spry despite the white-gray hair.

They exited the car.

"Is this the, um—" Jessica asked, flipping through their itinerary.

"The Oxenbould Bed & Breakfast," the woman said, clutching a half-finished crossword puzzle above her towering white hair. "I'm Cora Oxenbould. And you two must be the Gales."

"The Dugan-Gales," said Leah as she popped the trunk. "We hyphenated."

"Oh, dear yes, I'm sure I have that written somewhere," she said, shouting over the rain. "I'm not very technical. Can barely open *the email*. My grandson made the website. And here I am—can't even get on *the Google*. I miss the Yellow Pages."

As Leah started disassembling the *Tetris* game of luggage that was their trunk, a peal of thunder clapped through the clearing.

"Oh my," Cora said, giggling, "you'll catch your death in this. It wasn't even in the forecast, but here it is, raining cats and dogs. Came right out of nowhere."

"Speaking of," said Leah. "What's with those people down the road out in the storm. One of them jumped out in front of us. He nearly forced us off the road."

"People?" asked Cora. "Back the way you came?"

"Yeah," said Jessica. "The ones with the weird, tattered umbrellas?"

"Umbrellas?" Cora's expression darkened. "Were they old-fashioned looking?"

The Dugan-Gales glanced at each other through the rain.

"Uh-huh," said Leah. "Made of leather. They were acting sort of weird."

Cora forced a smile. "Never mind them, dear. Just some locals from down the road. Keep to themselves. Best to leave them be." Her gaze jumped to the sky, studying it with sudden interest. She stuffed her crossword puzzle into her apron and strode down the stairs, her mound of gray hair bouncing in the rain. "Let me help. Best get you both in."

Cora moved along behind them, grabbing whatever she could carry before darting back the way she'd come. "Let's get out of this weather."

As Leah handed Jessica a bag, she gasped. A trickle of blood ran down Jessica's forehead, staining her white-blond hair with a streak of crimson.

Leah moved to her, running her finger to Jessica's head, and lifting her bangs. "What did you do, Jess? Did you cut your head on the door getting out?"

Jessica touched her own forehead. "I—I don't think so." Her fingers came away bloody. "I don't think I'm cut."

A red splash dotted Leah's outstretched arm. Another dropped onto the shoulder of her green top, making a circle of greenish brown. Puddles at their feet, which had started with an iridescent sheen from the oil-stained driveway, were now being peppered with red rain which quickly tinged pink as the color diffused. The sight of it reminded Leah of dropping food coloring into water to dye Easter eggs as a girl.

A large drop of blood splashed on the back of Jessica's luggage-laden forearm. "What the—" she shouted, nearly dropping a suitcase.

It was all around them. Red streaks ran down the rear car window. The white walls between the exposed wooden timber beams adorning the English Tudor B&B turned first pink and then crimson as the rain washed down the sides of the house. In a span of seconds, their clothes, first soaked with water, were now running wet with blood. Leah's bright red hair was all that hid the downpour.

Movement at the end of the drive caught Leah's attention. Two thin women lingered there, watching them. They each held a tattered leather umbrella in one hand, and in the other an odd-looking knife. Instead of coming to a point, the blades were rounded half-circles at the end of the wooden handles—a silver half-moon pretending to be a dagger. They both wore faded yellow dresses unmolested by the raining blood, except around the hem where it splashed onto them as they slunk through the bloodied grass.

"Get in!" Cora shouted.

As they turned to run up the steps, a loud thud boomed in the clearing, echoing around the tree-enclosed yard. Where it came from, Leah couldn't tell, but a moment later another loud bang came from the roof of the house.

Leah grabbed Jessica's arm and pulled her toward the stairs. As they rounded the sedan, the front windshield's passenger side shattered into a network of spiderweb-shaped cracks. Jessica shrieked as they cleared the front of the car.

Something was stuck in the fractured windshield, and it wiggled, seizing like a worm on a hook. Leah stopped long enough to look. It was some deformed bloody thing, and it twitched and writhed, straining against the hold of the laminated glass. With a shudder, the thing worked its way loose from the windshield and lurched out onto the hood of the car. As it crawled across the metal, Leah saw it wasn't some wounded bird, but was some kind of meat-thing—a fleshy mass, shiny red like blood clots and smooth like raw chicken. As it crawl-walked down the hood, it left a trail of bloody phlegm.

Another chunk fell behind them on the pavement. This one, larger, bounced hard in rebound, rising back up a foot off the ground before landing again. When it gained purchase on the blacktop, it righted itself and scampered along the driveway amongst narrow plumes of steam rising off the hot asphalt.

More sounds careened around them. Heavy, wet thuds sounded as more meat-things fell on the roof, in the yard, and on a truck parked on the side of the house. The bowing sounds of metal popping rang as another dented in the roof of Leah's sedan. Small chunks of meat slid down the windows of the B&B. Heavy pieces of twitching meat fell out of the trees that had broken their fall, dropping like hellish hail.

They joined Cora beneath of the safety of the porch and watched in disgust as more bloody rain and meat-things fell from the sky. Where the two women had stood, there were now several others. All were in antique clothing carrying threadbare umbrellas.

A thud rang directly overhead, and Leah ducked out of instinct. Rattling sounds gurgled above them as a meat-thing scampered, dragging itself across wet shingles. An edge of redness appeared over the lip of the gutter, dripping red phlegm down in front of them.

It didn't appear to have eyes, but Leah knew it was glowering down at them nonetheless, and she pulled Jessica back further into the recesses of the porch.

The meat-thing slid over the edge of the roof and fell to the topmost step. It skittered toward them, leaving a foul streak behind it like the trail of a slug.

Leah stepped forward and kicked at it, sending it flopping down onto the driveway.

It slid a few feet before once again scampering toward them, undulating and distorting as it crawled. To Leah, the shapes it contorted itself into as it moved reminded her of the movements people's tongues make when they tie knots into cherry stems.

Three more meat-things slid off the roof and onto the porch, scrambling greedily toward them. More umbrella-carrying people appeared, stepping out of the tree line all along the front of the property, their silhouettes muted in the scarlet downpour.

"Inside," screamed Cora.

They rushed inside, and she locked the door behind them.

They could hear the intermittent thuds of raining meat on the third story roof. Wet, sucking sounds came through the walls as the things slid down the outside of the house.

They peeked out the curtains and saw the odd people were advancing toward the house.

"What the hell is going on?" Jessica screamed while uselessly trying to wring the blood out of her hair.

Leah held her and tried to calm her. "It's a fair question. Who are those people? They have some kind of weird knives."

"They're Head Knives," Cora said, through a pained exhale. "They're used in leatherwork, to make things."

"You do know what's happening," Jessica said, sobbing.

"They must be from the old town," Cora said, clenching her hands.

"Town? Rapture Town?" asked Leah. "Jess, didn't you say they all vanished?"

Cora's eyes grew wild. "They've come back. Come back for the deer."

"What deer? Are you saying they are the actual people from Lederwood? What do these pastel Mennonites want?"

More meat-things struck the roof. Leah could hear them scrambling around on the front porch, bumping into the furniture, and scraping against the front door.

"They didn't all vanish," Cora said. "My great-great grandfather, Henry Oxenbould, wasn't there that night. He was sixteen. Had eyes for a girl down in Smithland named Molly. He'd seen her on runs to the general store her family owned. As my mother told it, he was a bit of a tomcat. Molly agreed to see him *that* night, and he snuck out of Lederwood to meet her.

"They were courting when the earthquake hit. He rushed back to town, worried the elders would be woken by the quake and he'd be caught. They didn't allow the believers to marry outside the faith, you see. But when he got back, everyone had vanished.

"But he knew there'd be punishment. He broke the faith. The

gods had come along and took the true believers. Took them to their Dead City to get their rewards. After that night, Henry was plagued by nightmares. Nightmares he knew were sent by their gods. By the one they'd dedicated the town to. The one they worshipped the most."

"The Lord of Meat," Jessica said, breathing through a shuddered sob.

"He has other names." Cora nodded. "The Flayed One. The High Prince of Tallow. Others I don't dare say. Henry said he'd seen him deep in the woods, wandering by the rivers. Always a presence lingering when Henry would go hunting or when he walked the trails. He said he knew that the Flayed God would find him. That he didn't really escape. The folks down in Lederwood had a saying: *Sometimes a hunter wounds a deer, and it staggers off into the brush and hides. But a good hunter always finds his prey.*

"He grew up and had kids of his own with Molly. Then one day he went into the woods and never came home. All they found were his clothes and a splattering of blood. Mom always said the Lord of Meat caught up to him. He'd found the wounded deer that escaped and claimed him. Folk in our family have disappeared ever since. Not everyone, but enough of us that we've known we're cursed. But here I am, in my sixties. I thought I'd outrun him. That he'd skipped over me. But he's come for his deer."

A low singing came from the townsfolk. Leah peeked out the porch window. They'd all formed a circle in the yard, and she watched them sway in the red rain.

*"Praise unto the Meat, to the burning Tallow,*
*To the lamplight in the deepening shadow.*
*To the hunger, and to the hunt. To the gristle, to the fat.*
*To the drippings and the offal in which he sat.*
*To the boiling of the blood, and the sizzle in the fire.*
*To the steady thirst of relentless desire.*
*To the flesh, which is both cage and key.*
*Praise to the Flayed One, the Lord of Meat."*

"Local folk have seen him," Cora said, whispering over their chants. "Walking the woods in the high heat of the summer. Summer's his time, the Lord of Meat. And winter for his consort, the Lady of

Bones. Gods of the hunt. Of hunger and need. Of consumption. To bring down an animal or dine on flesh was worship of him. To use what's left—the marrow or the ivory, the horns, and the antlers, to make scrimshaw or tools of bone—that was sanctified by her. The heat of life was his. The frost of death was hers."

"That's what the professor said in the book I read," Jessica said. "Some gods they brought with them from the old country. But some they found when they got here. He said they discovered what lay hidden behind the bones of the world."

Leah couldn't stop looking at the townsfolk as they sang. The meat-things had gathered in the circle, and they jittered in rhythm with the singing.

"What the hell are those things in the yard?" Leah asked.

"My mother said to look for the Lord of Meat's signs, in case he was hunting. Signs in the rivers, in the fathoms of the earth, in the skies. So, I've kept an eye out for it. This has happened before."

"She's right," Jessica said. "A lot. There was the Kentucky Meat Shower."

"You've got to be fucking kidding me."

"Nope. Chunks of meat rained in Olympia Springs, Kentucky in 1876. Covered an area the size of a football field. More meat rained in Virginia in 2012. And it's not just meat. Jellyfish rained in England. Spiders in Australia. Worms in Scotland. Blood rained in India in 2001, and again in Colombia in 2008. Tornadoes have always been the theory, but it's never been proven."

"Shhh!" whispered Leah. "Listen."

The singing had stopped, leaving only the tapping rain. Leah risked another peek through the curtain. They still swayed in the circle. Then a shape moved into frame just outside, and she jumped back.

The man they'd nearly run over was standing on the porch, still wearing his ludicrous smile. "It's time to come home, Cora Bell. The Lord is truly good, and his harvest is plentiful. Praise unto the Meat. We've come to claim you."

"Do you have a gun?" Jessica whispered.

Cora shook her head. "Wouldn't do no good. I'm an Oxenbould. I'm marked."

"Come now, child. He'll free you. You can be like the Flayed God. See a world without sin or skin. See it as he does. Walk with us unto the Dead City, stripped clean. You've dreamt of it, have you not? The city by the lake. Its yellow flags caught taut in the wind beneath a black sun. All our gods—the host of Lords and Ladies—are seated there, in service to our Dead King. His name is on your lips. His color is in your mind. His song is in your heart. You're expected."

"Leave us be!" Cora screamed.

The man tapped the glass, and in answer, the chimney rattled. Meat-things crept down, bursting open the flue, and rained down into the fireplace. They slunk along the floor toward them.

"Not all manna comes from heaven, child," the man tittered. "Hell has its own manna. But you don't eat it, you see. It eats you."

While the man was tapping on the window, Leah decided to risk it. She grabbed Jessica's arm, unbolted the door, and burst out onto the porch. Before he could turn, they jumped down the steps.

Leah slipped on the slimy pavement but fell forward into the car door. As she opened it, she glanced at the townsfolk. They were staring at her, and in their center the meat-things were joining together, knitting themselves into something larger—a golem made of flesh.

"Get in!" Jessica screamed from the passenger seat.

Leah jumped in and started the car, ignoring the grinding sound the windshield wipers made against the broken windshield.

As she backed the car up and shifted into drive, the man stood by the stairs, leering down at them.

"What about Cora?" screamed Jessica.

"What about that?" Leah said, pointing to the writhing mass of meat-things.

They had taken on a vaguely human shape, though taller. It craned a head-like mass toward them. Fleshy bits rearranged themselves, a puzzle of meat trying to solve itself. Two narrow slits opened, and white eyes rolled and twitched before settling their gaze on Leah.

The townsfolk shouted, "Praise unto the Meat."

Leah floored it.

The sedan fishtailed in the grass before jumping back onto the pavement, and she aimed the car down the driveway. They squealed down the lane and jumped a ditch before bursting back onto the main road, bottoming out for a brief second and scraping metal on the as-phalt.

Despite the downpour, Leah took the curves in the road as fast as she dared. The trees and the kudzu and the ivy roared by in a blur. They raced back down the hill, and as they hugged the curve leading into the narrow country bridge, Jessica screamed.

Four children stood hand in hand across the bridge, bloodied um-brellas twirling in the rain.

It was instinct. Had Leah had more time to think it through, she might have driven right over them. But some impulse drove her to yank the wheel at the last moment.

To Leah, it felt like the sedan floated forever. At last, the arc of its flight did bend, and the creek beneath the bridge flew toward them, filling the narrow segment of the unshattered windshield. They skidded down into the narrow gulley of the creek bed. As the hood of the car disappeared beneath the water, the airbags deployed. The world went black.

Leah thought the blood was from her broken nose, but it was just the blood raining through the shattered driver-side window.

Then came the children singing.

*"Praise unto the Meat, to the burning Tallow,*
*To the lamplight in the deepening shadow."*

Leah tried to concentrate, but the airbag had left her dizzy. Jessica was unconscious. Leah shook her, but she mumbled incoherently.

"My child," the man said, opening her door, "poor little wounded deer. The Flayed One has chased his prey across worlds with yellow skies and black stars. He's stepped in and out of time to claim what is his. It's such a simple thing to corner such as you."

He opened his umbrella, shaking it in the rain. Its leather was new—bruised and bloodied—and it was freshly stretched around its wire frame. As she stared at it, her double-vision eased just a moment, and Leah could make out the delicate stitching around a mouth and eyelids, sealing shut the flayed skin of Cora Oxenbould.

Behind the man, a great mass of meat trundled down into the gully. Not a puzzle, but a regal god, flayed of his skin. He towered above them and stared down at her with horrible intelligence.

Two children came alongside the god, taking up each of his hands, and they sang.

*"To the flesh, which is both cage and key.*
*Praise to the Flayed One, the Lord of Meat."*

# A Thousand Forbidden Weddings and a Song for Dead Darlings

## by Ai Jiang

You are outside of your body, looking down at yourself on the hospital bed surrounded by family and strangers alike with smiles too eerie, too joyous, for the airlessness of the suffocating atmosphere.

Next to you, Mother stands, eyes rimmed crimson, lids both above and below swollen, purple veined, pulsing, twitching, bluing lips holding back their quiver, but the quakes are apparent none the less if you look close enough. Father, behind, stoic as always, teeth clenched beneath thin-pressed lips, hands clasped in front of him.

"My darling, my darling," whispers a woman who's not your mother, and you wonder who she's speaking to when she's a stranger, yet she's looking directly at you. Until— "You'll be perfect, *perfect*, for my son. He will be so, *so*, happy to have you."

A throat clearing, hidden in the crowd of gathered faces.

"*My* son would love her as well," says a man with his hands folded behind his back, chest tilting forwards as he regards you with narrowed eyes and a sly smile.

"Twenty thousand, if we can take her right now," says an elder as she prods aside those in front of her with a cane, the fractured design of the aged wood seems on the verge of splintering save for the fact the elder's birdlike frame holds only skin and little flesh beneath.

"Thirty-five," the woman who's not your mother says.

The man with the folded hands clears his throat. "Forty."

"Sixty." The elder.

"Seventy-five." The woman.

"A hundred." The man.

"Two-hundred and fifty." The elder.

A hush. A dead silence. A single shuddering breath from Mother and a disgruntled grunt from Father. The price is higher than the bride-wealth Father offered Mother's family for her hand: a hundred and fifty, which was far past a modest sum.

The elder, self-satisfied, prods the side of your hospital bed, wood clanging against metal, a gavel struck at the end of an auction.

"I will send for her at midnight," the elder says, then, in a whisper, "That should be enough time for you to say your goodbyes.

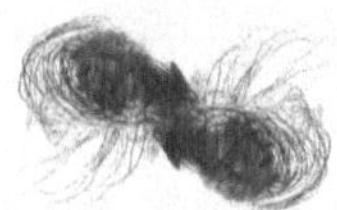

Before midnight, Mother and Father stand next to you, hovering above, your hand is enveloped in Mother's, and Father's settle overtop. You wonder what they'll be doing with the money, if they'll sell your belongings or keep them and make a shrine. You wonder how long they'll mourn you before they refocus their attention on your sister, less than two years of age, left at home with Grandmother. And you wonder what they'll tell her when she's older, how you'll be remembered.

The doctor arrives to pull the plug, expression hidden behind a mask they don't need to have pulled up, spectacles glaring so you can't see if they're bored or pitying, but before they do, Mother shows you a picture of a young man no older than you, maybe a year or two different, max. Couldn't have been a graduate, maybe halfway through undergraduate studies, like you.

"I heard he's a nice boy, and I know he'll treat you well." She strokes slow circles on the back of your hand, under Father's warm, clammy palm.

There's no way Mother could know that for sure, but she seems convinced, or rather, these words are for her own comfort, to convince herself her choice is correct.

When the heart monitor flatlines and the doctor offers their condolences to Mother and Father, your heart halts, as do your breaths. But you know you're not dead. Not yet. Not yet.

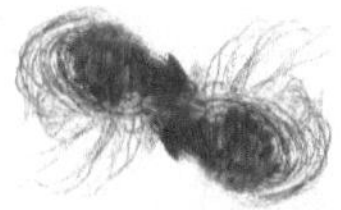

*Minghun.* You've heard about these. Weddings, marriages, that usually occur between the dead, though there have been forbidden cases where the living are forced, though not always and sometimes willingly instead, to marry the dead—sometimes to appease angry and lingering ghosts, other times to accompany them into their afterlife the way joss paper money and items and homes are burnt and sent to spirits in the netherworlds. Forbidden, because—

A matchmaker hands the elder your death certificate. She receives a more than a satisfying commission from the smile you see on her face, as she waves to the elder who is helped onto the car in which you're already resting inside a cushioned coffin—cushioned in appearance only because it felt as though you were laying on cement.

At her home, an antique-decorated manor with elaborate floral-patterned wallpaper and dark wooden floors, the handlers the elder hired treat you as though you're alive, but you can tell, even with their faces held expressionless in the elder's presence, that they want nothing more than to be finished with rubbing your cooling body with sweet chrysanthemum oils, redressing you in fine red silk embroidered with gold, painting your colourless lips with rouge and brushing a similar coloured powder onto your pale cheeks so you look as though you're in a deep slumber rather than an unawakening death.

The elder's hand roams across your cheek, your closed eyes, as she whispers, voice a grating rasp, "Beautiful..."

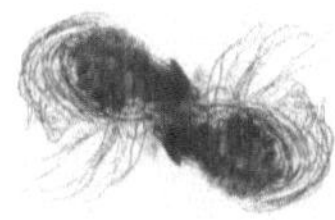

You thought your parents might be present, but they aren't, and neither are your husband's. After all, who would want to be present during such a ceremony to see their children dead?

Tassels sit dangling from the sides of your headpiece, a thin red veil thrown overtop. Your husband is a wooden effigy carved in what you think is a caricatured version of the photo of the young man Mother showed you—eyes larger, lips longer, thinner, cheekbones and jaw-line sharper. In your hand is a ribboned, fabric bouquet of a large crimson flower, the same is strapped over your husband's effigy's chest as a sash. Your wedding dress is a pool of scarlet; your husband's effigy sits in stiff garments with colours that match yours with midnight accents and gold.

You and your husband are facing the elder, seated in chairs that prevent your corpse from flopping over, behind a table filled with bowls of apples, oranges, pears carefully sliced and plated, steaming dishes with chopsticks set. Red candles, wicks lit, rest on each side of the table, wax dripping down the side like thick perspiration slowed by the dense breaths released into the air by the elder as she regards you both, separately, then together, her gaze scrutinizing, as though the two of you are still alive.

The elder lifts your veil with two steady hands, and that is when you feel yourself blink, and the elder, bewildered, jerks in her spot, your veil fluttering back down, the elder's hands resting on her lap, trembling.

Still, you cannot move. Your eyes do not blink again no matter how hard to try to will them to.

Next to you, a whisper floats with each vow the host announces. And appearing by your own hovering ghost is your new husband's—lank hair hanging into eyes with deep shadows beneath like soot crescents, lips cracked, cheeks gaunt—not at all like his photo: vibrant, alight, alive.

"My... love..." his voice is a harsh scrape against your eardrums, pitched as though he'd lost use of it and is only now relearning the feeling of sounds and the way each word wraps around the tongue, contorts in the shape of its will.

At first, you thought he's referring to you, but he wasn't looking at you but past you at someone who wasn't there.

"Help me," he says.

You don't know how—you can't even help yourself.

Parents fear that their children will die before them, and others fear their children will come back to haunt them, and some worry that their children will be lonely in the afterlife. There are a few who might even want to join their children, finding it too difficult to live with their own failure as parents, and yet, they're too afraid of death themselves to follow. But it's believed that certainly the dead would appreciate being loved, being needed, even after they're gone.

With this elder, this isn't quite the case. She'd wanted to appease her grandson, yes, because it seems he's been causing quite the haunting ruckus in her home—torn edges of portraits, overflowing sinks, ashes in the fine weavings of rugs and carpets, bulbs exploding after flickering like firecrackers—which she seems unamused about and lacking in patience for, rather than the mournful sorrow she should have been displaying for the recent death.

After the ceremony, the elder returns you to your parents in that same coffin you arrived in. A closed casket funeral followed by your lowering into a graveyard outside the city, up a lush mountain near an collapsed mine that took the lives of too many youths. Plots of lands have been diminishing in number and you're surprised your parents didn't cremate you instead. Apparently, it was the elder's idea, and she even funded part of the money for that expensive plot you now rest in beneath the soil.

It should have been obvious why. But you don't realize until later that night when the elder with hired handlers, the same ones who dressed you for the minghun, come to dig you back up from your grave, throws your body into a preservation coffin, the timeline of it all perfect for her wicked plans to resell you while you're still fresh, still complete, for two, three, four times the price she'd bought you at, and had a wooden effigy made to take your place in the cheap coffin she commissioned and returned to the gaping mouth of your empty grave.

A mistake.

And your husband's ghost laughs with you.

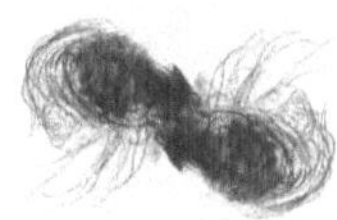

You have never fallen in love in the short years you were alive—your mother and father might have been the closest things to this foreign feeling, the nanny you had a close second, because she seemed to care more about your own childhood than you yourself, until she disappeared without a word, and you've always wondered if it was because your mother was jealous.

"What did he look like?" you ask your dead husband about his lover when you're loaded into the back of a truck with many other bodies halted in various states of decomposition—some missing a limb or two, some without eyes, some slightly bloated, some bearing scars that reveal their cause of death, unnatural. Surrounded by dead darlings, you feel as though you are being shuttled away like livestock in number yet treated like exotic species in price and packaging.

You and your husbands' ghosts sit cross-legged, facing one another, on top of the lid of your shut coffin.

His love is a young man from the mining community where your wooden effigy now rests. One that he has been waiting for, who had been already buried, only, it is in a place your dead husband cannot reach. Not like this, tethered to you.

You're about to ask if there might be a way to sever your bond, though it felt better to be together than alone, or at least better to wallow in the loneliness together, when an alive girl thought unalive begins to sing at the back of the truck—collapsed and wedged between two coffins with her broken limbs like a rag doll. You're surprised that the handlers haven't sewn her lips, though it might be for the sole reason of fetching a higher price since she cannot run anyhow.

She laughs, delirious, eyes locked on us both. She can see us. And after the song, she tells of how she had been buried alive, then dug up before death kissed and marred her skin, before the blood in her veins had even dried, where her makeup still sits fresh on her face—supple: alive. Her mouth opens, closes, opens again—a fish gasping for air, a bird with broken wings and talons drowning in water—

Minghun—forbidden because there have been those kidnapped, murdered, dug from graves, ashes stolen from funeral homes and graves, sold on the black market.

Unsettled ghosts rise like vapour, like wafting steam from their coffins, some stacked, within the truck to join in the chorus of vengeful voices like the unalive alive girl's—

Some were targeted because they were rejected by society, abandoned by their families, for the cruel reason of physical and mental imperfections.

Some were injected with heavy sedatives by those hoping to have them at the ceremonies alive, half conscious, only to have them pass away because of overdose.

Others were bullied into committing suicide—both before and after the minghun so they could not be wedded to another.

Improper burials—all.

All our ghostly heads turn to the only one among us still alive, as though this might be the only chance we have at escape, at least this way, both us and she would have a choice, no matter how limited, even if it feels as though we are choiceless.

"Will you marry us?"

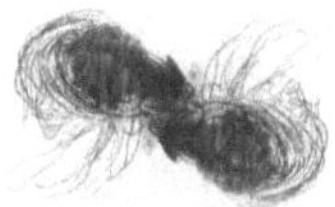

Before reaching the black market, the doors to the back of the truck are flung open, rattling the ghosts of dead darlings, among which your husband and you drift. Each ghost weaving themselves into our living vessel, the unalive alive girl, mending her broken body, half-tethered soul.

Our vessel rises, starts crawling, then walking, jerkily, a puppet yanked forth towards the elder at the yawning opening of the truck.

We sing, "My darling, my darling."

We sing, "You'll be perfect, *perfect*, for *us*. We will be so, *so*, happy to have you."

With hands folded behind our back, chest tilting forwards as we regard her with narrowed eyes and a sly smile, we hum, "It is midnight. That should have been enough time for you to say your goodbyes."

And as her cane falls from her hand, clatters onto the ground, and her mouth falls open, a maw from which drifts the scent of rot and musk and sour fear and bitter death, we smile, and smile wider, and whisper in a rasping voice, "Beautiful…"

The elder's scream resounds, but we swallow each of her echoes.

Then, together, we head into the night for the mountains, for the mines, for the graves—marked, unmarked, filled, emptied, empty—with a song for dead darlings trailing from our lips, words rattling like trains over tracks, the clicking of bone against bone, the dribble of blood like rusting tears coating our tongue:

Feet cold

Toes numb

Fingers bloodless

Expression fraught-less

Lapis veins

Iris lips

Eyes open

Eyes closed

Breaths held

Breaths gone

Whispered gasp

Gasped whisper

Dead darlings

Darling's dead

Undead dead

Dead undead

# A Dirty Job

**Patrick Hurley**

The human body releases over thirty chemicals as it decomposes. Cadaverine. Putrescine. Skatole. The smell clings to nearby surfaces long after the body has been removed. Even seasoned pros puke unless they line their upper lip with Vicks.

Crime-scene cleaning, or "biohazard services" as it appears on my business card, isn't for weak stomachs. You need good gear, a steady hand, and the ability to block out the most horrific crap you can imagine.

My crew had that. Hakim Benjamin was the steadiest of us, but he had a work visa of questionable status. Gabe Torres worked his ass off while sober, which was about 50% of the time. Frank Blutophsky, who did our heavy lifting, was a recovering junkie I'd known since high school. That left me: Sherine Jankowitz, half-Iranian, half-Pollack. The boys called me Hardhat.

We'd just parted ways with our former manager, Jimmy Catalano, over a minor disagreement. Jimmy thought because we slept together, he didn't have to pay my crew time-and-a-half. I thought who I fuck shouldn't come into it. Our disagreement ended with Jimmy's nose in a sling and me starting my own business so I could put him out of it. Luckily, my crew also had an issue with being screwed out of overtime and came with me.

We'd been open for a couple weeks when I got the call about a cleanup at Fairview Terrace, a high-rise in Uptown. Officer Matt Miller had died from a case of gun-in-mouth syndrome, and it was a couple weeks before anyone found his body. The call surprised me. Not how he died; for cops, offing yourself wasn't uncommon. What surprised me was that I got called at all. This was Chicago, and everyone already had a guy for stuff like this. Why hadn't Jimmy's new crew or one of the other cleaners snatched this up?

When I first saw the unit, I estimated a few days' work at most. We'd strip the carpet, scrub the floors and walls, bleach everything, and fumigate. It didn't go down like that. We stripped the carpet easy enough. The poor bastard's blood and brains had also stained the floor and nearby wall. No matter how hard we scrubbed, no matter how strong the chemicals, the stains stayed put. Luckily, my crew had some reno experience. We ripped out the flooring and wall, replaced it, and bleached the new surfaces for good measure.

The smell grew worse, creeping down the elevator shaft to spread through the second and third floors. Even though we had until month's end to finish, I was getting desperate. I had the unit checked for mold, but tests turned up nothing. Even weirder, the stains on the floor and wall began to come back.

So there I was, staring at pictures of those dark spatters, wondering if I was losing my mind, when my cell lit up with a number I thought I'd blocked.

"What do you want?"

"Heard you took the Fairview Terrace job."

Jimmy Catalano's voice sounded as deep as I remembered it. Half a year ago, that bass rumble seemed kind of sexy, but now it made me want to punch through a window.

"Yeah," I said. "So what?"

I heard him take a deep breath, then another. Jimmy had terrible blood pressure and used breathing exercises to calm down. "Listen, we had a thing, and I screwed up. I get it. You have every right to hate me."

"How noble of you, shitbag."

"That's got nothing to do with this," he continued. "If you got the gig, you should think about dropping it."

"What are you trying to say, Jimmy?"

His tone sounded almost ashamed. "Have the nightmares started, Sher?"

"What?"

"My new crew," said Jimmy. "They tried to clean the place, but the smell wouldn't go away. They started having nightmares. Three of them already skipped town."

Outside my place along the Chicago River, the wind screamed. From my patio window, I could see waves crashing against the corroded iron barrier far below. Jimmy was lying. Had to be. I'd seen what that apartment looked like when we went into it on the first day. No way another crew had been in there before us.

"You trying to mess with me?" I said. "You want another beatdown?"

"No!" he said. "This is professional courtesy. Maybe you should leave the job alone."

"Maybe you should mind your fucking business, cheap-ass prick," I said, and ended the call. Minutes later, I was still shaking. If Jimmy had straight-up threatened me, fine. Instead, I heard honest-to-god concern in his voice. That freaked me out.

Next day, the place smelled worse than ever. Gabe didn't show, and when I called his cell, he mumbled something about bad dreams and hung up on me.

"What do we do, Hardhat?" Frank asked. I gave him a once over. Big Frank had been on and off the wagon since he was twenty. Right now, he looked about two steps away from setting the wagon on fire. His eyes were wide and twitchy. His hair, normally slicked back, stuck up in greasy clumps.

"Why don't you take it easy for the day, Frankie?" I said and slipped him a couple twenties for his time. I leaned into his ear and whispered, "Get some food; get some sleep. Try to stay right for the next day or so."

Frank nodded his giant melon and said, "No promises."

Hakim watched Frank leave, smiling wryly. Even he looked a little worse for wear.

"What about me?" he asked. "Shall I also take cash and go home?"

I shrugged. "If you talk this out with me, could be something extra in it for you."

"Talk what out?" I could tell he wanted to see what I'd say.

"Stains that come back; smells that stay for no reason." I took down my mask. "Bad dreams and weird shit. Something's wrong here."

He bowed his head. "Very astute, Sherine, but why ask me to stay?"

I gestured for him to follow and we left the building. Outside, the air smelt like regular Chicago; full of people, greasy food, and icy-cold Lake Michigan.

"Because this weird shit annoys you, but it doesn't scare you. That tells me you're not surprised by it. That tells me you might know what the hell is going on."

Hakim nodded, as if conceding my point. "Let's say you're not far off."

"Is it some kind of hallucinogen?"

He looked a little disappointed. "You know it's not that."

The wind gusted around us; brown and yellow leaves gave a soft *tap*, *tap* as they rebounded off my parked van. The bastard was right; I knew what was happening but didn't want to say it. Saying a thing makes it real.

"Haunted?" I finally blurted out.

Hakim smiled. "Where I come from, it's understood when a man dies poorly, something remains, something that needs to be cleansed. Only in this frozen wasteland do people dress it up with disinfectants and chemicals. They forget Chicago is a city founded in blood and water."

It was the first time I'd ever heard Hakim talk like this. "So ... if the place is haunted, what do we do?"

"This is where our knowledge is the same, Sherine." He laughed at my groan. "What? You think because I'm from Lagos, I know voudons? I'm an atheist."

"An atheist who believes in ghosts?"

"Just so."

"Then what the hell do I do?" I asked.

"I believe that's why you make the big bucks," Hakim said, "and I wish you luck in finding a ghostbuster or a priest."

"Screw you," I said. My phone buzzed. I saw my sister's name on the screen and declined the call, hoping she'd take the hint. It was Mahin's fifth try this month. I hadn't told her about me and Jimmy and wasn't in the mood for another round of big sister judgement.

Hakim gave me an idea. I didn't know any ghostbusters, but I did know Donny "Second Chance" Brogan—or Father Don as most of the families in my parish knew him. Donny was another classmate. Back in the day, he was the guy who could outdrink and outfight any of us. At 16, he caused a three-car wreck while driving his pop's car. Somehow no one got hurt. Donny took it as a sign from God and became pure as the driven snow.

After dropping Hakim off, I rang Donny up and we met for lunch. He looked good, though he'd put on weight since I'd seen him at my niece's christening. Ever since Dad died, I didn't much go to Mass. I could tell Donny was curious, maybe even hopeful I'd had a come-to-Jesus moment.

We ordered food and traded small talk. I could see he wanted to ask what was up, but held back, waiting for me to broach the subject. I appreciated that. Donny was a good guy. If priests had been allowed to put out, I might have even asked what he was up to on weekends he wasn't giving homilies.

I finished my cheese-steak sandwich and laid out the situation with Matt Miller's apartment. The smells. The stains. Everything. After I finished, Donny took a long sip of water and stayed quiet for a while.

"So Sherine, what do you want from me?"

"Well," I said, "do you know any exorcists?"

Donny patted his mouth with a napkin. "Even if I did, I couldn't just put you in touch with them. They're not ghostbusters."

"I know!" I protested. "Look, I'm running out of options here. If you help me... I'll start hitting up Mass again. For one whole year."

Donny chuckled. "Eager as I am to get butts in pews, I don't think the Almighty would approve of quid pro quo. I'll tell you what, Sher. For old time's sake, how about I go with you to this apartment? If I see anything that warrants our diocese's exorcist, I'll contact him. You don't have to attend Mass. This is me, helping an old friend. What you do afterward is up to you."

I nodded, silently thanking the Almighty I wasn't locked in to going to Mass for a whole goddam year.

Fairview Terrace waited for us at the end of the block in Uptown, a half mile away from Lake Michigan. From outside, you could see old trees lining the street and a thin blue strip of water lining the horizon. Being within view of the lake meant posh, but a few blocks away, the neighborhood got sketchy real quick.

I took Donny up to the fourth floor via elevator. As the door opened, I gave him one of our masks. The sickly sweet-smell hit hard. Donny wrinkled his face, but didn't complain. I led him to the empty unit, the stink getting worse with every step. When I unlocked the door, it really swamped us.

"Mother of God," Donny said.

"It's even worse than yesterday," I said, "and it don't make sense. We've used every cleaning agent known to man. This place should smell like bleach."

I showed him where the policeman's body had been found, right in front of a tri-corner vestibule with a view out onto the street. The spray pattern of blood and brains was even darker than it had been the day before.

Standing next to me, I heard Donny begin to mutter the Lord's Prayer.

"So," I asked, my voice muffled behind my mask, "do we qualify for an exorcism?"

Donny didn't answer. I heard whispering; he had his eyes closed and was still praying. Then, as if waking from a deep sleep, his eyes slowly opened.

"We should leave," he said and took me by the arm.

I stayed put. "Do I get my exorcist or what?"

My priest friend glared at me. "Yes, but we need to get the fuck out of here."

Donny swearing did more to get me moving than if the blood on the walls suddenly spelled "Get out Sherine." We pretty much ran out of the place, skipping the elevator and taking the stairs all four flights down. Donny didn't say anything to me until we made it to the van.

"Didn't you feel it?" he asked me. "Whatever happened—it's bad, Sher. I've done the ritual before but never felt anything like ... that."

"Wait," I said, "*you're* the exorcist? Why didn't you tell me?"

Donny gave me a mean smile. "Because I didn't want to cheapen what I do. Besides, I thought you were exaggerating. Should have known better."

"What the hell does that mean?"

Donny laughed. "You never were sensitive, Sher. Remember your nickname in school?"

I laughed. They called me Hardhat because I could take a punch better than most.

"If Hardhat Jankowitz was worried, I should have known something was wrong."

"But you do exorcisms," I said, not wanting to let that go.

"It's not what you think," Donny said. "I've performed the rite a few times. Mostly for Catholic immigrants whose relatives have mental illnesses they don't understand."

"That's messed up," I said.

"You'd be surprised," Donny said, shrugging. "It may be a placebo, it may be real, but when someone believes, it can grant a measure of peace. There may have been a time or two where I felt something unusual, but compared to that apartment..."

"What?" I asked, ignoring the prickle down my spine.

"It's like comparing a breeze to a hurricane," Donny said with a shiver. "A guilt so powerful it literally smells foul. I don't know what happened, but it must be cleansed."

"So you'll take the job?" I said, eyeing the apartment window from the sidewalk. It might have been my imagination, but the room looked a little darker than all the others.

"It's not a—" Donny took a deep breath. "I will help you, yes."

"Solid," I said, clapping him on the shoulder. "Come by on Monday with whatever gear you need. Welcome to the crew, Father Don."

I don't remember my dreams. At least, I never did before. Near as I understand it, most dreams are just random junk your brain spits out while it's doing its nightly cleaning.

I still didn't quite get what was happening. Even after my talks with Hakim and Donny, I viewed the situation as a tough job that required some outside help. I'd have Donny say a few words in front of the boys, we'd clean the place, and that'd be the end of it.

Hardhat. Thick as an ox and just as stubborn, that's me. Always have been, ever since I was a kiddo. It would take a bullet or a mallet to drive a new idea into my skull.

Or this dream.

Maybe it was Donny's reaction to the apartment that opened me up to it. Maybe it was the prayers he said. Truth be told, it didn't feel like a dream. This felt like a movie; only in this movie I could smell and taste the scene as well as see it. Even worse, I could feel what the actor was feeling because I was inside his head.

Starts off with me—no, him—cupping his big, calloused hands beneath a running bathroom faucet. When they're overflowing with icy-cold water, he splashes himself in the face. Then he—I—look in the mirror. And it's not Sherine Jankowitz staring back, which I already guessed from the thick white-man's hands. The face staring back at me is pale and covered with stubble. The hair is thinning at the top; the eyes are bloodshot red.

It's Officer Matt Miller's face. I know it, even though I've never seen him before and won't Google his picture until tomorrow morning. Matt Miller is staring at himself in the mirror. Cold water drips from his chin. He starts crying. I get the feeling he's been crying like this for a while. He stares down at his hands, which twitch and shake. He stares back at himself in the mirror. He looks into his pale blue eyes.

I look into those pale blue eyes. And I'm taken somewhere else again.

This place, at least, feels more like a dream. Faded. Faint colors and blurry lines. I'm still Miller, but I'm in his memory now. Near as I can tell, we're in a large warehouse. There are vehicles in white with familiar blue and red stripes. There are cages. People are standing or sitting in them. Unlike the current Chicago winter with below-zero windchill blasting in off the lake, it's hotter than hell in here. The air's so thick you can taste it. I hear screaming. I hear shouting. I hurry to a dark room where I find a young black man lying on the ground, blood pooling on the floor from his mouth and nose. Standing over the kid is Miller's CO, Sergeant Peter Griggs.

"Little shit thought he could threaten me with a lawsuit," Griggs says, massaging his fist. His voice, the screams, they all sound like they're coming from far away, like I'm hearing them underwater.

"We gotta take him to the hospital," I—Miller says. "He's bleeding pretty bad, Sarge."

Griggs crouches down beside the teenage boy. The sergeant's face and hands are spattered with blood. There're dark stains on the nearby floor and wall. I immediately recognize the spray pattern.

"Too late," Griggs says. Even through the static, I can hear the annoyed disgust in his voice. "Fucking savages. Act all tough, but once you tie 'em down, they learn respect. This one didn't want to learn."

Miller doesn't respond, but he does help his sergeant pick up the body. They leave through a side exit, heading to an abandoned wasteland of cracked pavement that was once a junkyard. The place stinks to high heaven, but at least its cooler than the warehouse. Without saying anything, Miller grabs a shovel, finds a spot of loose soil, and begins to dig. Dirty jobs like this take a while. He can't wait to get home and wash the stink of the garbage, the warehouse, and the kid from him.

And then I'm back in the bathroom, staring at Miller's sad, twitching face. Only now, the face has changed. There's a distance behind those pale blue eyes. As if he's made a decision.

The thick hand reaches beneath the bathroom sink and removes a small black box. I know the gun's in there before he pulls it out.

Miller heads back to the living room, to the couch, to the spot on the floor in the apartment, right in front of that tri-corner window vestibule, the spot on the floor where he put the gun in his mouth and ended it—and I want out of this dream right now. I want to be gone. I can feel the anguish this guy's feeling, a waterfall of guilt drowning my soul.

I want out. I want OUT. But I can't leave, can't move as he slouches his way to the spot where it will happen. He stares out at the Chicago night sky, and for the first time I notice how pretty the view is. A few buildings, but a decent slice of Lake Michigan. Then he loads the gun. I scream at him to stop, do my very damnedest to take over that thick white hand, but he just stares out at the city and slowly brings the gun up.

I can taste the metal, feel the cold barrel poke the roof of his mouth. Feel the trembling, the adrenaline surge, the sweat, and the tears. And through it all, I can feel his guilt. That most of all. It stinks, it stains, and it will never really leave.

Then, just as his finger begins to tighten on the trigger, I break free, fleeing before the scene comes to its awful conclusion.

I woke up sweaty and trembling, but not screaming. Not yet.

Taking a few deep breaths, I got out of bed, headed into the kitchen, and poured myself a stiff drink. The booze burned, but it managed to wash away the taste of metal. I could still smell the guilt. For a moment I wondered if I should follow Jimmy's advice and find another job.

I hurled my empty glass across the kitchen. It smashed against the fridge as I sank to the floor and began to cry.

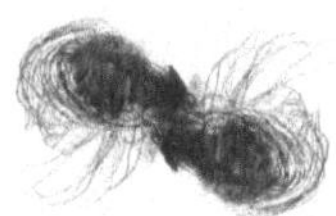

I could have Googled Miller, but I had a much better source.

"What the hell do you want?" The voice on the other end of the line sounded so icy it was a wonder my phone didn't stick to my ear.

"Now, Mahin," I said, "that any way to greet your favorite sister?"

"You're my only sister," Mahin said. "Last time we saw you, Sher, you got so lit you almost puked in my dining room."

"It was a party," I protested. "I had a few drinks!"

"It was my daughter's birthday party," Mahin pointed out.

"In my defense," I said, "maybe you shouldn't have celebrated on the weekend of a Cubs-Sox double-header."

Big sis paused. In a low growl, she said, "Tell me why you're calling, or I hang up."

I told her everything. My sister, Mahin Hogan nee Jankowitz, runs in different circles than I do. Our dad died of a heart attack while we were in high school, and we coped in different ways. While I was getting high, Mahin studied her ass off. While I almost flunked out, she graduated from Northwestern with honors and a degree in journalism. She met her jet-setting husband Carl Hogan while writing for the Trib. They're one of those Chicago power couples: fingers in several pies and eyes on a summer house on the Michigan side of the lake.

Mahin listened to my tale of woe without interrupting. I expected her to make fun of me, ask questions, or hang up. She did none of those things.

"You broke up with Jimmy Catalano?" she asked.

"Well, if you count knocking his teeth out, then yeah."

She was silent for ten whole seconds. "And you started this business on your own?"

"Guess I did."

I heard her breathe out again. "Okay, Hardhat. I'll get back to you this evening."

Mahin called later that day and told me what she'd found in a hushed whisper. She wondered if I'd bitten off more than I could chew but promised I could count on her help.

The sun set early like it always did in Chicago. The wind pushed tiny clumps of trash and leaves into the street gutter. From a block away, the ever-present traffic roared along Lake Shore Drive. My crew and I stood in front of Fairview Terrace. A few of the building's units' lights were on, but Miller's fourth floor apartment stayed dark.

"Here's the deal," I said. "I know things ain't been right since we started this job. I know some of you been skipping on account of the smell and the stains. I'm here to tell you what I intend to do about it. But first off, I'm giving you this."

I passed out envelopes to my crew. In each was $500 cash, decent wages for the work we'd already done. It nearly emptied my savings account, but I needed their help.

"Appreciate it, Hardhat," Gabe said, tucking the wad of cash into his pocket, "but why'd you call us out here?"

"This is my way of saying thanks," I said. "It's also my way of saying you can walk away no strings attached and no hard feelings, or you can help me finish the job."

"How?" Hakim asked. He looked curious rather than afraid.

"We clean the stain," I said. I knocked on the van door and Donny stepped out. "Some of you know Father Don—"

"What up, Second Chance!?" said Frank, giving Donny a high-five.

"—and some of you don't. Father Don Brogan is the priest for St. Mary's over in Lincoln Square. He's here to help us."

The crew exchanged glances. "We gonna do some supernatural shit?" Gabe asked. "Because I didn't sign up for that."

"We ain't doing an exorcism," I said. "We're cleaning a stain." I opened the back of my van where I'd left the shovels. "And to do that, we gotta do some digging."

I picked up a shovel and said casually, "I had the dream last night."

Understanding dawned on my men's faces.

"You okay, boss?" Frank asked.

"I'm good," I said, keeping my voice light. "Takes more than some dead cop's flashback to get to me. And I know how to fix the problem."

"Sher, you don't mean..." said Gabe.

"What happened to that kid ... it ain't right," I said. "To clean this place, we gotta fix that first. Whatever it takes. So who's with me?"

Credit where it's due, none of them backed out, Gabe included. We drove to the warehouse Mahin found for me, where rumor had it cops took suspects they wanted off the books for a while. The street was dark, the air frozen. A few police vans were parked out in front of the building, but it looked empty.

From there, it didn't take long to find the dump yard, which was through an alley across this street. No one saw us. If any police were on duty, they weren't watching the cameras. The rest of the block was an urban jungle of abandoned factories and empty garages.

As a group, we walked through the junkyard. Each step felt heavier. That sickening familiar smell hit right as we rounded a pile of used tires. It was the exact same stink in Fairview Terrace that refused to go away.

In a far corner behind an empty car husk, there was a pile of dirt swelling slightly above the ground. As one, we each put on our masks.

"All right boys," I said. "Get digging. I'll have Mahin make her anonymous tip. Father Don will be on prayer duty, just to be safe."

The boys started to dig, shovels breaking up the frozen dirt with steel spades. Donny's voice filled in the silences between. I sent Mahin a text, telling her to make the calls to the right people. Soon as that was done, I got digging as well. Wasn't long before we found the body.

Time hadn't done much to make him look better. I stared at the faint traces of blood trailing from his mouth and wondered if a bullet was too good for that coward Miller. I knew it was too good for Sergeant Griggs.

"Sherine." Hakim's whisper echoed in the junkyard. I looked where he was pointing—a little off to the side of where we'd recovered the kid. Another hand stuck out from the dirt. In the dim light, it looked gray. We stared at each other, realizing what it meant. Gabe started shaking. Frank wept. Hakim just looked tired.

There was more than one body. We didn't have time to find out how many. Very soon, this was going to be a very crowded dump. Minutes after we pulled away, several news vans flew past us. Mahin's cavalry.

My sister's story hit pretty hard. This was a few years before George Floyd and the shit year of 2020. Chicago PD had already been getting bad press. When news cameras showed sixteen-year-old honors student Gerald Jones being dug up from the ground, it was big. When forensics found dozens more bodies buried in the junkyard, it became the story of the year.

One dead Black kid, maybe they could have swept that under the rug with the usual character assassination bullshit. A mass grave next to an off-the-books police site? Someone had to take the fall for that. Sergeant Peter Griggs is currently on unpaid leave with a trial pending. Prosecution is hoping he'll name some names. Meantime, the warehouse got shut down. They'll probably open another in a few years somewhere else, but at least we got this one, right? That's what I tell myself, anyway.

Soon as we got back to Fairview Terrace, we could tell the difference. Nothing. That's what the place smelled like. Absolutely, positively nothing. The stains on the wall and floor were gone and none of us felt so much as a shiver. Just to be safe, Donny blessed the place.

I got a bonus check, which, after a slight bump to Hakim, I split evenly with the crew, including Father Don. We all met up for a celebratory beer. It was in the middle of that when Donny asked for my opinion on Officer Matt Miller.

"My opinion?" I said. "Guy was a coward."

"Yet by making his sins known," Donny said, "we may have put his soul to rest."

I polished off my latest beer. It was my fifth—or maybe sixth.

"His soul or the victims'?" I said. "We didn't do it for him. We did it because the place was dirty, and it was our job to clean it. We did it so Gerald Jones and the rest of those poor bastards could find peace. Some shit people have to know, Donny."

Donny nodded. He finished his own beer, stood up, and patted me on the back. "Come to Mass when you get the chance, Sher. We could use more people like you."

"People like me?" I asked, laughing. "You mean loud assholes?"

"People who do what's right," said Donny. He squeezed my shoulder and headed over to the bar to pay his tab. The juke blasted blues as the priest headed out into the night. All around me, my crew laughed, sang, and boasted about what they were going to do with their payday. I ordered another round, hoping that tonight I'd be able to finally get some sleep.

# Devil's Ridge

## by Jenny Kiefer

The moment of impact looped, over and over again, before Riley's eyes. Her fingers curled around the stone, then flexed, each tendon taut like a guitar string, ready to propel upwards. The chunk of rock *slipped*, sliding and scooping beneath her fingers. The granite disconnected and fell away from the wall. Her own voice yelled down to her belayer, that there was a rock incoming. Her eyes charted the line of the boulder as gravity pulled it down, heading straight for Samantha's face as if magnetized. The belayer's hands left the rope and as Riley dropped, she raised, a pulley that drew Samantha's face into the rock. Below, it collided with her skull, denting it like the thin siding of a car bumper.

Her face *crunched*. The noise exactly the same as crackling twigs in a campfire, the rock nestled into her skull. The sound repeated when her neck broke. The bones pressed inwards, shattering, the shards slicing through her freckled skin. Blood exploded in a round splatter, the exact shape of a dropped bowl of marinara sauce. Her cheekbones comprised the broken ceramic. For a second, the rock lodged there, burrowed into her gray matter, a granite mask, before it rolled away and tumbled down to the ground, taking her nose and the freckles on her cheeks with it. A bloody soup boiled there, ringed with hair, dumplings of teeth and brain and shredded sinew and plastic helmet and her untouched slug-like tongue floating inside.

Then Riley was back at the start, reaching her hand up to the chunk of rock, unable to stop what had already happened.

The only way to halt the loop was to shut her eyes.

The sun had already begun to recede behind the mountain face. Inklings of chill crept across her bare arms, the sweat drying into a tacky sheen. She kept her eyelids clamped shut against the revolving Rube

Goldberg gore machine. The harness holding her aloft dug bruises into the backs of her thighs, her rubber-encased feet scratching black against the rock wall as she hovered, swaying on the line.

Beneath her, a choking gurgle reverberated through the cooling mountain air. Riley's eyes flutter back open at the noise, no longer stuck in the loop, but still facing the same grim vision before them: her belayer's face had become a stringy mess of ripped sinew and muscle and popped irises, the goop settling on top of the blood like thickened fat. Tooth shards sat all over, some hovering where her forehead had been, some mixing with the eyeball gunk. Most of the front of her skull had been taken by the granite, had cascaded down the two thousand feet to the ground. Riley could see her pulverized brains, a shard of the plastic helmet jutting out of it like a neon horn.

And somehow she was not yet dead.

The gurgle rose again, a bubble popping in the middle of Samantha's face-soup. The vibrations of it snaked up the rope that connected them.

"I'm going to get help," Riley called down, knowing that there was nothing she could do until morning. That there was nothing to be done even if she had the emergency device in her hands this very second. Help would not arrive in time. But the sun had already retreated, silvery stars poking through the clouds. It was too dark to descend to the gear bag that held their lifelines, their food and camping gear and emergency beacons. All Riley could do was secure the anchor keeping them suspended, making sure that it wouldn't rip free or they'd both plunge down after the chunk of rock and the rest of Samantha's face.

They had been halfway through their multi-day pitch of Devil's Ridge, a difficult and technical route on the backside of a mountain in the Atacama Desert. The route sat on the backside of a mountain, a challenging climb with an annoying approach—meaning it hadn't been attempted many times and there wouldn't be much competition to send it, to climb it before anyone else. Riley had scouted this climb for months, wanting to be the first team of women to complete it. Another notch in her career, another accolade, another first.

The pair ascended the first few pitches without issue, their muscles stretching and contracting and locking, their finger tips attaching to the smallest bits of rock as if lined with super glue. They made good time and needed few breaks.

Soon the sun descended, the very tip poking below the face of the mountain.

"We should stop here and start setting up the tent," Samantha called up, holding tight against the rope, giving no slack.

"Let's push through this last bit and then we can stop for the night," Riley replied. If they stopped here, they'd have to make up time tomorrow.

"It's going to get dark really quickly."

"I can do it," Riley said. "It won't take very long."

At Samantha's hesitation, they pressed forward, continuing their ascent against the ticking bomb of impending darkness. But Riley was wrong; this patch of rock proved to be more challenging than anticipated, full of tiny ledges half the width of her fingertips and large swaths of smooth granite that even her rubber-soled toes could not grip. They had no choice but to continue, to pulse *up* to a spot where they could set up camp for the night.

And that's when it happened. Two thousand feet up in the air, a loose rock destroyed Samantha's face.

"Shit," Riley whispered now. The last bit of sunlight extinguished behind the mountain, the shadow shrouding the gore of Samantha. With it came a shuddering chill. Goosebumps settled along her bare skin, little beads for her sweat to pool around like a Plinko board.

Riley's echoing thought was not panged grief or even revulsion but: *the press are going to fucking eat this up.* She could see the headlines now: *Cursed climber Riley Dodge loses another partner.*

Her last partner had reached the crux of a difficult route, almost finishing the eighty feet of rock when her foot slipped and she fell to the ground. It had taken months for the heat to die down, for people to accept her story that it had been an accident, that the lock on the belay device had broken, leaving Riley unable to do anything but watch the rope marathon through, the friction scraping away the fibers. There had been no witnesses. She'd almost lost her sponsorships. But rock climbing was a dangerous sport. Freak accidents happened all the time.

Now, the last reaches of the sun extinguished, leaving pitch dark, only a splatter of freckled stars. Riley preferred climbing uninhibited—as much as possible without fully free soloing. She'd burden herself only with the gear necessary to anchor herself to the rock. Nothing more. Every piece of gear they lugged up the mountain suspended on a rope beneath the corpse of her partner, who now hung limp and silent. No more hideous gurgles. No more thrumming of the rope that kept them tethered.

With the settling cold, the goosebumps lining her bare skin transformed to daggers, each little dot a pinprick worming its way deep into her tissue. Stranded without her windproof tent and subzero sleeping bag, she had no choice but to endure, to shove her exposed fingers inside her armpits and hope she didn't awaken to black doll's hands the next morning.

She turned her face away from the wind, but she could still feel the pricks, the pins and needles of the water molecules living in her skin turning frosty, transforming to sharp crystals of ice. It started at her ears and nose and slithered in towards her cheeks, towards her clattering teeth like a worm shoving deeper into dirt. Crackling now, her sweat had become solid. It flaked away like shards of salt.

Amidst her body's violent shudders, against its wild attempts to keep every atom of her being moving, trying to generate some internal heat, Riley almost didn't notice the steady twang coming from the rope, a pulse that traveled up and through the rattling anchors and down to her own harness. Steady and almost rhythmic, as if intentional. As if a finger were curled and plucking.

Even through the darkness, Riley swore she could see this finger beneath her, attached to Samantha's limp body. She gritted her teeth. The constant pulse ending at her hips was unending. *It must be some sort of muscle spasm*, she assured herself. Something natural that occurred after death.

Every inch of her bare skin screamed, the mouth of each pore stuffed with needles. She hugged her limbs tighter against her. But nothing could save her tiny extremities, the mountain ranges of cartilage that she could almost feel hardening, turning into a black chunk of useless flesh.

A low noise started then, rising up to Riley's frozen ears. A low, throaty rumble. Almost a growl. It emanated from Samantha. Riley could no longer make out the shape of her belayer in the pitch darkness. Her eyes were useless now, unable to even distinguish her own shoulders, the frozen knob of her own nose. In a void of black, she could merely feel the steady flicking of the rope against her hips and the daggery chill, and now, she heard the rumble from below.

"S—Samantha?" she called into the emptiness. The condensation coating the words formed ice crystals on her eyelashes. "Are you—making that noise?"

A stone dropped into Riley's stomach, like she'd unhinged her jaw and swallowed the chunk that had decimated Samantha's skull. It did not seem possible that the body below her could still contain life. Even if the impact had not immediately killed her, surely in the hours—how much time had passed, Riley wondered, how much time had she spent in this shroud—that had elapsed, the belayer's busted brain would have stopped sending signals for her heart to keep pumping. Surely she'd lost more than enough blood, more than enough of it had pooled in the bowl of the remains of her face.

Still, the noise floated up to her. Unmistakably human. She imagined the soup of Samantha's face bubbling with each sound, the red orbs popping and splattering as each grumbling noise released. Stray teeth wandered in the goop with each eruption. If everything inside her did not feel like a frozen hunk, Riley might have vomited.

"*Rrrrr-iiiii-lllleeeee,*" the voice growled, the stray noise transforming to earnest syllables.

Somehow a shiver echoed through Riley's body, even beneath the numbing pinpricks, cutting through the frozen wind hugging the mountain. Punctuated by blood-filled burps and burbles, the corpse—and that's what it had to be by now; it could no longer be her belayer, no longer any bit of Samantha remaining—seemed to be forming words.

"*RRRiiii-lllleeeee,*" it repeated. "*I noooooo wwww-wwwattt yooooo ddd-iiiddd.*"

Trapped, needing to keep her hands packed into the relative warmth of her own armpits, Riley hovered, unable to stop the sound from squirming into her brain, unable to stop herself from parsing the noise, from putting the puzzle together of the syllables that kept repeating beneath: *I know what you did.*

She must have succumbed to sleep at some point. Suddenly blistering heat pounded against her face—every speck of bare skin sizzling and screaming with the exception of her nose and ears, three voids lining her face. For a moment, in her grogginess, in the searing pain of the bright sunlight, the events of the previous day were erased from her memory. She squinted against the newfound light, examining the new terrain of skin that sat on her hands like a glove. A patchwork quilt of purple and blue extended from her fingernails. Clear pustules polka dotted the swirls of her fingerprints, full to bursting on top of her calluses. Along the creases of her knuckles, the skin flaked away, peeling as though the new day's sun had already burned that layer away.

She examined her damaged hands, her money-makers, the two most important things she needed to do her job. How was she going to climb with these hands? She imagined that one single grip against the rough rock would puncture each one of these pustules simultaneously, would release the torrent of oozing serum trapped inside, leaving her fingers sticky, the screaming mouths of the blisters gulping up every speck of dirt, clogging and choking from every miniscule pebble lingering on the wall.

An odd noise bubbled into her consciousness, something wet and smacking, something like rubber bands being snapped. With each *snap*, the rope still tied at Riley's waist strummed, vibrated like guitar strings.

Perched on Samantha's dangling chest was a vulture. Its talons sank between the bones of her ribcage, bloody glops soaking into her shirt, slithering around the claws. Its featherless, red head bobbed. Chunks of her belayer's cheeks, some of the gore soup, slunk down the bird's throat before it bent for more, plucking away stray teeth and bone shards and dropping them into the air beside her head. With the next bite, it caught a stringy tendon and pulled it taut, stretching its head back until the string snapped. Samantha's congealed face bobbled on her limp neck.

Hovering above the bird and its meal, Riley could only kick and scream at the thing. The rope jangled and twanged in the commotion, jostling the corpse. The bird sank its talons in further on its swinging raft-meal, the crunching of bones between its toes forcing Riley to grimace, grinding the ones inside her mouth.

With enough wild shooing, flung arms and a hoarse throat, the vulture became spooked enough to abandon its meal, tearing one last chunk of flesh for its flight. With a stretch of its wings, the rope twisted and coiled around its wings, noosing around its neck. Squeezing taut with each of its movements. The bird's panged, panicked peals pierced through the numb exterior of her ears. Through pure instinct, Riley slapped her hands over the canals, the blisters lining her fingertips grazing the stiffened, necrotic flesh there.

It takes a moment for her to realize that she must untangle the bird, must free it from its wiry cage lest she be attached to two corpses, or, worse, that its wild, violent panic would rip out the anchors. The clips and cams shuttered against the rock in a metallic metronome. With each clack of the gear, little pebbles, tiny sprinkle-sized segments of the rock pulled loose. The gear shifted out of place. Each flap of the bird's wings moved the doomed party one step closer to cascading two thousand feet to the ground.

When she lowered her hands, something remained in her palm, curled and nestled in its creases. A crusty crescent, totally black. A foreign object that Riley couldn't decipher for a very long moment. When the realization came, it brought with it a cavernous  heaviness that settled deep in her guts. The little thing was part of her own ear, frostbitten, the flesh having escalated from pink to an enflamed red to an engorged purple to an eternal black. The top curve of her ear now sat inside her hand like a little piece of plastic, slick and hard as a doll's shoe. There was little time to mourn the lost appendage; the rattling gear and cracking rock shrieked in the remains of it. Riley slipped the stiffened slice of flesh beneath her top, unable to let even that piece of herself drop.

This was not how this climb was supposed to happen. They should be hundreds of feet higher by now. Her fingers should host calluses, not puss-filled balloons. She should be working the problem of the mountain, not the problem of unwinding her rope from a vulture's neck. Her belayer should be feeding her rope, not ragdolling at the end of it. It wasn't supposed to go so utterly wrong. She wasn't supposed to lose.

But she'd never get a chance for redemption if she didn't move quickly. She'd be spending another night naked to the elements if she did not untangle the bird, reset the anchors, and rappel down to retrieve the gear before the sun beat her to the punch, before it cascaded behind the pillar of rock. She had no idea what time it was or how much time she had to accomplish these goals. Her purple fingers, no longer strong and nimble, plucked at the rope. Each movement pained her, sent a million little knives through her fingertips and up into her elbows. The little pillows of puss popped, sticky serum slipping over the rope and her hands, each one gasping in stinging agony at the influx of air. Beneath her, the bird of prey continued its fervent flapping, its shrill shrieks, and the ensuing vibrations snaked up the rope, ensnaring Riley's wounded fingers.

The anchor slipped a full inch, the rock cracking around it. Ready to burst.

Beneath the tangled bird, Samantha was just a limp corpse, swinging gently at the whims of the rope's vibrations, at its tugging. Her arms hang at her sides, no finger to strum the rope in calculated time. No noises bubbled from her face soup, no syllables or sounds that could be mistaken for words. Any skin not decimated by the rock chunk hung taut against her skeleton, the underside purpling and sagging, a sack of rotten, stinking bacteria.

Finally, Riley untangled her fingers and then the bird's neck and wings, and with one last push against the complicated apparatus of rope and metal and flesh and rock, it departed. In its wake, it left a clear view of Samantha, who was very certainly dead. Maybe Riley had hallucinated the steady staccato on the rope and the distorted words. Maybe the sheer darkness had created a sort of sensory deprivation tank, the starless sky and numbing wind conjuring insanity.

Beneath her belayer's corpse hung the pack holding all the gear, holding the warm sleeping bags, the tent, the emergency radio. It seemed so close now, spinning at the end of a rope just a few feet beneath Samantha. Before Riley could retrieve it, she needed to fix the problem of the cracking rock, the tenuous volcano that could erupt at any time and send everything plunging. Fiddling with the anchor forced more pins and needles into her ruined hands, the whole process taking three times as long as normal. The thawed flesh there felt like rotten fruit, soft and sloppy and wet. By the time she was satisfied with her work, the sun had started its descent behind the mountain.

Rappelling now would be risky; the darkness would seep across the mountain shortly. But she might not survive another night with the elements. All the water inside her body might transform into icy crystals, every muscle and atom slowly morphing her into a hardened statue. She'd been lucky to only have lost her ears and nose the previous night.

Slowly and cautiously, she lowered herself. The scent of Samantha's corpse floated to her, more and more pungent the closer she got. The body itself seemed to be shuddering, flailing, a movement Riley could not decipher, could not determine whether it was moving on its own or whether it was still at the whims of the inertia pulsing through the connected rope.

The sky was a deep pink by the time Riley reached the dangling corpse, the sun's face hidden behind the mountain's peak. The putrid perfume reached its peak as she hung level with the rotting flesh. To retrieve the gear, she would need to get even closer. She'd have to touch it to reach the rope at the back of the harness still surrounding its hips. The thought made acid boil up to her throat and onto her tongue, searing the soft tissue there. She gulped one last breath of fetid air and started the dreaded task when the gurgling words came once more.

*"Riii-llleeeeee. I kn-now what yo-oou did."*

A smirk lived inside them, something Riley could sense. She could picture the shape Samantha's lips would have made if they had still been present. With pure, automatic revulsion, her body kicked away, scrambling back to the safety of the rock, the sneering cadaver swaying from the aftershock.

Then—clear in the lingering sunlight—the belayer's arm lifted from its side, the dead flesh rising. The congealed face-soup bubbled as if boiling, as if *laughing*, as its green-laced fingers pulled out Samantha's pocket knife and cut the rope holding the gear, which careened to the ground.

A scream erupted from Riley's throat, a guttural, primal roar that edged around the bile lining her esophagus. Scrambling, she tried to climb, sloppy and panicked, her feet scratching at the rock, slipping. The ring of skin surrounding each blister ripped, peeled away in purple curls as she slapped her hands against the mountain, scraping to find any ledge that might hoist her further away from the deranged corpse, from the *moving* corpse, at all costs, even at the bloody expense of her fingers. She even grabbed onto the rope, tugged herself upwards like a high school gym class. No longer thinking about compromising the anchor, only getting *away*.

Strangled laughter bubbled from the corpse at Riley's mad rush, the noise emerging from the congealed mess of blood and flesh and bone shards. Flaps of ripped skin hanging from the edge of the face-crater shook in time with each choked chortle.

"*I know what you did,*" it said, the words clear, somehow no longer muffled by the lack of tongue and palate. "*You let her fall. You held the lock open and fed the rope through. You did it on purpose.*"

Riley's limbs halted, an icy chill slithering over her skin, a sensation disconnected from the mountain winds.

"*No gear had failed,*" the corpse continued. "*You did it because she was going to finish it before you. You couldn't stand to let someone else take your glory. To place above you. To be better than you.*"

And it was true. Riley had been convincing, had even thrown the belay device against the rock until it did break. It was like the entity, this voice or corpse or demon or whatever currently inhabited her dead belayer had been there, right beside her, like it had even guided her hands as Riley watched her partner surpass the crux of the route. Like it held the sweat-slicked rope along with her when her climbing partner completed the route before Riley had even reached the halfway point in her own attempts.

Riley's heart had dropped. Anna, her partner, was a newcomer to the scene, some prodigy who appeared suddenly and racked up achievements, one after the other with ease. She'd been so new she had apparently not heard about Riley's cutthroat reputation, had not seen the footage plastered online of Riley screaming at other climbers to stop watching her, accusing them of trying to steal her beta. Anna had apparently not developed the magnetic repulsion that kept other climbers at arm's length from her, nobody wanting to partner with her—even if she was, on paper, the best. She wasn't going to apologize for being aggressive. It's what she had to do, who she had to be to get to the top. If that made her a loner, then so be it.

Anna was supposed to be a safe bet, a partner who'd be a competent belayer, but wouldn't overshadow her. Riley had been studying the route for months—Anna had never heard of it. So when this thin, short girl who had been climbing for just a couple of years, who hadn't put in her dues, hadn't done any scraping or hard work, reached the top before Riley, she grinded her teeth, there at the bottom. So when it was time to slowly lower Anna to the ground, she held the lock open, watched as the rope raced through, Anna's body cracking in a heap.

Now, the corpse laughed, a hysterical noise that ground its way through the gore. "*She was better than you. And she didn't even have to work half as hard.*"

Any hints of sunlight had been snuffed from the sky. The darkness crept in, a frigid shroud enveloping them.

"*You couldn't stand it,*" it said. "*You couldn't let her surpass you so easily. So you let her fall. You got rid of her.*"

The corpse sat up, leaned its melting, ruined flesh against the wall, only its inky silhouette still visible below Riley. Then it started to climb. Heading up towards her.

"*And you got rid of me, too,*" it growled. "*Where did that leave you?*"

"This time was an accident," Riley said, her words quiet and numb.

The rope swung wild, gaining slack as the thing ascended.

"*Now it's your turn.*"

Riley's heart hammered in her chest. She had nowhere to go; she'd reached the anchors. If she moved above them, she might as well free climb with no gear at all. Her hands scrambled along the rock, migrating back to the spot where the chunk had pulled free. Her stiffening fingers clawed around a sharp shard. It sliced into her flesh, spilling dark blood, a pain distanced from the seeping cold.

The corpse grew closer, growling and giggling. The darkness edged in, eclipsing even its silhouette beneath the moonless and starless night. The anchor she crafted should hold her aloft even if her belayer fell, and, her pulse pounding a mad rhythm against her skull, she got to work with the rock-knife, slicing through rope. The corpse climbed fast, the pungent, putrid scent of it growing, seeping through even the frostbitten nub at the end of her face.

But then it stopped. And laughed, an uproarious, gleeful noise that kept its distance.

Riley kept slicing.

The shard broke through the exterior sheath and snipped at the inner core. Only when a few measly fibers remained did Riley realize her mistake. She'd been slicing through the side that lead to her own harness.

Seconds later, a single *snap* echoed through the mountain air.

Her body floated down, gaining speed, the corpse's laughter following her even after she passed it. The wretched sound continued even after her body had halted, too suddenly and too soon, seeming to hover in midair.

From her belly rose a darkened silhouette of something thin and long, something that rose to a point above her. Her shaking, numb fingers could not determine whether she'd been pierced by rock or tree. But, she supposed, it didn't matter either way.

The sun stretched its arms into the darkness, brushing it away. Riley died slowly, her glazed eyes staring at the peak she wouldn't top, her partner dangling in the gentle wind.

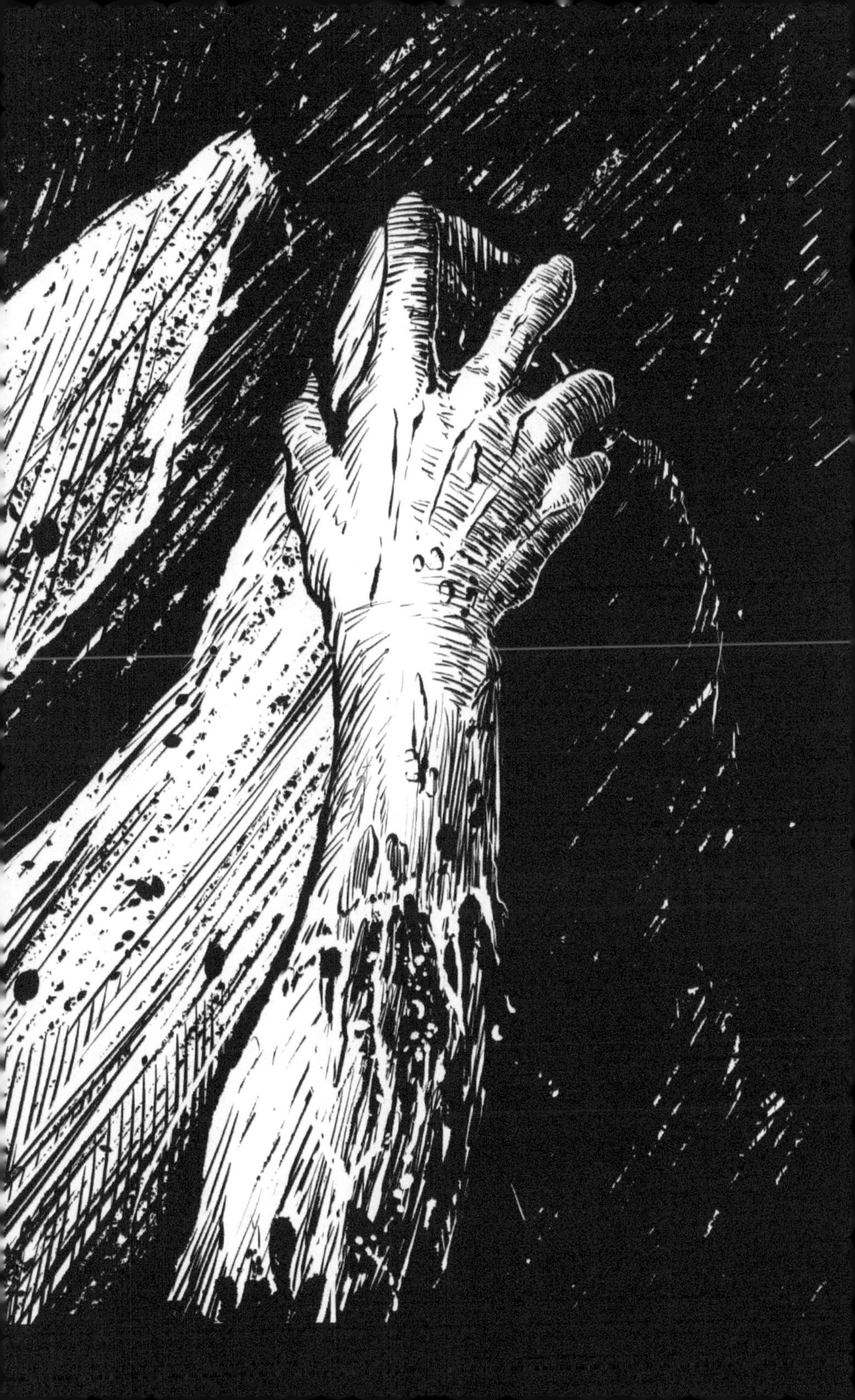

# Water Drops on Stone Hearts

## by Christopher O'Halloran

Water drops hit the carpet like tiny fingers behind a curtain. A soft, rhythmic *pat ... pat ... pat...*

Andrea hears the drops now that the sound of rushing water coming from the tap has ceased. She stops brushing, foam lathering between her lips and gums.

In grade three, Mrs. Johnson taught Andrea's class to conserve water for the sake of our planet. Turn the tap off while you brush your teeth and only turn it on to rinse. A lesson Andrea should have taught her daughter. A lesson Julián might have taught her.

*Pat ... pat ... pat...*

The sound comes from her right. In the walk-through closet leading to the room she shares with no one. The room where Clippy, the rubber duck, sits on her nightstand in his usual spot. Waiting patiently atop her old copy of *Anna Karenina*.

Andrea had once again crawled into bed forgetting to brush her teeth and had to rise with a groan to complete the arduous chore.

"That you, Clippy?"

He makes no reply. She knows he's not wet. He's not a bath time duck; he's a programming tool. Something she can bounce ideas off, a focal point for her troubleshooting.

Clippy isn't dripping. Something nearby is. Something that smells faintly of wood rot and skunk cabbage.

The bathroom is dark. A small night light in the corner glows a soft red. A calming tone that will help her fall back asleep. As different from the bright overhead lights as this condo is from the home she left, years ago.

The soft glow of the night light doesn't reach the closet. It barely reaches Andrea, casting her face in scarlet shadows that distort the features she hates: her long, pointed nose; her round face whose cheeks bounce when she runs; acne scars she shouldn't have picked.

If there's something dripping in her closet, she'll need to fix it. She'll need light. Sleep is long gone anyway.

"Grab the toolkit, Clippy." She leans down to spit and—economical in everything, even her motions—flips the light switch.

The bulbs fire up and fully illuminate the woman in the closet.

Andrea screams. She falls to the floor, banging her elbow on the way down.

The woman's neck stretches long, vertebrae sticking out along twisted flesh. Her head is cocked at a wrong angle, chin pointed towards Andrea like an accusatory finger. Her eyes are squeezed shut and her mouth turns down in a grimace. As if she ate something bitter. A wilted plant. A crushed aspirin.

Bloodshot eyes spring open. Full of pleading. Full of a desperate desire to live.

She's young, skin pockmarked with the acne scars from teenage years of popping and picking. Unshed baby fat turns her cheeks round.

Her mouth creaks open in supplication, but all that pours out is the harsh ringing of a phone.

Andrea screams again, neighbours be damned. She closes her eyes and holds her hands out in a feeble attempt to ward off the woman in her closet. Any moment now, she'll lurch forward. She'll come for Andrea.

What will her outstretched palms touch first? The soaking wet fabric of her jeans? The torn blouse? Her cold, pale flesh?

The phone rings again.

Andrea opens her eyes.

The woman is gone. Clippy makes no acknowledgement of the disruption. The neighbours don't even bang.

In a daze, Andrea climbs to her feet, nursing her sore elbow. The phone rings once more. She hurries to answer it.

"Hello?" Her voice is a whisper. She still tastes the mint of her toothpaste coating her teeth like a moss carpet over river rocks. Andrea clears her throat. "Hello?"

A man on the other end is crying. A high pitched whine slips out over the line.

Andrea looks at the phone. It's Julián. It's her ex.

"What's wrong? Julián? Are you okay?"

Andrea looks at Clippy. For a second, her eyes lose focus. The bright yellow rubber turns briefly green, and Andrea thinks she's going to faint.

Colours right themselves, and Clippy pops back into focus, lemon yellow. He stares at the closet, his bright smile the antithesis of the noise Julián makes from across the country.

"It's Mariana," he sobs. Their daughter—a woman Andrea doesn't know. The last time she saw her, Mariana was thirteen.

Andrea follows Clippy's gaze to the closet. Beneath the plain blouses, the heavy jackets, the featureless cardigans, there is a dark puddle.

Her daughter is in a closed casket, and nobody says why. Andrea can hardly blame them. Julián's parents, his co-workers, his friends. Mariana's peers all looking as if they stumbled out of middle-school and not like the college-aged kids of her time. They all peer at Andrea out of the corners of their eyes. Murmuring to each other.

*That's her?*

*Why do you think she left?*

*Didn't even talk to them anymore. Refused to.*

The refusal was Mariana's, but Andrea never pushed it. She had been more than okay with letting the contact dry up. The truth is, she was never meant to be a mom. According to everyone, she's cold, impatient, miserable. Trying caused more damage than leaving.

Andrea places her fingers on the lid of the casket. It's hard to the touch. Warm like something living. Like something inside is burning to get out.

What would she see if she threw open the lid? An elongated neck? Grey skin the colour of a fish belly? Soaking wet clothes?

No, they would have changed her. Put her in a dress she would have hated.

Does Mariana still hate dresses the way she did as a kid?

"We didn't know if you were going to come." Julián speaks at her side. His voice sounds shredded, as if he had torn his larynx to pieces over the grief of his lost child. "They told me not to invite you."

"You could have told me after the funeral," says Andrea. "A small part of you must have wanted me here." She reaches out and brushes a pinkie against his hand.

He pulls away.

"I wasn't the one to leave."

"You know it wasn't doing us any good," says Andrea. Her hand returns to the casket. She runs a finger along the crease between the lid and the body. Ready to fling it open. To see her daughter a final time. "Why the closed casket?"

"*No me hinches las pelotas*," curses Julián. "I don't need you coming back and casting your doubts on my choices."

"I'm just asking."

"You made your choice." He puts his hand on the lid of the casket. Holding it down. Making sure she can't take a look.

She wants to ask a million questions. What was she like? Was she abrasive like Andrea? Was she a little too honest, a little too critical, a little too sensitive? Did she like things done a certain way, or was she more like Julián? Going with the flow. Being okay with failure, with a half-assed job, with the bare minimum.

"How did she die?" is the question she settles on. Everyone made veiled remarks about how she was at peace now. How she had been so strong for everyone. The tip of the spear: sharp, but the first spot to blunt. Andrea has her suspicions, but she needs to hear the truth.

"You don't deserve to know," says Julián. His voice is quiet, but full of vinegar. People are looking. Talking.

"I'm her mother," says Andrea.

"*Me chupa un huevo*," curses Julián once more. "You didn't act like it."

"She wouldn't do something like this."

"How would you know?" Julián stares through her. His hair

bristles along his skull like the short fuzz of a peach. Efficient. Andrea had always admired that part of him. "How would you know what she would do and what she wouldn't?"

Julián's father approaches from behind and puts a hand on his son's shoulder. He whispers something in his ear. Something in Spanish. Andrea doesn't catch it.

Tears turn Julián's eyes glassy.

"She was starting to look just like you." The tears fall. They tumble down his cheeks, perching on the corner of his mouth for a second before dripping off to splash on his cheap shoes. "Just like you."

His father leads him away.

"I know," whispers Andrea. Since she was young, Andrea saw her own features in her daughter. She wished she hadn't. She prayed for Mariana to get more of her father, but her prayers went unanswered. Moving hadn't helped; distance was no match for genetics.

Andrea rubs a palm along the lid of the casket. It doesn't feel as warm as it did. The wood is dying. Ready for burial.

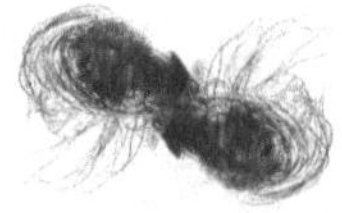

Mariana is not ready for burial. She is falling, pulled by torrential forces of water. Tugging at her clothes, her flesh.

On her face is the panic of a drowned cat. She pinches her mouth shut, trying to hold onto the air in her lungs. But it's a long fall. Her dark, curly hair flows upward as panic gives way to peace.

This is it. This is the end. An end to the suffering. The endless loop. The broken record.

But the end comes hard. She hits the rocky pool at the bottom of her fall. It's like hitting concrete.

Bones shatter. Her organs are torn apart as they rattle against the shards of her ribcage. The look of serenity on her face contorts. Becomes something like disgust. Swallowing what your mother told you was medicine but turned out to be arsenic.

Whistles and bells ring out from above the water. Though she can feel nothing, see nothing, she still hears it. Shrill noises passing through the water, cutting through the sound of the rush. Mingling with it until it becomes a cacophony more unbearable than the fall.

A rope, the end tied in a loop, hooks around her neck. It slips under her chin. Whoever threw it begins to pull, stretching her head away from her body. The weight of all that broken china sinking while someone tries to retrieve her.

Her neck stretches. The last thing she hears—the ticking of a metronome to the raucous sound of rushing water and shrieking whistles—is the vertebrae in her neck popping out of position.

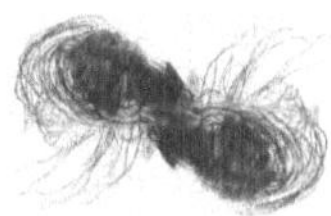

Andrea wakes covered in sweat. It's as if someone poured a bucket over her sleeping form. The sheets are soaked. She won't be surprised if it's reached all the way to the mattress. Maybe the hotel has some sort of protection over it. Maybe she'll just have to tip extra before she leaves.

The amount of water is too much to have come from her.

Her chest heaves with the breath she's been holding. As if she had been both observer and observed. Herself and her daughter.

She looks over at the glass of water on her side table. It's empty. Clippy sits on the other side of it, happy, white eyes unblinking.

"Was that you, Clippy?"

He doesn't answer.

"If I wanted a wake-up call, I'd have asked the hotel for a dryer one." Andrea slips out of bed and goes into the unfamiliar bathroom, groping for a towel. Not turning on the lights. Wanting to go back to sleep.

Not learning her lesson; anything can sneak up on you in the dark.

Her eyes buried in the fluffy texture of the hotel towel, Andrea stops breathing.

Drops of water splash against tile. One for every twenty heartbeats rushing through her ears. A cold sheet falls over her. Like a live wire, her body hums, stuck between collapse and escape.

*It's nothing,* she thinks. *It's the bathtub.*

Andrea is logical. She doesn't make decisions based on emotion. She doesn't see ghosts in every shadow.

When she pops her head out of the towel and turns on the light, she sees drops of water forming on the mesh of the sink faucet. Molecules coalescing, building until their combined weight pulls them away from one grill and down another.

She breathes a sigh of relief.

"I'm losing it, Clippy."

She turns the bathroom light off. Something glows from the main room. Her laptop sits on the desk. It's no longer in the bag she clearly remembers putting it in at the end of the night.

On numb legs, Andrea shuffles out of the bathroom. The towel falls forgotten onto the floor. When she sits in the chair in front of her laptop, her pyjama pants make a wet squelch that sends rivulets over the fabric and down the cheap wood of the legs.

"They never told me how you died." She's not talking to Clippy anymore.

She opens her web browser and clicks on the search bar. Her cursor blinks at her, waiting for her query.

"How did you die?"

Andrea types. *Death Vancouver 2024.*

Too much. Too vague. The results encompass too much, most of it celebrity related.

*Suicide Vancouver 2024.*

Again, too vague.

*Girl drown Vancouver 2024.*

That does it. As soon as she sees the headline, Andrea knows.

*Rescue team pulls body of woman from bottom of Cascade Falls.*

"It's you," she says. "That's how you died."

Something shuffles at her legs. A body moving closer. A cold girl attempting to find warmth at the lap of her mother.

Andrea closes her eyes.

"What were you doing there, Mariana?" It's a dumb question. She knows why Mariana was there.

Andrea raises her hand and holds it over her daughter's head. The moisture in her hair tingles against her palm though they don't touch. She holds her breath again. It's been so long since she's given comfort. Will she be able to?

Her hand falls and passes through flesh like mist. If Mariana was there before, she isn't now.

It's been almost two decades since Andrea visited Cascade Falls. The roar of the waterfall is deafening from this close. She's had to climb a barrier to get here, one that wasn't in place when she came with Mariana.

Back when she was still a mother.

That had been one of the last good days. Julián had encouraged Andrea to take Mariana out for a Mommy/Daughter Day. Something to bring her closer to her six-year-old. Something to break through the anger. The depression. The weight of expectation manifesting in her body like ice on the wing of a plane.

Nothing was ever as perfect as Andrea wanted it to be. She couldn't be the mother the world demanded. She was doomed to be just like her own. Cold. Distant. Happiness always out of reach.

But when she had sat in sight of the falls with her six-year-old, it all seemed to slough away. The roar of the rushing water was greater than the roar of her disappointment. The roar of her responsibility. They sat together, closer than ever. Mariana lay   in her lap, and Andrea stroked her long, beautiful hair.

She had looked more like Andrea every day. Andrea remembers pretending that Mariana was herself as a child and giving herself that love and acceptance that had been non-existent.

But outside of the falls, Mariana continued looking like Andrea. It became an irritant. A reminder of every flaw, every failure in her own life. A mirror that reflected every ugly part of herself.

Leaving was the only option. Her toxicity would have infected her family if she didn't. Like her own mother said, she was never meant to be anything but alone. Maybe if she could have lived at the waterfall in the midst of that roar, she could have been the mother Mariana deserved.

Is that why Mariana came here? Did she have the same thoughts, feel the same weight of the world infesting her?

"She didn't do it," Andrea says, standing by the water. Clippy is back at the hotel room, but she speaks aloud out of habit. "She wouldn't."

The smell of wood rot and skunk cabbage slips inside her. Death, and life that smells like death made somehow pleasant.

Something bobs in the river flowing past. A misshapen chunk of forest-green rubber. Rotating in the current, head breaching the water.

A rubber duck. Not hers—not Clippy—but another piece of Andrea's past. A gift they had received at her baby shower. An expensive toy made with cruelty-free rubber. Not the cheap yellow thing Andrea talked to, but something to save. Something to cherish.

Something to keep out of reach of little girls who might ruin it.

It flows past, a toy denied to Mariana for six long years. Andrea wants to grab for it, but it's out of reach. A dead tree hangs over part of the river, but anyone who would use that to lean down to scoop up the passing duck would be...

"No." Andrea covers her mouth. She doesn't know why she's seeing the duck.

It goes over the falls, dropping out of sight. There's nothing left to suggest it was there to begin with.

"Did you see it, too?" Andrea asks. "Did you try to rescue it?"

Another flash of green appears at the corner of Andrea's sight. Another duck. It bobs in the current, passes under the tree again.

Something follows it. Dark, soaked in the water. Long like a log but many limbed.

It bounces against a jutting rock and rolls over.

Andrea cries out.

Her daughter's face pops above the surface of the water. Her eyes are closed, and her mouth is twisted in a scowl. She looks exactly like Andrea did in her twenties.

Andrea can't move. Mariana—how can she be in the ground and here at the same time?—floats past. Dead, but not at rest. The water jostles her, violates her. Takes her over the edge of the falls and out of sight.

Tears fall from Andrea's eyes. Her knees shake. She wants to collapse.

"I should have given you the duck," she whispers. "I should have given you the duck. You wanted it so bad. You..." Her voice fails, though her lips make the motion. She can barely breathe. Her lungs cry out for oxygen.

Another duck goes past. Another Mariana.

Another.

Another.

A never ending loop of suffering daughters, of floating women reaching for their mother's love.

Andrea moves. She can't stop herself. For once, she's not thinking. Not calculating. She's sprinting for the tree, inching out along it. Feet on the bank's edge, leaning over as far as she can.

The falls pound in her ears. It threatens to burst her eardrums, makes her eyes shake.

She needs to do this. She needs to break the cycle.

The forest green duck goes past, but she ignores it. She's not here for the duck. It drops over the edge, only a few feet down river.

Mariana is coming. This close, it looks like she's moving at highway speeds. There's no way she can grab her. Not without falling in herself.

Andrea redoubles her grip on the branch and stretches toward the water. It sprays up at her.

Hard, jagged bark cuts her fingers. Blood flows over her hand and down her wrist, snaking its way to a screaming shoulder.

One shot. She can do it.

"Come on," she says, gritting her teeth. "Come on, baby."

Mariana is under her suddenly.

Andrea grabs her shirt, gets a good handful of fabric.

The river pulls Mariana, trying to lay claim to her, but Andrea will not let go.

Something in her shoulder pops. Agony shoots out along Andrea's collarbone. She screams, the noise louder than the falls. Louder than the whistles of someone out of sight. A rescuer noticing the struggling woman.

Andrea screams again and lurches away from the river, pulling her daughter out. Mariana's limp form falls on top of her, heavy with the weight of the water she's absorbed. It flows over Andrea, soaking her pants.

"Oh," she moans, the sound lost. "Oh, honey."

Mariana's head is in her lap once more. That grimace points up at the sky. As if the brightness is too much for her eyes, even closed.

Andrea rolls her so that she's looking over the edge of the falls. Off into the distance. She can pretend like that. Pretend her little girl is with her again. That the world has no expectations for either of them.

"I've got you, baby. You're okay. You're all right."

With Andrea's shawl over that broken, distorted neck, she can pretend her daughter is sleeping. They're just in the moment between breaths. Waiting for the inhale.

Andrea runs her fingers through Mariana's wet hair. She gently works the tangles out. Careful not to pull too hard. Her arm hangs limp, the shoulder throbbing and misshapen, but that's why Andrea has two.

"I'm here, baby."

The blood from her ripped fingers runs down Mariana's cheeks.

"I'm here."

The rushing water is clear. No bobbing duck. Nothing.

# When The Fox-Bells Ring

## by Ally Wilkes

London went slowly.

There wasn't a single point when it all went bad. The weather grew worse, then became strong enough to kill, a newly awakened giant. The floods drowned the city, then receded, and thousands—*millions*—of mosquitos began to hum their razor songs in the dusk.

One year, the lights worked, supermarkets had food; the next year, none of that was true.

Five years on.

Ten years on.

She's learned to mark the passing of time by simple events, now the seasons don't really turn. Today, she stands at the back door, pouring out a cup of rusty water. There's always a damp leaky patch in the corner of her daughter's bedroom, the colour of blood.

She'd brought the cup from her Nana's house. It's a collectible: painted on it is a winsome fairy-child wearing a hat made of foxgloves, peeping out from behind a spray of those reddish purple trumpets.

Nana had always believed in the fairies.

Now Mairead is old enough to be a nana herself, and she's still never seen one.

Standing at the kitchen sink, swilling out the fairy cup in a basin of settled water, Mairead thinks she might be the only resident left in the borough; she knows she's the only one left on this street. It ends at the Thames, now, the swollen-banked Thames, glittering and shimmering three doors down. It had crawled over number 23's garden wall last winter, sucking and lapping, then onto the lawn like a thief in the night. It had engulfed the abandoned trampoline, the pond—already full of mosquitos, singing like the plague—and progressed up to the kitchen door, inviting itself in.

There are whole streets drowned like this. More, in the aftermath of a storm. She can walk for hours and see not another living person. Her back garden is a forest, drooping a little in the summer heatwave, the relentless pounding of forty degrees or more, and looks more like a jungle than a suburban garden. Dock-leaves the size of dinner-plates. Parakeets, keeping a wary eye in the thickets, sometimes exploding out of the undergrowth with their hoarse and frightened chirps. A massed stand of foxgloves, waving purple trumpets.

There's something so fertile, so ... fleshy ... about it all.

When she shuts the back door again, the ceaseless din of the mosquitos fades away, although a few, sun-drunk, bat themselves against the kitchen window. Mairead has lived through the swinging Sixties, the greedy Eighties and the recession Noughties, and finally the big pandemic ... that was meant to be the last pandemic. She's lived this long by being immune to whatever had come to the British Isles in 2030, buzzed in on a wave of new fauna, ridden in on tiny wings. But she doesn't believe in taking chances.

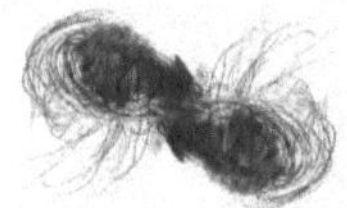

Mairead goes to bed when the sun goes down, because London is overwhelmingly dark now: you can scavenge all the tea-lights you want from Ikea, but eventually they'll run out. Padding through the gloom, she goes automatically to check on Vee.

*She isn't there.*

*I'm getting old.*

Vee has the room that used to belong to Mairead's *real* daughter; the room with the patch of red-brown rust and the dribbles of water that slowly, over time, fill up the fairy cup. Mairead stands at the threshold in the gloaming, looking over the neat blankets, washed and dried and washed and dried, until the cartoon characters are only a homeopathic trace. The bedroom walls used to be a gentle white, but now they're covered with Vee's drawings, bright and stark as cave paintings.

Mairead closes the door on her adopted daughter's room.

For a moment, the memory of her own true child is enough to

make her squeeze her eyes shut tight—*purple and swollen and terrified at what was creeping up her arm, the smell of rotten flesh*—and in that additional darkness she makes her way up the small flight of stairs to her attic room. Up here, the house is even warmer. There's no air. The city outside is luminous and dank under the full moon, and she can see the Thames gleaming at the bottom of the garden.

A fox barks.

"Hello, Mr Fox," she says quietly, just as she has for the last thirty years or so: thirty years of listening to London's urban foxes, clawing their way to the top of a blooming and uncertain food chain. She can remember when she arrived in the city, startled by the flash of orange fur, their lack of fear, yellow eyes in the dark.

As humans descended, foxes ascended.

Bork-bork-*bork*.

They're the only thing that speaks to her consistently, because Vee is a girl of very few words.

*Come outside,* they say.

*The moon is wild,* they say.

But the night-time city is a hunting-ground, and Mairead would make a gristly, bony meal for the people-trappers. She lies on her sweltering bed and listens to the foxes barking in the plague-filled, malarial dark.

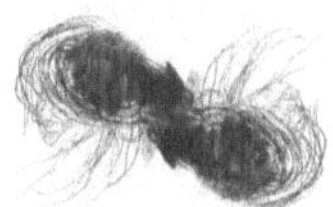

Vee returns the next day in a roar of siphoned diesel fumes. "I thought you'd be gone longer," Mairead says, and she snorts.

"Sorry to disappoint."

She's leaning, larger than life, against the kitchen counter, making everything around her seem small and petty and faded compared to the magnificence of her curly hair, her bronze-dark skin, her creaking leathers. Vee is too big for the indoors.

"That's not what I meant. Did you ... was it okay?"

"As okay as ever." Vee takes a swallow of water—Thames water— and winces. "I'm having to go further and further out, you know that, yeah? Everything in the inner city is totally picked over." Her gaze follows Mairead's to the two stunted, spindly basil plants growing on the kitchen window, baking in sunlight, and she snorts. They'd tried every seed packet they could get their hands on, but nothing grows predictably any more.

"I'm sorry."

"It's not your fault," Vee says, hard.

"I never said it was."

Ten minutes back and they're already bickering. Mairead unloads the motorbike panniers in silence, determined not to comment on the dirt tracked into the front hall, the great Machine ticking gently as it cools down, leaving the smell of diesel and dog shit everywhere; it's not as if they can afford to leave it outside. But somehow not commenting is the wrong thing to do, and Vee slams her glass down on the counter. "What?"

"Nothing." Mairead thinks about putting her arms around the child—now young woman—with her flaming red curls and eyes drawn on long and vulpine with eyeliner. She doesn't.

"We should leave," Vee mutters under her breath. "I keep telling you."

"What?"

Vee kicks at the kitchen bin, frustrated. "Only there ain't much more out there to find! The city's been picked *clean*, you understand."

"I don't know why you think it'd be different anywhere else."

"You're just saying that 'cos you're scared. Maybe you *should* be scared. More scared of starving. Look at yourself."

Mairead folds her arms. The texture of her bare skin startles her for a moment, and she rubs her elbows. Chicken wings, the flesh is sagging gently from the bone, and the skin is spotted and marked. Sunblock had run out early, after all. And she's thin—thinner than she knows is healthy. Sometimes she longs for the simple abundance of childhood. Peaches and condensed milk in her Nana's garden. Spotted Dick and custard.

"We won't starve."

"Only 'cos of me," Vee mutters. Her bristling daughter.

The foxes had brought her Vee.

This was a few years before total collapse, when it was only London that had been abandoned: no-one wanted to risk its swampy embrace, and the financial crash had happened so quickly Mairead's bank hadn't even got in touch. She'd lived quite happily as the bin collections stopped, and the neighbours' cars disappeared, and the streetlights stopped coming on: no sense illuminating a drowned borough.

If she'd thought about it then, maybe she'd have left. But now she's left it too late: there's nowhere for her to go, even if she manages to cling to the back of Vee's motorbike, coughing and spluttering, her old bones threatening to break.

Dusk.

She'd been gathering nettles when she'd heard a noise on the silent street outside. A clatter, like bins being knocked over.

It wasn't unprecedented. Sometimes there were news crews, although now, most often, they came by air. But what was happening the other side of the fence didn't sound like a car, or human voices. It was a dragging sound. Ponderous.

Even then, she had more sense than to say, "Hello?"

Dusk, and the light was coming in pink-and-honey and syrupy over the fences. Suspended in it: buzzing mosquitos and giant horseflies, as large as your hand, with their iridescent wings—*like fairies*. Mairead stayed very still, her garden shears dangling from her hand. Nettles were the only thing her garden was really good for. The other weeds, the inedible ones, came back every year, thicker than ever.

People were ceding their territory, bit by bit.

The noise continued, and then—with rising terror—Mairead realized she could hear something else. It sounded like a sniffle. A snuffle.

A *grunt*.

It was unmistakably human, and very young.

She put her hand over her mouth. *Nothing*, she thought, *could induce me to make a noise as vulnerable as that.*

The people-trappers had been rumour, then gossip, then word of mouth. Finally, when Mairead saw a convoy moving through the city on bikes, guarding an old, black-windowed prison van, they'd become an uneasy amalgam of gossip and fact, something that—if not reality— certainly sat alongside.

The noise out on the street became *sobbing*.

Afterwards, Mairead told herself how stupid she'd been. There'd been no reason to think it anything but a trap: someone parading a child on a leash, bobbing it from side to side like an angler-fish's lure. But when she pressed her face to the hole in the fence, she could see no other humans around, and a toddler in the centre of the road, crying its grubby little eyes out.

And the foxes.

A flash of burnt-golden fur behind one of the abandoned cars. One fox.

Another trotting at the toddler's heels, making a low growling noise whenever the child dropped the pace. Two foxes.

And a third up in front, keeping the snuffling child's red-rimmed eyes fixed on it.

The skin had crawled on the back of Mairead's old and sun-scarred neck. The light was all wrong, and the foxes weren't hunting the lost child so much as ... escorting her.

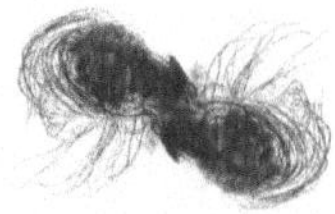

Vee won't talk to her about leaving, or about staying, and they eat dinner in absolute silence. It's not true dark yet, and Mairead can make out the hard glint in her daughter's eyes as she pokes at the tinned food on her plate. She thinks of that toddler, all swollen cheeks and snotty nose, and wonders when Vee had stopped being soft.

When Vee goes upstairs, Mairead feeds the foxes.

The supply of cat-food never runs out. Not the tinned stuff—that's too good, too palatable, and Mairead can remember early years when they'd done quite well for themselves after a raid on the local Sainsbury's—but the dry kibble that sounds like teeth when it jingles into the bowl. She can find that within walking distance, no need to send Vee, so she regards it as a harmless little practice.

The foxes have kept her company over the years, after all.

Bork-bork-*bork*.

When she opens the back door she doesn't see them at first: the garden is too overgrown, and the shadows play tricks with her eyes. She squints into the mellow humid dark, wondering if she needs glasses, then dismissing the thought. A mosquito tries to buzz in behind her, and she steps out quickly, closing the door behind her. They don't know if Vee is immune to malaria, or whatever they'd called it in those later days.

"Here, Mr Fox," she calls gently, putting the saucer of dried kibble down on the doorstep. Usually they materialise within moments, skulking out of the gloom, long bushy tails wagging.

Tonight, though, there's only the moon. It hangs low and soft in the sky, swollen and fit to burst. The air is so thick she could cut it with a knife. Around her, there's nothing but the hum of insects in the gloom, and there's a crimson cast over the undergrowth, rustles like something is moving inside. The city is pupating.

"Mr Fox?"

Nothing there.

And then: a single fox comes padding up on silent feet. It's larger than the ones she usually sees, its bruiser shoulders wide-set, its tail fluffy and curled at the tip like a question mark. It walks like it's got a purpose.

Mairead holds her breath.

The fox stops a couple of feet away. Belatedly, she thinks to worry about rabies, about disease—nothing works any more, not even antibiotics, and if it bites—

It opens its mouth in a wide, vulpine smile, revealing sharp teeth.

"Good fox," Mairead says.

It comes even closer then, and sniffs disdainfully at the dried kibble, nosing it around in the bowl with that sinister toothy tinkle. Mairead is so close she could touch it.

"Where are your fox friends?" she asks, stupidly. "Where have they gone?" But there's nothing in the garden except rustling leaves and the spill of moonlight over the Thames. A spray of foxgloves catches silver.

It looks up at her and bares its teeth again. She can see dried smears of blood. This time, its muzzle draws back, and its snout draws back and there's nothing friendly about it at all, its tail is flat to the ground and there's a low hard *growl*—

Mairead flees inside, slamming the kitchen door behind her. She puts her back to it, unable to forget the horrible yellow glint of intelligence in the animal's eyes.

*We see you.*

A few minutes later, she hears the call from Vee's room. It's unmistakable.

*Breeeeeee-oooooo—*

*How's that one got in?*

She makes it up the stairs as fast as she can, because Vee knows she's not to open the bedroom window. All sorts of weird and nightmarish scenarios present themselves: a fox standing over a baby, in a lace-decked cradle, its muzzle wide and curious.

Something *else* standing over a cradle, one of the fairies her Nana had told her were quite, quite different from the ones found in paintings.

The sound comes again by the time she's got to the landing, *breeeeeee-oooooo,* that lilting little trill that means foxes are happy and playful. It's coming from inside the bedroom.

When Mairead opens the door, she finds the bed pushed to the window. The fairy mug has been overturned in the process, spilling a couple of drops of fox-red water onto the decaying floorboards. Vee is kneeling on the bed, head and shoulders out of the window, all the mosquito nets draped over her hair like she's about to walk down the aisle—

Teeter, sobbing, down a street at dusk—

And she's crooning gently to the foxes.

Mairead closes the bedroom door and stands on the landing, breathing hard. She feels a sudden impulse—never felt before—to bash in the head of this little changeling in her house. To poison her with foxgloves, or drown her in the bath, for the unforgiveable crime:

"I'll be fine without you," she lies.

Vee doesn't say goodbye. She just puts her head to one side and stares straight into Mairead's eyes like an animal looking at the snare that nearly had it.

She's a girl of few words. She says English is a dying language.

Now she knows for sure that she's the only resident left, the nights seem a little more threatening. Mairead's no fool: she keeps a weapon by the front door, makes sure there are no signs of occupation from outside. Despite these precautions, the evening air takes on a pregnant, threatening quality. Summer thick, summer dark. She sometimes thinks she hears the cough and backfire of Vee's bike, a long way away.

She keeps herself busy.

She always keeps food in the house for the foxes, although none have come—none since the day Vee left. The shadows roil in the increasingly swampy back garden, under plantain leaves the size of machetes, brambles which climb the walls and tear down the useless window-boxes. Mairead watches the shadows from the back door, silently willing each one to be a fox.

She hears them, sometimes, when she's in bed.

They sound like they're right outside: like she could run, childish and barefoot, down the stair-carpet to find them waiting at the door. Screams, howls, and yips. They're more vocal than before, but she's sure they're still singing the same song:

*Come outside / the moon is wild*

*The night is juicy and sweet*

She's been cheating a little on her 'no human food for the foxes' rule. Although there's no longer Vee to go on scavenging trips, there's no Vee to eat her out of house and home, either. Mairead can survive on very little: she's a tough old bird, her Nana would say. And downstairs, on the back step, is half a tin of chicken chunks, pungent in the warm night air.

The night before, it had been a bird. Nothing sinister—it had flown, sun-drunk, into the window, and Mairead had wrung its neck before she'd known what she was doing.

"Can't take the country out of the girl," she'd whispered.

She lies in bed, paralysed and resentful, knowing that her window is angled wrong for her to spy the foxes outside, knowing that she won't make it down the stairs in time to see them. They're eating the food, though. She has that much at least.

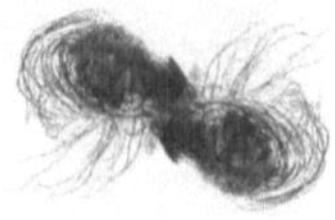

It's a few nights later when she catches one of them at it.

Mairead had sat up in the armchair in the front room, so reminiscent of the first days—or weeks, or no-one really knew how long—of the end. Back then, she'd closed the blinds and locked the windows, turned off all the lights, and sat up with a weapon in hand, ready to take on any looters. She'd been one of the sensible ones. She'd prepared.

Ten years on, she sits up in the same chair, waiting to see the foxes come to her door.

There's a clear line of sight from the armchair through to the back garden, and the night is light again, shading to lilac. She can see the massed hunched shapes of the plants, the pooling water at the bottom of her garden, thick and warm and unforgiving.

And then there's something beside them. Another set of shapes, large and—

Wrong.

It crawls up to her door on all fours, towards the offering of chicken. She's too scared to make a sound. It moves stealthily but clumsily, as though it's just getting used to things, and the moonlight hits its bare grubby feet as it tiptoes. She counts a few less than ten toes, each one tipped by a fingernail so long and brown that it might be a thorn. The hair on its legs is matted, longer than she's ever seen before, and leads up along stringy calves to disappear into the bush of thick undergrowth at its crotch.

It's not a fox.

The man has some sort of wound on his arm, as though it's been caught in a trap, and when he uses his hands to scoop up the chunks of food—using all fingers and thumbs together, like a rough shovel—she can see that the skin is rotting away. There's a damp red smile in there, which lips open and closed as he flexes the muscle underneath. He's wiry like a puppet. Mairead presses her hand to her mouth, thinking of her daughter, her true daughter, who'd died too young when one of the *superbugs* had taken her arm.

The heat that had come off her, waves and waves of heat, as if foreshadowing the burning London to come.

She must have let out a noise. The man looks up, wide mouth still working, and regards her.

She almost expects fox eyes. But no, they're human, squinted and pale, the rest of the face invisible under a shaggy beard. Mairead is aware of the thinness of the back door, the mosquito screens, the paucity of her weapons.

The man crooks his neck to the sky, the colour of meat on the turn, and lets out a loud, guttural bork-bork-*bork*.

Fairies, her Nan had said, thrive on chaos. They're creatures of the in-between times, the old age dying, the new age struggling to be born.

Mairead rinses out the abandoned flower-fairy cup in the kitchen sink and examines it carefully. After so long, the china is a little stained inside, and she knows her Nana would be disappointed with how she's kept things. But what else was she meant to do?

She fills the cup with water, and puts it on the back step.

When the foxes return that night, they're still speaking a recognisable fox-language, of night and moon and hunger.

*Come outside*, they say.

Mairead folds her arms and waits.

She waits until she doesn't think anyone is coming. The foxes fight, but it seems like a play-fight. No blood is drawn. Mairead thinks of the fox-man, and how his teeth had been stained and horrible, fit to give you death in a single bite.

She waits, under the blowsy moon. Finally, there's movement in the undergrowth, and her heart skips a beat.

It's Vee who slinks out of the shadows, towards the dish of steaming cat-food on the back step: her daughter on all fours in the darkness, eyes gleaming like a fox.

# The Empty After

by M. Edusa

I came back from Kandahar with a brand-new twisted smile made of scar tissue and a dead right eye.

"You're lucky to be alive," they told me. The doctors and lawyers and physical therapists and shrinks all told me, as if no-one had before. From some it was a joke, from others, a solemn declaration.

I listened, and nodded like I agreed with them, and looked them dead in the eye while I did it. With only one eye intact, my non-dominant one at that, they all looked a little blurry.

They patched me up alright, I guess. They did their best. It's not their fault they missed something vital. A cut artery they couldn't see.

But they did miss something. There was a wound in my head now.

I moved gingerly, protectively, cradling it like a gut-shot. Sometimes that was enough. Usually, it was not. Sometimes I moved wrong, and the edges I'd thought were healing over started to split, and seep, and bleed. I didn't know how much blood I could possibly lose before I lost myself.

In some religions blood is holy. It represents life, or some bullshit approximation. I've always been a little skeptical of those convictions. They're the war stories of men who have never been to war.

When you're singing monosyllabic nonsense to someone who used to be your friend, who isn't your friend anymore, but only a body with missing limbs and staring eyes, you know a little more about what blood means.

I tried church once. This was during a strange period in my life, after the Army, when I was finally left to my own devices and cut free to roam the earth. It was the empty after.

During the limbo of this first year or so I wandered. I stumbled through catholic castles, Buddhist temples, and fragrant mosques. Casting out like a prisoner in the dark of an empty cell, knowing there are no keys lying around. Thinking you've got to go through the motions, and check for one anyway.

A single-story brick building, emblazoned with a cross and some version of "redeemer," was my last stop.

I sat in the back row. I listened. I took a little cracker and a thimble-sized cup of grape juice when they made the rounds, and I listened to the snake-oil salesman who had never been to war. He stood behind the podium, unhinged his jaw, and spewed out a tired script about salvation and the body and the blood.

While everyone in the front rows drank, I stared down at the tiny plastic cup of liquid I was holding between two fingers. Purple more than red. I tipped the cup over. Poured the purple shit out on the white carpet. I stood up and walked out.

Drugs came next. Pills I knew the names of and plenty I didn't. Some of these offered me temporary reprieve, and others left me heaving in the toilet. I ate mushrooms. Smoked a few blunts. Drank the spicy tea. Popped tabs under my tongue with a variety of cartoon characters printed on the back. A stranger would hand me something, declare it "good shit," and I would simply ... take it. Playing Russian Roulette with chemicals and Mickey Mouse faces.

Once I woke up in the emergency room with no memory of what put me there. That didn't stop me from revisiting the same ER four weeks later. There were cops that time, but I kept my mouth tightly shut when they questioned me. Despite my silence, the officer that talked to me was an old vet, and it didn't take him long to piece together my story without assistance. He had some stern words for me, recommended a sober shop, and cut me loose.

Another time I woke up in a pool of my own sweat, with two men and a woman as naked as I was sleeping beside me.

I didn't find God. I didn't stop bleeding.

*Drip, drip, drip.*

On it went. Like the incessant clicking of some giant, cosmic clock in my head. In the dead of night, in the endless, unsleeping hours, I listened to myself bleed out.

"There's a place out west," some old fuck at the bar tells me.

We are both drinking alone, and with feeling. For this reason, we are instant friends, though I never caught his name, and he never caught mine. The way the night was shaping up, I wouldn't have remembered it if he'd tattooed it on my forehead.

"They sitchoo down in this sweaty tent," he slurs. "You smoke somethin' ... name escapes me. It's good shit. Then you go out there in the desert and you walk."

I wait for him to continue, thinking there will be more to his story. There isn't.

"Just walk around?" I frown, my tongue thick with liquor, my head fuzzy. "Fuck is the point?"

"Don't know." His shoulders draw up in an exaggerated shrug. The words strike him as funny, and he starts giggling.

Riding a pleasant buzz that warns of an incoming unpleasant morning, I giggle with him.

The bartender, who is wearing a tight t-shirt with a fire department logo, shoots us a weary and disapproving look. I know he is going to close out our tabs and bring us receipts to sign if we don't shut up, but it doesn't feel important.

We are just two grown men, strangers and friends, giggling and sloshed at a dive bar. The music is loud, the whiskey is strong, and for a brief, blessed time, I can't hear the sound I make while I'm dying.

I hear it the next morning, Lima Charlie, loud and clear. It's the sound vomit makes when you half-miss the toilet and your brain swells up to knock at the sides of your skull. It's the sound of a different kind of dying.

I languish on my bathroom floor for a few hours, rising long enough to make offerings to the porcelain bowl, flush, and drink water.

Eventually I even make it all the way up to the medicine cabinet. I chew aspirin like candy, because it tastes better than bile, and because I hate myself.

When life resumes the sun is setting again. I feel groggy and sore and a little ashamed. I always feel ashamed to some extent. It's a feeling that sharpens in the wake of a bad hangover for reasons I'm never able to pin down.

I make a perfunctory sweep of my personal belongings, a little surprised to see I've made it through the fog of another drunken night intact. Keys, wallet, phone (dead), and lighter all accounted for.

I find a business card in my wallet and examine it. It's labeled "wellness retreat" and is decorated with some gaudy Native American symbols. The kind of dreamcatchers-and-feathers imagery white people always use to make a dime off some cultural pickpocketing. On the back is an address in Nevada. There is a phone number listed and a website.

I plug my phone in. Brush my teeth. Force myself to scarf down a few slices of stale white bread. I brush my teeth a second time, but my mouth still feels fuzzy. My entire body feels that way, I discover, so I shower.

After I shut off the water, I can still hear a dripping noise. Faint but incessant. A ticking death clock.

I return to my couch feeling, and smelling, a little better. My phone has blinked back to life. I swipe away the usual barrage of automated text messages and voicemails, all warning me of upcoming VA appointments I have no intention of attending.

I open the browser and type in the address on the back of the card.

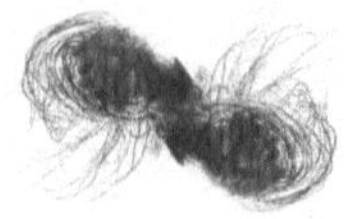

*Well, it's not peyote.*

I'm thinking this as I smoke with mixed interest and disappointment.

I'd been all geared up to say, "I already tried this shit, what else ya got?" I don't get the chance.

Weed gets passed around first. I shake my head and pass it on, buyer's remorse blooming in my mind.

I'm still holding out a little hope that there's something here, some little desert secret, that will be worth the effort. Otherwise, I'll be out three grand and the cost of a plane ticket to boot. Just another idiot who got taken for a ride.

Worse still, I'll be out of options. I'll bleed to death.

What comes down the line to me next is not weed. Or peyote. I've tried the former many times, and the latter only once—didn't much care for it—but I'm still fairly certain it's something else. Some herb I've never seen or smelled before, packed into a wooden pipe with a huge bowl.

There had been a time in my life when I might have asked. I might have been concerned, even distantly, about whatever I was about to put in my body.

I'm not that person anymore, and I won't be him again. I'm someone else now. I'm a dying man.

I smoke.

We listen to an old Indian man beat a drum. Staff workers load big stones into a fire pit and douse them with buckets of water. Four or five other dark-skinned men join in with the drummer, and then they're all chanting something in some variation of a native language.

I don't know for sure. It's hard to care. I'm blazed.

The temperature stands at about ninety-five outside and picks up another twenty in the tent. Rivers of sweat are running unobstructed down my bare skin. The men present have lost their shirts; the women are down to sports bras.

Now that the initial fog of steam has dissipated, I can see the others. I'm sitting in a circle with maybe twenty other people.

There are a lot of veterans here. I realize this as I look around at them with the unselfconscious eyes of a man dipping into a hallucinogenic trip. Three or four of these are scarred like me. One looks like something blew up directly in his face, taking his eyebrows and most of his nose. Others have artificial limbs or bare stumps, no prosthetic in sight.

Most are whole, physically. I know they're bleeding, though. Like me.

*Drip, drip, tick, tock; there goes your death clock. Wind her up, boys.*

I'm not surprised to see them here. Not surprised that a place like this might be the final stop on a soldier's personal farewell tour. One that began with service, derailed, and ended with a steep drop off a tall cliff. I have images of a literal train track in my head, the rails all bent and twisted and jutting over miles of nothingness.

I know from experience that soldiers, ones who aren't soldiers anymore, will try just about anything before they try support groups. Take away a man's structure, leave him spinning in orbit, and then hand him his consolation prize: *Soldiers Anonymous.*

*Hi, my name is Greg, and I'm a recovering soldier. I'm missing my leg. Or both arms; my dick, my brain. I'm missing me! Have you seen me recently?*

*Anything but that,* we think. We try drugs, sex, rock and roll, even religion. Anything but *Soldiers Anonymous.*

So here we are. Displaced refugees, outcasts and misfits and statistics in the flesh. Willing to smoke whatever is being passed around and wander off into the desert on some kind of goddamned hallucinogenic vision quest, no questions asked.

We are soldiers for whom the track has run out. We're desperate gamblers on our last dime; all or nothing. We are dying.

A woman introduced herself at the beginning of our visit, welcoming us to the "spiritual experience." She'd said some generic shit about pain management and healing and self-discovery, hitting all the buzzwords.

She'd carefully avoided the big no-no label: PTSD. Smart lady. We don't like that. We'll get up and leave if you start throwing that one around.

Truthfully, I hadn't absorbed most of what she was saying. I was waiting for the good shit.

She reappears after some period of time. Maybe hours. By this point we're all sweaty messes, but floating and no longer worried about the sweat, or anything else.

She has more words, all very professional, all very reasonable, I think. I don't hear a single one. I'd be surprised if anyone did.

I remember what she tells us at the very end though, before we start walking.  We have our clothes back on, including sturdy hiking boots, and hydration packs strapped to our backs.

"Remember," she tells us with sparkling eyes and her schoolteacher voice, "we have state of the art medical staff here! Should you find yourself experiencing illness or injury, simply return to camp to avail yourself of our emergency services."

She tells us this while we're all high as fucking kites. This is a fact I will later think of as both unethical and brilliant.

For now, it's the last thing on my mind.

A desert canyon yawns before me, fluorescing brilliantly in shades of orange and yellow and pink and gold. A dirt road stretches away and winds through it like a river made of diamonds.

It's the most beautiful sight I've ever seen, sober or not. The only thing on earth I want to do is walk into it.

"Good luck!" She sends us off with grating cheer, hands outstretched. "Go forth and find yourselves!"

We go. Whether we find ourselves or not is open to interpretation.

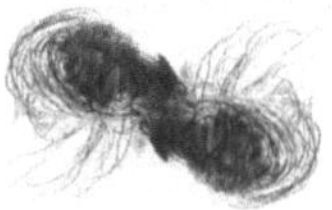

As far as business plans go, releasing us into the Nevada wilderness, a four-hour bus ride from the nearest airport, blitzed out of our minds on some kind of desert shroom dust, is maybe the dumbest fucking thing anyone has ever done.

Maybe it's the smartest fucking thing. Who knows.

It's the equivalent of letting a kid get all doped up on sugar before releasing him into a lion's cage. Yeah, of course he's gonna have a great time. At first.

I go bouncing away into the canyon with a big dopey grin on my face and not a care in the world. I'm not thinking about Iraq, or Kandahar, or the blood that is sometimes gushing in my brain, and sometimes dripping like a leaky faucet.

I'm thinking it's a beautiful day and I don't even know the names of most of the colors I'm seeing.

I spend a couple of hours chasing butterflies. At some point I realize there are no butterflies, and I chase something else. A lizard, maybe.

The sun sets, and now *that's* the prettiest thing I've ever seen. Hands down.

I climb to the base of giant red rocks that rise high up into the air like chimneys, and I sit my happy ass down to do something I've never done before. I watch the sun set.

I have no concept of time. The sun goes down, and I stare at the place where it sank out of sight, all glazed-over and content.

After that I wander around in the dark, getting a new burst of *ain't-this-the-shit* happiness when a big white moon comes sailing out to light up the desert.

The rainbow brilliance of the day has gone, leaving a surreal white alien landscape behind. The jutting fingers of the chimney rocks cast long moon-shadows, and strange little birds chirr in the darkness.

At some point I remember that I have water, and I drink some.

Maybe that's when I start to sober up. Just a little, enough to recognize that I'm in a strange place. A very strange place, and maybe it's a little scary now, too.

*Scary? Beautiful? Exhilarating, terrible, thrilling?* All of the above. "What the hell did we smoke?"

I ask this of a cactus, and it's the first time I've heard my own voice all day. It makes me feel a little more sober still, and I don't like that much. I want to keep riding this wave as long as I can, because I have a lot of desert left to explore.

I haven't discovered myself yet.

With this mission now firmly in mind, I amble back down to the dusty road, mostly cloaked by the shadow of the canyon. I set off with the long stride and purposeful step of a man who has somewhere to be, though I don't have a clue where that place actually is. Gotta get going, though. *Chop, chop.*

I'm sweating a little when I finally stop, breaking myself away from the hypnotic waves of moonlight shimmering just overhead, at that dark place where the cliffs stand against the night sky.

I hear a noise. Or, I think I hear it.

Because I'm still buzzing pleasantly, but mostly maybe, because

I'm an idiot, I step into the grass to investigate.

Something heavy hits my leg. I look down in dumb surprise and stand there as a thick snake goes buzzing off into the grass.

Buzzing. Rattling. *Rattlesnake?*

I look back at the road.

A man is standing there. I'm fairly certain it's one of the guys who was sitting down the line from me in the sweat lodge. Now he's wearing jeans, and a button-up over a white t-shirt, and staring at me with the same awestruck lack of comprehension that I feel.

"A snake just bit me," I announce.

"I saw that," he says.

We stare at each other for a long time.

I'm trying to access anything that might be stashed away in my brain referencing snakebites, and wondering if maybe I just imagined getting bit, when the man approaches.

"Should probably sit down," he says slowly.

I think that's a good idea.

I take a step, and that seems alright. Then another one. Maybe I didn't imagine the snake, because now my right leg is feeling warm. Two more steps, and I realize that I don't know where I'm going, and that my leg is now very warm.

Flannel-shirt man grabs my elbow and leads me to a long, nearly flat slope of rock at the base of the canyon wall. It's safely out of range of the grass, which I think is pretty smart considering recent events.

He lets me hold onto him as I sit down. That's good, because now I'm feeling vaguely ... shitty. As soon as I sit, I feel even worse, and I lie back against the ridged stone. It's warm.

The man whose name I don't know pulls up my pant leg.

"What's your name?" I ask him.

"Charlie," he says. "Stop moving."

I do, not because my self-preservation instinct has engaged, but because I think Charlie is pretty damn good-looking, and I'm enjoying doing the looking.

I prop up on my elbow, watching with interest as he works. He's missing two fingers on his left hand. Where his jeans have pulled up above his tennis shoe, I can see the glint of metal on the same side.

"Army?" I take a stab.

"Marines."

I watch him take his flannel off, tearing strips out of it and wrapping them around my leg. I'm not surprised to see he's a little clumsy and uncoordinated as he does this. I think he knows what he's doing anyway. If he doesn't, he's doing a good job of faking it.

"Are you gay, Charlie?" I ask him this because I'm high, and apparently whatever demonic cocktail I have whipping through my veins is turning me into a chatterbox.

"No," he answers, a little too quickly. A pause, a look, and then, "Are you?"

"Nope," I drawl, popping out the "p" sound for no reason except that I feel like doing it.

His answer, and mine, are the answers expected from soldiers. I think later I may call his bluff.

If I get a later. It's looking less likely as time passes. I'm feeling squeamish now, my stomach performing all sorts of interesting acrobatics below my ribs. What started as a distant warmth has matured into a searing burn and spread. It's all the way up to my knee.

Charlie is watching me as closely as one high man can watch another. I catch him staring at me when I open my eyes, and I try for a grin. It's harder to muster up than it was an hour ago.

"You didn't tell me yours," he says.

I blink dumbly at him. "Army," I say, thinking that was obvious.

He laughs. It's a surprised sound, and loud in the night.

"Your name."

I think about it and realize he's right.

"Jake," I announce. "Light infantry. Three tours."

"Combat medic. Two runs."

Medic. That explains a lot.

"I'm bleeding."

Charlie's face, all harsh angles in the moonlight, twists into a frown. He looks down at my extended right leg as if to verify this.

"Not that much, actually."

"In here." I tap my forehead, then my temple. I hear myself slur a little. "In my brain."

Maybe because he's still coming down himself, Charlie seems to understand perfectly.

"Oh," he says simply. "Yeah. Me too."

We say nothing else for a while.

I lie back against the warm rock, although the heat of it seems to be leaving little by little as the moon climbs above us.

*Maybe I'll die out here,* my brain suggests in a lazy kind of way. The thought brings no dread, but a sense of exhausted relief. Like a marathon runner glimpsing the finish line somewhere far ahead.

"Get up." Charlie, the one-legged combat medic commands it.

I have no idea how much time has passed.

"Not supposed to move," I protest. I'm not sure if this is true, but it feels true. It's hard to think.

"True, usually. But nobody's coming. We have to get back on our own."

That seems like a terrible plan, but I do as instructed. I pull myself up. Charlie helps, and neither one of us is very steady on our feet when the job is done.

I hope that he knows where we're going. I sure don't. I walk, letting him support me. I know I need to keep my weight off my injured limb, but it's hard to remember this. There's less pain there and more of a swollen discomfort, like my leg has turned into a balloon and wants to float away from me.

"Snakebites can be fatal if left untreated." Charlie feeds me this bit of trivia with encyclopedic frankness.

I laugh, but there's not enough breath in me to make it a good one. "No shit," I retort. I catch my breath, and add, "I'm not gonna die. Not yet. Not from this."

In my right mind, I would have said less. I would have said nothing and left nothing open to interpretation.

"You're one of those, huh?" Charlie's quick deduction, and his question, are both oddly calm.

This time I do manage to stay quiet.

"If this one doesn't work, this last hurrah, *then.* Then I'll kill myself."

He says this like a man reading a quote, but I hear the truth easily enough. He's quoting me. He's quoting every other wounded man who sat around the circle with us, smoking mystery herbs and listening to drums and chants. He's quoting himself, too.

Again, I stay silent. My verbal restraint tells me the high is fading a little. In fact, by this point I think I'm really sobering up. I'd peaked, wasted the plateau portion of my high dealing with rattlesnakes, and now I was probably in for a hell of a steep downhill slide.

I don't know the half of it.

The moon crests the peak of the sky and stands directly above us, a silent witness to our slow progress down the dust road. I think later that it hung there a very long time. Longer than it should have.

Watching. Waiting. Waking things up.

Charlie stops moving before I do. I'm leaning on him pretty heavily now, every step a bolt of lightning up my injured calf, and the solid weight of his stop draws me to a jarring halt.

I grunt, in pain and in question.

I look at him, and then past him. In the weird half-light the shadowed canyon walls seem to be dripping. Little streams of dark water. The water has all come bubbling out of the cracks and is running down the stone in trickles.

This is a strange sight to me, even half-delirious. I start to tell Charlie. His shell-shocked eyes pull me up short and I follow them.

The road has changed, gone all crooked and rippled and twisted. It moves as I stare at it.

The earth opens up, and whatever is kicking around in my bloodstream thinks I am watching that horrible wound in my head split open. I can see the blood welling up out of it, and hands. Hands wearing armored gloves with little Kevlar patterns across the knuckles, and the fingers torn and singed, and they're attached to arms—

Charlie's grip on me tightens, reminding me that he's there. I don't think I can look at his face, which I know is like mine. Full of wide-eyed terror.

We stand clutching on to each other, watching in disbelief as soldiers climb out of the earth.

Greeley. Vick. Cortes, Wilmer, VanHorn. More.  Soldiers I don't recognize wearing Marine Corps camo patterns. I think Charlie recognizes those, because a strangled noise comes out of him when they appear.

He sees them too, then. We both see them.

The places where their boots land on the earth becomes something liquid. Or maybe the soldiers are the liquid, and the earth is soaking up the blood pouring out of them. Not in drops. Not in the *tick tick tick* of a clock running out, but in rivers.

I think we would have stood right there and let them take us, out of dumb shock and mindless fear.

The earth shakes, a tremor first. Then a burst. An explosion.

I lose my grip on Charlie and tumble, landing in the rocks. A shower of debris and sand strikes the earth around me, but it doesn't sound right. It sounds like loose pebbles falling into water.

My ears ring. My vision doubles. I taste sand and iron.

I look down and see Matt Jeris lying across my legs, or the part of him that I could grab onto after the blast, anyway. That's most of him, but he's missing his leg. Not just his leg, but his entire hip, a huge portion of his abdomen with it. His right arm is gone below the elbow. His left one is all twisted up wrong, like a rag that's been wrung out. His eyes are staring up at me. Dead and glassy. I can see the moon in them.

I scream.

I scream now like I wanted to scream back then and couldn't. Back then I'd clutched onto his body like a drowning man. Now I push it away, scrambling backwards.

The weight of him falls halfway off me, his torso twisting. His eyes seem to follow me, and they're full of accusation.

He bursts.

Like a sack full of liquid, his body swells, eyes bulging, flesh tightening. He explodes all over me, and I feel the slick warmth of his blood as it splashes into my face.

I choke, my mouth now full of another man's death, and make a half-retching motion. Thick, warm gore comes spilling out.

I scramble away in the dirt, my hands clawing blindly behind me.

My mind is blank with horror, my leg pulsating with pain like a neon sign in a bar window.

I know this is not real. I know, because it can't be. No amount of denial seems to stop the blood.

Charlie is screaming like I screamed. The dead soldiers made of blood are screaming too. The earth itself is screaming, releasing noise and IED blasts and ghosts of men we couldn't save, and couldn't die beside.

I twist like a contortionist, my eyes casting around wildly for some escape. Blood is rising from the desert floor, seeping from every stone, dripping from every gnarled finger of growth.

I see the slope of rock, a giant smokestack stone rising above it. It's the same point where I'd felt so high and happy a few hours ago, watching the sun blink out.

I lurch to my feet and run to it. Adrenaline carries me most of the way, and then the pain of my swollen calf, full of venom, catches up. It cuts my leg out from under me, and I go sprawling.

Still, I don't stop.

I scramble and claw and rip chunks of brush out by the handful. I scrabble onto smooth rock, up and up and up. My stomach heaves as blood wells up from the little cracks and fissures. More than once, I lose my grip and backslide. More than once, my fingernails crack and peel.

I am possessed by the pulse in my leg. It's an engine, powering me up the slope, warning me that it is overheated and overtaxed, and time is short. I can hear the heavy sound of shifting Kevlar, the slurp and suck of blood on boots. At any moment I think, a dead hand will close over my dragging leg, and that will be it for me. I'll be sucked down into the blood, into the earth; I'll be gone.

Once I think I even feel it. Cold, gloved fingers land on my ankle. I jerk my knee up and kick back with the strength of desperation. It connects with a helmet, or a rock. I never look back to find out. I'm moving again.

It takes minutes, or hours, to climb on my hands and knees to the chimney rock. I sag against the pillar of stone, breathing in horrible, whistling gasps.

When I look down, it's instinct. I never would have done it consciously, if I'd stopped to think.

Below me the dead soldiers stand or lie. Some are on the road. Others have crawled halfway up the slope after me. They no longer pursue. They only stand in the bubbling red earth, looking up at me with the wide, unblinking eyes of a lost war.

I'm still afraid. Still half-mad with the kind of terror that reaches down your throat and gets a grip on your spine, igniting every nerve, lighting up your neurons like Christmas lights. Only, now I'm something else, too. I look into the shell-shocked gleam of round, sad, terrified eyes, and my heart breaks a little for these dead men. For the first time in my *empty after,* I am grateful that I'm not one of them.

I'm alive. And I'm startled to realize I think that's a good thing.

Pain sweeps this sentiment away from me. It takes the moonlight, the sky, and the terror in a single brutal tidal wave. It takes me and leaves only my harsh breath. My clawing fingertips.

The stones beneath me are dry, but they're cold. The ghost of the sun's warmth has bled out.

I think I might bleed out, too.

I lie there until the sky turns light, waiting for death.  Death is a fucking flake. He never shows up.

The police do, though I never find out who called for them. Cell phones were confiscated before we entered the sweat lodge, but someone had one. Someone had been a smart little rebel. The cruisers come with the sun, in waves of red and blue light and the crunch of big rubber tires on sand. Fire trucks, next. Ambulances too. There are many of these, but only two men left to occupy them.

I see Charlie, as if from a great distance. He's sitting up on his gurney, but he's staring into space with empty eyes. His white shirt is red now.

I think maybe he'll turn to look at me. I think maybe I'll get that silent flicker of unspoken meaning: *I'm okay.*

But he doesn't. And I don't.

I watch them load him up. The ambulance doors close between us. I never see him again.

The snake bite doesn't kill me, though at times the pain makes me regret that. Other times I feel lucky. I spend a few days in the hospital, suffer a lot of injections and IV's, and get a lot of attention from cops with questions.

*What happened?*

I guess on paper, that's simple enough.

We all handed some con artists a couple grand. Doped ourselves up on some kind of mescaline mushroom cocktail. And we walked off to die. I think this racket worked for the "retreat" many times before. The lost souls who wandered in were on their last lap around the track, after all. No-one had anyone left to miss them when they vanished.

In a roundabout way, I'm almost certain that snake is what saved me. Whatever is in a diamondback's venom had some neutralizing effect, or a partial one, on the other poison inside me. The two had some kind of neurotoxin standoff, tried to kill me, and tapped out. Both combatants left the battlefield, tails tucked. No winner.

Something else had a standoff in my head too. Maybe it was one kiss of death that canceled out the other. Maybe it was a hard knock to the head sustained somewhere along the way, and that was finally enough to jostle something back into place that had come loose.

Maybe it was some strange and nameless nightmare drug; maybe it was a rattlesnake, and maybe it was lightning. I don't think I'll ever get that answer quite straight.

I only know that the bleeding stopped. The itch of an unhealed wound stuck around a while longer. Then it flickered, faded, and found the door.

My right eye never sees sunlight again. My right leg never loses its unsteady half-limp, and my lips will always be twisted up wrong on one side, even when the scars mostly fade. All of those things stay with me.

I never hear the dripping sound in my head again after that night, though. After the bleeding desert, the bleeding in me is cauterized somehow. The faucet turned off.

I had wandered far and wide in the empty after. I found many places where gods do not live, and places where devils do. I found a place where the desert turns red, and my past and future wait for me. My nightmare. My destiny.

They stand around my bed at night. Watching me with big, round, white eyes. Their faces stained with blood and soot. Their blood dripping on the floor. I know someday they will take me. Away from my stolen life and down to the place I had always belonged but had escaped.

I roll over and look at them. I remember their names. I sleep.

They will not take me tonight. Not yet. After all, I haven't discovered myself.

In some strange corners of the world, the earth bleeds in the night. But I don't. Not anymore.

# VAPORCOIN

## Jonathan Louis Duckworth

### THE STREAM

The comments are a deluge, multicolored names cascading down the window, all-caps screeds and litanies bombarding his eyes.

*What's up with vapecoin?!*

*Vaporcoin, vaporcoin, vaporcoin!*

*Will y'all shut up?*

*He's stalling cuz he doesn't know shit.*

*You promised you'd find the truth.*

*Click link for nudes!!*

"I've said all I'm going to say about Vaporcoin," says Vic. "Seriously, chat, shut up about it."

*C'mon Prof.*

*WHAT ARE YOU HIDING???*

He sees his own face in a square in the bottom left corner of his screen: pale, sweaty, a thousand-yard stare in the middle of his headset. He watches his lip quiver.

"As I've said, Vaporcoin is nothing, it's bullshit," Vic says, raising his voice as if the chat is an audible roar he has to shout over rather than a silent spray of text. "It's a regular PoW blockchain, it's not magic or mysterious—the story is there's no story at all."

The incredulous messages roll down the textbox, hundreds of viewers calling bullshit all at once. Maybe they can see in his eyes that Victor Parkhill, AKA VicPark95, AKA "The Coin Prof," has finally found a lie he can't sell to his followers.

Still, he persists. "Fuck you if you doubt me. I'll say it right now—Vaporcoin ain't worth your mental bandwidth. I don't care that it's traded on Coinbase, it's barely worth a cent. It's not—it's not ... it's..."

*Are you okay, Prof?*

*He's deadass crying. LOL.*

*Maybe someone died.*

*Bro found out he got cucked.*

*Fuck, is he wearing guyliner?*

*Grown ass man crying on live.*

*WHY ARE HIS TEARS BLACK THO??*

He's crying in front of his 22,000-strong live audience. He removes his headset and wipes his eyes. Black seepage like crude oil beads from his fingers.

## TWO WEEKS EARLIER

Vic arrived at a little past midnight, bedtime for most, but not for someone who grinds like Vic. The building was a monolith of blue glass, reflecting the gray arch of the Sam Rayburn tollroad overpass rising over downtown Plano. This was where all of Vic's research (well, his assistants' research) led him. The old U-Mii satellite campus, abandoned when the U-Mii company got shut down by a government regulatory body five months ago for vague "anti-labor" practices—Vic remembered because he got quite a lot of engagement railing against the overreach from his social media pulpit. Before its shuttering, U-Mii had specialized in high-end robotics and synthetic companions—talking coffee makers, robot dogs, sexbots, even a line of surrogate mothers. Truly a company ahead of its time, now only a memory.

According to government records, the office was currently vacant and off the market, and yet he'd barely crossed the street from where he parked his Tesla before Vic saw signs of activity. A half dozen cars in the parking lot, including a sweet lime-green Bugatti Veyron.

"Mr. Satoshi, I presume?" Vic muttered under his breath.

When Vaporcoin first started popping up three weeks ago in investors' wallets and on exchanges, no one including Vic, knew anything about it. It was such a mystery that many in the cryptoverse began to assert (with varying levels of seriousness) that Satoshi, the faceless creator of Bitcoin, had struck again. But more than the mystery of its creation, Vaporcoin had attracted attention because of the weird "messages" that obsessive coders had discovered by digging through the blockchain's code. There was what appeared—to a paranoid sort of person looking for hidden messages everywhere—to be a cypher built into the blockchain's script, and some other influencers had made videos where they teased out phrases like "the air is gone" and "we climb over each other," and "it's all gray here." Vic had responded to these videos on a stream where he explained that if you wanted to find a pattern or message you could find one in any code or sufficiently long, complex kind of text. Still, his followers weren't satisfied. Being the Coin-Prof, Vic staked his reputation on finding the truth, and now here he was, about to enter the building that hundreds of hours of sleuthing had tracked the blockchain's origin to.

He found the glass doors open, the lobby lit up and waiting for him. The air inside was wintry, so cold his forearms started to shiver. U-Mii's lobby bore all the hallmarks of the once thriving tech giant: sleek design, ostentatious building materials (the reception desk made of tropical wood, an intricate "waterfall" statue made from rods of crystal), and LED screens everywhere proudly flashing the company's logo.

Until one of the displays shorted out. When it blinked back to life, it flashed a different message: WELCOME, COIN-PROF!

Vic stared at the message for a long time, mouth open, gawking like an imbecile. His arms quivered, and one hand slid to his belt where he kept his Glock (thank God for open carry) on its holster.

*Think about this rationally, Vic—you had to hire a lot of people to track this operation down, someone could have blabbed. And besides, what do you have to worry about? It's probably people just like you.*

He took a deep breath—what he was doing was in the name of science. His followers were counting on him to find the truth.

The display changed again.

TAKE THE ELEVATOR, VIC.

And again:

FIFTH FLOOR, VIC.

"Nah, fuck this," Vic said. He turned around, intent on leaving and coming back with a friend, maybe Fuckhead Trey or Gilbert, but as soon as he'd turned, he saw the doors had shut behind him.

He tried the handle. Locked.

*Okay, okay, don't panic...*

Two seconds later, he was shrieking, "Let me out!" while pounding on the tempered glass with both fists, each blow probably damaging his bones more than the glass with how badly his arms revibrated.

Thinking a little straighter, he got his pistol out, ready to shoot the glass.

"Dude, that's bulletproof, it's just going to bounce back at you."

He turned around, heart pounding, and leveled his Glock at a small man in a hoodie.

No, not a man. A woman. Where had she come from?

She lifted her hands. "Whoa, bro, easy. No need for that."

"Who are you?" Vic asked. "How did you know I was coming?"

She smiled, and even in the tense moment and with so much of her face obscured in the hoodie, he could tell she was cute. Not *hot* or anything, but possibly bangable if you squinted.

"You parked a limited-edition Tesla with spinners across the street with a license plate that says 'Coin-Prof.' Not exactly cloak and dagger, bro."

Her voice was familiar, though he couldn't tell why or where he might have heard her. He searched his internal database of exes and fans but none of them matched. He was still pointing the pistol at her, and she wasn't the least bit worried. She was gutsy—had to give her that much.

"My name's Sammy," she said. "I'm part of the group behind Vaporcoin. That's why you're here, yeah?"

He lowered his arms so that the pistol pointed at her feet instead of her center mass. "You knew I was coming."

"Bro, you were telling the whole internet you were investigating us. Put the gun away, no one's dangerous here."

A fringe of icy blonde hair fell over her forehead, and then it clicked why he recognized her voice. She wasn't wearing any makeup, and the frumpy hoodie did a lot to obscure her best assets, but he knew who she was: Sammy Kohl, AKA SamSunGal, 600,000+ followers on TikTok and close to 100,000 on Instagram. Until a few months ago when she dropped off and stopped posting, she'd been a major mover in the cryptoverse, well known for giving (mostly) sound advice on crypto strats while wearing crop tops and sports bras that flaunted her impressive cleavage.

"Holy shit, SamSunGal?" He puts the gun back in its holster. "What are you doing here?"

"Follow me, Vic," she said, and the way she smiled meant he'd do just that (not that he was a simp, or anything). "There's some people who'd love to meet you."

She walked toward the elevator. A girl had cake for sure when you could even see it through sweatpants. He followed her—but again: he was expressly not a simp.

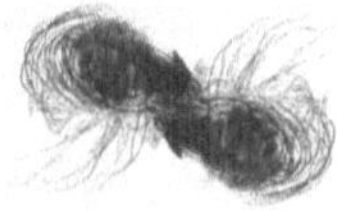

On the fifth floor, in what used to be a breakroom, Vic found himself walking into a circle of chairs like some loser A.A. meeting. The people who filled those chairs (with one exception) all got up when he entered. They all wanted to shake his hand, and their greetings came in a deluge:

"So cool to meet you, Vic." "You look just like in your streams, Vic." "You helped me make my first million, Vic."

To the uninitiated eye, these smelly, dumpy little men with bad fashion sense and uncombed beards would seem like classic basement dwellers still living with their moms, but Vic knew his people. Basement-dwelling losers didn't wear limited edition Audemars Piguet platinum watches or rock game-worn Jordans on their feet. And who had time to shower when there was so much grinding to get done?

"Who are you guys?" Vic asked, feeling a smile stretch his face.

It was the guy who didn't stand up to greet him who answered. "We are the Watchers of the End," the man said.

The warm, fuzzy feeling of having his ass kissed drained the instant Vic glanced at the seated man. Even sitting down, it was obvious the guy was tall, much taller than Vic. That was already a problem on its own, but what troubled Vic more was his smile—somehow too wide, too elastic. The dude was dressed in slacks and a cardigan and wore aviator sunglasses as dark and opaque as eclipse glasses.

"That's The Captain," Sam explained. "He's kind of our leader."

*The Captain?* Shit, that sounded cool. Not that Vic would admit it.

"Hey, hold up," Vic said. "Watchers of the End? What kind of name is that?"

"A descriptive one," The Captain replied.

"We're those blessed to foresee what's coming," said the guy with the watch.

"Our wealth and foresight will spare us from the tribulations," said another, a guy with eyeglass lenses as thick as dinner plates.

"We can escape before the Earth really starts to bleed," said the fat guy wearing the Jordans.

Maybe he'd misread these guys—they were sounding like a bunch of whacked out envirocuck libs.

"Is this a cult? Is this some cult shit?" Vic asked.

He looked to Sam. She shrugged. "Kind of?"

The Captain stood up from his chair, and as Vic surmised, he was huge—six-five, easily. "The word cult is a word that's taken on nasty connotations, but I like to remember that its root is the same as *to cultivate* and *to care for*. That's what we Watchers are about, Mr. Parkhill."

"Uh-huh." Vic took a small step back. "This is some cult shit."

Sam came alongside him and took him by the wrist, squeezing him reassuringly. "You wanted to learn about Vaporcoin, didn't you?"

"Ask us anything," The Captain said. "Really. We have nothing to hide from you, Victor Parkhill."

There was something unwholesome in the way he pronounced Vic's full name. Vic managed to brush it aside, his curiosity and personal mission overriding his apprehensions.

He asked some basic questions first, some of which he already knew the answer to, but which he hoped would tell him if they were being honest with him or not. He liked the answers he got. He asked if they were okay with him sharing this information with his followers.

"Of course," The Captain said. "As I said, we're not hiding anything."

"How is it produced?" Vic asked. "What kind of rig do you use?"

The Captain held his silence, while suddenly the others avoided Vic's eyes. And there it was—so much for the "nothing to hide" bullshit they were selling him.

Sam was the first to speak up. "We could show you the origin," she said. "But I don't think you're ready yet."

"What's that supposed to mean?"

"If you saw it, you'd know," Sam replied.

Before Vic could say anything else, The Captain appeared suddenly beside him, only inches away even though a second ago there'd been entire yards between them. It made Vic's heart jump.

"Tonight's meeting has concluded," The Captain announced, still grinning wide, showing teeth—more teeth than should be in a human smile. "We do hope to see you again tomorrow night."

As if he blacked out, Vic next found himself going down the elevator with Sam.

"It's good you found us now—we're leaving soon," she said. "Maybe we can escape the End together."

He was tired—asleep on his feet. That's what Vic would tell himself when he got to his home in Highland Park an hour later to explain why he doesn't remember putting up more of a fight when the weirdos brushed him out of their hair the second he started asking a question they didn't want to answer.

But he knew where to find them. And there was a new number in his phone's contacts, listed under the name "Sam ;)."

He didn't post anything before falling asleep. What could he have told his followers? *So listen, I found a cult...*

No, he needed to understand more before he spoke. He had a reputation to maintain.

His sleep was a nightmare reel of visions too solid to be called dreams. Vic never really remembered his dreams, but these nightmares stuck with him long after waking. Deep into the afternoon when he showered and had breakfast and checked the markets, he could still smell the burning plastic he'd whiffed while sleeping. That was the dominant sensation of his visions: a stench of burning plastic with an undercurrent of roast pork. The details he could recall: barren fields of sunbaked, cracking earth, wide fissures from which black tar gurgled up, poisonous watering holes where teeming hordes of stick-figure skin-and-bone people waddled and wallowed to escape an unrelenting sun. Then something worse: skies turning black, the sun vanishing, but the heat only intensifying. No more green, no more blue, just a palette of browns and grays. He woke just before he could glimpse what came after the skies turned black.

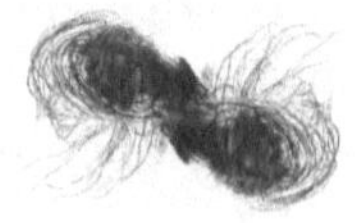

This time, he parked in the main lot, next to the Bugatti that he was pretty sure belonged to Sam. They were all waiting for him in the break room on the fifth floor with its circle of chairs, sour-smelling coffee, and sickly-yellow fluorescent lights.

By the look and smell of them, none of them had changed their outfits from the day before. He wondered if they were living here.

Despite his best efforts to pay close attention and keep his ears open, Vic found himself succumbing to a kind of hypnosis born of boredom as the "Watchers" took turns sharing their visions of the future. It was like they were speaking words he understood but which left no impression on him, so much code that wouldn't save.

"What does this have to do with Vaporcoin?" he asked after a while.

The chubby guy in the Jordans sniggered in that way that precedes a "well, actually."

But it was Sam who spoke up. "Vaporcoin isn't just a crypto—it's a ship in a bottle."

"It's from the future," said the guy with the giant watch.

"You're fucking with me," Vic said.

The whole time, The Captain seemed to be watching him—or so he felt, it was hard to tell with those sunglasses hiding his eyes. "It's natural to be skeptical," The Captain said. "Although, I think you know more than you suspect. How were your dreams last night, Mr. Parkhill?"

Like flipping up a stone over an anthill, the question kicked up a swarm of sense impressions—sights, sounds, smells, all from his nightmares. Vic tried not to let it show. "Don't see how that's any of your business."

"We're not trying to make you uncomfortable, Vic," Sam said. "Really, we see you as one of us. We want to help you."

The others leaned forward on their chairs. The circle seemed suddenly smaller, closer-knit than he recalled, like a manacle cinched around him.

"Help me?"

"Everyone's going to die," said the guy with the thick glasses.

"Some of them quickly, but most slowly," said the Jordans guy.

"We don't want that to happen to you," said Sam. "You're too special to die like one of the ants."

When he was younger, Vic did a lot of personal research on cults and how they operated. He was fascinated with cult leaders, with devoted followings, with the communities so entirely tied together by a powerful personality that they became like a homeostatic organism receiving its commands from the brain. He knew how cults operated, how they grew and gathered new members. It always started with making even the most worthless and weak mark feel special. He looked past Sam to The Captain and understood the game.

"Sure," he said. "So, 'The Captain,' do you also think I'm special?"

The Captain's already freakish smile somehow managed to widen. "You're cagey. I like that." The Captain then looked around at the others. "I don't think we're going to convince a natural-born free-thinker with just words. I think he needs to see the genesis block."

"Is he ready for that?" asked Glasses.

"He needs to see," said Wristwatch.

"He'll see; he'll know," said Jordans, as if reciting a mantra.

All three of them were blank-eyed, their pupils as tiny as poppy seeds.

Vic looked at Sam. "What are they talking about?"

In answer, she reached over and took his hand. Her eyes looked normal. "You wanted to see where Vaporcoin comes from, right?"

He followed them out of the breakroom, into a stairwell, where the lights flickered and the off-white paint was peeling in big strips. They went up two flights, The Captain leading the way. Soon, they were standing outside of a reinforced metal door with a sign that read PRO-PRIETARY MATERIAL. The Captain opened the door, and gestured for Vic to enter.

"You first," he said.

The Captain had to duck his head to clear the doorway. Vic followed, then the rest behind him. As soon as he crossed the threshold, the air changed, becoming stifling hot, like he'd stepped into a furnace or into an animal's throat.

The room was dark. All except for two small blue dots of light. It took a moment for his brain to catch up with what his eyes were seeing. But if his eyes lagged in comprehending, his ears got the message instantly, the second the *thing* screeched.

There was only one thing in the dark room: what looked like a human torso and head, pale, naked skin illuminated by the glow of two blue eyes set in a skull-like face. The body was butchered; legs cut off at the mid-thigh, bits of flesh hanging off the nubs like bits of loose red upholstery. The arms were gone too, gnawed off—yes, *gnawed*—a few inches past the shoulders, humerus bones sticking out like jagged broken stakes of white wood.

The thing rested against the wall, its bald head craned upward so that its blinking blue eyes strobed off the white ceiling. Its mouth was open wider than any human mouth could open, and as Vic entered, it let out a powerful exclamation somewhere between a human scream and the screech of an ancient dialup modem. A tangle of black wires stuck into its flanks and back, life-support keeping it alive against its will.

Vic recoiled, trying to back out. "The fuck is that?"

He walked into a wall of human bodies. The Watchers pushed him forward, gently.

"Don't be afraid," Sam said. "I know it looks gruesome, but it's not even a person. It's an android—*was* an android."

Vic's heartbeat galloped on as he looked at the thing again. It was undoubtedly the source of the oppressive heat. The wires weren't life support—they were a power supply. For a crypto-mining rig.

Vic's disgust turned to fascination, and he moved closer, even though the heat was making him sweat through his shirt and his eyes water. The creature's screech ceased, and it began to cough instead, ribbons of black tarry discharge spurting from its lips onto its chin and naked chest. The android's face was familiar, but it wasn't until Vic looked at The Captain again that he understood why: the facial structures were identical: same jawline, same cheekbones.

"This is the genesis block," Sam said. "This is the source of Vaporcoin."

"A prototype that never saw production," The Captain said. "U-Mii planned to call it the Learn'd Astronomer. Unlike their other synthetic lines, it had no commercial applications."

Vic nodded along, his mouth hanging open.

A stream of random numbers interspersed with terse words ("cold," "hunger," "cancer," "hunted," "shelter," "shrinking") dribbled from the android's tar-stained lips.

"What is it doing?" Vic asked.

"Calculating, working, mining," The Captain said. "We believe it mines Vaporcoin by calculating future events."

Vic's eyes, now adjusted to the gloom, began to pick up strange details from the room. It was not entirely empty: scattered around the floor were articles of discarded clothing. Shirts, pants, underwear, a pair of eyeglasses.

"We weren't the first to find this," Wristwatch said.

"Another group must have set it up," Glasses added.

"We think they're the ones who ate the genesis block's plastic flesh," Jordans said.

"There's something in the Astronomer's synthetic protein that resonates with a different reality, and metabolizing it allows one to shunt there," Sam said. "It was how they escaped this world. We can escape the same way."

Finally, Vic snapped out of his trance. "Escape what?"

"The End," all the Watchers said in unison.

"Right. Sure."

"You can join us—plenty of room at our feast," The Captain said.

Sam walked away, disappearing into the murky other side of the room. When she returned, she had a paper cup, the kind from an office water cooler. Somehow, bundled in that hoodie of hers, she managed to go closer to the android and its heat, close enough to hold the cup to its lips and collect the tarry discharge dripping from its mouth, until the cup was nearly whelmed. She stood up and walked carefully, slowly, toward Vic. She held the cup with its black broth to him.

"Drink it," she said.

"I'm sorry, what?"

She smiled and lifted the cup to her lips. "It's safe. See?" She took a sip. Her lips were a gothy black now, and shimmering.

"No thanks, I think I'm straight on that," he said.

The other Watchers clustered around him. "It's the only way you'll see—*really* see."

Sam was closer now, all but pushing the cup into his hands. "Come on, Vic," she whispered, something in her voice doing things to him, sending blood to low places. "I promise it's safe."

*Oh, what the Hell.* He'd imbibed weirder substances, like that fermented cat piss drug he tried last summer in Costa Rica.

There was no odor to the liquid, though it gave off a certain warmth when he held it to his nose. He took the tiniest sip possible. It tasted bitter, but not nearly as disgusting as he'd expected, with minor notes of recognizable flavors: iron, and three kinds of salt. At first, nothing happened. And then—

He sees out of both eyes. In one eye, a glimpse of green, in the other, a dull vision of broken brown earth.

With one eye he sees himself—a younger Vic—kayaking across Lake Lewisville, his dad's lake house looming on the shoreline behind. This is a happy memory, one of the happiest in fact. He's 14, still in school, no idea what he'll do with the rest of his life, no idea of the fame and wealth that awaits him.

With the other eye, he sees the same lake, only its water is all but gone. Not a lake anymore, but a constellation of miserable brown puddles where bands of things that could only charitably be described as human—no clothes, hair matted, bodies filthy with dust and ash—huddle in what little water remains while their heads jerk back to regard the skies above with fear. What are they checking for? What are they worried will find them? The vision expands, and he sees the ruin of the earth, the broken ground, cracked and ulcerated by the unrelenting ire of an endless summer. Only at night, when the sky's merciless red eye closes, does the black blood of the earth ooze from the wounds carved into its skin. The people bathe in this, too, and drink it—much more plentiful than the water.

He snapped out of it when someone grabbed his arm and asked him what he was seeing.

He couldn't answer. Words wouldn't come. Looking around at his surroundings, everything felt unreal, having only a second ago been pulled between the unfathomable immensity of past and future.

"The first time is always hard," Sam said. She hooked an arm around his waist, and she guided him out of the room.

"What did you see when you drank?" he heard himself ask her as they walked together down the stairs.

"In one eye, I saw my ninth birthday party," she said. Without looking at her, he could hear the smile in her words. "I was eating a dirt cup—you know, chocolate cake, pudding, gummi worms—and my mom was singing to me. Me and my friends were about to go on the slip-n-slide. The grass was so green."

"And the other eye?"

"I saw people in little groups, tribes maybe. They were walking across ground that'd lost all its topsoil so that it was just bare rock, like the moon. They kept looking up at the sky, because they were following clouds. I think that's what they do in the future—nomads following clouds around, hoping they'll make rain, but they never do, and even if they did, the rain would just be hot plastic that sticks to the skin."

Walking with her, hearing her share her vision, collating it with what he saw, he wondered if everything he'd ever done had been a horrible mistake, and if there was still time to do something about it.

An hour later, they were in his bedroom and he was fucking her with a kind of automatic, joyless intensity. She didn't even bother to take her hoodie off or he to remove his shoes. She lay on her back and stared past him at the ceiling, maybe thinking of rainclouds, or of eating a dirt cup. After he came, he stripped off the condom. The bulge at the bottom of the latex sleeve was a swell of viscid black.

Somewhere in the night, Sam asked him a question, and he said Yes, but he wasn't really paying attention. It was always difficult to listen when women talked, or really people in general. She repeated the question; he didn't answer.

"Are you sure?" she asked.

"Yes," he said, and he took her hands in his and squeezed them, but he didn't know what he'd agreed to.

Sometime later, he was alone in his bed, shoes still on his feet. Whether he opened his eyes or closed them, the visions he'd seen wouldn't leave him. Fires burning as high as skyscrapers, vast salt fields left where oceans receded, babies emerging from the birth canals already cancerous and dying, tumors swelling their limbs like grotesque water-wings under the skin. He understood what work the "rig" was doing to mint new Vaporcoin—it was calculating future suffering. How many people would die, how soon, of what causes. He decided he'd rather not think of it anymore. Somewhere deep in the night, he deleted Sam's number from his phone and decided he was never going back.

The stream that Saturday was a disaster. It started out normal enough, lots of ass-kissing, cascades of idiotic questions, a nice chat with fellow influencer Baecoin about the recent dip in Ethereum and whether it should concern anyone (spoiler: nah), and all through it, Vic managed to smile at his webcam and look and act like he had his shit together. Managed to act like the visions weren't playing on loops in his head-space cinema. But midway through the stream, he noticed a recurrent question in the chat from a username that was just a strand of numbers.

"Do you know how it ends??"

He tried to ignore it, but the question became more persistent, the commenter somehow spamming it multiple times per second. The chat moderator kicked the account, but then there were two of them repeating the question, and this hydra trick carried on until the chat was nothing but that one question.

He ended the stream an hour early.

He'd thought staying away from the Watchers would make the images go away, but now he could recall them even with his eyes open.

His phone buzzed—another call from an unknown number. He rejected the call, and when the same number tried again, he went for the nuclear option and turned his phone off.

Vic thought maybe he could blitz the visions out of his brain with the right cocktail of pills and a generous guzzle of vodka. This did not banish the images, but it did nullify all the parts of him that cared. At about seven p.m. when it was still sunny out, Vic settled down into his bed and drifted off into a blessed oblivion, broken only by a brief dream where he imagined a figure standing over his bed, whispering to him, but whatever they were whispering couldn't reach him all the way down where he was.

When he woke up, his body was clammy and aching at every joint, and his head throbbed with a buckshot-grade hangover. His tongue was like a dry kitchen sponge. He waited for the visions to return, but they didn't.

When he closed his eyes—nothing. That should have made him happy.

When he got out of bed about two hours later, he noticed something that chilled him. On the handle to his bedroom door were smudges left by fingers, black and inky. Or like tar. He thought of his dream, and realized the person who had tried to wake him had been dressed in a hoodie.

A strange, quiet, cold fire impelled him into his car. It was late in the afternoon, the sun low over Dallas's skyline. He drove to Plano, to the office he swore he wouldn't visit again.

The cars were all there in the parking lot. The front door was open, inviting him in. But something gnawed at his gut, a misgiving he couldn't pin down. The first time he'd come there, he'd sensed from the jump that he was not alone, perhaps even that he was being watched. It didn't feel that way now.

The break room was empty, just a circle of chairs. He went up the stairs to the room where the genesis block was housed, and each step he took up the stairwell felt like an impossible exertion, his throat shrinking, him feeling like he was breathing through a coffee stirrer.

When he touched the metal door, it was cold. And that's when he realized he was fucked. When he opened the door, wintry air greeted him, and darkness. He had to use the flashlight on his phone, and as he swept the weak cone of light side to side, it surveyed a scene of bloodless carnage.

All that was left of the genesis block was a plastic skull, the bare blue eyes now lidless and lightless. Realistic white teeth smiled starkly in an eternal grin, one identical to that of The Captain. Speaking of The Captain, Vic found him next. There wasn't much left of him either. All his skin and flesh gone, stripped clean, but someone had put his sunglasses back onto his skull, which was connected to a long column of synthetic vertebrae flanged with fiberoptic wires and circuitry. About a yard away, The Captain's bare ribs shone under the flashlight's glare, tooth marks exposing bits of metal under the enameled surface.

Not a scrap of meat left for him.

He swept his light across the filthy floor, scuffed by the grease of knees and elbows, and surveyed the piles of clothes left behind. Some of them were the same articles that were here the first time he entered the room, but he recognized some of the items: a $50,000 Swiss watch, a set of dingy game-worn Jordans, thick eyeglasses, and a sweaty hoodie that when he picked it up stunk of many of weeks of built-up grime and sebaceous odor.

He searched on hands and knees for anything he could eat, for the merest morsel of android flesh. He cursed his own stupidity, his fear, his inability to listen. He was going to die, he was going to die like all the other poor, miserable idiots on this planet. This wasn't right; people like him didn't suffer. He started to cry.

That's when The Captain's jaws gnashed together.

"Do you know how it ends?" the skull in sunglasses asked.

Vics face was in his hands. Through the darkness, through his fingers, he watched the grinning robot teeth snap open and shut, a kind of laughter.

"Do you know how it ends?"

One piece of meat remained: the tongue. He scrabbled on the ground like a lizard, seized the skull, and pried the jaws open with his fingers, cutting himself on the sharp incisors. The tongue was like muscle taffy. It had no flavor at all.

It took many minutes to chew the leather-tough morsel enough that he could force it down, and once it was down, Vic waited for something to happen. But all that happened was that while one of his eyes filled with more visions of that dark and terrible world of ash and raining hot plastic, out of the other eye he saw where the others had escaped to: a colorless place where nothing living ever grew, and nothing could ever die. Where the numbed digits of an unfeeling appendage sifted through gray dunes of silicon to collect its newly minted currency.

# I Think My Treehouse Is Haunted

### by Philip Fracassi

## PART ONE – THE TREEHOUSE

Yeah, I'm pretty sure my treehouse is haunted.

My mom and I moved into this new house a few months ago. We used to live in the city. A small apartment on the $12^{th}$ floor of a building downtown. We'd lived there my whole life, and I loved it. I had lots of friends in the building and taking the city bus to school was always interesting. I didn't like to take it alone, but that only happened a few times, when my friends were out of town, sick, or for whatever reason got to school a different way that day. Strangers were funny when you had someone to watch them with. They were a lot less funny when you were by yourself. They could be downright scary.

When my dad was killed in the accident, my mom decided we'd move to a house in the suburbs. Mom worked from home and Dad didn't work downtown anymore (obviously), so she said we'd use the insurance money to buy a house where it was quiet and less dangerous.

So, I'd be starting junior high at a new school, which sucked, but I wasn't going to be a jerk about it. My mom had been through a lot, and my friends and I could still hang out online, which is what we mostly did anyway, even when we lived in the same building.

I have to admit, so far the house hasn't been all terrible. It's pretty nice—much bigger than our apartment—and having a yard is pretty cool. I hadn't thought about it before, but now that we live in a house and have a backyard with a fence I wonder if we can get a dog.

(NOTE: Possible birthday present?)

The best thing about the new house, at least at first, was the awesome treehouse in the backyard.

First of all, it's big. Like four closets put together if you took out the walls. There's a rope ladder that goes up through the floor that you can pull up once you're inside. Keeps other people from invading. It also smells nice. Like wood and leaves. There are a couple cutout windows—one that looks into the neighbor's yard and one that looks back at our house. If I look through the one facing the house I can see my bedroom window. I can even see my bed, which is neat. Like spying on myself.

There's no light in the treehouse, but Mom bought me an electric lantern that I kept up there in case I wanted to go up at night, which I thought would be kind of cool. I thought maybe I could even spend the night out there.

But yeah, that's not going to happen.

And that's why I'm writing this. I want to see if maybe other people have had similar experiences as me. Also, I want to write about it because there's no other way I can talk about what's going on. I tried to tell Mom, but of course she thought I was being dumb, and then she started looking at me funny, like I was nuts.

No help there.

I tried to bring it up with my friends, but they just laughed their asses off and teased me. Trying to play Call of Duty while getting called "ghost boy" is not as fun as it sounds. Every time they'd call me that, laughing, I'd think about the little girl and feel sick all over again.

Right. The little girl.

The first time I saw her we'd been living here a couple weeks, I guess. Lots of stuff was still in boxes, but for the most part we'd moved in. My room was almost totally unpacked except for a couple boxes with toys and books that I just shoved into my closet. I'd already met a couple other kids who lived nearby, but we hadn't really become friends yet. I knew when school started I'd meet more kids, so I wasn't worried. But otherwise living at the house is pretty much the same as the apartment. We just hang out. Unlike the apartment, though, my mom started telling me to get outside all the time. When we lived downtown, that *never* happened. And now it's like she's desperate to prove how much better it is living in a house. She'll be like, "Go outside and play!" or "Go ride your bike!" She has no idea how ridiculous she sounds when she says stuff like that. As if there's a circus in the driveway or something.

So, whenever she'd get going on the "go outside" thing, I'd usually just head to the treehouse. I'd bring my phone or a book or my Warcraft cards. I had a sleeping bag up there already, and an old couch pillow Mom said was "okay to ruin."

It was probably my fourth or fifth time going up there. Mom was working in her office, which was still *really* messy, so I grabbed my stuff and went out back. I'd already gotten pretty good at climbing the rope ladder, which swings around a bit if you don't balance right. But I'd had a lot of practice by now.

When I pulled myself up this time, though, the treehouse wasn't empty.

There was a girl sitting in the corner.

Holy shit, was I freaked out.

"Hey!" I said, kinda loud and mean because her being there surprised me, and not in a good way. I assumed she was a neighbor kid I hadn't met yet, but I was annoyed at her coming into my treehouse without being invited.

She didn't answer me, and she didn't look at me when I climbed up. Not even when I spoke. She just sat there, her knees tucked under, playing with something I couldn't see. Like she was playing with dolls, but the dolls were fake. Imagined. Or invisible. She wore a yellow t-shirt and jeans. The shirt said something on it that I couldn't read because it was super faded. Her hair was long and dark brown, and it hung down over her face while she played with her invisible dolls. I say she was little, and she was. Young, I mean. Maybe six or seven. Like a second grader.

She was humming something, but it wasn't really a song. More like a part of some old rhyme. I tried to think about what it was, as it sounded familiar, but I never did come up with it.

"Hey," I repeated, more gently this time. I moved over to my sleeping bag at the other side of the treehouse. Opposite the girl. She still didn't look at me or do anything but play with the dolls and hum her weird tune in a way that was becoming more and more creepy.

"You're not supposed to be in here," I said, not wanting to be a jerk but more to get her to pay attention to me. "Hey, can you hear me? This is my treehouse, okay? You should go home."

It was when I said that last word – *home* – that she finally stopped playing and looked up.

She didn't look at me, though. She was glaring at the corner next to me. As if someone else was in the treehouse with us.

"Just me and Mommy," she said.

"You and Mommy what?" I was now feeling very, *very* freaked out. The back of my neck prickled, and my stomach felt queasy. It was seriously weird.

It was something about the way she looked into that other corner. The empty corner. Like she wasn't answering me, but somebody else. Talking to someone I couldn't see.

I started to ask another question, but honestly? I couldn't talk. For some reason, I was getting really scared. Which didn't make sense because, other than the neighbor kid sneaking into my treehouse, there was nothing all that spooky going on. The day was warm and bright. There were no weird shadows or anything. And the girl wasn't really scary, she was just a little kid.

Then she spoke again.

"I don't want to," she said, and then *she* looked scared. Frankly? She looked terrified.

"Hey!" I yelled, and it was so loud inside that little treehouse that I jumped at my own voice. "What's your deal? Who are you talking to?"

And then it was like ... I don't know. It's hard to explain. I'll try.

Okay, so my dad used to play records all the time. It was sort of a hobby, I guess. My mom sold his collection when we moved. She asked me if I wanted them first, but I didn't. That was his thing and I figured the records sort of died when he did. Anyway, one time he was playing a record and I was sitting with him doing homework, and the record started to *repeat*. Like hiccups. The same little bit of music played over and over again, and then after a minute or so it fixed itself and kept going with the song. Dad cursed ("Damn" and "Hell" were allowed in our house), and when he saw me looking at the record player he kinda smiled. I think he was embarrassed.

Then he said, "It just skipped a little, bud."

Point being, that's what happened to the little girl.

It was like her whole body sort of ... *skipped.* One second she was looking into the empty corner of the treehouse, wide-eyed and frightened, and the next second she was playing with the dumb invisible dolls again, hair over her face, humming that strange melody and not paying attention to me at all.

Like she'd been reset.

That was it for me. I crawled to the top of the ladder, which was about halfway between us, and climbed down. I dropped the last few feet and sprinted for the house, not looking back once at the treehouse.

I went straight to my mom and told her. "There's a weird little girl in there!"

She seemed annoyed with me at first, but something in my expression must have bothered her, because she stopped typing on her laptop and followed me into the backyard. She laughed at me when I stopped at the little patio just outside the house. I didn't want to go any further.

It was almost funny watching Mom climb the ladder, but she did a decent job, actually.

I waited to hear her scream.

But the scream never came, and she didn't go all the way inside, but I could tell she was looking around, her head and shoulders having gone up through the floor while she hung onto the ladder.

When she came back down, she walked over to me kinda quiet. Then she looked at me, not making fun, but serious. It was the look I would come to recognize when I tried to tell her about the other stuff a couple months later - the one she gave me when she thought I was nuts.

I hated it.

"No one there, pal," she said, and cocked her head a little, like she was studying me. "Were you making it up? Like a joke? It's okay if you were. But be honest."

I started to shake my head, but then I glanced over her shoulder, at the treehouse window.

I could just see the top of the little girl's head.

I swear I could even hear her humming.

"Yeah," I said, not even sure what I was saying. "Sorry, just screwing around."

I don't think Mom totally believed me, but after looking at me that weird way for another few seconds, she just ruffled my messy (and sorta sweaty) hair and went back inside.

"Good one," she said from just inside the house. "Since I'm apparently taking a break, why don't we have lunch?"

"Okay," I yelled over my shoulder, my eyes still fixed on the treehouse window.

Where the little girl was still playing.

I took a deep breath, then followed my mom inside.

After a while, I calmed down. Told myself it wasn't a big deal and to stop being such a baby.

Of course, all of this was before things got *really* scary.

## PART TWO – THE BLEEDING MAN

Luckily, I didn't see the little girl every time I went in the treehouse.

Once school started and I'd made a few friends, a couple of us would hang out there sometimes. But the little girl never appeared then, either.

Apparently she's shy.

The first time I had a friend over, this guy Jim, he saw the treehouse in back and freaked. "No way," he'd said, already jogging toward the ladder. "A real treehouse!"

I tried to persuade him not to go inside—begged him really—but the more I protested the more he wanted to check it out.

"You got a secret porn stash in there or something?" he asked, whispering too loudly only twenty feet from where my mom was distractedly heating up a couple burritos. "I wanna see it."

"Fine," I told him. I was super nervous, but part of me was a little curious, as well. Not that it mattered, because when we finally climbed up there it was fine.

No little girl.

Man oh man, was I relieved.

Still, during those first couple months in the new house, she continued to appear when I was there alone. It happened at least a few times. Maybe more. Honestly, after a while, I just kind of forgot about her. I'd just read a book or listen to music, and she'd play with the invisible dolls, constantly humming that weird tune.

Every now and then she'd start up with the "just me and Mommy" stuff. But since it seemed triggered by my talking to her, specifically by certain words ("Home" being one of them), I basically didn't say anything, and she'd stay quiet.

So, even though it was obviously weird, it was also not really a big deal. It was just another new thing I'd have to learn to live with. Lately, it seemed there was a whole bucketload of things I had to learn to live with, but I guess that's part of growing up.

After a while, I figured it would be fine. That her presence there wouldn't be a problem.

But then, just like that, it *was* a problem.

A nasty one.

Looking back on it, I realize that the mistake I made, what broke the fragile peace between us, was going up into the treehouse at night.

The first time I did that, it had been a hot day in late summer. Or fall, I guess. But it *felt* like summer. I mean, it was crazy hot for being almost October. Mom called it an Indian Summer, which I thought sounded racist, but I didn't say anything. And, of course, our air conditioning broke, and Mom said the repairmen were busy and it would be a few days until they could come fix it. So the house was *hot,* and being outside - maybe even sleeping outside - seemed like a good idea.

At the time.

So that night, after dinner, I packed up a couple books, my iPhone, a bag of candy and a bottle of water. The plan was to sleep in the treehouse. Something I'd never done before, but times were desperate. Besides, by that time I hardly noticed or cared about the little girl. If she was there goofing around, that was fine by me.

Once the sun went down, I put my stuff in my backpack, walked across the overgrown grass of the backyard to the big tree, and climbed the rope ladder.

Inside, the treehouse was wonderfully cool and breezy. Since it was nestled within the shady tree all day, it never really heated up like the house did.

But it was also dark. There wasn't any moonlight coming through the windows, and I could hardly see my hand in front of my face. I managed to crawl over to my sleeping bag, where the electric lantern was shoved into the corner along with some other stuff. I'd never used it, having avoided the treehouse after dark, but figured the batteries would be just fine.

I knelt on the sleeping bag, feeling like a blind man. I dumped my backpack next to me and fumbled around in the corner until I found the lantern.

I could already hear the girl humming from the other side of the treehouse.

Honestly? In the dark? It was creepy.

I started breathing faster, feeling a little panicked as I hurried to find the switch for the stupid lantern, thinking if I could at least *see* her doing her thing it wouldn't sound quite so ... *menacing*.

I finally found the knob on the side of the lantern and twisted it. The light popped on, and the treehouse interior lit up.

Sure enough, the little girl was there, hair in her face, playing with those dumb invisible dolls.

"Hey you," I said, wanting to keep it brief. Then I settled back against the wall.

And that's when I saw *him*.

I couldn't move. I mean, I literally could not move. I couldn't even breathe. I was scared shitless, to be honest.

In the corner of the treehouse to my left, just a couple feet past the edge of my sleeping bag, was a man.

He was sort of sprawled in the corner, his legs loose and bent. One hand was pushed against the floor, the other was holding his stomach, like he was sick. He wore dark jeans, heavy boots and a black leather jacket. The jacket was unzipped and spread open, exposing a gray t-shirt underneath. He was pretty old. I'd guess at least in his forties, because he was older-looking than my mom, and she was thirty-something.

The t-shirt, beneath the hand that covered his stomach, was stained and slick with blood. The hand clutching his gut was also wet and red, like he'd dipped his fingers into a can of paint.

He was bleeding. Badly.

His dark hair was long, stringy, and sweaty, plastered to his forehead and cheeks. He had pale, sickly skin and dark eyes.

The eyes were fixed on the little girl.

"Don't be scared," he said. His voice was deep and rumbly, but it was also muffled, like he was speaking through a pillow. "Do you live here?"

Still frozen, my eyes darted to the little girl, who had stopped playing. She was looking up at him.

At the *corner*.

"Shit," I said, whispered really. I was shaking. I just wanted to leave, to turn off the lantern and run back into my house. But I couldn't. I know it sounds weird, but I honestly don't think I could have moved if the whole tree was on fire. It was like my blood was ice, my muscles locked up. I could only watch, and listen.

The little girl stopped humming, and her hands dropped, lifeless, supposedly having let go of whatever invisible toys she played with. She stared at the bleeding man and, after a long hesitation, nodded. But her face looked different. She looked scared.

I don't think she knew the man.

"You and your family live here, is that right?" The man spoke slowly, carefully, as if he didn't want to spook her into doing anything... sudden. "You, Mom and Dad? Do you have brothers or sisters?"

The girl shook her head. "Just me and Mommy."

I looked back at the man in time to see him smile. When I saw that, and I hate to say it, my bladder let go. Urine soaked the crotch of my pants, and then I started to sort of moan. Like whimpering, I guess. I don't know why. There was something so terrible—so *off*—about him. I felt like I shouldn't even be there. Like it was wrong to be sitting with them, seeing this play out, pissing into my jeans like an infant.

"I see," the man said. He shifted his weight then, brought his legs under him, like he was going to crawl. His face got even more white, and he looked, for a second, like he might puke. Blood dripped off his stomach and onto the treehouse floor.

I'd never noticed the small, dark stains there.

I did now.

"Come here, sweetheart," the man said.

The girl shook her head. I could see tears on her face. "I don't want to."

"It's okay," the bleeding man said. "It's going to be just fine."

And then, faster than I would have thought possible, he scrambled across the floor toward the little girl, like a spider who'd caught a fly in its web and was moving in to feast. The little girl started to scream, but I screamed first.

I yelled as loud as I could, and only then realized that I was also crying. I jerkily kicked the lantern and it somehow freed all my muscles, made my blood start pumping again. I dove for the hole in the floor.

The lantern was rolling on its side, creating a weird lighting effect inside the treehouse, like a wobbly spotlight.

I only looked back once before my hands and feet hit the ladder. The man and the girl were joined together. It looked like he was giving her a hug.

I climbed down as fast as I could, tripped on the last rung and fell. I got back up and sprinted toward my house, screaming for my mother.

I'd never been more scared in my life.

Later, after I calmed down, I babbled about the man in the treehouse and repeated my vision of the little girl. Although my mom assured me it was just a nightmare, she still went out and checked for herself, gripping a hammer from the toolbox. I watched from the patio as she climbed up into the illuminated box, knowing she'd find nothing there.

Because they weren't there, of course. The little girl and the bleeding man. They weren't there because they weren't real.

They were something else entirely.

I didn't know if I was going crazy or what, all I knew was that I would never, ever, go into that treehouse again. Standing on the patio, watching my mother climb the treehouse ladder, a hammer in one hand, I swore it to myself.

I promised. Never again.

Unfortunately, this is a promise I would break.

## PART THREE – THE SLEEPOVER

After the incident with the bleeding man, I tried my best to forget about the whole thing. About the girl and the treehouse and what might have happened there.

But I couldn't let it go. And after a few days, when the events of that night sort of dimmed and became less frightening to think about, I started to get more and more curious about what, exactly, had happened to the girl. I asked a few of my neighbor friends, but they all sorta shrugged and said they didn't know, and obviously didn't care. But I kept it up, asking whenever I thought it would seem natural and not like I was obsessed with it or something. I even asked a few teachers about it, and the postwoman when she dropped off a package one morning for my mom. But the adults seemed to know even less than the kids, and were a lot more reluctant to chat with me about it.

As it turned out, it was my neighbor's mom who finally caved and told me what happened to the family who lived in our house before we moved in.

Honestly, it wasn't that hard to get her going. Apparently "everybody" knew but nobody liked to discuss it. She said it wasn't polite. That it scared people. Which makes more sense after you know what happened.

Because it's horrible.

Okay, so one night, Jamie, who lives three houses down and has sort of become my default best friend in the neighborhood, invited me over for pizza, a movie, and a sleepover. My mom seemed pretty excited about the idea of having a night to herself, which didn't bother me in the slightest. If I had to make me dinner and bug me about taking a bath and doing homework and going to bed every day I'd want a break too.

"Was awful what happened there," Jamie's mom said while filling our milk glasses. She was sort of the exact opposite of Jamie, who was tall and skinny with black hair and brown eyes. His mom was short and had a big bowl of blonde hair on her head. I found myself staring at her bright pink fingernails while she poured my milk. I'd never even met Jamie's dad. "I mean, it's a beautiful home, and you guys will be happy there, no doubt. But, geez, the people who lived there before you?" She shook her head and pursed her lips, which were bright red. "Did not end well."

I pretended to be enjoying my pizza when, in fact, I was really just doing my best to simply gag it down. My throat felt like it was closing and my face got kinda hot when she started talking.

*She's going to tell me,* I thought, and the idea of finally knowing was both exhilarating and terrifying. I could feel myself sweating as she talked, and hoped she or Jamie didn't notice that I was having an anxiety attack or whatever.

"I've heard a few things," I said, and took a long sip of milk. "But wasn't sure if it was real or not. I didn't want to ask Mom about it because I was afraid she'd feel bad."

Part of this was a lie. I hadn't heard anything about anything. Obviously, there must be something wrong with the house. *Something* happened, and I just couldn't contain my curiosity. Seeing a ghost, I've learned, makes a person question all sorts of things.

"Well, that's considerate," she said, and sat down at the table with us, nibbled at the end of her lone slice of cheese pizza. "And I don't want to, you know, speak out of school or anything. I mean, are you sure you want to know this stuff? It might freak you out."

Jamie looked at me with wide eyes, and I wondered which one of us it would freak out more. As for me, I'd seen some insane stuff already. Stories weren't going to make it any worse, but they might explain some things.

"No, it won't bother me. I don't scare easy." I wasn't sure if this was true or not, but part of me hoped it was. Then, of course, I remembered the bleeding man crawling toward the girl, moving like a giant spider as she started to scream, the spill of warmth in my pants as I pissed myself...

"Okay," she said. "Well, no need to go into all the gory details. And I'm sure your mother is well aware of the basics, as they probably told her before she bought the place. It's the law or something."

I nodded along, not fully knowing what she was talking about, and getting the sense that Jamie's mom wasn't, as my dad used to say, "the brightest bulb."

"So, first of all, you should know this happened a while ago. That house sat empty, God, for at least three years. Which is crazy in this neighborhood, but it was tied up in legal mumbo-jumbo for a while, and then was purchased by a bank and renovated, which is why you have the nice floors and those new appliances."

I kept nodding, hoping she'd get back to the stuff I cared about. Jamie was finished with his pizza and was studying his phone, so I had the feeling time was short before he demanded more movie and less dinner conversation with his mom. "But someone lived there before us," I said gently. Prodding.

"Oh yes honey, of course. And, well, that's the thing. See, the people that lived there ... gosh, I don't know if I should be telling you this."

She looked at her son, saw his attention was diverted, and shrugged. Maybe giving me nightmares was okay if it meant spilling local gossip, but I don't think she wanted to deal with Jamie screaming in the night.

"Look, first of all, you need to understand that this is a very, very safe neighborhood. And that what happened, my gosh, was a total anomaly. You know what that means?"

I nodded. I had no idea.

"Right. Well, there's no sugar-coating it. One night there was a break-in. A burglary, you know? An intruder."

The word "intruder" conjured up an image that raised the hairs on the back of my neck, the image of the man in the corner of the treehouse, breathing heavy, covered in blood and sweaty, holding his torn guts.

I set down my pizza, but met her eyes, willing her to continue. I needed to know.

"I'm sorry to say, but the man—this intruder—he, okay, he killed the people in that house. But remember," she added hurriedly, "this was many years ago. We had just moved in, hardly knew a soul. Hadn't even met the woman."

"Woman?" I asked, intrigued despite the crawling dread in my stomach.

"Yes honey. A woman and her little girl." She leaned closer to me, as if we were in public and she didn't want to be overheard. As if saying something quietly makes it less true, less horrible. "They'd been strangled."

I tried to swallow but couldn't do it. I noticed my hand was trembling and tucked it into my lap beneath the table. "The little girl, too? She was..."

Jamie's mom nodded.

"Horrible," she said.

And it was.

"Where did they die?" I asked, realizing I'd unconsciously matched her strained whisper.

Jamie, meanwhile, had stopped playing with his phone and was staring at his mom as if she was telling me about the end of the world, letting me in on a hot tip that it was coming in just a few days. He looked plenty scared, and I hoped his mother wouldn't notice. Not yet.

She looked away, as if debating whether to answer me. I pressed the issue.

"Did the little girl die in the treehouse?"

Her head jerked back to me, her eyes shining with what I could only describe as anger. Like I'd insulted her cooking, or her looks. Or her kid. She was angry, but I think she was also afraid. Yeah, looking back on it, I'm almost sure of it.

"How..."

Then she shook her head, her face reddening. I knew it was all the information I was going to get. But it was enough.

More than enough.

"Dinner's over," she said, and then just stood up and left the room.

At least now I knew, knew for sure, what happened back then. And why the ghost of the little girl was trapped in that treehouse, reliving the same night over and over.

With me as her sole audience.

Later that night, I convinced Jamie to let me use his computer, and together we looked up stuff on ghosts and haunting spirits. It was actually Jamie who found the information that proved most useful, buried deep within a website devoted to hauntings around the world.

I had never told him what happened to me, or what I'd seen. I think some part of him knew—had pieced it together from my questions and our following information dive for hauntings—but he never asked. I don't think he really wanted to know what I'd experienced.

I didn't blame him.

"It says here that some ghosts are forced to relive their deaths over and over again, for eternity," he said, reading off the screen. "Like an old film replaying a traumatic event from the past."

"Let me see," I said, and read the passage he was referring to. There was a bold section break that read PSYCHIC IMPRINT. I scanned the paragraph below it quickly, getting excited. It made perfect sense, and fell into line with what I'd seen. Unlike many of the other described hauntings, my ghost wasn't interacting with me. It was just doing whatever it had been doing that night.

So why was I seeing the bleeding man? Was that part of some sort of show the little girl was putting on for me? To let me see for myself what had happened?

To see if I could do anything about it?

"I wonder if there's a way to help them," I said, scrolling further down the page, desperate for answers. "If there's some way to, I don't know, *release* them."

Jamie spun off his chair and flopped down onto his bed. He gripped a pillow to his chest and faced the wall. "I don't know dude, but I don't want to talk about this shit anymore. It's stupid."

By stupid, he of course meant scary. And it was, but I felt like I was finally getting somewhere. I wanted to help that little girl. Free her.

But how?

While Jamie had his back turned, I googled one more thing before shutting the topic down for the night.

I typed my street address, city and state. Then I typed the word MURDER.

I got multiple hits.

One was a local news page that had a two-paragraph article and a photo of a woman hugging a small girl.

I recognized her instantly.

My skin tingled unpleasantly, as if I'd been lightly touched by someone I couldn't see, or was suddenly covered in baby spiders.

Scrolling down, I passed by a few links that had nothing to do with my house at all. Then I saw a link to the city's homicide department website. I clicked on it, and it brought up the same incident the news article had, but it was more technical, like a crime report.

They were asking people to come forward who had information on the murders of the woman and her daughter. There was a form you could fill out to respond.

The page was old. Dated almost four years ago. But it was still active. They hadn't taken it down. They were still looking for information.

They were still hunting the killer.

## PART FOUR – SALT AND CANDLES

The rest of the fall was pretty tame. I dug around a bit more here and there, but didn't learn anything more about the murders than what I already knew.

School was fine. The usual. I was making more friends, and even joined a drama club, which made my mom happy.

I never spoke to Jamie's mom about the murders, or much of anything else, again. The next few times I saw her she acted really different, like I'd tricked her or something. I asked Jamie about it once and he mumbled something about nightmares.

He never invited me over for another sleepover, and we don't hang out much anymore.

I still visit the treehouse, but not very often. It's getting colder now and if I'm out there for more than an hour my hands get icy and my nose runs.

I have seen the little girl a few more times, though, and even saw the bleeding man again. Only once.

Like the first time, it was at night.

I hadn't meant to be there after the sun went down, but I'd fallen asleep while reading a book.

It was his voice that woke me up.

"Don't be scared."

This time I didn't stay for the end. I didn't want to see him crawling across the floor again, watch him pull the little girl into that deadly embrace.

The only thing I heard him say, as I was scrambling for the ladder, groggy and terrified, was the same thing he'd said that first time:

"Do you live here?"

By the time the girl started to respond, I was already three rungs down the rope ladder, heading for the warmth and safety of my bedroom.

Still, as weeks passed, I couldn't let go of the idea that I could somehow free the little girl. Let her eternal spirit rest or whatever. Go to heaven.

I spent a lot of time on the internet, looking for more information about ghosts, especially those trapped like mine was. It was hard to find stuff that was helpful because there was, like, tons and tons of stories and supposed facts about ghosts that had nothing to do with what was happening in the treehouse.

She was a very specific haunting.

There was, however, some information about getting *rid* of ghosts, like certain things you could do to free them into the spirit realm, which was interesting. But even that came with its own series of problems.

For instance: burn sage. What the hell is sage? And how do I burn it? I considered asking my mom, but like I said, she was already thinking I was getting too weird, and plus I didn't want to have to answer a bunch of questions.

Another option, one that was much easier, was salt.

Salt I knew.

Apparently, if you put salt on the floor, or across a doorway, it keeps the ghosts out. I'm not sure if it would work, because the ghost was already *in,* but I swiped the salt container–the one my mom uses to fill the little ceramic shaker we keep on the table–from the pantry and hid it in my room. Figured it couldn't hurt.

Another idea for banning spirits was to burn white candles. Okay, I thought. This was also something I could handle.

I knew we had a stash of emergency candles in the laundry room, along with a wind-up flashlight, bottled water and some first-aid stuff. The candles were white and heavy, plenty big. I took three.

So... I had my salt and my candles. I was feeling pretty good about things.

There was only one snag. I wanted to do the salt and the candles when I knew the bleeding man would be there. I'd pretty much decided that he wasn't really a ghost-ghost, but sort of a part of the little girl. Like she was *showing* him to me using her own ... spirit energy, I guess.

I don't know what makes me think that. But there's one obvious fact: If he killed the girl, and then her mom, it would mean that he probably didn't die in the treehouse.

Unless he killed the mom first, of course. And maybe that's why he was bleeding? Maybe she'd stabbed him or something. Defended herself.

Or maybe he'd already been bleeding. I thought of a hundred reasons why, but the ones I went back to again and again were these: he had robbed a bank, and the police had shot him while escaping; there was a drug deal and the drug dealer shot him or stabbed him when he wouldn't pay; he'd been bitten by someone's dog when he tried to rob their house and had gone to the treehouse to hide, not knowing the girl would be there.

Or, did the girl come in after he arrived? Maybe he was the one who was surprised.

Or, maybe he knew the little girl.

Maybe he was the mom's boyfriend.

I know the police always think it's the boyfriend or husband, though. He definitely would have been a suspect. There's no way he could have escaped if he was someone they knew.

So, a stranger.

Or, as Jamie's mom put it: an intruder.

Whoever he was, I wanted him gone along with the spirit of the little girl. And since he only appeared, at least so far, when it was dark, I figured I'd have to go out there at night.

Again.

The only thing that still sort of confuses me is something my mom said a few days ago.

"I was talking on the phone earlier with the realtor. He'd called to check in," she said one night while the two of us were watching a movie. I could tell she was trying to be all cool about it, but she was obviously nervous. "You know, the guy who sold us the house."

"Uh-huh," I mumbled, my eyes on the screen. If she could pretend, so could I.

"It's just … well, I don't want you to be mad at me, but I mentioned that you'd been having nightmares. About a little girl, and the man?"

She said this like a question I was supposed to answer, or at least reply to, but I kept my eyes forward. I didn't want her to see my face.

She went on anyway.

"He stopped talking for a moment... I thought we'd lost the connection at first. Anyway, he said something kind of strange."

Okay, now she'd got me. I turned to look at her sitting at the opposite end of the couch. But now *she* was the one looking away, pretending to watch the movie.

"What'd he say?"

She was quiet a moment, and when she finally answered, it was more like she was talking to herself.

"He said, 'Tell him to sleep in the treehouse. The fresh air will do him some good.'"

I swallowed hard, ignoring the chill that ran up my back at the very thought of such a horrible idea.

"Why is that strange?"

My mom turned to me then, her face half-lit by the light from the television. Her eyes were wide, and worried.

"Because when we bought the place, he'd said the exact opposite."

"I don't get it," I said.

"At the time, he told me you should probably stay away from the treehouse. He said, and I remember this clearly, that it wasn't safe."

Which brings my story up to date.

As I type this, I'm readying myself for what I need to do next, and I've already figured out when I'm gonna do it.

I'll do it tomorrow.

I'll go out there after the sun sets, when it's dark, and I'll finish it.

After all, it's just a ghost and her memories. There's nothing out there that can actually hurt me—scare me, for sure-—but not actually *hurt* me.

Right?

# PART FIVE – THE LAST NIGHT

## 7:36 PM

Okay, tonight is the night.

I'm gonna time code this entry. If it works, it might be something to keep the details of, like a science experiment.

So, I've got three of the heavy white candles in my backpack. Plus the container of salt I swiped from the pantry.

I'm writing this on the laptop at my desk. If I look up, I'm staring straight through a big window that faces the backyard, the giant oak tree, and the treehouse.

The sun is about to go down. Mom and I just had dinner together, and she seemed weird, like distracted. I made sure not to do or say anything that would worry her, but she was worried anyway.

"How are you doing?" she'd asked, sitting down across from me as I ate. Watching me.

"Fine," I'd said, maybe a bit too enthusiastically. I dipped my grilled cheese into the hot tomato soup, took a big bite and smiled at her. "Why?"

She tried to smile back, but it didn't really work. I could tell she was bothered. Nervous. Like she wanted to ask me something.

"I think you've lost weight," she said. Which, to be fair, is probably true. I haven't been eating well. And, being honest, I haven't been sleeping too well, either. Not since the time I was in the treehouse that night, when I'd fallen asleep and woken to the bleeding man talking to the little girl; her timid, frightened responses as I ran away.

Plus, these last weeks, I'd been focused on my plan. On releasing the girl so she could move on. Stop reliving her terrible death.

I guess, for a kid my age, maybe it's a lot to take in. A lot to accept. And maybe it was making me anxious. I had nightmares almost every night, and lately I've noticed my hands shaking for no reason, or the repeated tug of a weird twitch on my left temple. My grades have been slipping, and I haven't been hanging out with my friends much.

Okay, at all.

It's like all I can think about lately is the treehouse. About the restless spirit that lives there. Her stifled screams. Her terror.

"I'm fine," I said, repeating myself. "I'll try to eat more."

Thankfully, Mom let it go. I forced down the rest of the soup, hoping it would make her relax. But the truth was I couldn't wait to get away from the table. To put my plan into action.

And now, at my desk, writing all this down so that ... well, I guess so that if something goes wrong, I want people to know what I've been dealing with. What I've experienced. I'd be lying if I said I wasn't scared, but I try to remind myself that there's nothing to be afraid of. Her ghost has never so much as *looked* at me. All she does is play dolls and hum that crazy, weird tune.

And the bleeding man, like I've said, is just an extension of her. I'm sure of it. Her way of showing me what happened. Of what she has to live through again, and again, and again.

But tonight, very soon, that ends.

I just need to wait for the sun to finish going down. Until it's full dark. Then I'll go out there, up the ladder, and into the treehouse. I'll exorcise her. Drive her away so she can be at peace.

I know I can do this. I just know it.

## 8:15 PM

The sun's down now. Nothing out there but a dark red horizon. From my window, the treehouse is nothing but a giant shadow amid the blowing leaves and creaking branches of the big oak tree.

It's time to go.

Wish me luck.

## 8:33 PM

Shit!

Shit shit shit shit shit motherfucking SHIT!

I screwed up. I screwed up big time. I got it all wrong. I got it ALL WRONG.

I'm back at my desk, but I don't have much time.

Hold on.

Okay, I just looked out my window. All the lights in my room are turned off, so I can see the treehouse pretty good. No one came down the ladder. No one followed me.

Oh my god I really messed up.

But I think it's safe. I think.

I need to put down what happened. I need to tell you guys. Someone needs to know.

Okay.

Like twenty minutes ago, I grabbed my backpack and went out to the backyard. I had my phone, a box of matches, the candles, and the salt. All of it in my backpack.

The electric lantern was already up there, but I wasn't too worried about that. My plan was to light the candles, throw salt fucking everywhere, especially on the floor where the girl always sits, and at the corner where the bleeding man usually appears.

There's hardly any moon tonight, and when you're under the tree, looking up at the floor of the treehouse, at that black square at the top of the ladder, it's so dark you can hardly see anything at all. But I didn't want to risk a light in case my mom happened to look out the kitchen window and notice me. I didn't want her to worry.

It was windy. A cold wind that reminded me of Halloween, of the beginning of winter. The tree was making a lot of noise. More than normal. Creaking and swaying. The rope ladder swinging in the breeze. The wood handles tied to the rope were cold to the touch. But I grabbed on and started climbing.

Up toward that black square.

I pulled myself inside, and immediately felt a little better. The walls did a good job of blocking the wind, and even with the windows it wasn't too cold in there. I crawled, all but blind, toward my sleeping bag in the corner.

I couldn't see a damn thing. It was literally pitch black. But that was okay, I knew what to do, and had been in there enough to know my way around, even in the dark.

I slung off my backpack and sat down on the sleeping bag, my back tucked into the corner. I unzipped the pack and pulled out the three candles, the box of wood matches, and the cylinder of salt.

I took a couple deep breaths. I was confident that this would fix things. I wasn't scared.

Not yet.

I set one of the candles on the floor in front of me, figuring I'd light one and then spread the others around. Wait until the little girl appeared—if she wasn't already there, sitting in the dark and playing with her dolls—and then spread the salt everywhere. I hoped that the salt wouldn't hurt her. Like garlic on vampires or something. The image of her smoking and screaming was an awful thing to think about, so I shoved it away.

It wouldn't be like that.

This would work.

I slid open the box of matches and pulled one out.

I was just getting ready to strike it, when I heard the bleeding man speak.

"Don't be scared."

I froze. The hand holding the match, even though I couldn't see it—couldn't see *anything*—started shaking. My teeth began to chatter, so I clenched my jaw hard.

His voice came from that near corner, the way it always did.

I decided to ignore him. I would finish this.

Willing my hand to steady, I struck the match against the side of the box.

It flared. I quickly turned my head to the left. I wanted to see him, but the match fizzled and went out almost immediately.

Here's what I saw: the shadow of a man. A flash of white teeth. Like he was smiling.

"Do you live here?" he said.

I knew this dialogue by heart now, and I refused to let it frighten me to hear it again.

I dropped the spent match, cursing under my breath, and pulled out another. I started to strike it against the side of the box...

Then stopped.

My hand hovered in mid-air. My breath was trapped in my chest, and I felt a burning in my throat. I was like a statue, there in the dark. Frozen in time.

Because, right then, I realized something.

I realized that something was wrong.

Something was missing.

The humming.

The little girl wasn't humming. I didn't hear the strange tune that she made—that she *always* made—when playing in the treehouse.

I stared at what I'd begun to think of as "her side" of the tree-house, and I was right. There was no humming sound. Just the dark.

But that wasn't all.

There had been no reply. She hadn't answered the man's questions like she always did.

She hadn't said anything at all.

Because the little girl wasn't there.

And the man wasn't speaking to her.

He was speaking to *me*.

I threw the candle as hard as I could toward the sound of the voice and scrambled for the opening. I heard a grunt, but not the sound of the candle hitting the wall. Because it hit something else. Something made of flesh and blood.

I threw my legs over the hole and dropped, not even thinking about the ladder.

I landed, ten feet later, and my legs buckled. I slammed down onto my side against the hard, cold ground. My breath shot out of me, and my ankle hurt bad, but I didn't care. All I cared about was that black square above me, about the thick shadow putting a foot on the top rung of the ladder.

I got to my feet and sprinted for the house. I threw open the sliding door and ran straight for my bedroom. I slammed the door shut and turned the little lock on the handle.

Only a few seconds passed while I ran from the door to the window, and the lights of my bedroom were still turned off. I looked through the window, into the backyard, at the treehouse. I waited to see a shadow moving across the yard, or to see someone staring back at me through the glass, eyes wide and feverish and angry.

Murderous.

But I didn't see anyone. Just the empty backyard, filled with shadows.

After a few minutes, I started to calm down. I sat in my chair and wiggled the mouse. The laptop came on—way too bright—and I dimmed it as low as it would go.

I've been writing this ever since, and so far nothing has happened. Nothing...

Wait.

There *is* something out there.

Inside the treehouse.

At one of the small windows, the one facing my room, I can see a face. A small, pale face.

It's the little girl.

She's never done this. She's never acknowledged me in any way. Never once spoken to me, or even glanced at me when I've tried talking to her.

But now ... she is.

She's looking straight at me.

Oh fuck. She's talking, from the window ... she's yelling something. I can't hear...

She's screaming. She's screaming at me.

Why now?

What's different? What changed?

I can't understand...

Oh God. I just heard a loud thump from the hallway. Someone's inside the house.

Heavy footsteps.

A door opening.

My mom is talking to someone. She's angry.

Who is she talking to?

I have to go. I'm sorry.

I have to see if it's the man.

I have to see if he's bleeding.

# A Mousy Little Thing

by Christi Nogle

Visitors knew not to ask for her at Orville's drugstore, Dessie's Ice Cream, or at the library made out of a little cottage. They knew only to hang around those places until she happened to stop by. Sometimes they'd have to spend a night or two at the strip motel before she found them, and they would grow self-conscious about the looks from towns-folk. This was no vacation destination, after all. Why were they hanging around?

When visitors finally spotted her, they would give each other looks. *Could that be the girl? Surely not.* Too young, too unassuming. A dress so old-timey that at first they took her for an underage bride from one of those compounds you hear about down in Utah. Seventeen, they had heard, eighteen, but she struck them as more like thirteen, fourteen. Apart from the thong sandals, she looked like someone out of an old western. Clean but none too composed, not a lovely child at all. How would she do this thing?

They would move tensely, looking around. She never spotted them right off, or never seemed to. They would twist things in their hands under the table if it was at the ice cream spot, handkerchiefs or napkins. If it was at the library or the drugstore, they would turn away from the girl, pretending to browse. Their heart rates would rise and they would think about leaving. Sweat would spring up around their hairlines. They would consider freezing until she was gone and instead turn back to her. They would catch sight of her hands ruined from the digging, cracked and stained with grave-dirt. They would make eye contact. Hers were pale hazel, didn't look real. Clear their throats, try to smile. That's how it always got started.

They always ended up at one of the burger joint's outdoor tables, no matter where things had started. They would buy her a meal to pick at while they made arrangements, talking low. She needed the food—bones showing in her chest, hard and knobby wrists and elbows. Up close they saw her teeth were uncorrected and her calico dress was not so modest after all. It revealed too much tanned skin for her to be in one of those religious groups. How had they thought that? Well, it was only her long hair and that demure flower print. Up close, her eyes looked even more like murky pondwater with the moonlight reflecting on it, a seer's eyes most certainly.

The smell of the ketchup, burger, and fries, her brown hair so sun-bleached it sparkled when she leaned out of the umbrella's shade. She didn't say much. "Oh, yeah?" "Well, you heard right," "Might work, might not," "No trouble at all to try." Her dad could not know; that was the one thing. She drew them a map on a napkin and told them where to park and wait. She took a much-reused Ziploc out of a pocket and smashed her leftover food down into it before leaving.

There the visitors waited on a country road at sunset. They knew the girl's dad's house was out of sight at the end of the driveway lined with skinny wind-break trees, and he would be busy doing chores after supper anyway. Pigs, they wondered, cows? It smelled like pigs, maybe. She'd said she would sneak away and come to them, soon as she could.

Their arms were goosebumped though the weather was mild. A muted sunset left the surroundings grainy pink and gray and lovely like the way things are when you need new glasses. She came through the pasture in her dress, in tall black rubber boots. She was warmer with them now; they were her guests. She hugged the woman lightly and took her hand.

"Careful to pay attention how we go," she said. "We'll have to come back in the dark."

That did not seem like it would be too difficult, but the walk was long, through that same pasture for a bit and veering into a copse of trees and down, looping past some old farm equipment and an abandoned outbuilding, its insides black. Flies were biting. The man and woman began to feel some dread.

Past the pond, past a few cows—those big-eyed golden ones—slowly chewing and staring, down to a place where the ground dipped into an armpit-shape lined with cattails, filled with mud. She moved into the trees and crashed back through hauling a couple of tattered lawn chairs, unfolded them, turned.

"Where you going?" said the man.

"Got to get ready for bed. I'll sneak out again soon as I can," she said, and then they were alone.

Sunk in that moment of wishing they hadn't come, wishing it wouldn't work and wishing it would. They said none of this to each other, just patted each other's knees and complained about irrelevant things—the flies were biting, they hadn't dressed warm enough, hadn't had enough to eat, had a bellyache—keeping their eyes off of that mud. The man paced around and went into the trees for a piss.

"There's a rusted out VW back in there," he reported when he'd returned to the lawn chair.

Sunset came and they listened to sounds of livestock and birds. They had been raised in the country and had often vaguely wished to go back. They both wondered if they would ever mention those wishes again, after this.

She came back very soon after moonlight replaced the last glow of sunset, and that was good. They told themselves they might not have waited much longer. She held a dim flashlight and wore the boots over a pair of faded overalls she promptly slipped out of. Underneath she wore tight black bike shorts and a tank top. She sat cross-legged in a space where there were no cattails, on the very edge of the mud, and after a moment, gently sank her fingertips into it.

"Oh, it feels charged tonight. It feels living," she said, turning her face to them. "That's good."

"Should we do something? Should we get down there with you?" said the woman.

"Only if you want to," said the girl, sinking in past the wrist, half-way to the elbow. Her top rode up, revealing her knobby spine.

The woman didn't need a firmer invitation. She stood and unbuttoned her blouse.

"Surely you're not going to—" said the man, but something in her stance or her face stopped him.

Soon they were both perched at the edge with her, the man fully clothed apart from his shoes and socks, the woman in her heavy-duty white bra and briefs. They were all three reaching into the mud, which was not so soft and not so wet as it had looked. Sand in it scraped the visitors' soft and citified skin, and there were rocks and other things— shells? bits of rope? The earth *was* charged. They felt it through their arms—like raging hot pepper on the tongue. Lemon-bright, electric, quivering.

The mud felt like water now, thick with eels and catfish. Fighting, sliding. The man withdrew his hands and wiped them on his knees. He was weeping. They both expected the girl to cry out at him to reach back in the mud, but she said, "It's fine. You all can sit back if you like."

She seemed distracted, like she wasn't really talking to them. She was up well past her elbows now, chin dipping in and out—she was that flexible—but after a while she withdrew one arm to reach around behind her for the flashlight. When she shone it over the surface, they all saw the mud was bubbling like a slow boil, and out of those bubbles came a thick and oily blood.

"Oh *yeah*," she said, switching off the flashlight and passing it to the man. "She's real close now. When we bring her up you've got to shine this on her and see." With that, she reached down farther than before, sparing just her eyes, and the woman reached deeper too.

And the woman said, "I feel her."

"Shine it and see what?" said the man. He was quivering.

"I feel her hair," the woman said.

"*Don't* bring her up by the hair," said the girl. She stood and squatted down closer to the woman. She ran her muddy arm down the woman's and surpassed her reach. "Her shoulders are right there. Good work. You want to get back, I'll pull her up for you."

Hesitantly, like she didn't know whether to trust the girl's promise, the woman withdrew from the mud and pushed her body back. Her fists were clenched now.

The man flicked on the light, saying "Shine it and see—"

The girl, her body contorted and one leg in the mud, whipped her head toward him, scowling. "See is it really her," she snapped. She bent again, more deeply than before, heaving the body up and out in one heroic motion. The body—the person, for it was a full-grown person— lay on her back, coated in mud and blood and gasping, wheezing like someone who's held her breath far too long. The man ran the light over her face, her tightly closed eyes.

"Yes," he said, though it wouldn't have mattered what he said. Her mother was lying beside her already, trying to rub the mud from her face.

"Don't," said the girl, taking the woman's wrist.

The woman turned to her, overcome. The face held joy, sadness, confusion.

"The dirt don't come off," said the girl. "You can touch her, but you can't get it off."

"How long do we have?" said the man. He hadn't touched her yet.

The girl shook her head slowly. "I don't know." She took the flashlight from him, switched it off.

So they spoke to her, saying her name often. It was Audrey. After a time, the man held her too. They were lying on either side of her, saying things. She was only gasping at first, and as the gasping slowed, she began to try to speak. She said she'd had a terrible dream and tried to describe it, but her voice was croaky, and after a minute she asked for water. They helped her to sit up and the girl brought a milk jug filled with dark water.

"Is that from the pond?" the man asked.

"Does it matter?" said the girl. Her expression was firm. She eased the pitcher to the dead girl's lips, and they saw more clearly the large pores and fissures in her and the mud and blood streaming out of them, thick and oily at first and then running thin and fast as she took in the water. Blood streamed out of the eyes, which still didn't open. They saw earthworms wriggling out of her, little stones and bits of leaves and straw and twine. A button, oddly enough.

After the long drink, she gasped again, and as her breathing settled, they tried to coax her to speak of where she'd been all this time. They were wanting her to say it was someplace nice.

"Hungry," she said, and the parents looked up at the girl, who had gotten away to the pond at some point and come back cleaner. She was back in her overalls and seemed to be naked under them. She reached into a pocket and withdrew a wadded Ziploc, scooped out the contents, and passed them to the mother.

"You can chew on it for her if you want," she said, and the mother did. Cold and sitting out all day as it was, she did it gladly, did it quickly as she could, a handful in and a handful out, soft enough for her daughter's toothless mouth. The daughter took it in until there wasn't any left.

What a good mother.

With the food had come some greater awareness, it seemed, because now, in a great passionate gush, the dead girl apologized for all she had done wrong in life and told them how she loved them. The nightmare she'd mentioned earlier had been something about running and hiding in terror, but now she spoke only of going back to sleep. She spoke of perfect rest, bunnies and kittens, beautiful colors you can't see in life. Her voice grew softer and softer as a child's does, fading into rest, and yet her body began to move, began to slowly ooze and reach back toward the muddy divot.

The body couldn't really be called that anymore. It was like a slug, like a moving sack of earth, and the parents seemed to know—as all of them did by this point, when it worked—that they had to help her back before the movement ceased. They grew frantic, pushing and pulling. A part came off, and the woman shrieked very briefly. She held a slightly moving thing in her hand, the shape of a hand.

"It's okay," said the girl. "Just get it all back in." She wasn't helping. It wasn't her place.

When it was over, she walked them back to their car. She'd have liked to let them make the trip alone and get back to her bed that much sooner, but you never knew with these city people. They could fall or even get lost in the dark. They could come back to a drained battery or a flat tire.

When they opened the car doors and the dome light shone on them, the woman gasped. She'd put her blouse back on, but her arms and upper chest were crusted with blood, and the man's jeans were a deep rust red. No mud anywhere. All of that had gone back in the ground.

They settled themselves in the car anyhow, and only then did the man take out his wallet. He leaned and passed the thick fold of bills out the passenger window to the girl.

Sometimes visitors said things like how talented she was, how blessed. Or the opposite, how dark and wrong this was. She ought to stop this, listen to her dad and stop. He didn't approve, did he, or she wouldn't have to sneak out to do it?

This man only sighed, started the car and turned up the heat.

"Thank you, baby," said the woman, patting her hand. She was in a daze, but, the girl thought, a happy daze.

"You can tell someone," she said. "Tell them what you were told. They can come to town, to the places you were told—not here. One other person, someone who needs it, someone you'd trust with your life. And they can bring one other or come alone." No one ever came alone.

This instruction didn't affect the woman any sort of way—she gazed straight ahead in confusion and joy, like she was still looking at that other face—but the man was nodding like he knew just who he'd tell, like he maybe already had.

"Tell them whenever you like, and they can come in a couple of weeks or so."

He nodded again, the girl stepped back, and the car pulled away.

*Take me with you*, she thought. She didn't allow herself to think it until she was too late. They were a quarter mile up the road before she thought it.

She turned to cut across the tall pasture grass and up the long driveway to the farmhouse where her dad, with any luck, would be snoring in his bed.

She thought of the souls in their underground river of blood and wondered if there were other places they came up—in the city, even. If they had the right one calling, could they come up anyplace at all, or was it only here in this place? She'd never had a chance to see.

That warm car, that good mother. *Take me with you*, she thought again, looking back, half expecting to see the headlights heading back this way, but of course there was nothing.

Sometimes new visitors came too soon, and she worried. Her dad wasn't smart, but he *was* suspicious, and she had been caught before. It was why she needed to use the flashlight and be ready to throw back the catch.

The worst was when no one came. She would wonder if the visitors had failed to pass on the invitation, or if those receiving it had chickened out or were waiting for a particular date. Sometimes they did wait for a birthday or an anniversary of some sort.

She would hang around town more and more, awkwardly watching and waiting. No one liked her there. They had not liked her mother, either.

She didn't do it only for the money. She needed to do it, and after a while with no visitors, she would start to notice the locals. *You don't shit where you eat*, her dad had said—everyone said it—but the locals would start to pull at her, like the pretty green-eyed woman at the video store, her face all sad and hollowed-out now since her young husband had died in a drunken car-crash. Wouldn't she like to go out to the mud-pit and see him once more? Kiss him and then beat the shit out of him for wasting his life?

Sometimes the girl thought she knew enough to never do something like that, and other times she wasn't sure. She didn't trust herself. No one came and she would find herself browsing in the video store even though they had no VCR at home.

The green-eyed woman with the fluffy perm, she wasn't cruel to the girl like some people were. She looked her in the eyes and asked if she was looking for anything in particular, especially after the first time the girl lingered in the horror aisle. This woman wouldn't have the money to pay, but maybe she could offer something better.

And all that exhaustion and confusion in her face; what would feel like to change that? The girl thought of her wad of bills, buried and safe, ready to go. She looked at the woman's brown Camaro parked outside. Whole fantasies she spun of conversations:

*You out of school? How come he doesn't have you working on the farm, then? You're always hanging around town.*

*He's afraid of me. Thinks I'm too stupid to do anything else, and he's too afraid to make me work, and so there's only this. There will only be this forever.*

*Don't you want more?*

*I do—and you do too.*

*Let's go, let's run away.*

Of course she would have to show what she could do. She would have to let the green-eyed woman visit the mud and say goodbye to the man before she'd say goodbye to the town, but after that she would see the girl differently. They always did. And then she just might be able to start that conversation.

*Does it dry up, in the heat of summer? Or freeze in winter?*

*No, it never does.*

She was close to trying. She was so close to beginning the conversation that would lead to the city, and then she saw them in the drugstore, just where she'd found them the first time.

"This isn't the deal," she hissed at their backs. "It's one time," but he was already turning to show the fold of money twice as thick as before.

Everything about this time felt different, felt wrong. She ate the entire meal without noticing what she was doing. The man was already standing, about to go to the window and order more food for the ritual.

The woman looked to be on something. That, or the glow from weeks before had not subsided. "Get her a cheeseburger, no onions," she said, and her eyes were full of water, her smile so open and unselfconscious. Not a smile for someone else at all but only anticipation—she was thinking of later, when she would chew the meat to feed her daughter. The girl noticed that she was wearing a blue and aqua swimsuit under her half-unbuttoned black blouse.

Something about it made her blood boil.

"We don't need you to take us through this time," the woman

said, gazing off into the distance. "We can find it."

What was wrong with this woman? The girl imagined her going about her days in this stupor, raising questions everywhere she went.

Answering them.

She insisted on walking them across the field and settling them in their lawn chairs as before. The pasture grass soaked their legs, and the couple acted different this time, bubbling over with humor and expectation. She made the walk during her dad's bath, as always, and when he came out of the bath, she was already back and ready to go in and pick up his clothes and rinse out the tub, as always. Scrub his shit-skids out of the toilet bowl.

He was settled in front of the television in his puffy robe, as always, when she brought the laundry down. "Sleepy tonight," she said as she moved past him.

"Better turn in early," he said.

She put the laundry in the washer and moved to the kitchen to put away the few dishes in the rack, looking out the window to the trees separating the house from the back pastures. She liked to keep a neat house, and maybe that was something she could do in the city, too. Her mother had cleaned motel rooms for a time and had lots of stories about the fun she had with the other young maids.

The sink was filled with cool water. She reached in to pull the plug and stilled her hand a moment, felt the stirring like little fish nibbling her fingers. This was why she showered, never bathed. It was why she thought that maybe, even in the city, she could still…

"Go on up to bed if you want," he called.

She kissed him on the forehead on her way by. It wasn't something she'd done in some time.

Upstairs, she changed into a sports bra and bike shorts under a gray sweatsuit, then lay down to wait. It was only nine. The television would go off around the time darkness fell, he would visit the bathroom, and then he'd be out within fifteen minutes, snoring hard. She waited, and it did not happen. None of it. She waited until eleven o'clock, and the television still hadn't gone off. When she tried the door, it opened just a tiny crack, even when she pushed. It had been braced with a chair and would not budge.

By the time she'd gotten the window open and crawled out onto the porch roof, she knew it was too late, and yet she had to do something. Strong and wiry, she eased her way to the roof edge and lowered herself down as far as she could before dropping into the bushes. She had her flashlight but didn't use it. She hoped she wouldn't need to.

There was a time once before when he'd caught her. He'd snuck up behind her and her visitors—oh, she couldn't think about it—but that was why you had to check the bodies and make sure they were who you wanted.

The people thrown in the mud there had fouled it, in a way. Not irredeemably, but they had fouled it. They were stronger than the others, whether due to being murdered or due to the place or time of their death, she couldn't say, and for a long time they had been the first and sometimes the only ones to come up. Two women, an old one and a young one, as well as the little boy they had come all this way to see. They would bob up out of the bloody mud, reeking of meat, faces full of anguish. Never anger, and that surprised the girl. She would pull them halfway out and thrust them back down again and again until she caught the one she was supposed to catch. Or until, catching nothing of use, she had to send the folks back to town to wait for a more propitious night.

He had knocked her out with a blow to the head, that time. She'd known and seen nothing.

Not this time.

This time he had left them for her to clean up.

He had butchered the man first, it looked like. He still sat in his chair, legs splayed and looking almost relaxed. His neck had drenched the left side of his trucker jacket.

The other chair held a pair of Keds topped with a neatly folded black blouse and jeans, topped with the brown paper takeout sack. She was face-down halfway to the pit, as though she'd been trying to play in the mud all alone and then had rushed to try to save her man. Her arms were coated, as was her backside. The girl could not easily see her death wound, even after clicking on the light, but she lay in a thin puddle of blood.

"I'm so sorry," said the girl.

It was the kiss that had tipped him off, wasn't it? Stupid. She pulled at her hair.

She would drag them into the mud. It was all she could do, and it was the best place. She took off her sweatsuit and lay it on the chair with the other clothes. She put her muck boots back on and started with the man. It was a longer distance, and he was heavier. She was always one to do the hardest thing first.

It was hard, even with the ground halfway slick. All the time she dragged, she thought of her fortune buried under the rusted-out car back in the trees. It wasn't right to think of it, wasn't respectful, and yet she could not stop. She had the terrible thought that her dad had found it, but what if he hadn't? What if he waited right now, somewhere close, to see where she'd hid it. Was it safe that she should go to it now—after putting these good folks to rest, of course—or not?

She did feel him watching, him or God. She thought of that blow she'd taken and the soft spot that had lingered in her skull for so long after. Maybe he was watching for another purpose?

The man sank so quickly, she suspected he was being pulled down. She turned to the woman, suddenly aware of her own sick-smelling sweat. It had to be done, though.

She turned the woman over, and her heart leapt—*she's not dead.* The woman's mouth squirmed, then came the long gasp. The girl tried to brush the blood and the mud away from her eyes so they could open, but they couldn't open. They would never be clean enough. And her belly *was* opened, and her neck.

She was dead, only animated from all of the mud and wetness, or from the touch of the girl, or the combination.

"Hungry," she croaked.

The girl focused on the paper sack, and she rose to get it. It was the least she could do. Strange to chew and not to swallow, to pass the softened mass to a dead and muddy hand. The woman moaned softly. She took another wad of it, and another.

"Audrey?" she said, as though waking.

The girl did not answer. She only held the woman tight, and after a while, the woman held her back, stroked her hair.

"He's in *our* car," the woman said, and laughed in surprise. "He's nowhere near here. Going to dump the car."

They weren't always honest. She thought they usually weren't. Still, it was good to hear.

"He hasn't found the money," the woman said. "He's looked."

These insights felt like a last energetic surge. After she'd voiced them, the girl felt her beginning to weaken.

"Let's get you to bed," she said, rising. She grasped the ankles and threw her weight back. One hard yank and another. Doing this made her feel strong.

"She'll go with you, your green-eyed girl," the woman said. Unbelievable that she still spoke, so close to the pit's edge. She was saying something more, but it was so faint that the girl had to bend down to hear. The woman whispered of what to say, how to prove herself, what messages to pass on from beyond. When she lost speech, they started their journey once more.

When they reached the lip of the mud-pit, the girl went ahead and stepped back into it. She had not done this before, and it was silly to do now. How would she get the woman in with no leverage? But the woman sat up, smiled weakly, and scooted her way to the edge, where four greedy arms reached up to ease her in headfirst without another word

The girl felt the living mud flicker around her like tails and tongues and fingers. No one hurt her or seemed to want to. She breathed out in relief and was not pulled under.

Soon she would go to the pond and rinse off as best she could, put on her sweatsuit, and go to see if the money really was there, but first she would linger in the mud just a little while longer, just to see if anyone wanted to be caught.

# Dolly Rocks

## by Em Starr

There were at least twenty ways to die on the mountain.

Snakes and parasites aside, there were landslides, and rockfalls, and seasonal flash floodings—plenty of reasons to sell up and head south to less tumultuous terrain. But Rosie was bound to her hinterland home, with its saw-toothed rock ledges and silty-sweet rainforest damp. She lived in a cedar pole-house, on tank water and septic, and ate root vegetables and herbs from her mother's garden.

Rosie didn't live like most girls her age. In the mornings, she meditated to whip birds and woodsmoke, cross-legged in the dirt with the funnel-web spiders, the water tunnels of the giant earthworms churning below. In the evenings—if the creek beds weren't rushing—she took the backtrack to the bloodwood tree, at the bottom of her property, and fossicked for thunder eggs. As was her duty.

She was raised in reverence of the tree's sacred gift bearing, her Ma taking her to kneel at its base, as soon as she was of an age to dig. *Old Mallory is as deeply rooted in our family as you are,* she had said, handing her a ceremonial trowel and pick. Old Mallory was named after her great-grandmother, a war widow who'd discovered the rocks beneath the roots. *She's our matriarch, our sister, our goddess, our child. As she gives, so she must take. You understand?* Rosie hadn't understood—not then—but she took the tools and set to work, determined to make her Ma proud. That was the day she inherited the burden of excavation, passed down from mother to daughter. It was her earliest childhood memory, and no matter how she tried to cast her mind back, she could only recall things from that moment forth—as if there had never been life before digging.

Now, she had the same calloused hands as her mother, the same tired brow—spent most of her hours unearthing the treasures buried beneath the tree, a giant as far as bloodwoods went. Every night, she would take her pick and till the sacred ground, taking care not to disturb Old Mallory's precious roots, knowing how they oozed red sap if they were damaged, like blood from an open wound. She'd fill her bucket with thunder eggs, big as baseballs, and carry them back to the house; brew herself a pot of home-grown peppermint tea, drop the stylus on something from her mother's vinyl collection—Nina Simone, or Ella Fitzgerald, usually—and turn the volume right up so she could hear it over the tile saw. One by one, she'd cut them open, *carefully, carefully,* to find the worlds of stone within—opal snowstorms, and agate mountain landscapes, and sunsets of red-yellow jasper. Then she'd sell them at the local artisan market for thirty-five bucks a pop.

She always took a few raw stones to cut and polish onsite, so she didn't have to make conversation. Her mother had been the talker of the two of them, a gifted saleswoman who knew how to turn lumps of lava into prehistoric treasures—but Ma had been missing for some time now, and Rosie wasn't good with people.

No matter. The eggs sold themselves.

When she cut them open, and the customers saw what was inside—sceneries and starbursts as vivid as a Picasso—she sold out every time. Better yet, when the other artisans were packing up, a crowd would gather at her stall to watch her split the last stone, and a bidding war always broke out. On a good day, there'd be three or more people, driving the price to double and triple the value.

On the day she found the eye, there were six bidders. Little wonder. It was a beautiful eye, as real as she'd ever seen. Made of translucent chalcedony. Blue, just like her mother's.

"It's not for sale," she told the disappointed bidders, packing up shop, then and there—and she wondered, if she took the stone home and placed its broken halves side by side, would it watch over her as she slept?

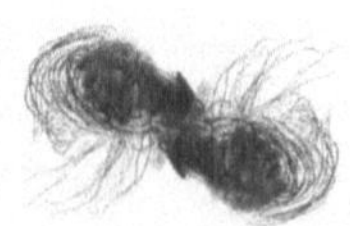

The insomnia had started when Ma disappeared. Before that, Rosie would sleep all day, smashing the snooze button on the alarm clock as many times as she could get away with. Now the sun shone too brightly against her mother's silent sawblade, spilling light into her eyes so it was impossible to find restful slumber, and on the rare occasion she did, she was plagued by nightmares—of being buried alive beneath Old Mallory. But she slept soundly that afternoon, and woke that evening, deeply rested and somewhat disoriented.

The stone halves were perched on the mantel, where she'd left them, two perfect eyes, wide and unblinking. The resemblance was uncanny. Such a rare color blue. She moved to the fireplace and reached out to touch one, tracing the unpolished inner where the pupil and iris converged. *Is that you, Ma?* It wasn't, of course—no more her mother's eyes than any other rock—still, she swore she felt something staring back, willing her to hurry up and get to work, even as she mixed herself a lazy salad and dressed it with lemon and rock salt. She found the thought comforting and decided she didn't care if it was crazy.

When it was time to gather her tools, she slipped the stone halves carefully into her satchel, so she didn't feel so alone.

The path to the bloodwood tree was shadowed in dusk, growing darker as she moved deep into sub-tropical terrain. She was well prepared with heavy boots and a reliable torch, having walked it enough times to know that brown snakes often crossed when the sun was setting, heading home to their burrows as she headed to work. The torch light caught the reflection of wild eyes in the scrub, possums in trees and pademelons in the grass, but Rosie left them to their business, sidestepping from rock to rock until she reached the furthest corner of the property, where the soil was rich with Old Mallory's blessings.

She knelt at the foot of the tree. Gave thanks and kissed the trunk. Took out her pick and started to dig. The recent rain had softened the earth, so the soil was malleable and easy to excavate. She stuck to the spot where she'd unearthed the eye-stone, a six-by-six-foot pit that was almost as deep—not that she expected to find anything like it again. In all her years of fossicking, she had never seen a rock so ... human.

Still, when she kept digging, falling ten inches deeper into the earth, there was an electricity in her fingertips that she hadn't felt before. She used her bare hands to scoop dirt from the twisted tubers, searching for Old Mallory's sweet spot. *Careful of the roots, lest they bleed,* Ma's voice echoed, and she was wondering if the words had come from her mind or the satchel, when she saw something peculiar in the dirt—a row of thunder eggs fused together like vertebrae on a spine. She picked at the earth, loosening it enough to pull one of them free. The stones were laid so compactly, the other twelve came with it, like a string of old pearls. She held them out, at arm's length. The cord measured three feet, maybe more, but that wasn't the strange part. The thing was moving—writhing—like a giant earthworm. *Are you seeing this, Ma?* It squirmed from her hands and dropped to the ground, floundered at her feet like an angry snake. Instinctively, she struck it, her pick severing the head of the spine. The remaining cord thrashed wildly. Rosie didn't stop to wonder. She went to work, hacking vertebrae from vertebrae, not stopping until the eggs were spread out, and still, in the dirt. She wiped her brow, and filled her bucket and gave thanks to the tree—as was her duty.

When she arrived home, she didn't play any records, didn't brew any lemongrass tea, just sat down and got straight to work. The hum of the tile saw drowned out the sounds of the rainforest, hushing the cicadas and lyrebirds. She reached for the first egg—felt the tingling in her fingers again, pins and needles creeping up her arm to the back of her neck—lined it up for the blade. When she cut it down the center, the stench of rancid meat was undeniable. She opened it up, recoiling.

Inside was a human hand ... two hands, now the stone was split in half.

But unlike the eyes, they were nothing like Ma's. They were skeletal and twisted, with boney fingers of miriam jasper that stretched through the rhyolite towards her—

"No fucking way," she whispered, recognizing them in an instant.

She hurried to the bureau, lined with the photographs of her fore-mothers. There was a shot of Nana Mimi in the sixties, standing in a pit at least seven feet deep; she was grinning amongst the bloodwood roots, reaching towards the camera with long and dirty fingers. The picture had always terrified Rosie—the way the old woman's hands seemed to stretch out of the frame. She held up the stone to compare. It was a direct imprint. She turned the photograph over. Written on the back in Ma's cursive loops was Nana Mimi's real name—Miriam. Like the stone.

*What the fuck is going on, Ma?*

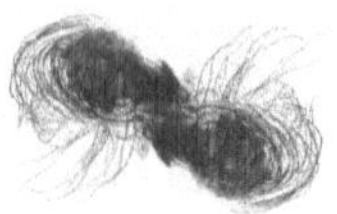

Rosie didn't dig that afternoon. She spent the day cutting her yield, forgetting to eat or rest. By nighttime, the blade was blunt, and the workbench was scattered with a cornucopia of body rocks. Agate footprints and lungs made of plume stone; an amethyst vascular system complete with an apple-sized heart. There were random limbs in various sizes, opal femurs and tibias, and red jasper arms that didn't quite go with Mimi's hands.

She matched the stones to her family photographs until the early hours of the morning. Waited patiently for a sign from her mother—a wink of a chalcedony eye, a gust of wind, a whispered warning—heard only the kookaburras, welcoming the dawn.

When sleep finally found her, she was still at the workbench, surrounded by the unusual anatomy. She dreamed vividly—a recurring scene where Ma showed her an old incubator hidden underneath the stairs.

"Put the eggs inside," she said. "And you'll never be alone again."

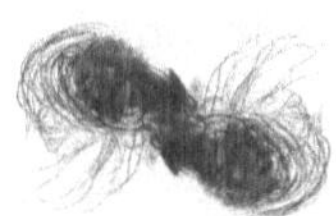

The incubator was real. Rosie found it behind a stack of old boxes, under the stairs, where her Dream-Ma said it would be. It was a round vintage one, made of galvanized metal, with a copper heating element and a wire turning rack. She dragged it across the lounge room floor, and set it up in the bathroom, for extra humidity, leaving it to warm as per the yellowed instruction manual. When it reached one hundred degrees, she gathered the body rocks and laid them out on the interior rack. Her mother's eyes, her Nana's hands, her great-grandmother's ailing hipbones—she didn't think to place them in an orderly fashion, just scattered them like a genetic jigsaw puzzle, and closed the lid.

She showered, and fixed herself a snack, and set the timer on the wall oven. The manual recommended a twenty-one-day incubation period for chicken eggs, but Dream-Mother had given her strict instructions: *wait six hours and open in the dark.*

While she waited, she browsed the vinyl collection, flicking through classics until she found one with Dean Martin on the cover, all porkpie hat and cheesy grin. She slipped the record from its sleeve and placed it carefully on the turntable, dropped the stylus and closed her eyes. The opening crackles were familiar and comforting—she was suddenly six years old again, dancing on her mother's feet and singing about moons and eyes and pizza pies. They used to play *That's Amore* when the harvest was bountiful, so it seemed only fitting Rosie played it now.

She must have drifted to sleep, because when she opened her eyes again, the room was dark, and the needle was caught in the record's last groove, scratching and scratching to get out. There was a repetitive trill coming from the kitchen—the oven timer letting her know that six hours was up.

Rosie kept the bathroom in darkness, save for the dappled moonlight that spilled through the window. The incubator felt pleasantly warm to the touch. She fumbled with the clasps, and lifted the lid to peer inside...

In the first instance, she thought it was a trick of the light—she couldn't possibly be seeing what she was seeing. But as her eyes adjusted, things became horrifyingly real. There was a child—a living child—coiled inside the incubator. A girl, no more than five or six years old, with Ma's blue eyes and great-grandmother Mallory's flame red hair. Her facial features were smooth-skinned and non-specific, as if the traits were in limbo, stuck between this nose and those lips, and her skin pulsed with veins that were branching into new pathways, even as Rosie looked on. She started to stir, disturbed by the moonlight, her shoulders and neckbones cracking, fingers stretching and snaking their way over the rim of the incubator. She pulled herself into a sitting position and scanned the shadowed bathroom—saw Rosie gaping and smiled.

"Momma," she said, holding out her arms.

"Nope," replied Rosie. She lowered the lid and snapped the locks back into place.

When the shock wore off, and the reality that she had a child locked inside an incubator kicked in, Rosie took the lid off again. The little girl was still in there, arms wrapped around her knees. Her face had finished forming, so she didn't look so frightening, and her skin was peachy soft and clear of spreading veins.

"Where did you come from?" Rosie asked, incredulous.

"Momma," said the child.

"I'm not your mother," she replied. "But if you're hungry, I can make you a sandwich and we can try and figure this out."

The girl smiled, holding out her arms again. "Momma."

Sighing, Rosie hoisted her out of the incubator and onto her hip. She carried the child into the kitchen, where the oven timer was still sounding. Sat her on the cedar bench and gathered ingredients, doing her best to make sense of the situation as she spread butter onto bread. The kid must have wandered into the house, somehow, and crawled into the incubator—that was the most likely explanation. *So why was the lid still locked from the outside? And where did all the eggs go?*

The girl watched her intently, swinging her legs. "When are you taking me to the tree?"

Rosie paused, mid-spread. "What did you say?"

"The tree. When are you going to take me?"

She put the butter knife down. "How do you know about that?"

"We all know about the tree, Momma. She's our matriarch, our sister, our goddess, our child."

"Who told you to say that?" Rosie was suddenly dizzy.

"As she gives, so she must take. Those are the rules." She held out her arms again, blue eyes twinkling. "Can you take me there now, Momma?"

"I'm not your mother," Rosie repeated, but she wasn't as sure when she said it this time; the child's features were so positively familial, the urge to nurture her so strong. Ma had always talked about the power of maternal instincts, the intensity of the bond between mother and child. Rosie imagined taking the path to the bloodwood with child in tow, teaching her the way of the dig, raising her in reverence of the tree's blessed gifts. An alternate reality, where she named her Dolly—short for dolomite—and they spent years digging and cutting, side by side, until—until...

"Take me to the tree," the girl said. "And when it's time, I'll do what must be done. As is my duty."

The maternal hallucinations fell away to white noise. Rosie picked up the butter knife and returned to the sandwich-making. "Once I've made you something to eat, I'll call the police. I'm sure your parents will be looking for you."

She phoned the local station while the child ate her food, picking at the crust and dripping jam onto the floor. The landline rang out. There was no message service after midnight—she knew that from when Ma disappeared. She turned to the child, who was still chewing and leg-swinging.

"What's your name, little one?"

"It's Dolly," she replied.

Rosie felt dizzy again, jolts of white electricity bursting behind her eyes. Visions of her and Dolly, digging side by side, until—

"Are you okay, Momma?"

"I think I need to rest," Rosie said, making a beeline for her bedroom. *It's another bad dream, is all.*

"And then, can you take me to the tree?" Dolly called after her. Rosie didn't answer—the girl shrugged and took another bite of her sandwich, legs swinging contently.

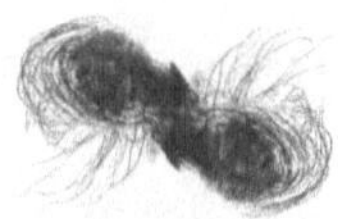

Rosie woke at dawn to find Dolly by her bed. She had peanut butter smeared on her face, having clearly found the jar in the pantry. "I'm bored, Momma," she said. "Can we go to the tree now?"

"Why do you want to go to the tree?" asked Rosie, reaching out to wipe the excess paste from her mouth, like it was second nature.

"So I can learn how to dig, silly," said Dolly. She giggled and threw herself into Rosie's arms, hugging her with ferocity. Rosie, who had never been hugged by anyone but her mother, balked at first, then felt the intense maternal pull again, that overwhelming need to nurture. *Is this what you meant, Ma? The impenetrable bond?* No sooner had she returned the hug, than Dolly was pulling away, jumping on the bed with boundless energy. "Let's go down to the bloodwood tree," she said, bouncing and bouncing. "You can teach me to dig like your Ma taught you, and when it's time, I'll do to you what you did to her."

Rosie's breath caught in her throat, like wet dirt. "What?"

Dolly kept jumping, her (*Ma's*) blue eyes shining as she repeated the words in singsong. *I'll do to you what you did to her, I'll do to you what you did to her*—and then, quick as a brown snake, she was off the bed and down the hall. Seconds later, *That's Amore* was blasting on the record player. Rosie ran to the living room and found Dolly attempting to dance—she was cracking and contorting at unnatural angles and failing to find her rhythm.

"You have to teach me, Momma," she said. "You have to teach me everything." She ran to Rosie, and stood atop her feet, and a wooden waltz ensued. "You have to teach me how to dance and dig, and when the tree calls you home, I'll do what must be done."

She suddenly felt impossibly heavy on Rosie's feet, crushing her toes as she shuffled beneath her. "What do you mean 'what must be done'?" she asked.

Dolly looked up at her, smiling. "What you did to your mother. Don't you remember?"

Rosie shook her head, losing her favorite parts of the song to the white noise of her failing memory.

"You restored her to the earth," said Dolly as they spun around the living room. "You hacked her into tiny pieces and buried her beneath the roots. Remember how she screamed her blessings, when you took up your pick?"

"No," replied Rosie.

"As the tree gives, so must she take. Remember, Momma?"

"No," replied Rosie. They danced faster. *I wish you could see this,*

*Ma. You always wanted a granddaughter.* She whirled Dolly in circles, spinning around the hardwood floors like a record, turning and turning until they lost balance and stumbled into the music cabinet—the song skipped and scratched to a halt. Rosie wept, when she saw the deep groove etched across the vinyl.

"Your grandmother used to dance with me to this song," she said to Dolly. "It was our favorite."

"I know," said the child. "I have her eyes."

When she asked to visit the tree again, Rosie didn't argue. She promised Dolly she would take her to visit Old Mallory—teach her how to dig, *carefully, carefully*, as was her duty. And when it was time, she would gladly sleep amongst the bloodwood roots with her ancestors, and hope she was fit to be re-harvested.

"We'll go when dusk falls," she said, and that seemed to satiate Dolly. "Now come—let me teach you how to make peppermint tea."

The little girl hugged her again, and this time, Rosie saw the veins still writhing beneath the skin surface. They walked to kitchen, hand in hand.

"I hope I forget too, Momma," Dolly said, "when it's time to hack you into pieces."

The child had never tasted peppermint before, so she didn't notice the difference when Rosie brewed up a concoction of valerian, lavender and chamomile and crushed half a valium in the icing of some passionfruit slice. She devoured it all, not even complaining about the obvious tang of the pill.

"I love you, Momma," she said, yawning.

"I love you too," Rosie said, waiting.

When Dolly was asleep, face down on the cedar bench, Rosie scooped her up and carried her from the kitchen. Outside, the skies warned of an impending storm. Soon the creeks would be rushing.

She tucked the child into bed, placed a picture of herself on the bedside table, next to her favorite thunder egg—a sparkling rose quartz geode—and ventured into the looming night.

The rain had turned torrential by the time Rosie reached the backtrack, the path slick with mud that rushed down the mountainside. She hurried, half sliding, half-stumbling, the torch light useless in the downpour—her tool satchel snagged on a tree branch, and she fell face first, tumbling and cutting her knees and elbows, went back for the pick and kept going. When she reached Old Mallory, the excavation pit was already half-filled with water, the rain coming down in sheets.

Lightning struck close by—electricity surged through the ground and in her ears, illuminating the tree and its twisted limbs. She lowered herself into the pit, blood spilling from her wounds as she went—she arced the pick and struck, aiming for the roots. She hacked and hacked, blinded by the relentless rain. The water levels rose in the mud pool, and still she hacked, reveling in the red sap that oozed from Old Mallory's roots, the tortured moans of the sacred earth. Lightning cracked again, this time hitting the tree. The canopy erupted in flames, and one of the main boughs crashed to the ground, blocking the mouth of the pit.

Rosie clawed at the dug-out walls and found only bleeding roots and branches—she slid into the mire, trapped and exhausted. The crimson sludge of her ancestral pool rose around her, as she watched Old Mallory burn and prayed the rain wouldn't dowse the fire. She let the mud fill her mouth and her throat and felt the comfort of her Ma's presence for the first time in forever.

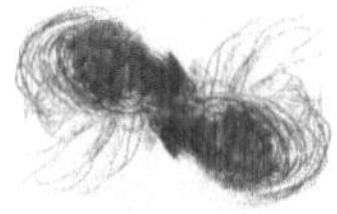

There were at least twenty ways to die on the mountain—her own mother having perished in a mudslide, when she was younger—but Dolly adored her hinterland home. It had been in the family for generations and she didn't mind the isolation.

She spent her hours growing mangoes and bottling relish to the scritch-scratch vinyl tones of Eartha Kitt, using a recipe she found beneath the stairs, in a box beside an old incubator. The preserves were a hit with the locals, and her roadside honesty box was always stuffed with cash.

Dolly didn't often leave the property. It had everything a girl could want. There was a creek for fishing, and a herb garden for brewing tea, and at the bottom of the plot stood the most glorious bloodwood tree, half blackened by fire, but still thriving. She found herself drawn to it, even in her sleep—sometimes waking to find herself kneeling at its base with dirty feet, resisting the inexplicable urge to dig.

# Godslingers

## by Joe Koch

He hurls his meat into any open mouth. I rip him apart and make him a god. Love is like that sometimes: callous, sudden, excruciating.

"You should take better care of yourself," I say. "You're a good-looking kid."

The god-boy gently snorts, nearly finished getting dressed. I'm stretched out on the hotel bed wearing my black Versace briefs, the ones with a Grecian gold trim that makes my abs look regal. No small feat past forty. I stand to face him, trying to punch through that distracted fog that hovers around him as if he's haunted by his own presence, uncertain in his skin. He doesn't quite fit inside of it. Or maybe he's made out of fog, blurry on the edges, opaque for a moment and then disappearing in the next breath, dispersed by sunlight over the horizon.

"I'm serious. I'm a physician. You'll bounce back after tonight, but too much of this rough stuff will catch up to you someday. I feel, I don't—I guess I don't want to let that happen to you."

"You don't even know me."

"I could."

The boy drops to his knees, lifts his chin, and spreads his arms. "If you want to help me, piss on my bruises and make them sing."

I can't help but smile at the theatrical gesture, the invitation to kink, and the adorable error that conjures iconography. "You mean sting."

"Piss on me and dump me out on the highway to die."

The bruises aren't all mine, only the whispers of fingerprints encircling his neck. Certainly this encounter is consensual, or started that way, as an experiment to test the limits of what I suspect about myself and the peculiar way reality bends every seven years for me. Is it the same for anyone else? Or has it all been coincidence and I'm cursed with incredible luck? It's true that people have always said I was lucky.

"What are you talking about? God, you're a slut. At least take your clothes off first."

"No." The boy grabs my cock through the snug cotton. I swell. His teeth are clenched, grinding near the tender head. His hair is a mess. It smells like dirty cypress. A pearl soaks through my briefs beneath his teeth, the dark spot blacker than the black fabric. He says, "I swear if you don't drench me, I'll bite it off."

Fingers tangled in his hair, I pull him up into a kiss.

Later, I drop him off on the old highway, the one with rusted-through signage and ghost-town remnants of failed homespun businesses, shacks built of scrap that must have been barely fit for habitation even before they decayed. I've read that whole towns were submerged here over the years as levees were built, concrete smothered the cities, and acres of wetlands vanished leaving the land vulnerable, unstable, no longer resilient to sudden floods.

I should do something, say something more to him; convince him to come back to the hotel, at least for as long as I'm here. Buy him a meal. But he won't even take my cash as he slides out of the rental. The bills flutter down onto the passenger seat. He empties his pockets, showering the upholstery with crumbs of dried mud.

"Burn that for me," he says, moving swampward. His long eyelashes deny me even a final glance of gratitude.

What can I say as he drifts off into the weeds? Who am I to question how people live down here, to judge another man's choices?

In the rearview mirror, he's quickly indistinguishable from the skeletal stumps, grey devil fingers reaching up from brown water between the trees. Further on, an eerie green coating of algae lends the still expanse of liquid some semblance of life. I wonder where he will go in the middle of nowhere, how he will sleep safely or find something nourishing to eat. I imagine a camp or a boat, a tent city or derelict craft shared with other boys, hidden deep in the clogged wilderness. It's an instantly exciting idea of unbridled freedom such as I've never had, of a life with the pack instead of my sham of a respectable life. He'll return to the secluded encampment with my scent on him, my semen, my spit, my urine mixed with the fragrance of his own filth. Will the other boys notice? Will they revel together in sucking and sodomy, craving my mark? I picture them coming after me, crashing the well-lit hotel lobby like a dirty band of mongrels and storming into my room, into my bed, into my body, making me like them; or maybe they wait in the wild for me, daring me to track them down in a sacred hunt. Maybe they succor at some woody flame even now, incanting me to abandon my hypocrisy and seek them out.

Beside me, the car seat smells of cypress and urine. I breathe it in.

Too hard to concentrate on the road; no streetlights, no cars or trucks for miles, nothing but the ghost of our shared secretions and my yearning thoughts. I pull over to leave an offering to the swamp gods.

My shoes sink an inch in the muck beyond the berm. Weeds conceal me to my knees, but otherwise I'm exposed, as a supplicant should be. There are no lights except distant industrial blinkers, pink and green pinpoints. Frogs hum rhythmically. Mosquito squeals make my shoulders twitch. I dump my sperm like hot toxic waste, unsure after the act if I'm elated or ashamed.

Hoping the taste of me was sweet enough to reach the god-boy through the thick oozing waters, I zip and buckle up. I'm scraping my soles on the asphalt when the headlights flash. They creep up from behind, pull in beside me, and stop.

"Evening," a bearded man in a ball cap calls out from a red truck. The model is old enough that he has to reach over the passenger side to hand crank the window. "Everything all right?"

"Oh, no. I'm fine." I nod and open my car door. His truck rumbles beside me.

"Lost your way? Out of gas?"

"Thank you. I've got GPS."

"GPS don't work out here, not always. Where you headed?"

"Um, I had to take a leak. Just cleaning the mud. I do appreciate your concern."

He cocks his head to the side in alarm. "Aw, no, no, no. Don't do that. You got to go, don't leave the road, you mind? Gators snatch your pecker clean off. Take a foot or something, too, you know? Drag you down."

I try not to laugh at the comic emphasis of his warning. "I ...did not." I clear my throat. "Well. I guess I got lucky."

"You got to watch for them crossing the highway, too, no joke. Won't see them until they're right up under you. Take it slow, okay? You hit a big one full speed he'll flip you." He cranks the window up. "All right. You take it easy now."

Then I think of the boy walking out into nothing. I shouldn't ask but I can't help it. "Hey, would you say you know the people who live around here fairly well?"

He pauses, the window halfway shut. "Are you a process server, sir? Or an officer of the law?"

"What? No, of course not. I'm a physician. I mean, I'm on vacation, and I met a ...friend ...in the city. He had me drop him off a few miles back that way, and I realize I forgot to, uh, tell him something important. I suppose there's some sort of campground nearby, or a boat you know of where kids hang out?"

The bearded man stares at me, betraying nothing. He seemed eager a moment ago, so I try again. "You see, I'm visiting, I'm not from here, so I didn't realize how isolated it was when I dropped him off. He was quite specific about the place, but I've grown a bit worried. You mentioned alligators."

He pulls off his ball cap and rubs his hand through surprisingly thick chestnut hair. Sighs. He's younger than me, probably by a few years, despite the hokey way of talking, the antique rust on his old geezer truck. As he ponders, I notice his beard is trimmed with care, no stubble or stray hairs. I'd expect a man out in the country to have fur straggling down his neck, hairs sprouting wild like the unruly weeds that surround us on both sides of the road.

"Ain't no campground out in that mess," he says, eyes on the swamp. He frowns into the humid stillness. "Ain't nobody live less than thirty, forty minutes off either way."

The night trembles with frog song, with the rumbling of his truck.

"I saw him walk out. Right down the road."

He targets me with knowing eyes and a fearful gravity in his voice. "I only know of one kind of soul asks to be left out here, and one sort of man inclined to leave them. Same that picks them up in the first place. Sir, let's be clear now, you and me. Are you telling me you're that kind of man?"

I choose the boy because he's invisible. I can't stop thinking about him, even though earlier I passed him quickly, without registering a conscious impression. Outside, he faded into the wall. Inside, on the dance floor, I find myself hoping for a glimpse of him between the bodies, but he remains missing, like a ghost.

We didn't make eye contact, but the idea of him unsettles me like a memory. I'm not sure what he looks like, not sure I saw enough of his lean shadow to distinguish him amid the fantastic swirl of faces, shoulders, and asses; and once I'm moving in the crowd, I become part of one great sweaty beast, priming its own sex, rubbing all its components in an extended frenzy of pleasure. Handsome men pay attention to me, vie for me, and I know I look good and eat it up. The hands that grab me, cup me, muscle me; cocks barely trapped by leather jockstraps frotting me, in front and behind, men I've never met making intimate moves on me like welcome lovers, speaking body to body with animal language, taking liberties with intimacy, and giving me anonymous rough affection devoid of inhibition or pretense, and it all feels perfect, normal, and right.

For the first time in my life, I kiss another man in public. No hiding, no shame. I'm drunk on the freedom of it, on the verge of tears over the life I have missed.

Making out with a stranger on the edge of the dancefloor, a dirty blonde on the not-too-muscular side of slightly overweight, exactly my type, full, substantial, with receptive lips—but I keep thinking of the invisible boy outside. His presence worries me like a splinter. Move a certain way, and I feel him under the surface.

Then the surface thins into a film, and the joy and lust of the club is no longer mine. I'm finally at home, but I'm an outsider to this world. I have a wife up north that I love, in a way. She's smart and talented. Her anxiety disorder prevents travel and most social outings, providing me a certain clandestine freedom, such as this trip. People say I'm too generous in our relationship, but the truth is, she benefits as much as I do from our arrangement.

When I fuck my wife, I'm highly competent. I stop when she needs to stop without the resentment she's met from other men. I stop fucking and hold her or stop touching and bring tea, or a snack, or I leave her alone, whatever makes her feel safe. We love each other in our way. I don't mind the occasional sex, though it seems more about proving desirability for her than orgasm. She's always been like this. The eating disorder that plagued her through college has been in remission for years, though. Our only reminder is her shame about her front crowns, her horror of the rotted nubs below the surfaces that are her real teeth.

I don't blame Synthia—or Sin as I call her, our inside joke since we've grown to despise the church—for stabbing me with her palette knife last week. I suppose I should have lied about this trip, continued hiding my affairs, my existential conundrums and desires, but Sin is the one person in this world I thought I could trust.

Fondling the dirty blonde and smearing his neck with my lips, I feel responsible for her. Yet in my whirling mind, her face conflates strangely with the boy, calling me outside like a long lost yearning, impossible to eschew.

How do you explain to someone you love that you're not who they think you are? You tell the truth, and you sound crazy. But I told her. About the men, and the deaths.

The first time I died I was seven years old. Being a child, I didn't know it was a remarkable experience—or gift, or curse—to be rejected by death. I assumed that everyone went through the same thing.

When I was murdered at fourteen, I woke up with a mouth full of dirt, buried in a shallow pit, my father insisting upon my silence. My memories made very little sense. By the time I turned twenty-one, I vaguely expected it. The same cycle replayed at age twenty-eight and thirty-five. Tomorrow I'll be forty-two. As I explained to Sin, finding myself repeatedly, unbelievably alive has changed what I want from this life.

Some sort of ghostly obsession undermines the thrill of the club, dampening it down with a curious veil. I've a sense of something I missed outside, a gap I need to fill. The mood is oddly similar to those intense yet joyless instances when I've emerged with urgent animosity from the emptiness of yet another death. My memory and language break when I think too hard about those paradoxical moments, neither unalive nor undead, when I'm thrust from one reality into the next as if in an uncontrollable madman's dream.

"I have to meet a boy," I blurt out, abandoning my sexy dirty blonde with a final embrace of quick regret. His lips still shine with my spit. I rush outside even though who or what I'm after isn't clear to me yet. The ghost or god leaning against the wall has yet to show his face.

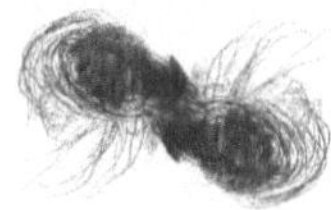

My lip will be bleeding. That's the first thing I'll notice. Fascination with the taste of my blood will coax my tongue to stroke the cut as I wake up.

I'll be moving already; running or fucking or driving the man's red truck, impossible activities since I won't be conscious in any ordinary sense, head heavy with indefinable impressions like the last lucid glimpse before a coma. Impossible since my cracked skull or broken back or splattered guts will have killed me.

I'll be alive after he's murdered me, the same as the five other times a man or lover has murdered me. Alive, in the black grip of physical agony, I'll be in the midst of fulfilling some universal law of revenge, like a vow I don't remember taking. Either in the act or fleeing in its aftermath.

Whatever forces this involuntary miracle or mythological anomaly to occur, I'll know I'm back from death by the fractured memories and unconscionable pain. Imagine every cell in your body is a separate prisoner undergoing invasive torture, and as your consciousness charges with false confidence into the dungeon of your reconstituting flesh, it flees from chamber to chamber finding no single corner, cleft, or compartment of rest. You cannot endure, but you cannot escape. Your body is the only place you can go. With the urgency of a burn, cold hard emptiness flares in every neuron that twitches back to life.

These seconds last for eternity. Time squeezes me. Panic wrenches my senses at every turn, compounded by seizure-like impressions of my violent death, painting me black and red with mortality's shock, grief, confusion, rage, and idiocy.

Then I'll laugh.

The absurd idea of my scattered limbs, organs, bones, and body fluids crawling back into cohesion seems more comical than profound. I know what it feels like, but I can't picture the medical process without scoffing. What a shame no one has ever thought to murder me on film. Mail my head to Iceland, my kidneys to France, my feet to the Bahamas, and so on, and leave the tape rolling.

I'll be running or fucking or stabbing, awash in my murderer's blood, laughing. Nameless emotions, nothing as simple as my own thoughts to sort through, but rather a confluence of multitudes that crowd me, like a flood. Every dead thing within miles has been in me and at me and is trying to hitch a ride.

Sunken in this swamp, there are so many.

Memories: something black yet bright, sparkling like a concussion that glitters behind my eyes. A sudden separation of femur from socket makes me vomit as my limbs are bitten. I'll taste swamp in my nostrils, in the spaces mending between fascia and bone. I'll see huge jaws in quick cudgels of disjointed memory, aquatic monsters clamping down and quartering my violated and discarded body, and I'll sweat as I grip the steering wheel and laugh harder with hysterical agony, laugh that my handsome parts have been digested by alligators, and this running fucking sweating body is nothing more than a thing reborn of shit.

I'll leave my unrecovered memories to rot by the side of the old highway. I'll floor the accelerator on this rusted truck. Soon, when I stop laughing, I'll hope for quiet and pretend I'm not crying when I think about the boy.

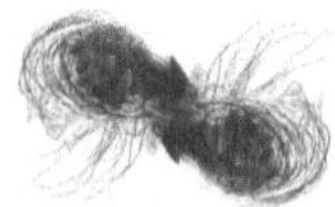

"I'm sure I don't know what you're implying."

"I reckon you know about half, and don't want to admit what you know of the rest. Let me put it to you this way; was this friend of yours traipsing off into the swamp a real young kid, one you just met?"

"What? I can't imagine—look, never mind. Thank you. Have a good night."

"Nah, you got no idea."

He brushes his beautiful chestnut hair back from his forehead, puts the ball cap on, and whistles. Not a pop tune or a bird call, but something fragmented and atonal, barely audible over the sound of his engine and the calling of small frogs.

As the long string of off-key notes unfolds, I pause instead of leaving as I intend to, need to, stuck in an atemporal mire. Sin likes to sing when she works. Though she forbids me to listen, I tiptoe up to her studio and lean my cheek on the cool wall outside, delighting in her unrestrained pleasure when she thinks I'm not home yet. I love her voice. I've told her so. We used to read out loud to each other, poems and stories, sometimes plays, but she refuses now. Over time Sin's grown more introverted, more ashamed. She blushes with rage when she catches me eavesdropping, yet even her scolding tones ring with inadvertent beauty.

Discordant whistling tangles with the sound of Sin, infecting her beloved tone. I can't help thinking of her right now, far away from this nearly alien landscape where I've gotten foolishly stuck, raising her voice happily in my absence. The humidity of the night, the sag of the broken tree line, the godlessness of my frail attempt to appease the swamp deities leaves me wondering what is left between us after all this time besides the deception of memory.

The bearded man's hollow breath weaves around me, keeping me in place when I know I should leave, must leave to save my life. Despite my past, I'm not certain that my life will save itself every time I die. I'm not fearless. The horrid whistling drowns out the nighttime quiet. It's a bad sound, as if he's blowing air through flutes made of my innards, scraping his teeth across my living bones.

Finally, he stops.

"You got no idea, yet here you are. Shoot, the hell did you find this place?"

I'm shaken and drained, immobile. The night has finally caught up with me, this trip, this life; my many shattered lives. This life is slipping away. I have nothing to say.

"I don't hold it against you you're a faggot. Bigger problem than that. You got some ghost in you."

Anger sullied by exhaustion. "What do you want from me?"

"That friend of yours."

"He wasn't a child. I wouldn't do that."

He spits out of the driver's side window once and hooks an elbow over the back of the vinyl seat. "Well, sir, he was and he wasn't, he is and he isn't, and I'm afraid to say you pretty much did. But I'm talking about you. What's got me riled is how did you manage it lest you come from some such place, and what need be to put the matter to rest. So here's what's gonna happen. We're gonna go on up the road and meet my buddy Slick—"

All at once, my phone buzzes in my back pocket. The car alarm on my rental blares. The far off industrial lights flicker and grow brighter, flaring across the expanse of the barren landscape. At the same time, the headlights of the man's truck burn my retinas, turning everything white. I shield my eyes. Light scorches the night sky, illuminating the swamp in sickly, surreal contrast like the oversaturated negative of a photograph.. The edges glow brighter until they sear black, curling inward.

The light is blinding. I can't find my keys. The car door handle feels like it's on fire.

I run. I'm in good shape. I can run a long time. I can't outrun a truck, but the bearded man probably can't see any better than me, sunspots, shapes, strange outlines. On foot there must be some path into the soggy woods, enough brush to hide until daylight, a shack or pile of lumber I missed. I run back the way I came when I left the boy. Maybe he's waiting with a weapon. Maybe he'll shelter me in his secret hiding place.

Maybe he'll explain to the bearded man that it wasn't like that between us. Or that I didn't mean it to be. I recognized something I'd lost in the boy, in the way he was disappearing, and I had to grab for it and try to hold on.

Or maybe he's not out there, the god choosing to become faceless in my moment of need, the truck headlights swerving round to follow me, the slow crunch of tires creeping patiently behind. I dodge to the side, try to lead him off the asphalt into the sucking mud, but he knows the precise limits of his vehicle and the tendencies of the swamp.

I'm wasting my energy flapping in the headlights like a moth against glass. I stop.

Memories clipping in and out of darkness. A green fire with liquid flames drips upward. The corpse of a small mammal like a beaver or oversized rat disemboweled on a concrete floor. Something charred and acrid fills my mouth, a swollen object, solid but pliant, with another taste underneath, a metallic tang of iron. Duct tape seals my lips. I can't spit. Tape binds my forearms and wrists, pressing them against hard surfaces on either side, spread out, holding me up.

Hands of men—they must be men, large, calloused hands, and the air reeks with the intentions of men, men in seclusion, not the sweet musk of the locker room, but something more beautiful, threatening, and rank—press from all directions. Praying hands, the inverse of the communal joy exchanged freely on the dancefloor, a hard mockery imitating my recent fragile discovery of shameless self-expression, of love; yes, I'll call it love, though in the club I was surrounded by strangers. These strangers, these new hands silence, bind, and isolate. My stomach heaves and I shudder deep in my marrow with fever. Snippets of their nonsense prayers erupt through clouds of miasma.

"...Son of river and starry waters..."

"...The first to exist is the light..."

"...The egg ascends not from the soil..."

"...His heart in twain, a seed in each thigh binds the demon and births night..."

"...Lay him to rest, to rest, to rest..."

Chanting, prayers, hands heaving me, rocking me, fondling me with hate, replacing love with disgust. I love my body but it is killing me. It is a monstrous anomaly. It is a sweating thing hurled to and fro by a sea of hands, crying out for release from consciousness, begging in its forlorn weakness to escape their loud petitions. They yell. Press harder. Dark, light, dark, light, clipping in and out, on and off. Sounds of strangled geese. I'm not sure what happens next. Please, don't let me remember.

Something hits my face to wake me.

They tilt my lolling head downward to make me watch. A scalpel crosses my chest twice, cutting the T of an autopsy incision. It's cold where my blood pours out, warm below where it soaks my crotch. They peel my skin back, hack through muscle, and crack the sternum to open me up. Let me die, let me die. They pull out my slippery heart, which isn't beating. I'm already dead, though I feel every cut and crack, feel the sickening snap of the organ evicted from my chest cavity, the pain of life leaking out of me long after my life is gone.

Carefully, they turn the wilting heart around and around, seeking some specific shape or angle. They slice it vertically in half. A long gash sliced in each of my thighs, deep pockets of quad wrenched apart, and the halves of heart are stuffed inside. They duct tape around each muscle, sealing the tissue within. My torso they leave open like a torn flag.

The last thing I'll remember before I'm tossed into the swamp and torn apart is an enormous white bird flapping, struggling, squalling, held up by its feet. Again they chant. The bird screams. They wring its long neck, pour its blood out over me, and then tuck the feathers from its limp white body into my orifices and wounds.

Soon I'll be devoured. Soon I'll come back. I'll decide as I'm flooring the red truck, hurtling away from the scene of the crime—the scene of several crimes, theirs and mine—that I'm not responsible for whatever happened to the bearded man and his tribe. Or congregation, coven, whatever they are. I won't remember how he died. I won't want to know, don't want to know how I killed him. Inevitably, that's what I'll have done.

The wrath of some god I don't believe in and don't understand demands it.

I'll be shocked several days later when I get home to find the locks changed. Recovering the information from my cell account while at yet another hotel, I'll get Sin's message. "Don't come back. You're insane. I thought I was the one who needed help. They should revoke your license. If your father were here he'd be appalled."

The irony that Sin can't appreciate is that if my dad were alive, I wouldn't have taken this trip. I wouldn't have told her about the deaths. In retrospect, I'm glad I didn't get the chance to go into more detail. Who knows what she'd have done with a full confession. I'm still living out of a hotel, even though as his only child and sole heir, I have the legal right and responsibility to take possession of my father's house.

He passed away just over two weeks ago. Two weeks before my birthday.

I'd be lying if I said grief overwhelmed me. Grief rolled in slowly, like a tide, and it's still fucking with my mind. I don't know who I am, but did I ever? All these choices made to please him, lies to hide what he disapproved of, my whole existence constructed to adhere on the surface to his expectations and desires.

I wanted him to be proud of me. Of course we fought; who doesn't? I learned early on how to hide what I needed to hide. I never confronted him with who I am. I loved him. I didn't want to hurt him, disappoint him, hear him call me a slur and find out he never loved me. If he were still alive, I'm not sure I'd have told Sin anything.

He was gone, and I was about to turn forty-two, and that meant that at some point soon I'd die and occupy those strange liminal spaces where all the dead things nearby congregate. They'd be exposed to me, be part of me, and I'd be part of them, in all my naked emotional monstrosity.

So I ran.

I long to see him again. The possibility is within my grasp, but I can't let him see me. I turn away, though the grief of choosing this loss is agony. I'm longing for all the people I've lost as the joy of the club and the freedom of the dancefloor erodes, as I abandon my dirty sexy blonde after my first public kiss in anticipation of finding the invisible boy outside. We didn't make eye contact, but the idea of him unsettles me like a memory. I'm not sure what he looks like, not sure I saw enough of his lean shadow to distinguish him amid the fantastic swirl of faces, shoulders, and asses, yet something absent in him draws me like the water that flows into an empty furrow, nourishing, inevitable. I work my way through the crowd and breach the humid evening to touch what is intangible.

Inexplicably, a parade is ending as I exit the club, despite the late hour. Streamers and baubles litter the street. Children scrabble for paper and plastic prizes in the damp gutters. There's a light rain, almost mist. I wonder that there are no parents anywhere, no signs posted restricting traffic, and no holiday that I'm aware of. As the sound of percussion fades with the colorful marchers turning a corner, the children yell, laugh, and shove, taking off to follow down the street with the ebullient tumult of a river.

There he is. Fading into the wall, obscured by a thin curtain of water falling from a damaged roof. I jog through the mist. Like the sweat on my skin, it hardly cools me. Slicking back my hair and shaking water off my hands, wiping my brow, I join him under the awning.

"Muggy, isn't it?"

He startles, eyes darting back and forth. Long lashes flicker. "Yeah?"

"I guess you get used to it. So, uh, what did I miss?"

He seems puzzled. The smell of gunpowder lingers from recent fireworks. I say, "What was the parade for? What are we celebrating today?"

"Oh. A funeral."

"I'm sorry."

"I'm not."

Slumped against the wall, head hanging, he retreats behind a veil of indifference, nearly vanishing. I lean in beside him and bump shoulders, and then instead of pulling away, I settle in, staying close.

He's shorter than me. His head tips against my left shoulder. My arm goes around him. He rests his cheek against my chest. I rub his arm and press my face into his hair, smelling the green smells of mud, rotting lichen, and dirty cypress. We stay this way for a long time, my pulse caressing his skin, his hands in his pockets.

I whisper, "Come on."

When we get to my room he tells me I can do anything I want. He asks me to hit him, to choke him, because it all goes right through him. Because he hasn't felt anything in so long and he wants me to do it all. He wants new bruises to prove I saw him, because, he says, "I'm a ghost." He twists and points to a dark welt on his hip. It hurts to look at it. "I've had this same one since nineteen eighty-five."

Navigating between brutality and tenderness, I grasp his neck with my right hand and push him down into the mattress. "If you're a ghost, how can I do this?" I spit on my fingers. "And this?"

And he gasps and moans and does the same to me, and for several hours he doesn't answer, in fact he never answers or mentions it again. We fuck as if this is our first and last chance in a lifetime, in several lifetimes, and only later when I'm flooring the truck and laughing like a deranged maniac racing away from the swamp do I realize that it is.

# It Is the Night!

## by C.M. Forest

Kari Bowman checked the time. "C'mon." She was technically early, but waiting never came easy to her.

The phone call had been brief. "Mr. Fletcher has granted you an interview. A car will pick you up on the corner of Bay and Adelaide at 6pm sharp. Recording devices will be prohibited; your phone will be confiscated for the duration of the interview. A note pad and pen will be provided if required."

Under different circumstances, Kari would have balked at such a demand. But for the chance to talk to Ronson Fletcher, the reclusive billionaire, she would have taken notes on an Etch A Sketch if requested.

A warm, dry front which had travelled up from the southwest had decided to take up temporary residence in Toronto. Whatever breeze might have existed was kept from reaching the streets thanks to the buildings lining the roads. Kari brushed her bangs aside, her fingers capped in sweat, as she peered up in time to see a flock of birds slip between skyscrapers; their number momentarily doubled in the mirrored windows of one of the buildings. Vapour trails criss-crossed the azure sky beyond.

She looked at her watch again. 5:58 PM. "Calm down, Kari," she instructed herself. Her nerves were like a pack of wild dogs running unbidden through her body. She had spent the better part of five years making a name for herself as a journalist at the expense of Ronson Fletcher. And now she would have to sit across from him, look him in the eye.

A soft jingle began to issue from her purse. Digging past the note pad and four pens—just in case one ran low on ink—she freed her cell phone.

"Hey, Tony," Kari said, answering the call.

"Are you there yet? Wherever *there* is?" Her publisher, Tony, was a tiny man with a huge caffeine addiction.

"No, not yet. Still waiting."

"You don't think it's bullshit, do you?"

"Hard to say. If Fletcher knows me well enough to ask for me by name, then he knows the stuff I've written about him. Which begs the question: why me?"

Tony sighed. "Yeah, it's pretty suspect. Still, I hope like *fuck* this is legit. We could use the boost in traffic."

"Who knows, maybe he wants to get me alone to kill me. At least you'd still get a helluva story out of it." Kari laughed as her boss snorted. Tony had been very good to her over the years, had even stood up and fought when the cease-and-desist letters came from Fletcher's attorneys.

"Don't even joke about that shit, Kari. Just let me know what happens, okay? If nobody shows up, still shoot me a message. My fucking ulcer is fit to burst over this whole thing. And if this is the real deal, you're gonna be a goddamned superstar!"

"Fingers crossed." Kari ended the call. She knew he was right. An interview with Ronson Fletcher was a golden ticket.

"Ms. Bowman?" The voice was deep, strong, it caused Kari to jump.

Turning on her heel, she saw a black BMW with heavily tinted windows nestled against the curb. A man in a dark suit and short hair looked out at her from behind the wheel.

She cleared her throat, straightened her posture. "That's me."

The man stepped out of the car and opened the rear, driver's-side door. "Mr. Fletcher's flight has just arrived. He is waiting for you."

"Where are you taking me?" she asked, as the BMW pulled into traffic. "Secret hideout? Black site? Illuminati sex dungeon?" She hoped the last would garner a laugh. It did not.

"Mr. Fletcher is at the airport."

"Yes, as you've said. But where is the interview being held?"

"At the airport. His private jet, to be more precise."

The car turned onto Yonge St. and started south toward the Gardiner Expressway.

"His jet? You're joking, right?"

"I never joke while I'm working." The answer was so ridiculous that it caused Kari to roll her eyes, until she realized he was serious.

"We're staying on the ground, though, correct? We're not flying anywhere?" The idea seemed absurd. But then again, she was meeting Ronson Fletcher. A man so erratic in his behaviour over the past half-decade that applying any logic to him was fruitless.

Kari caught the driver's eyes in his rearview mirror. A small collection of lines creased from the edges revealing a smile, but he remained quiet.

The drive was uneventful. Traffic on the Gardiner was moving for a change, which made the trek to Pearson International Airport quicker than usual.

"Don't we need to go inside? Pass through security?" Kari asked as the driver directed the BMW through a gate at the far end of the airport and onto the tarmac.

The man snorted and shook his head.

"Here we are." The driver put the car into park, near what she assumed was Fletcher's jet, and opened her door.

She took a step toward the aircraft before stopping. Looking over her shoulder, she asked, "Are... are you going to be here when the interview is over?"

The man smiled, but did not answer. He climbed into the car, put it into drive and slowly rolled away.

"Oh, that's not ominous or anything," she said with a sigh.

The artificial thunder of nearby planes taking to the sky caused the air around Kari to vibrate. She suddenly felt very small, which was not a sensation she was used to. Staring ahead, she took in Fletcher's jet. It lacked any of the flourish she expected from a billionaire's private aircraft. No giant corporate logos, no crazy paint job; Fletcher's name was completely absent from the exterior. It was quite ordinary. As ordinary as a personal jet could be. Stairs had been affixed to the side of the craft; the door at the top was open. From her position, and due to the brightness of the day, the space beyond the door appeared black. A hole into nothingness.

The illusion was broken when a man appeared in the doorway. "You must be Ms. Bowman," he called down.

"Yes. I mean, I'm Bowman, er, Kari Bowman." She cursed herself. She was already flummoxed and she hadn't even laid eyes upon Fletcher yet.

"Excellent," the man said. He hurried down the steps, his shoes clanging on the metal stairs as he did so. "My name is Aaron. I'm Mr. Fletcher's personal assistant. Thank you for taking the interview."

"I would be a fool to turn down such an offer."

"Yes, well. Mr. Fletcher is a very private man." Aaron stood impossibly straight. Kari wondered if it was his natural posture, or some tactic to make her uneasy. "And speaking of privacy, I will have to take your phone. Don't worry," he added quickly, when she opened her mouth to respond. "You will get it back after the interview."

She grudgingly handed over the device. Aaron tucked it into his pocket.

"Please, follow me. Mr. Fletcher had to step out for a moment, to stretch his legs, but will be back shortly. In the meantime, he asked that you make yourself comfortable. We have drinks and hors d'oeuvres prepared."

"Is this an interview or a date?" Kari laughed at her own joke.

Aaron, a man with a slightly better sense of humour than the driver, also chuckled. "Mr. Fletcher prides himself on being a good host."

"In that case, lead away."

As she followed him up the steps, Kari was hit with a sense of foreboding. The darkness resting inside the aircraft had yet to dissipate. She wondered if it ever would. As silly as it sounded in her head, she imagined the jet filled to the brim with darkness. Dense, unforgiving blackness. A void she would become lost in.

Aaron must have noticed her trepidation as he stopped on the top step, looked down at her and asked, "Everything okay, Ms. Bowman?"

"What? Oh, yes." She took a breath. "Just excited for this opportunity."

The darkness finally peeled back as she reached the topmost step. Kari shook her head and mentally chided herself for being a child.

"Please, this way." Aaron guided her into the craft.

Kari was impressed. The interior walls of the jet were a mixture of rich wood paneling and gold trim. A section of shelves held a library of books that would have been impressive in a proper home. Housed within the tight confines of the aircraft, they looked downright excessive. Thin, silver bars held the books in place. "Wow." Kari whistled.

"Ah, yes. Mr. Fletcher is a very well-read man." The pride in Aaron's voice made Kari want to gag.

She perused the titles of the books. "'Lore of the Ancients', 'Pre-History Civilization', 'The Nine Doors'. Jeez, and here I pegged old Ronson as a James Patterson kind of guy."

Any levity Aaron had showcased previously, dried up. "Some of these books are literally one-of-a-kind. Mr. Fletcher's collection is priceless."

"Maybe storing them on a jet isn't the best place for them."

Aaron cleared his throat. "He likes to have them nearby."

Kari's reporter sense was tingling. This guy was keeping secrets.

"Now please, this way."

Beyond the bookshelves, the jet opened up into a more familiar sight. Four plush seats, two on either side of the craft, awaited her. The seats on the right were positioned front to back, while the ones on the left were turned to face each other. A table with a silver platter sitting on the surface rested between them. A collection of finger foods adorned the platter.

"Have a seat. Enjoy the hors d'oeuvres." Aaron stood just beyond one of the facing chairs and held out a hand.

Kari had taken many flights in her lifetime. Some, even in first class. Nothing compared to the luxurious comfort the chair afforded. She couldn't stop the sigh which blew past her lips as she sunk into the seat's embrace.

"Would you like a refreshment?" Aaron nodded to a drink cart loaded with bottles, an ice box, and several glasses.

She would love a drink. But thought better of it. "I'm good for now. Thanks."

"Mr. Flecther will be arriving shortly. I have a few arrangements to make before take-off. Please, if you need me, press the call button."

"Just so we're clear. When you say 'take-off', you mean after the interview, right?"

"Buzz if you need me." Aaron bowed slightly and went through a narrow door at the front of the cabin.

"It's like pulling teeth," she groaned.

In preparation for the interview, she removed a pen and the note pad from her purse. She placed them next to each other, with the pen on the right, on the table. Unsatisfied with the placement, she then shifted the pen to the left. Afterwards, she pulled a crab cake from the tray and popped it into her mouth. "My God," she mumbled around the food. "Money *can* buy happiness." She ate another.

Kari was surprised to notice that the most prominent feature in the jet was not the luxurious chairs, or even the library, it was the clocks. Two-dozen large, round clocks covered most of the walls. Beneath each time piece, engraved into thin, gold plaques were time zones. Somebody, Fletcher, she presumed, had drawn on the face of the clocks with a black marker. Two thick lines, all between five and ten, slashed across the glass.

"Weird," Kari whispered to herself.

"Yes, I suppose it would seem odd, Ms. Bowman." A voice wafted up from the rear of the jet.

Kari's heart leapt. Leaving the clocks behind, she turned in her seat to see a man in his mid-fifties walk stiffly through the aircraft.

"Mr. Fletcher," Kari said, hurrying to stand. She raised her hand. "It is nice to meet you."

His handshake was frail, weak. Kari knew men like Fletcher. Rich, powerful men. They loved crushing her hand whenever they got the chance. She wondered if he was ill. He certainly looked it. Before his self-imposed exile, Ronson Fletcher was something of a playboy. His physique, his looks, that of a much younger man, was constant tabloid fodder.

"In person, don't you mean?" Fletcher continued to grip her.

"Excuse me?"

"It's nice to meet me in person. I feel we've become very well acquainted through your work." His hand was hot. It trembled slightly.

Breaking the hold, Kari cleared her throat. "Yes, well. Articles don't count."

"Oh, I think they do. A story, say, like the ones you've written, go out to millions of people. They form untold opinions. People who don't know me, don't think about me, suddenly become aware of my existence."

Kari held her breath, waiting for the other shoe to drop. She imagined Fletcher having her removed from his jet, the entire thing an elaborate joke. A chance to gain some payback against her.

"Please, sit." There was no malice in his voice, only weariness.

"Nice jet you have here," Kari said, returning to her seat.

Fletcher nodded, but remained quiet. He approached the seat opposite her, but did not sit right away. First, he stretched his back, eliciting a choir of pops and cracks. It sounded painful, and given the sudden grimace that came across his face, it must have been.

He sat with the care of a man lowering himself onto broken glass. Once settled, he smiled thinly, his lips strained, and said, "It's the best money can buy. Fast, too. It can circle the globe in less than twenty-four hours."

"Are you okay, Mr. Fletcher?"

"I've been better. It's hard being cooped up all the time."

Kari wasn't sure what to make of the comment, but filed it away for later questioning. She had bigger inquiries in mind. "First, I would like to thank you for granting me this interview, Mr. Fletcher."

"Please," the man said, waving a hand through the air. "Call me Ronson."

"Okay, Ronson, then let me ask you, where have you been for the last five years?"

"Ah, always the eager beaver. I think that's what makes you so popular; you don't waste time." Ronson leaned back, crossed his legs. The overhead lights created dark pools of his eyes.

"People don't want small talk, Ronson. They don't have time for it. This is the social media era. Information delivered in thirty seconds or less."

Ronson Fletcher shook his head and sighed. "Of course. Nobody takes time to breathe. If you only knew how trivial this all is, you would never go online again."

Kari ground her teeth. She had encountered such attitudes from the wealthy before. "Well, when you have billions of dollars, it makes it a bit easier to sit back and enjoy the sunshine."

She expected a retort, but instead, the man sitting across from her laughed. A big, belly laugh. One that transitioned into coughing halfway through. "I'm sorry," he said, wiping tears from his eyes. "You don't know how close to home that comment hits, Ms. Bowman."

The narrow door at the front of the cabin opened and Aaron stepped out. He appraised Fletcher for a moment, concern writ across his face. "We're ready for departure, sir."

"Thank you, Aaron."

Kari felt a moment between the two men, a sadness. But nothing was said. Ronson's personal assistant simply bowed his head, and left.

"So ... we *are* flying? I wasn't informed of this when I received the call." Kari did nothing to hide the annoyance in her voice.

Ronson tilted his head, a mischievous grin on his face. "You're not afraid of flying, are you Ms. Bowman?"

"Of course not. I just wasn't expecting to do so today. Will you be bringing me home afterwards, or am I going to have to catch a flight from wherever we land."

"Don't worry, you'll be back at Pearson in a few hours. I have no destination in mind. I just need to keep moving. Once in the sky, you may ask me anything. For now, let's enjoy the silence."

Take-off was smooth. Kari watched from the nearest window as the pilot circled once over Toronto before heading west. Aaron returned shortly after the craft reached cruising altitude. He retrieved the drink cart from its place off to the side and deposited it next to Ronson's seat.

The billionaire gripped the man's hand. "Thank you, Aaron. That will be all."

"Yes, sir." Kari thought she saw tears in the personal assistant's eyes as he scurried away.

"Let me pour you a drink," Ronson said. His hands shaking as he reached for a bottle of scotch.

"No, I'm fine. Thank you."

"Nonsense. I drink alone too often. I need the company."

"Fine. But no ice," she quickly added when she saw the man reach for the ice box.

"Ah, you like it neat. So do I."

Ronson half-filled the glass before handing it to her. He filled his own to the brim. Afterwards, he reached into his pocket, pulled out a small pill bottle, liberated two yellow tabs and popped them into his mouth. "Cheers, Ms. Bowman," he said.

Kari raised an eyebrow. "Mine isn't poisoned, is it?"

"No, Ms. Bowman, yours is not poisoned."

"Salute." She lifted her glass and took a drink. The scotch warmed her throat. It coated her stomach like honey. She had no doubt the bottle cost more than a month's salary for her.

Ronson knocked back his own drink in one slug. He sucked in a bit of air through his teeth before pouring another two fingers into his glass. When he offered to top her up, she declined.

"You've been a good host, Ronson. But I think it might be time we get down to business." As Kari spoke, the jet banked slightly. Outside the nearest window, she could see the sun hanging heavy in the sky.

"I suppose we do. The day's almost over. So, Ms. Bowman, you have me at your mercy. Time is short. What is it you want to know?"

Kari straightened; her pulse quickened. "As I asked earlier; why me?"

His eyes narrowed, a smile on his lips. "Ask me again at the end. What else do you have?"

"Fine," she cleared her throat. "Where have you been these last five years?"

The billionaire rolled his eyes. "With your reputation, I was expecting for you to go right for the throat, Ms. Bowman, but I will humour you." He raised his arms out to his sides. "I've been here."

"Travelling, you mean? Hiding out in one of your dozens of mansions?"

"'Hiding'. I like that. But yes, and no. I have been travelling. All day, every day. But, and this is sadly true, I have not visited a single one of my homes. When I said I've been here, I was being literal. This jet, and a few more like it, have been my exclusive residence."

Kari waited for him to elaborate, but he seemed content with his answer. She decided to dig. "You're telling me, that for five years, you've lived on this—"

"Can we move along, already?" Ronson interrupted. "As much

as I enjoy your voice, Ms. Bowman, I'd like to get this over with. Stop beating around the bush. What do you really want to ask me?"

She looked up from her note pad. There was a twinkle in the man's eye. He was enjoying this. "Fine. You want it? Okay. Ronson Fletcher, did you kill your girlfriend, Cleo Lane?"

"Ah!" Ranson leaned forward and clapped his hands together. "There it is! I have to admit, I'm shocked that you were able to restrain yourself for so long. After all, you've written many articles declaring me a murderer over the years."

"I've never once accused you of murder."

"Oh, of course not. That would open you up to litigation. You're too smart for that. But you've implied it quite well."

"I'm sorry, Mr. Fletcher, but what is the point of this? Clearly you do not like me, and honestly, I don't like you. As you say, I've never outright called you a murderer, but I think you are one. I think you killed Cleo Lane."

He began to cry. Nothing big or dramatic, just a subtle tremor in his jaw, a bit of moister in his eyes. "I loved Cleo. I loved her so much. I know that's going to be hard for you to believe. To the rest of the world, she looked like another trophy girlfriend. Beautiful. Half my age. But she was so much more. Cleo had a lust for life that rivalled any I've encountered. She was fearless. If you think my status, my wealth, intimidated her, or even impressed her all that much, you would be wrong. She was incredible." He stared off, his gaze unfocused. "And, to answer your question, yes, I killed Cleo Lane."

There was moment of turbulence, or so Kari thought, but it could have been the seismic shock of the confession she had just heard. Her fingers began to tremble as she tried to make notes. Her mind racing for the appropriate follow-up question. Already, she was imagining the places the story would take her. It would be an international headline. Within days, she would be the most known journalist in the world.

"Just to be clear, you have just confessed to the murder of Cleo Lane? Is that correct, Mr. Fletcher?"

Ronson brought his attention back to his empty glass. Kari thought he might pour a third, but he left it empty. "I would never hurt Cleo; she was the love of my life. No. I didn't murder her, but I did kill her. At least, I did through my actions."

"What does that mean?"

Small beads of sweat began to form below Ronson's hair line. "Have you heard of Doggerland?"

Kari shook her head. "What is that? Like an amusement park for dogs?"

"Very humorous, but no. It was a section of land that long ago connected Britain to Europe. A vast chunk of earth that was lost after the last ice age. It's funny, we grow up looking at maps of the world and think that we know everything, and meanwhile, those same maps only show us a brief moment in time. This world looked much different in the past.

"People lived on Doggerland for millennia. Can you fathom that? A history far larger than our own, washed away by the world. Forgotten. Excavation is, as you might imagine, quite difficult given the submerged nature of the area. But archeologists are a persistent people and a recent discovery had been made. A temple, carbon dated 13,000 BC was found at the bottom of the North Sea. When Cleo caught wind of the find, she demanded that we see it."

Kari raised an eyebrow. Her knowledge of Cleo Lane was of a twenty-something with perky breasts, blonde hair and a million-dollar tan.

"You didn't know that about her, did you? Cleo was an adventurer. She was obsessed with archeology. Not really my thing, I prefer the here and now.

"I organized an expedition to this newly found temple as an anniversary present to her. We went down in a submersible. A cramped box with a domed window in the front. The water was dark, murky, but when our lights fell upon the structure, I could feel Cleo go electric with excitement."

Ronson wiped his sleeve across his forehead. The sweat had progressed beyond beading and now dribbled from his skin.

"Are you okay?" Kari asked.

He nodded once.

"I have to tell you, Ms. Bowman, this place was like nothing I had ever seen before. It was built in a way to trap air within. Almost as if the architects knew, someday in the impossibly-distant future, their temple would be sitting at the bottom of the sea. We entered through an opening beneath the structure; one that rose up into a pool at the center of a massive chamber.

"I paid just a smidge over four million dollars for Cleo and I to be the first people to enter. This garnered some ire from the team working on the find, but archelogy is not a cheap venture, and four million goes a long way.

"We needed to wear oxygen masks, in case the air had grown toxic, but that was all. It was incredible."

Kari's notes were short, clipped. She didn't much care about the lost temple or Doggerland. When Ronson's story stopped, she glanced up. "What is it?" she asked, following his gaze toward one of the cabin windows.

"It's getting late."

A visible shiver cascaded across his body before he returned his attention to her. "The temple was ... alien. And I don't mean that in an extra-terrestrial sort of way. I mean, it was very clear to me and Cleo, that it had belonged to a people far removed from anything we recognize today. The pool exited into a nine-sided room with a doorway on each side and a pedestal in the middle.

"I wanted to check each doorway, see what secrets lay beyond, but Cleo, God bless her, ran for the pedestal. Her camera highlighting the object stored there in flashes of white."

"What was there?" Kari asked.

Ronson bit his bottom lip, his teeth yellow, in need of dental work. "It was a triangular tablet carved from stone. The surface was decorated with various characters; symbols that made no sense to me. At the time" —he shook his head — "I was more interested in Cleo than whatever gibberish had been etched by long-dead hands. You see, I was going to propose to her."

Kari's pen jumped slightly on the page. Everybody in the media, herself included, had always assumed Ronson was using Cleo for her body, her youth, and that he would discard her as soon as those things began to fade. But marriage? That was unexpected.

Ronson reached into the collar of his shirt and pulled out a dainty, silver chain wound through a ring. The jewellery was simple but elegant.

"What happened, Ronson?"

He blew a sigh that sounded half pain, half heartbreak. "Cleo approached the object. She touched it."

Ronson closed his eyes, took a deep breath. "Have you ever seen a person get electrocuted, Ms. Bowman? Like, a musician touching a faulty mic stand, or a child reaching for an exposed wire?" Kari nodded. "It was like that. Her body went rigid, stiff. I thought she was joking, until her eyes rolled up in her head. Soon after, she fell to the floor and began to seize.

"I thought I was going to lose her right then and there. Her skin was so cold. It felt as if she had just stepped out of a freezer. Her eyelids fluttered like mad butterflies. Her mouth, behind her oxygen mask, opened and closed. It took me a moment to notice she was speaking. With her head in my lap, I leaned forward and listened."

Kari realized with a start that she had stopped taking notes. Ronson's story had swept her up and was threatening to carry her away completely. Taking a moment to center herself, she brought her pen back to the note pad and asked, "What was she saying?"

"She was repeating what she read on the tablet."

"But" —Kari cocked her head — "you said it was gibberish."

"Yes. And yet, I'm certain, the moment her skin touched the stone of the tablet, she was able to read it."

Ronson was shaking. His hands quaked in his lap. "If you'll excuse me, I think one more drink is needed." Kari watched as the man attempted to lift the bottle of scotch from the tray.

"Let me help you." She poured a healthy measure of the amber liquor into his glass. An act which netted her a tip of the head and a wink in thanks.

"We rushed Cleo to the nearest hospital. She was stable, but unconscious. I wanted to stay with her, hold her hand, caress her cheek, but people like me, at least at that time, always had somewhere to be. On that day, it was Los Angeles. I recall that flight. My stomach in knots. My thoughts a tornado of worry. The plan had been for Cleo to accompany me. I'd made reservations at her favourite restaurant. A celebration for our engagement." He laughed, but it was low, closer to a humorous sigh. "How sure I was of the future. In my mind, she had already said yes to my proposal. Such a fool.

"The phone call came in just after I landed. She was awake, coherent. But also terrified. I tried to calm her, but she wouldn't listen. I think, looking back, hearing her in that state was scarier than watching her fall in the temple. Cleo was a matador; she waved the red flag at life, daring it to charge her. She was not one to give in to fear."

"What was she afraid of?" Kari asked.

Ronson leaned his head back, his Adams apple jutting from his neck like a tumor. "The truth, Ms. Bowman." He brought his head back down, his eyes boring into her own. "The truth of the world we live in. The truth inscribed on the tablet.

"She told me, then, in full detail what the ancient writing had revealed. It was wild, insane. I thought she must have suffered a stroke. I really did. I'm sorry to say, I became short with her. I demanded she call a doctor. It was too late. Her screams filled the phone. They grabbed me, gutted me. The line went dead. When I called back, there was no answer. I had the hospital staff check on her. She was gone. Vanished. Her bed was still warm, but the room was otherwise undisturbed. The windows and door were closed.

"This happened just before 1pm Los Angeles time. Almost 9pm in the UK. Sunset."

"Jesus." Kari's mouth had grown dry. She eyed the scotch, but refused to give the man the satisfaction. "You still haven't told me what the tablet said."

Ronson's lips had grown slick with saliva. His skin, pale. "A secret, Ms. Bowman. There is an entity, a being that defies our very limited understanding of life. Long before this world produced its first single-celled organisms, this being took refuge here. It hides from the sun. It is invisible to us, and us to it. Until we become aware of its presence. Once that happens, Ms. Bowman, it sees us, it hunts us."

All the tension, the suspense growing like a weed inside Kari, wilted. She blinked; three rapid flutters of her eyelids, before bursting into laughter. "What? Like a vampire? You have got to be joking. All this, all this bullshit for a stupid prank."

Ronson Fletcher was not laughing.

"No, nothing like a vampire." He had slumped fully into his seat. Sweat had mixed with the saliva from his lips; it hung in small globes from his chin. "The secret written on the tablet damned Cleo, and cursed me.

"I spent four million to get into that temple, and another one-and-a-half billion to erase it from existence. I can't let people know the truth." He began to cough. A spattering of red spots appeared briefly on his bottom lip, before being swiped away by his tongue.

Kari prided herself on seeing the bigger picture, and when the pieces of the Ronson Fletcher puzzle fell into place, it was quite a revelations. "You actually believe all this, don't you? The clocks, the jet, the reclusive life style. Are you...? Are you trying to run from the night?"

"Not trying, Ms. Bowman," he slurred. "Since the day Cleo vanished, I have lived exclusively during the daytime. A march, forever West along the equator, chasing the sun. I land briefly, to switch planes, appreciate the ground, but the majority of my life is lived in the sky."

It was all too much. Kari looked down at her notes, the words, the confessions, practically jumping from the page.

"Five years. Five years you've been flying around the world because you fear a monster that lives in the night." She couldn't hold it in anymore. "That is the stupidest thing I've ever heard! But you know what? I'll take it. I came up here expecting ... *something*, but *this*, this exceeds my wildest expectations."

Ronson's breath was short, shallow. His hair stuck to his head in sweaty clumps. "I'm sure it has, Ms. Bowman. But you are wrong about one thing: the entity that has me running for my life doesn't simply live in the night. It occupies it fully. For all intents and purposes, it *is* the night."

His answer caused a ripple of goosebumps to climb her arms, to dance across the back of her neck. "Okay. Fine. Let's say you're telling the truth. Then why reveal this now?"

Ronson leaned into the side of his seat. His eyes barely open. "I'm tired of running," he wheezed. "But I'm too scared to stop. If you heard the sounds Cleo made, you would understand. So, I chose another way out." Tears slid down his cheeks.

"'Another way out'? What does that mean?"

"No more time." His lips barely moved as he spoke. His words jumbled together. "Ask me again. Ask me why you."

"Okay, Ronson." She licked her lips. "Why me?"

"Because..." His head bobbed as if it took everything he had to keep it up. "Because I fucking hate you." His neck gave up the fight, and his head lolled forward, his wet chin resting on his chest.

"Mr. Fletcher? Ronson?" she asked, reaching across the table to give his shoulder a shake. Her actions dislodged him from his seat, sending him folding onto the floor.

"Holy shit!" Kari jumped up. "Hey," she yelled. "We need help!"

Something rolled out of his pocket. It was the pill bottle from earlier. Ever the reporter, Kari scooped up the plastic container. Although it looked like a prescription bottle, no pharmacy label adhered to the side.

Aaron entered through the narrow door.

"He took something!" Kari sputtered.

"I know, Ms. Bowman. It was cyanide." Aaron's voice was tight, clipped. He crouched next to his employer and checked Fletcher's pulse.

"Fuck! Is he dead?"

"Yes," Aaron said, standing back up. "We will take you home now, Ms. Bowman." He turned on his heel and left Kari alone with the dead man.

"Jesus." Kari sat heavily in her seat. She glanced down at her pad. The pages of notes she had written looking back up. "Jesus!" she said again, rising back from the chair, this time with some gusto. "I'm going to be famous."

The private jet banked to the right. It caused the setting sun to leave orange streamers across her eyes, before heading back toward Toronto. As soon as they landed, she would get her phone back, she would call Tony. He wasn't going to believe this.

Trying not to look at the man on the floor, she began organizing her notes. "Crazy," she whispered. But then her eyes came across a couple passages.

*It's invisible to us until we become aware of its presence.*
*It is the night.*
The jet bounced, causing Kari to grip the back of her seat. Tur-

bulence. Although, if felt different than usual. It felt localized. As if something had pushed on the hull directly above her. Sitting down, she quickly buckled. Outside, the sky continued to darken. Ronson had said he was the only person in the world to know the terrible truth, but that wasn't true. He had told her. And now, even if she thought the man insane, the idea was alive in her thoughts.

A second wave of turbulence jolted the craft. For just a beat, she was sure that the windows, all of them, had been obscured. Sweat began to roll down her face. The jet continued toward Toronto. Toward the night.

Toronto

# Holes, Souls

## by SJ Townend

### December 2nd

Once Martha, her husband Jack, and Allison settle in an empty booth—a discreet table in the corner of a cafe—with a hushed voice, Martha uses language like 'poorly' and 'sleepy' and 'heaven,' not 'flesh-consuming stage four endometrial cancer' to explain her situation to her daughter. To wrap the diagnosis up softly, this is what a mother must do. Cushion the blow. Although, Martha has seen how it ends—premonitions have haunted her fitful sleep for weeks—and it is not the ending she would have chosen, not at all, but the last moments of her life, she holds faith, are in the hands of the Lord.

Years ago, Reverend Gabor had told Martha her sleep visions were a blessing, 'revelations from God', when she'd confided in him how she'd predicted her conception of Allison. Messages from Jesus had told her that her daughter would be special. And special Allison is, indeed. So, so special. But the *déjà vu*-adjacent visions infiltrating those liminal moments between wakefulness and sleep which always play out in reverse, have felt anything but a gift to Martha. So she keeps what she fears may be her denouement to herself.

Martha unfurls the bad news: her final round of treatment has not worked. Young Allison rubs the weft of crimson velvet on her sleeve with increasing ferocity and asks quietly about end-of-life care and the intricacies of the ceremonial processes of her mother's cremation, all without making eye contact.

"We aren't just complicated machinery that can always be put back together again then, like clockwork, like Lego?" Allison asks.

"No, darling. Sometimes, people can't be fixed, and, I guess, when Jesus calls, it's time for their souls—for me, this time—to fly home." Martha reaches for her glass of water and takes a gulp, forgetting the cancer has robbed her of her ability to swallow so much so fast. She splutters. Jack thumps her back with a fist.

"You okay?" Jack asks.

"Yes, fine." Martha replies. "Fine."

Allison's freckle-dusted brow furrows as Martha, on catching her breath, explains the concept of the Christian soul once more. God-given. Immortal. A blessing. Jack shakes his head and pulls out his mobile phone.

Under the tabletop, out of sight from her daughter and husband, Martha grapples at her midriff. A throb of pain. She grimaces as her sweet, perplexed Allison fidgets. The turning of inquisitive cogs in her daughter's mind is almost audible.

"And they burn the coffin. With you inside?"

"Yes. But it's not really me... My spirit will've floated up to Heaven by then. It's just an empty vessel inside. My corpse."

Jack clears his throat and frowns at his wife, but Martha understands, as best she can, that her daughter's questioning, and the answers Martha must provide, bring her daughter reassurance and calm, even if sometimes, Allison's questions are peculiar. Even if Allison's obsessive queries about intravascular catheters and curtains and urns might raise alarm bells in other, more typical families.

If Martha had all the time in the world to respond to her daughter's string of enquiries about the tragic news Martha has just divulged, she would give her daughter that time.

But Martha does not have time. The cancer—which had initially presented as a heavy, relentless menstrual flow—now rampantly webs monstrous mutated wings throughout her womb.

"Can I ask another question?" With her head bowed and shoulders hunched, Allison's unblinking eyes drink in the very essence of the swathe of soft velvetine dress cuff she strokes over and over again with the pad of her thumb.

"Ask away." Martha crimps the fabric of the waistband of her own skirt in an attempt to massage away the pain as she responds to her daughter.

"After you die, you'll go to Heaven? And Jesus will be there on His crucifix, just like He is on my duvet cover, in the same pose, with that look of unending love in His pained eyes. And Daddy and I, when we die, we'll all be together again? The three of us, with Jesus?"

A waitress delivers a chocolate milkshake to their booth and Allison slides the glass close to her face to squint and examine the contents before taking a knife from the pot of cutlery at the side of the table. With the blade, she jabs at the shake. "No lumps, no lumps."

Jack places down his phone and restrains Allison's hand while she wriggles in her chair, shirking from her father's proximity. "Not now, Allison. Not here. There are no lumps, we checked when we ordered," he says. Allison's bottom lip quivers.

"Just leave her be." Martha bashes Jack's hand away. "Yes, darling. We'll all be together again, in Heaven. And it's a beautiful place. Jesus will be there, yes. With that look of eternal love in His pained eyes. Heaven is full of fluffy clouds and angels, and everything will be bright white and velvety soft. There'll be music, harps–the angels play those– and only happiness. No pain or tears."

"Just harps. No drums." *Clang.* Allison drops the knife. Jack picks it up and places it away from her as she rams her index fingers in her ears. "Just harps."

"Just harps," Martha says. "Just harps, darling. And Jesus."

Jack downs the last of his coffee then sighs before smiling with tight lips at a *tssking* elderly couple sitting at the table to his right.

After angling the bendy straw propped up in the thick shake towards her daughter's lips, and offering a few words of Grace, Martha pushes back a wisp of hair from Allison's cheek. Allison scowls.

"Sorry, Poppet. Didn't want you to get hair in your milkshake.

Drink up." Martha forces a smile and adjusts the floral scarf she has tied around her now-bald scalp. Three failed rounds of savage chemotherapy stole not only her autumn, but also the blonde waves Jack had once used to run his fingers through in moments of passion.

Allison settles, cups her small hands around the glass, and slurps.

"Do you have any more questions?" Martha asks.

Allison twirls her straw in the milkshake dregs in a repetitive figure-of-eight motion and sways slightly in her seat in time with her stirring and asks what Jesus looks like, and why, if Jesus can come back from the dead, can't her mother. Martha clutches her silver cross pendant and stumbles over her words as she tries to answer.

Jack shifts in his seat, side-eyes his wife. "You look tired," he says to her, his concern interrupted by his phone ringing. "One moment. Got to get this, and then we're going home. Allison, stop hounding your mother with ridiculous questions." He leaves his seat and steps outside to take his call.

Allison's eyes dart to the cafe door then back to the bottom of her empty glass. "One more question?"

"Sure, darling. Go ahead."

"Where is Heaven, exactly. Where in the world is Heaven?"

"I'm really not sure *where* exactly, darling," A knot of unfathomable sadness tightens in her heart. How will this small thing, this baby she grew in her now-rotting womb, cope when she's gone? She is special, so precious. Different to other children.

Words of diagnosis, descriptors of Allison, have been bandied about by various teachers and medical professionals over the years, but Jack disregards it all, tells his wife a diagnosis is not worth pursuing. "God will protect our daughter, and she's doing okay at school." And Martha agrees to some degree: what advantage will labelling a child provide? Jesus will guide them, Jesus will protect. But now this. Where is Jesus now? And where is Heaven? "I don't think anybody really knows, Sweetheart. Some people say Heaven is up in the clouds, above the clouds—"

Allison rocks in her seat. "But the stratosphere is seven to twenty kilometres away."

Martha pauses, tilts her head. Yes, she supposes, the clouds are a long way away, and she wants her daughter to believe she is close, will always be close, watching her, watching over her. With Jesus.

Jack returns, his cheeks flushed, a takeaway coffee in hand. "Come on, I need to get you two home. I've got to go back into work. If you want to know more about Heaven, I suggest you read your bible properly each evening during silent time, madam."

While Jack paces around the cafe, in whispers, Martha responds to her daughter's concerns, because she knows her daughter inside out. Knows Allison will only worry and rock and dwell on the distance of the stratosphere and the precise location of Heaven if Martha does not offer alternative information. "Heaven's not really anywhere, not in a literal sense, darling. The Bible tells us we all have a seat there though, by Jesus' throne, if we have faith... Some people say Heaven is all around us, within our hearts, scattered in nature, hidden in plain sight–but wherever it is, I'll always be watching you, watching over you. With Jesus. From wherever Heaven is. I promise."

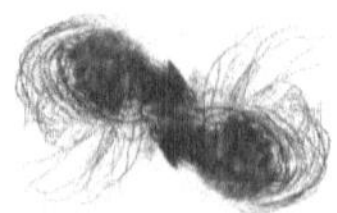

That night, Allison tosses aside her crucifixion duvet cover her parents had given her last Christmas, folds it up to hide its bold poly-cotton image. Screen-print Jesus, with each of His pained eyes, has been staring at her. She cannot sleep. Her heart races with anxiety, and her mind is spilling with questions. She creeps into bed with her mother. Jack will no doubt choose the sofa on his return from work, as he has done ever since he took on all the additional shifts, ever since his wife got ill. He tells Martha he does not want to wake her, she needs her sleep. She must sleep as much as she can, for as long as she can. He tells her this often. The sofa has become his make-shift bed.

Despite her pain, and even though her daughter is not one for hugs and physical affection, to watch her daughter sleep, to hear and see the rise and fall of each breath brings warmth to Martha's heart through the cold December night. And Martha does not mind, not really, when Allison wakes, full of nightmarish panic. Martha answers her daughter's midnight questions, regales biblical stories about the realm of Heaven in all its glory, reads verse from her Bible, and sings quietly to Allison of the Lord's love.

And before Allison drifts back to sleep, while rubbing the edge of her velvet comforter on her cheek and lips, she tells her mother she will build her a Heaven, a place for her to spend her afterlife. So she will know where it is. So they all will. Even if they can't see each other, or perhaps, even if they can see each other, but can't tell anyone for fear of getting into trouble, Allison will know Mummy is nearby.

With the empty shoebox in which her most recent pair of patent t-bar dolly shoes came delivered, with Mummy's help, Allison will build her mother a place to rest in peace, until Allison and Daddy can join her.

# December 5th

On returning from school, Allison, sulk-faced, heads straight for her mother's bedroom. It has not been a good day.

Martha has lain there all day, in bed, floating without ever leaving the dank sheets, drifting in and out of a most unheavenly cloud of Fentanyl-spiked delirium, the emotion of the day before and the short trip to the cafe having exhausted her.

"Miss Bastion will be Zooming after dinner, to chat about Allison's attitude in class today. Says she wants to speak with us both," Jack shouts up to Martha from the bottom of the stairs before returning to the kitchen to fix an evening meal for himself and his daughter. Martha tries to respond but no sound emits from her throat. She has felt out of control these last few months. Jack has attended parents' evenings and school trips and sports days without her, has been taking his daughter to and from school. Now, largely housebound, Martha feels useless. A burden. She has not even met Allison's Year Three teacher, Miss Bastion, before.

*Have the carers been in recently to change my pads, switch my opiate patch? They must have,* Martha thinks. But each day melds into the grey cloud of the one before; time itself, is near obsolete. Martha's nutrition is now prescription bottles of fortified beige-flavoured milk, most of which, she's unable to hold down. A near-full bottle rests on top of the Bible on her bedside table.

Martha sees the outline of Allison at her bedroom door. Yellow light from the late afternoon winter sun shines behind her daughter from the window on the landing and makes a ring of amber around her child's head: a Renaissance painting halo. Allison's hair is a mess; a blonde, tangled crown of thorns. Martha startles as she rouses, rubs her owlish eyes. Her daughter now stands over her, closer.

Allison holds in her hands an empty shoebox, a selection of pens and scissors and tapes. She places her collected items on the floor and perches on the side of her mother's bed. Martha pulls herself up to sitting position, withholding a gasp as her bad womb, razor-blade-weighted, and the burning in her now-cancerous spine and pelvis slow her down. She points at the glass of water on her bedside table. Allison passes her the glass.

"Thank you," Martha says, once the water has soothed her dry throat enough for her to be able to speak without rasping. "You found the shoe box? Well done, darling." Martha glances at the other items Allison has scattered on the bedroom carpet, then at the cream walls of the bedroom itself. *This bedroom is also a box of sorts,* Martha thinks, *a practice coffin with walls that feel like they're pressing in.*

Jack had said to her that morning, or perhaps the day before, that she should stay in bed now. He will bring her everything she needs. No need for her to get up, walk around, it is all too much for her now, at this stage. Once he had left, to take Allison to school, Martha had cried, realising the cafe may've been the last venture outside of the house she may ever take. He had, at least, moved the bed closer to the window a few weeks ago, so Martha has a view of the garden. Birds, grey sky, winter foliage.

"Mummy, do you have some fabric? To make the curtains to close you off for Heaven, when your body, your corpse, gets sent to the fire."

Martha swallows hard, rubs at the discomfort in her neck. Her daughter's literal interpretation of the cremation service she had asked about with such gusto yesterday in the cafe jabs at Martha's heart.

"Perhaps Daddy can help?"

"Daddy's cooking dinner and then going back into work, after the meeting with my teacher," Allison says. Jack has been working late, working early, is worried about finances. "He hasn't time for crafting. Has to keep a roof over our heads." Martha sighs. Her daughter hears everything, takes everything in. Martha wishes Jack would spend more time with his child, with her, despite the poor company she fears she now is.

Martha gestures at the pile of head-scarves draped over her dressing table mirror, gifts from old work colleagues she may never see again. "Take your pick," she says.

"No, I've got cotton-wool for the clouds. And tin foil for the angels." Allison points to each item she has gathered from the house as she explains. "I really need white velvet for the curtains."

"Of course, velvet. Well, I suppose we could use your old Christening blanket." Martha directs her daughter to a drawer to retrieve the blanket and together, using the inner card tube from the roll of foil and a needle and thread, they fashion a pair of functioning curtains, theatrical drapes, to decorate the front of the upturned shoebox. A string of paper dolls, decorated in foil, in glitter, and a bed of cotton-ball clouds fill the shoebox Heaven. The girl busies herself as Martha tries to contain her pain, until Jack calls Allison downstairs for supper.

"Can we keep it in here, Mummy? So you can look at it? Look after it, until you need it?" Allison carefully lifts her creation and places it on her mother's dressing table.

"Of course, darling. It's wonderful. It truly is."

"Wake up, Martha, Liz is on the line." Jack is in the bedroom. With one hand, he squeezes Martha's shoulder, and with the other, he carries his opened laptop. Martha stirs, moans, then draws herself slowly to a seated position.

"Who's Liz?" Despite fuzzy thoughts, she eventually recalls the meeting Jack had mentioned earlier. "Miss Bastion?"

"Yes, Liz, Lizzy." Jack preens his hair in the bedroom mirror then sits on the chair beside the bed and places the laptop between them. "She's calling now." Martha flusters. She feels in no state to meet teachers or be present in meetings, but her daughter is her priority. A mother's love is unending. While she can still participate in her child's life, she knows she must.

Before Jack connects to the incoming call, Allison is at his side, her mouth covered with bolognese sauce. "I don't like Miss Bastion," she says. "She's not Christian and she has a squealy voice. She laughs like a horrible piglet. And she laughs at me a lot. I hate her."

"Go to your room," Jack says. Martha feels her daughter's anguish in her chest, but is too weak to counter her husband's harsh tongue. Or offer emotional support. She will make it up to her daughter, must do, in some way, tomorrow. She will sing to her, talk of Heaven again, give her quality time while she can. Allison slopes off, her bedroom door banging in her wake as Jack clicks 'connect'.

From the screen, a young brunette smiles with just her mouth. Heavy black lashes. *Too much make-up. Prim,* Martha thinks. *Cold.*

"Hello Mrs. Newbury. Thank you for meeting with me. I'm Miss Bastion, Allison's teacher. I'm so sorry to hear you're unwell—"

Martha forces a smile in return but can think of nothing more to say than a simple, "Hello, please, call me Martha," in response. Martha can't help but agree with her daughter—this sharp-looking woman does have a grating tone.

"I wanted to speak to you directly because I'm concerned about Allison and some of her ... schoolwork. In particular, her current art project."

"Go on," Martha replies. She tries to summon strength for what she feels may be the commencement of battle. Allison has frequently disliked other classmates before, often preferring to work alone, to stay in and read rather than charge around in the playground at break, but she has never *disliked* a teacher before, never *hated* anyone.

"I've already chatted with Jack about this. At length. He said he'd handle it, but considering the nature of your situation and the discussions you've been having with Allison, my line manager insisted I speak with you both. In our art session this week—woodwork—we gave our pupils a chance to design and create something. Jewellery boxes or nick-nack pots, you know, to be given as a gift to someone for Christmas. And, well ... Jack mentioned you've Allison embroiled in some sort of, quite frankly, odd project at home—which might explain why she's constructed this."

Miss Bastion holds up in the palm of her hand a small balsawood coffin. Six small nails have been hammered into each side. A loose-fitting lid rests on top. Jack shakes his head and tuts. "Quite," the teacher responds.

"I don't know what to say," says Martha. "It's really quite well built, from what I can see."

"It's a bloody coffin, Martha," says Jack.

Miss Bastion clears her throat and straightens in her seat. "We're concerned for Allison's mental health. Our safeguarding lead would like to meet with her this week, with your consent."

"I'm not sure why this is a problem. I'm sorry if it's caused alarm but it's really just Allison's way of expressing herself. She's ... special—"

Jack snatches up the laptop and apologies profusely to Miss Bastion as he carries the face on the screen out of the room. "It's just Allison's way of processing what's happening to me," Martha calls out as Jack storms downstairs.

Martha reaches for her tablets. "Am I in trouble, Mummy?" Allison is, again, at her mother's side.

"No, dear, no," Martha wipes her eyes with her nightie sleeve. "No, not at all. I understand. Really, I do."

"It's for you. The coffin. For our Heaven in the shoebox."

"I figured it might be. You've done nothing wrong, darling."

"I don't like Miss Bastion, Mummy."

Martha swallows three pills, grimacing as pain ricochets down her oesophagus. "Do you want to sleep here tonight, darling. With me?"

Instead of answering yes, Allison stares out to the garden. "What happens to animals when they die, Mummy? Do animals go to Heaven. Will Skippy be there? To meet you?" Skippy had been the old ginger tom Martha'd brought home from the rescue centre a few years ago. "Did it hurt when Skippy died? How did he die, out in the garden, under the holly bush?" So many questions. But Martha knows this is her daughter's way of saying *yes, yes Mummy, I feel safer here with you than alone in my room.*

"Skippy had felt unwell and wandered into the garden, to be amongst nature." That is how creatures die. Return to the earth. He found his peace out there, amongst the shelter of foliage. "No, it hadn't hurt. For an animal, to die is just to fall asleep and not wake up," she tells her daughter.

In truth, a neighbour had found Skippy at the side of the road, the poor cat's hips smashed to smithereens, his orange fur drenched with clashing vermillion. Kindly Mr. Rogers from Number Four had taken Skippy's body, had cleaned Skippy off, had clicked the cat's displaced joints into a shape to make him look more at peace then placed Skippy under the holly bush in Martha's garden. Martha, Allison and Jack had been out when it had happened.

"I'm sure cats also go to Heaven," Martha whispers. Allison strokes her chin with a strip of velvet fabric, a remnant from the shoebox curtains.

"And did Skippy get burned, too? In a coffin?"

"No, we buried him out there, under the holly bush. His soul took … a different route."

"I did a good job, didn't I? Making you a place to stay when you die. Building you Heaven."

"Yes darling. The best. It's perfect. It really is."

Later, Allison falls asleep, curled on the edge of her mother's bed. And as her medication kicks in, Martha recites the Lord's Prayer until she drifts off too, and returns to that liminal place far, far from Heaven, and her dreams play out her ending again.

# December 24ᵗʰ

"Not much point," Jack says to his daughter. "Mummy won't appreciate anything, she's too unwell now, and the roads are blanketed in snow." Allison has asked Jack to take her into town to purchase something to give to her mother tomorrow, for Christmas. From the constraints of her bed, Martha hears them arguing and weeps. Plumbed in to pain-relief drips and waste bags, despite being largely bed bound, she still has all of her senses. *Hearing is the last sense to go.* The nurse who visits four times a day to add morphine to Martha's driver, to change urinary bags and offer sips of ice cream and water from a spoon, had told Jack this in the hallway earlier in the week. Allison insists, screams, and demands her father takes her to Debenhams, so he grabs coats and keys and takes her out.

From her bed, Martha desperately scans her prison cell. *Where has my Bible gone?* Jack has moved things around, cleared out most of her clothes. The shoebox Heaven now sits in Allison's bedroom. Jack said it gave him the creeps. In its place, on Martha's dressing table, boxes of medical equipment are stacked. Medication, needles, catheters, bleed-out kits. The nurse had also informed Jack that Martha will most likely go by 'mass haemorrhage'. *Her tumours are so large, they're pressing, pushing against major veins and arteries.* Martha had heard that too, all of that. She has also witnessed her finishing a thousand times before, playing out backwards and forwards in her head at night, her insightful 'gift' from God. An explosion of cancer-riddled tissue. A lagoon of opiate-wet blood. But her final moments are in God's hands now, and through the pain, through the torture of muddled thoughts, she gropes for her cross necklace, feels its silver between her fingertips, and prays. *God, Jesus, guide me, protect me,* she asks.

But today, trapped between four ever-looming walls and trapped within an emaciated body full of progressive malady, Martha is fed up of dying, and equally fed up of living.

She looks out of her bedroom window. How the velvety blanket of snow shimmers on her lawn. Crisp and clear in the last of the afternoon light. Bright red holly berries pop through the white. The sun is setting.

*Jack and Allison will be home soon,* she thinks. *This is the last opportunity I will get, to try and get up, to walk, to breathe in fresh air and be amongst nature.*

In a wave of rare energy, adrenaline-fuelled perhaps, Martha pulls free the needle plumbed into her arm, yanks out the catheter from beneath her night dress, yelps at the pain of both, but needs to seize this chance. The ice-crunch of snow underfoot, to walk amongst the nearest nature she can find, these are sensations she desires. Easing herself out of bed, she steadies herself with frail hands, and makes her way slowly out of the cage her bedroom has become.

Death will hurt, this she has accepted, but death will bring her life again, an eternal life with Jesus. Soon, she'll find Heaven.

But before she passes, she wants to make a gift for her daughter. After all, her daughter has made something for her: the string of shining angels, cotton wool clouds, velvet Committal curtains, the coffin which now forms centrepiece in the shoebox Heaven. Martha wants to wake on Christmas morning and be able to tell her daughter she has a gift for her child, has created something, a contribution to Allison's art project.

*I must go to the garden and gather holly, ivy, maybe a clip of mistletoe from under the apple tree, and fasten it all together. A decorative wreath. I'll place it by the shoebox, a winter bouquet to crown my daughter's creation with,* she thinks.

She moves carefully down the stairs, gripping the bannister tightly, and opens the front door. The chilled air is a welcome slap to the face, the crisp white lawn, an old friend. She steps out barefoot onto the snow. This is how it happens, and she has known so since she first became ill. God has shown her how it ends, in dreams, in premonitions.

Pain rips up in her groin as she stumbles towards the holly bush beneath which Skippy's bones lay buried. With each step, agony jabs, throbs, grows, until something red within her bursts out hard. Her arms drag down through the holly bush, scraping her thin flesh as she collapses. She lands on the snow-topped grass, curls there, writhing, and bleeding out. A balloon of widening crimson spreads around her hips as she slips out of consciousness. It is as if the white earth itself bleeds red this Christmas Eve.

And this is how Jack and Allison find her a moment later, her body still warm, but her brain unconscious. With shaking hands and heart in throat and his daughter rocking at his side, there, in the garden, surrounded by frosted nature, on bent knee, all Wise Man at a manger, Jack discovers his wife still has a weak pulse.

Jack and Allison follow Martha into the hospital as she is blue-lighted in. They wait for her in the waiting room. Fluids are pumped in and sutures are attempted, but it is too late. Martha is too ill. She passes at midnight.

## Christmas Day

Allison wails. Jack does not. He drives his daughter home in the early hours of the morning, his wife's body still warm on the hospital gurney. Dead there, her body lies. Dead, yet still riddled with energetic processes, as cells and tissues and organs wind down.

Father and daughter walk up the path to their house, passing the blackened lagoon on the lawn, which, at dusk, had been as bright red as a robin's breast.

Did Jesus bleed like that on The Cross? Is there no chance at all Mother will resurrect? How long will it take her soul to reach Heaven? Allison asks many questions. Jack ignores them all. He raises his voice and speaks to her only once: "Stop asking questions. Go to your room." He needs time to think, to make some calls. Allison does as she's told, and sits awake all night, alone in the dark, on top of her crucifixion duvet cover with her a Bible and a teddy placed strategically over Jesus's roving eyes. There, Allison rocks, flicking open and closed the velvet curtains of her shoebox Heaven which rests on a small table by the side of her bed.

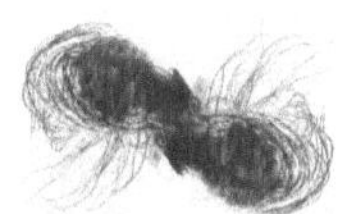

Martha's emptied corpse lies under a sheet at the hospital mortuary now. But there is something of her still present. She feels this. Or whatever this is that is left of her does. Her presence, her cognizance perhaps, retains a weak connection to this world. Is it a longing? An all-consuming urge to be close once more to her daughter? She finds her thoughts amidst the particles of the air in the mortuary hallway, as if part of her essence remains there, between the spaces in the atoms, inside of holes within holes. *Is this my soul?* she wonders. She can feel no physicality, cannot touch or move the objects she senses around her. But she still sees, still hears, has become some transient form of energy; an energy which will oscillate for an eternity, backwards and forwards, as the universe expands and contracts, all in some dimension divorced from time.

Light matter becomes dark energy, and then light again, and then, both at the same time, and then neither at all. Martha, or the energy that conformed into her shape and powered her predetermined Will, has always rattled forwards and backwards, here and there. She has always and will always witness the same infinite narrative unique to her as she pans out in all linear directions. Martha has seen and heard all of this, her life and death, before, forgetting it at her point of singularity, then revisiting it as consciousness expands in bodied form, again and again. And so she will continue to, like a videotape jammed in its slot, lurching between play and rewind, until the electrical supply fails, until all the energy in everything. all matter and antimatter, is composed of dissipates entirely.

Martha, or her esoteric imprint, sails over a quiet road in the dead of night, is in a field, by a meadow, part of the air, on a bird's wing, throughout an oak canopy, amongst the leaves of a holly bush beneath which her discharged blood has frozen and the bones of an old family pet rot, and then, Martha is inside of her home.

She drifts up the staircase, drawn on by a sound—the nurses, correct; hearing is the last sense to fade. Pulled onwards, outwards. Her awareness entwines with her daughter's sobs. Martha, or whatever this is that remains of Martha, senses her daughter, perched there on the edge of her bed, sometime in the early morning of Christmas Day. Her daughter rocks gently, then faster, while opening and closing miniature velvet curtains. Her daughter lifts the lid of the sparrow-sized coffin which sits on a bed of cotton-wool clouds, then closes it again, as if waiting, waiting, for a sign.

But there is no sign. There are no ghosts, Holy or otherwise, and there is no Heaven or God, and as Allison realises this, her faith shatters like punched glass. The young girl screams in silence from the edge of her bed and hurls her Heaven and all its contents across the room.

Dribs and drabs of Martha, or the last of her earthly sensations, linger in Allison's room, the staircase, the downstairs of the house, and over the balloon of red-black which sinks like ink into an otherwise white lawn. The last thing What Is Left Of Martha is aware of, before she repeats her existence in rewind, and then forwards, and then backwards again, until her essence becomes nothingness and returns to the Big Sleep, before her contact with our world thins, becomes puckered with holes, threadlike, snaps completely, is the sound of a knock at the door, the squeal of a high-pitched voice, the swoosh of bare feet on deep-pile carpet, the clunk of her husband opening the door and letting the squeal-voiced lady in, the wail of her daughter crying and rocking on the floor of her bedroom as she opens and closes the curtains of a broken Heaven as if caught up in a loop of her own, and then, from the living room, the sound of Jack and Miss Bastion fucking.

# To the Bone

by David-Jack Fletcher

It was in his shirt, scurrying around. Scratching at him, exploring his skin with its tiny feet. Bryan swatted at his back in the places he could reach, shuffling his shoulders around as his hand wound behind him, slapping at the creature to no avail.

The creature—an ant—had lodged its attack during his sleep. Those precious few hours where his mind ceased to exist, when he could recharge, ready for the next day. It felt purposeful, like the creature had climbed into his bed just to walk all over him. Wiping its feelers all over him. He wouldn't have called it a phobia, but when anyone showed him pictures of bugs—spiders, scorpions, bees, grasshoppers, ants—he had to turn away. He couldn't oblige their interest, and would grimace with a tight smile as he excused himself from the conversation.

Bryan jerked around, rubbed his back against the wall in the dark room, cursing the tiny thing. It moved so fast, like it knew his next move. Ants were always like that, though. Dodging boots and drops of water with expert ease.

*Not tonight*, Bryan thought, and raced for the ensuite shower. Flicking the light on, he shimmied out of his jocks and pulled at the shower door. Twisting the tap to hot—*I'll burn the mother fucker*—he stood under the water until he saw the tiny black creature circling at his feet.

The hot water coursing over him was refreshing, relieving the itch from the ant's feet, feelers, cock—*Do they even have cocks?*—whatever against his skin. As the ant circled once more, he pushed at it with his foot, directing it to the slits in the drain.

Just like that, the ant was no more.

Turning off the tap, his body drenched, Bryan reached for his towel. Dabbing the fabric at his eyes, and wiping at his midsection, he returned to bed, dumping the towel on the floor.

With a heavy sigh and a yawn, he rolled onto his side and closed his eyes.

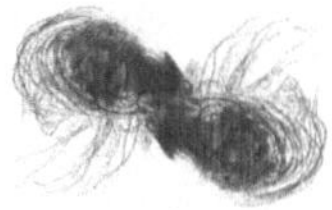

It felt like the morning sun was giving him the middle finger as it streamed through the blinds. An intense heat burned at him, the yellow light filtering into his eyes, and he pulled the duvet over him.

*Go to work.*

The voice in his head was always there, but for once it wasn't saying nasty things. The usual rantings of *you're worthless, you're disgusting, you're nothing, you're a fucking piece of shit* were absent today. So far. Instead, just his rational brain reminding him that he needed to get up and get his sorry ass to work.

Rolling out of bed, he almost tripped on his towel from the night before, and grabbed hold of his nightstand to steady himself. He shivered at the memory of the ant, invading his private space. Invading his bed, the worst sin of all. Scooping his towel with one hand, he headed to the shower again—the previous night did not involve soap, which he *tsk tsk*ed himself for now.

After a lengthy shower, scrubbing at all the parts the ant had stepped on, Bryan felt ready for the day. A pressure building behind his eyes told him the voices were on the way, and that his medication was due sooner rather than later.

As he stepped out of the ensuite and pulled on fresh underwear, Bryan paused.

*It's back.* He kneeled at the wall, reached for his glasses on the nightstand, and slid them into place. *Another one.* He gulped as he watched it crawl in and out of the crack in the wall. The crack, less than a millimeter wide, had let the creature in.

Swallowing again, he stood. Got dressed, his eyes peeled to the ant the entire time, and considered his options. He knew if he called an exterminator about a single ant or two, crying infestation, they'd laugh at him—again. He knew if he called a friend or a neighbor, they'd hang up at the sheer ridiculousness of the situation.

*It's never just one. Same as fucking cockroaches.*

Unclicking the lock on the back door, he headed outside. Right there, by his bedroom window, a nest. Thousands of the things burrowing into the dirt like they paid rent there. Hollowing out his backyard, making tunnels and destroying the very land he walked on.

A few stray ants had found a crack in the brickwork; they must have burrowed through the cement to get to him in his room.

Bryan breathed hard at the idea these ants thought they could just do whatever they wanted. In his yard. To his land. To his house. He knew, though, that this was how his brain was when he hadn't taken his pills. It was a truth he'd had to live with for the longest time—the voices in his head didn't just despise him, they took issue with the whole world.

"I'm going to take my pills," he said in the direction of the ants, "and then I'm coming back to deal with you lot."

The verbal confirmation was something his psychiatrist had made him do, a few years earlier. The habit had stuck. Say what you're doing, make your *real* thoughts *real*. It sometimes helped drown out the *you're fucking worthless, Bryan, you're fucking worthless, BRYAN, fuckingworthlessfuckingWORTHlessFUCKINGWORTHLESS.*

He could feel them coming, his forehead was burning and aching. Sometimes his ears itched, too, and he knew it was a physical manifestation of his mental state. He rushed to the kitchen, where he kept his medley of medications, popped the caps on what he needed and threw them down his throat. He'd emptied one of the bottles, made a mental note to fill the prescription on his way home from work.

Swallowing hard, he reached for the kitchen tap and put his mouth under the stream of cold water. It would take a few minutes for his mind to settle, but in the meantime, all he thought about—to focus on anything but his infinite worthlessness—was the anthill. Hill, nest, tower. Whatever it was called, it was going down.

He stomped back to the yard, grabbed the hose, and turned it on. Aiming right at the heart of the nest, he watched water drown the ants into nothingness, their tiny bodies carried in a stream of good ol' $H_2O$. Corpse after corpse shrunk up into beady black balls under the power of the water, others fleeing for their worthless little lives. Bryan smiled, stepping closer to the destruction, intent on sticking the hose nozzle into the mouth of the nest. To make sure those tunnels were flooded out. A trail of ants scrambled away, and Bryan made a note to get them after he'd destroyed this nest. He didn't want any survivors.

An ant stood at the mouth, the last defender of a ruined kingdom. He sprayed it with the water, watched it careen away like a swatted fly. Splatted against the wall of his house.

He smiled again.

Kneeling in the wet destruction, he peered into the nest. Just inside, an ant larger than the others, watched him. And he knew. The queen. He was about to kill the fucking queen. It filled him a great sense of purpose, though somewhere inside him, he also knew his pills hadn't kicked in yet. That the sense of purpose would flatten into a feeling of even satisfaction.

"Goodbye, my queen," he said, and turned the nozzle downward.

He left it there for a few minutes, to be sure he flooded the whole nest. As he finished watering and wound the hose around the tap, he remembered the stray ant trail, the survivors. Searching the house, the garden, the crack that had started it all, he saw nothing.

*Better make sure I don't find you.*

Suddenly, he felt less than impressed with his behavior. Felt an evenness that meant he was ready to greet the world. The voices were in check, for now, stowed deep in his consciousness for another twenty-four hours. Exhaling slowly, he was ready to leave for work.

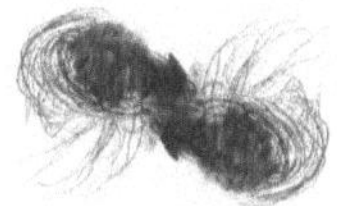

"I'm so sorry, we're out of these tablets," the pharmacist said, frowning at Bryan over the counter.

He stared back at her. "What do you mean? You can't be out, you're a pharmacy."

"You could try another pharmacy?" The pharmacist offered.

"Everything is shutting," Bryan muttered, "you know that."

The pharmacist cleared her throat, stepped around the counter, and rested a hand on Bryan's shoulder. He shuddered at the touch and reminded himself he didn't hate her, he didn't want to stab her eyes out or rip the lips from her face and make her eat them. That was the voices in his head, nothing more.

"I know how important this medication is for you," she said, her voice low and soft. She looked him in the eyes as she spoke, the gaze pleading and apologetic. "I can put a rush order in for overnight delivery, but that's the best I can do."

"But..." Bryan looked away, the eye contact making his heart hammer. "I'm prone to hallucinations. I... The voices are..."

"Should I call the after-hours psychiatrist? They might be able to arrange an overnight stay in the...uh...the *ward* until we can get your prescription?"

Straightening, Bryan shook his head, and shrugged away from the pharmacist.

*WORTHLESS WORTHLESS WORTHLESSWORTHLESS-WORTHLESSWORTH—*

"Bryan?" she asked.

"I'll be fine." He started to walk away, then stopped. He didn't feel it coming this time, couldn't stop it. He opened his mouth. "Can I please come back please first thing in the morning please and get my pills please because I think by the time morning comes I'm going to really, really, really need them is that okay please?" He could hear himself, blinked away a frightened tear, and continued to avoid the pharmacist's pitiful glance.

*FUCKING WORTHLESS.*

"They'll be here first thing, I promise." She tried to touch his shoulder again, to reassure him, but he moved away. "Are you sure I can't call someone?"

Breathing hard, Bryan walked out of there as fast as he could, ignoring the rattling, raving voices screaming at him.

By the time he got through his front door and had thrown open every cupboard in a search for a spare pill and collapsed on the lounge, Bryan was ready to rip someone's throat out. The pharmacist would be ideal, but his rational brain throbbed away in there somewhere.

*Sit down and breathe. Make your* real *thoughts* real.

He tried, reciting every U.S. state in alphabetical order, and every president in order of power. He even recited lyrics to old songs he'd heard on the radio. Liam Lynch's *My United States of Whatever* wasn't really the best choice, but it was all he had in that moment. In a way, the song was about power. It was about doing what *you* wanted to do. It was about being secure enough in yourself to follow your wants and needs.

"I went down to the beach and saw Kiki and she was like ewwww—" His wandering eyes caught sight of the things as he tried to remember the rest of the lyric.

Ants.

*Hundreds* of ants.

Crawling up the walls in the living room.

He jumped from the lounge, wiped sweat from his face, and stared at the invading ants. As he stared at them, the voices screaming his worthlessness in his brain, he noticed something strange. The ants weren't just crawling up the walls. They were in a series of straight lines.

Ordered.

Controlled.

"Nope," Bryan said to himself, and frowned. "This isn't real."

The hallucinations didn't usually start so fast, the pills were supposed to work for an even 24 hours. Yet, here the ants were, taking advantage of his earlier anxieties by appearing to walk in straight lines. His brain really was a cunt.

He breathed deep, sucked in air hard, squeezed his eyes shut.

Released.

Opened his eyes.

"Fuck."

Still there. Scurrying up the walls.

Squeezed his eyes harder, until he saw red and the voices moaned in the pleasure of his pain.

Opened.

Still there.

"You aren't fucking real!" His screams were a whisper compared to the ones in his mind. Hounding him, goading him to touch the ants, to lick the ants, to *FUCKING DO SOMETHING YOU WORTHLESS PIECE OF SHIT!*

Squeezed again, his eyeballs aching at the pressure. His head was heavy, the way it always got when the voices were too loud and grew in number. He'd learned long ago to stop counting them, and he wasn't game enough to try now. He just knew they were in there, eroding his sense of self.

"You. Are. Not. Real."

Opened.

The ants were gone.

"Thank Christ," he whispered through a heavy sigh, and collapsed back onto the lounge. *I can do this. I can beat the voices until morning. This is my United States...* Checking his watch, he saw it was only 6:15 p.m. "Fuck."

*Fuck. Fuck. Fuck fuck fuck FUCK—*

"Stop it," he begged, and held his ears.

For a few seconds, the voices were gone. It had never been that easy before to silence them. A win was a win, and as he raced to the kitchen to swallow two sleeping pills, Bryan couldn't help but wonder if the key to his victory was that stupid song—*Cause this is my United States of whatever!* He sang it again as he put the pills away, intent on going straight to bed.

He'd get his pills in the morning, the best thing to do was to sleep through the torture.

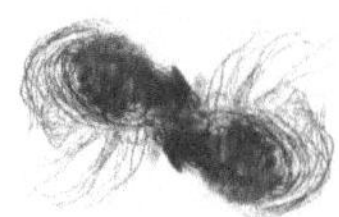

It wasn't the howling wind that woke him, or the torrent of rain striking the earth. He normally loved storms in the middle of the night, but this night was different.

It was the itch that woke him. All over him, under his skin, inside him.

Bryan flung the covers off him and scratched hard. His red skin indicated he'd been scratching in his sleep, too. He'd scratched until his forearm was bleeding, and Bryan looked away. Bugs and blood were his two kryptonites. He didn't have time to let the blood sink into the voices in his mind, feeding them again with his pain. He had to get to the pharmacy, but it wouldn't open for hours.

Sleeping pills would have to do, but the ones he'd already taken hadn't lasted. The thought of having to stay awake made his chest tight, and he scratched at his arm again.

As he slithered to the edge of the bed, his feet touching the carpet, Bryan's head felt heavier than a few hours before. Groggy, he rubbed at his eyes. The movement of lifting his arm, the sense of his fingers across his face, was uncomfortable. A slight pain in his upper arm and shoulder. His neck was stiff, and the itch ran down his nape like sweat.

Even so, he enjoyed the quietness of the room. Of his head. Some mornings were like that, when the voices were still asleep and he could shower in peace. This was *his* time. His world. "Cause this is my United States..." he mumbled.

*Shower,* he thought, and it was his own voice that had said it. He sometimes did that, have a shower in the middle of the night. Sometimes it calmed him, but as he scratched more at his arm—the other one now—his skin felt wet already.

Smiling, Bryan stood.

His left leg was dead, and he collapsed at the knee. Grabbed his nightstand to steady himself. He shook his leg to wake it, the pins and needles intensifying with each outward kick. His neck itched more and more and his upper arm began to seize.

Bryan clutched the nightstand, trying to wake his leg, to wait out the pain shooting in his arm. He started to breathe in short, focused bursts.

*In, two, three, four... Out, two, three, four...*

And he coughed.

Just a little cough, clearing something in his chest.

Another cough.

He felt it. Squirming around, scratching at his throat. He hocked a few times, pooled some saliva in the back of his throat, and spat whatever it was onto his nightstand.

An ant.

"What the hell?" Bryan coughed again.

It struggled in his spit, upturned on its back. Little legs running a mile an hour, but going nowhere. With his sore arm, the pain throbbing now and heading to his elbow, Bryan raised a hand. Slapped the nightstand hard with his palm.

He coughed again, spat into his hand. No ants. No nothing. Just dirty, wet saliva.

*...worthless...*

The voices were waking. Bryan should have been in the shower already, but as he tried to take a step, the pins and needles made him feel as though he were walking without limbs. Letting go of the nightstand, Bryan steadied himself, his feet throbbing now. His hands and fingers trembling with pins and needles and an itch he couldn't scratch.

*Worthless.*

"I am not..." Bryan muttered, but he didn't believe it. Never believed it. "This is my United States... This is my... This is..." The song wasn't helping. Not with the itch, not with the sense of worthlessness.

Another step, the pins and needles reverberating up his leg. Throbbed at his knee.

Another step.

Bryan's shoulders were aching now, the itch in his neck traveling down through his entire body.

Another step.

His chest was heavy.

"This is my... *Whatever.*"

Step.

Cough.

Scratching in his mouth again. A tickle. Moving. He knew it was an ant. Maybe more than one. And he wanted to spew. He wanted the creature out of him. The pins and needles made it hard to move, and the pain in his shoulders was traveling down, down, down into his abdomen.

He stepped again, lost his balance. Tipping down, he grabbed for something to hold onto. His fingers didn't work. Falling face-first to the floor, Bryan smacked hard against the tiles of his ensuite. His cheekbone throbbed under the skin, and he heard a slight crack.

"What is happening?" he asked, eyes wide.

*Worthless. FUCKING worthless.*

"No. I am not!" He tried the song again, tried to take back control. Take back his power. "...of whatever..." Bryan shed a tear.

Tried to move. The itch was all through him now, the pins and needles prickling away at him until his whole body was numb.

As he lay on the tiles, the itch crawling through his body, voices yelling at him, Bryan could do nothing but cough. It was as though his chest smacking against the floor had dislodged something. He could feel it now.

Feel *them*.

He knew, without seeing more, that his body was full of ants.

*It's not—*

*WORTHLESS PIECE OF SHIT!*

*—pins and needles.*

The familiar scratch at the back of his throat was working its way up his esophagus now, and he pictured the ants on the wall, only hours earlier. The way they marched in lines of single file. The way they were doing now, inside him.

In his legs.

In his arms.

In his neck.

He felt them everywhere and couldn't move. Could just cough and stare at the bathroom floor.

A flash ran across his eye. Just a blur at first. Another flash, slower. He blinked it away, felt the tiny feet on the skin around his eye. Running over his face.

Another one. Tickling at his eyeball.

Bryan blinked again, felt a pressure under his skin, behind his eye. Blinking once more, he felt the scampering of hundreds—thousands— of ants spilling from his eyes. Could only watch as the ants ran across his eyeballs. Felt them scurrying around his face, in his nose, out his ears, exploring his body like a nest.

"My United States...of whatever..."

He tried lifting his hand again, struggled to get it off the tiles, but he managed just enough to plant it face-down and push.

*WORTHLESS WORTHLESS.*

His chest came up, just a little, and he managed to grip the tiles with his other hand. The shower was just a few feet away, he only had to drag himself inside and flick on a tap. The ants would fucking drown.

The itch intensified, and his shoulders felt weak, his bones brittle.

He dragged himself, coughing and spluttering, and blinking away ants from his eyes. Pulling the shower door open, Bryan passed the threshold and reached up for the tap.

His fingers had just enough sensation to feel the metal of the tap, but only by a hair. Coughing again, he felt ants pour from his mouth, scratching at his lips.

He reached again, strained hard, his shoulder blades cracking and breaking. His arm fell to the floor with a dull smack and Bryan screamed from the pain and the anger and the fear.

*Told you. You're fucking worthless.*

The voices were awake now; they'd eaten his brain for breakfast and were ready for the day. They were right. He couldn't even reach the fucking tap. He was worthless. Even the ants knew it, taking his entire body for a ride.

With his other arm, Bryan pushed hard against the tiles, twisted himself into a sitting position, breathing through the never-ending coughing, and the growing pain throughout his body. It was like his bones were falling apart inside him.

"Help..." His voice was weak, his plea non-committal. *I don't deserve help.*

*YOU ARE FUCKING WOR—*

"I know," he said. "I know I am."

With that, he rested against the shower wall, the tap just above his head, and let his bones crumble under his skin. Through the blur of ants over his eyes, Bryan saw a line of the things exiting his body from a newly-formed hole at his left wrist. Like a dirt mound, made of his own skin and veins.

The ants came out of him, *bled* from him as though they were the only things keeping him alive. As they ran from him, he saw each one carried chunks of something, red and yellow. Spongy.

"Is that my...bone marrow?"

*YOU WILL LET US HAVE YOU.*

The voices were persistent. They'd won.

*We are not voices. I AM NOT A VOICE.*

Bryan stopped breathing, held back another cough as the ants continued streaming out of his wrists like black, gooey blood. With each passing second, he felt more and more empty, like his body was just a shell.

*I am the queen.*

"What..."

*I am the ant queen.*

"Why are you doing this?"

The voice in his head laughed. It echoed through him, and Bryan realized it wasn't in his mind. It was in his actual head. Lodged in there somewhere, an ant. The laughter stopped and the queen moved. He felt it, the pressure against his brain as she shuffled about in there.

"WHY???" Bryan screamed.

*You killed my family. We will now kill you. Because you are right, Bryan. You are fucking worthless.*

A single tear fell down his cheek, and Bryan felt ants shift out of its way.

His spine began to crack and crumble now, and Bryan felt his body deflate a little, his back sliding down the wall, a hollowed-out thing belonging to the ants.

"I'm sorry," Bryan mumbled through another tear. "I'm sorry."

*Humans have said this for millennia. Stomping on us. Destroying our homes. Killing us by the billions like we're nothing.*

"I didn't know..."

*Didn't know what?*

"I didn't know you were...so human."

The queen laughed again, it was as hollow as Bryan's body was becoming. *We are anything BUT human. Humans are the scourge of this planet.*

Bryan couldn't disagree. He wanted to, but he knew it was true. Humans had fucked the Earth, destroyed forests and the oceans. Bled the earth dry. Destroyed wildlife. Even ants. It was time to let them take it back.

*It is time,* the queen agreed. *But we can use you.*

"Use...me?" His throat was collapsing now, Bryan felt it was harder to breathe, harder to think.

*You will not be worthless.*

Bryan almost skipped down the street that morning.

He walked by the pharmacy, a brief thought entering his mind, before continuing on his way with a whistle.

"Excuse me!"

Bryan spun at the voice, a wide smile greeting the person. "Hello," he said.

"Your, uh,"—the pharmacist looked around, lowered her voice—"*pills* are in."

"Oh," Bryan replied, and grimaced. "Well, thank you. But we don't need them."

The pharmacist raised an eyebrow. "*We?*"

"I." Bryan smiled again. "*I* don't need them."

"But last night... I mean... You seemed..."

"It's fine," Bryan said, patting her on the arm. "I'm not worthless anymore." He left her to scratch her head and continued on his way. There was a lot to do, a lot to see. Many, many people to visit.

He was getting used to his new body, the way it moved, the way it felt with his new family burrowing through him. His bones were tunnels now that his marrow was all gone. His body, a nest. A beautiful nest for the generous queen, who had instructed the family to rebuild his body. To silence the voices.

Whistling again, Bryan looked up to the sky with fresh eyes. The sun was shining, the air was so still and clean. He stopped a few times to admire his neighbors' gardens and to search for signs of ant farms. Or beehives. Or wasps nests.

They were all equal under his queen's watchful eye.

# When the Moon Turns Red

## by Mark Towse

Maud's fingers tap at the cool glass of the bay window, her mouth opening and closing. George nods but has no intention of moving away from the flickering flames. A tumbler of bourbon in hand, he's still lost in thoughts of the farm's earlier times, nostalgically fuzzy highlights emerging from the usual smog of decades gone. Half-closing his eyes, he inhales, imagining the scent of wildflowers and perfume carrying on a summer breeze.

*Different people. Different times.*

Maud snaps her head towards him, glasses at the end of her nose.

"Yes, love," he says, unable to hear a single word. He takes another sip of bourbon, smiles, and nods, letting the memories play for as long as he can. Dementia has taken so much from him, but the little snippets withstanding the test of time, he hangs onto them for dear life. "Huh-huh," he says. By the shape of Maud's mouth and the redness of her cheeks, he knows she's bellowing his name, the intended harshness exploding in his mind like a disturbed murder of crows.

*George! George! George!*

*"What was that love?" he says, putting his bourbon down and groaning as he pushes from the couch. "A cup of tea?" By the time he turns up his hearing aid, the curtain has well and truly come down on his wistfulness.*

*"—anything like it, George. What is it?" She prods at the window again; her eyes screwed almost shut, every line on display. "It looks as though the moon is—"*

*"Bleeding." George wipes at his breath cloud. In the present, his skin prickles with a different excitement. "Come on; we'll have a better vantage from the porch."*

*"But it'll be freezing out there." Even the thought causes Maud to*

*shudder, a flare of goosebumps running up her arm. "I don't like it, George."*

*"Put that blanket over your clothes, love." George grabs his jacket from the rack and coils his fingers around the cold door handle. "When did you get so soft anyway?"*

*"Soft in the head to marry you." She grimaces as she stoops to collect the crocheted blanket—last year's special project that took her far longer than it should have. "What do you think it is, George?"*

*"Dunno, love. Nothing in the papers about it." He opens the door, the icy breeze immediately trespassing and stealing all the warmth. "Didn't see anything on t'internet either."*

*"Well, I don't like it. What if it's aliens?"*

George ducks his chin into his collar and steps onto the porch. "Don't worry, love. One taste of your cooking, and they'll be on their way back."

"Cheeky bastard."

"Always."

"I don't like it, George."

It looks even more impressive from the porch, the sight bristling the hairs on the back of George's neck. "Would you look at that?" he mutters. "Hurry up, Maud. Come over here." Not another property for miles to pollute the night, the fields in all directions carry the moon's sinister red tinge, as though the earth is bleeding. He steps forward, wrapping his bony fingers around the railing. "Would you look at that," he repeats.

Wrapped in swirls of brown and yellow, Maud tuts and follows. She coils her fingers tight around the walking stick, almost going ass-over-elbow as she squeezes between the couch and the coffee table. "I don't like it, George." She makes an about-turn at the doorway, going back for her phone and cursing under her breath. "I don't like it," she mutters again.

"Hurry up, Maud." Unable to tear his watery eyes away, George is mesmerised. "Bloody beautiful." And it is, hanging in the night sky like the world's rarest and finest jewel. "Maud, come on, it's one in a million."

"Oh my." She finally huddles up, peppering the air with quickly dissipating clouds of breath as she aims her phone at the sky. "I don't like it."

"You don't like it? You should have said something."

She gives him a nudge through the blanket. "I'm serious; it doesn't look right."

"Maybe you're right. Better get on the phone and let NASA know."

"Do you think?"

"Oh yeah, for sure." George digs his aching hands in his pockets as the cool breeze cuts across. "I can see it now: Maud Devlin, pensioner and amateur crocheter, saves the world after the big red moon falls into the blind spot of the world's most powerful telescopes." He clears his throat and, in the highest voice possible, says, "Well, I noticed something wasn't right. I said to our George that it might be little green men up to no good."

"Have a day off, you sarcastic sod!"

He leans across and kisses her on the forehead. "Besides, I think we replaced NASA on the speed dial with—Ow!" He winces, feeling his wife's fingers digging into his arm.

"Over there," his wife says, extending her right arm towards the barn.

"What? Where?"

"There!" She waves her arm, the heavy blanket pooling on the floor. "There, George! There!"

"What? I can't see a—" He squints, trying to put the moving object near the entrance gate into focus. "Is it one of the horses?"

"George, we don't have any horses. Bernie was the last, and he died over twenty effing years ago."

"Well, shit." It's his life now, his mind a poorly edited movie full of continuity errors and too many deleted scenes. Some days are better than others, but it scares the hell out of him. Still, he's grateful for the memories that do stick, the precious ones.

"What is it, George?" Maud says, huddling even closer. "I don't like it."

George leans forward, straining his eyes for a better look, the grip on his arm getting tighter still. "Not sure. One of the cows?"

"We don't have any cows either, you silly bastard." Maud shakes her head and offers a deep sigh. "It's got two legs, for Christ's sake. It's aliens; I bloody know it, George. Just like the documentary that we watched."

"That was a movie, Maud." He surprises himself with the recollection. "Body Grabbers or sommat."

"I'm scared."  She gives him a tug, almost taking him off balance. "George!"

"Just a minute." The chill of the air works through to his bones, spiking adrenaline. A cool breeze blows across the long grasses, making them resemble a fast-flowing river of blood. George squints, but his vision isn't what it used to be.

"I think it's human," Maud says, no relief in her voice. "George, there's someone on our property!"

George does his best to focus on the blurry figure, a blanket of fear and cold wrapping around him. He had a six-pack in the day. Arms like legs and a neck like a bull, what with all the farm work. But he was just a wrinkly shadow of his old self now, the thought of confrontation causing his balls to shrivel. "Hello?" he shouts. "Hello? Are you lost?"

Nothing.

Perhaps a hundred feet away, give or take, the human silhouette continues approaching. It moves sluggishly, head occasionally snapping left or right, one of its legs dragging behind. Trying to will the fog from his head, George tightens his grip on the railing, but pain bites, causing him to release. A knot develops in his stomach, further emphasising his vulnerability and frailty. Nothing much phased him in the old days; he could stay calm in all sorts of situations, but with a broken mind and riddled with arthritis, it's a different playing field these days. "We've got guns!" he yells.

"It's aliens, George; I know it."

"You said it was human a minute ago."

"Like that documentary."

"It was a bloody movie, Maud! I thought I was the one with dementia?"

"Zombies then."

"Fuck's sake."

"The red moon," she says in a quivering voice. "Not a coincidence. They've come for us, George."

"For what?"

"Information. To plug into our minds."

"Maud, I can't even remember what I had for breakfast." George does his best to stay calm for his wife's sake, but the chill is getting to his brittle bones. "I reckon it's just a straddler, someone looking for work."

"But it's after ten, George." Maud leans in further, her face taut and pale. "And it's been nearly thirty years since we hung a 'Help Wanted' sign on the gate."

"Jesus. Really?" The fields had been bustling with workers in those days, mostly drifters passing through looking to make beer and cigarette money. Over time, a shortage of labour and increasing cost of production meant they got to the bare bones, with only Maud's money and the inheritance from her sister keeping their heads above water. Now it was just acres and acres of uncultivated land that George couldn't bring himself to sell, afraid the last of his memories would go with it. "All those years," he mutters.

"Never mind that, George. What the hell do we do?"

"Let me think, Maud."

Huddled together, they watch the approaching silhouette, sometimes losing sight as it merges into the shadow of the treeline that splits the fields.

"George!"

"Okay, okay." The breeze blows across again, offering the slightest hint of something other than wildflowers and smoke. "Call the police," he finally says, shuddering as he glances at the moon. "Call the police," he repeats, louder for the sake of the approaching silhouette, and adding with gusto, "We've got guns!"

Maud's already fumbling at the keypad, clouds of mist spitting out faster than ever. She holds the phone to her right ear, her eyes widening. "George! There's another one," she cries. "Over there!"

George follows his wife's trembling bony finger, only to see another silhouette approaching from the west. "In the name of horseshit."

Maud shakes her head and tries again, punching the keys with urgency. "I can't get a signal," she croaks. "I can't get a signal, George!"

"What are you talking about?" George snatches at the phone, squinting at the blur of artificial light. He manages the numbers on the second try and holds the phone to his ear. "Not possible." But after thumbing the keys again, the skin around his skull tightens. "The police are on the way," he yells at the top of his voice. "Best leave now, and there'll be no trouble! We've got guns. Loads of the fuckers."

"George, they're still—" Maud's arm extends again, but in a new direction, only a rasp leaving her lips this time. "More."

"Jesus Christ!" Six of them now, approaching under the blood-red moon. "Get inside, Maud," he says. "WE'VE GOT GUNS! BIG FUCKERS! PUT A HOLE THE SIZE OF BARREL IN YER!" But as his mind swells with fog, he struggles to remember his own name. He waits for Maud at the door and swings it shut behind them. "Where do we keep the guns, Maud?" he says, working the bolts across and wincing as arthritis nags.

It all becomes too much for her, her tears splashing onto the wooden floor. Her shaking becomes more vigorous. "You sold them, George."

"What?"

"With the grandkids coming over sometimes, we agreed we'd get rid of 'em."

"Goddammit!" He presses his face against the bay window, hoping the bluff might have been enough. "Shit! Shit! Shit!"

"Are they still coming?"

"More of them."

"Oh God, George. What do they want?" Maud reaches for the couch, trying to stop the room from spinning. "George, what do they--"

"I DON'T FUCKING KNOW MAUD!"

Silence falls.

It's the first time he can remember raising his voice at her. Not that he can remember much. Regret is instant as he studies her pale face and quivering lips. "I'm sorry, petal. I'm so sorry."

"I'll get cash and jewellery," she croaks, planting her stick down. "It's probably drugs."

*Fuck!* George peers through the bay window to see the closest silhouette less than seventy feet away. Fear wraps around him and squeezes, something telling him they aren't coming for their worthless valuables. *What do you want?* He backs away towards the coffee table.

*What the fuck do you want?!* After dousing his dry throat with whisky, he shakes his head, still trying to dislodge the mist. "We're leaving," he yells, marching to the counter and grabbing a knife from the block. He slides his hand into his jacket pocket, relieved to find the keys to the truck. "Maud, we're leaving. Let's go!"

Maud emerges from the bedroom, a handful of cash and jewellery clenched in the bony fingers of her left hand, her face appearing even paler than before. Her wide eyes draw to the knife in George's hand. "Two more near the fruit trees out back." She places the handful of treasure against her chest, swallows hard, and tries to catch her breath.

"We'll be safe once we get to the truck," George says but remembers the one approaching down the driveway. *Run the fucker down if I have to.* He marches past her towards the laundry, keen to check if the coast is clear. "We can easily make—"

"George?"

He blinks hard. And again.

"George!"

He wipes his breath cloud from the window, tears forming in his eyes.

"George, what is it?"

The shadow of the house extends well beyond the truck, but there's no mistaking the silhouette of a bony figure sitting on the hood, baseball cap turned the wrong way around. "Fuuuuuuccccck!" George marches back into the living area, his grip tightening on the knife, pane flaring up his arm.

Maud sobs again, her body entering the initial stages of full-on convulsion. "We don't deserve this; we're good people."

George tosses the keys against the wall, almost throwing the knife after them. Vulnerable, weak, and confused, his head plays more scenes from the past but offers nothing helpful for the present. "The basement."

Maud drags an arm across her damp face. "What?"

He often went down there when Maud was sleeping. No distractions. Quiet. "Go, Maud. NOW! And take this."

"But my legs, George."

"Just take it steady. You'll be fine."

Maud refuses the knife. After several snivels, she lifts her stare back to her husband and tries to speak. "What do they want, George?"

"Please, love. I'll be down in a second."

"I won't go without you."

"I'll be straight down; I promise." He marches back towards the bay window. "Just going to make sure we're all locked up."

"I love you."

"I love you too."

Maud shakes her head as she begins backing away. She turns, groans, and reaches for the handle. A cold rush of air highlights her tears as she pushes the heavy door ajar. "Promise me, you'll come."

"I'm no hero, Maud." He swallows hard, surprised his legs still support him. "I'll be down shortly."

"We are going to be okay, aren't we?"

The glass is cool against his cheek as he surveys their land, silhouettes getting larger under the blood-red moon. He opens his mouth to respond to his wife's repeated plea for hope, but only a garbled croak emerges. His attention is elsewhere. In disbelief, he watches as, perhaps thirty feet from the bottom porch step where he planted begonias for his wife, a small patch of the earth begins lifting with almost mechanical precision. "Go, Maud. NOW!"

The click of the door follows her whimper.

Maud presses the switch, shuddering as a single bulb offers a dirty yellow hue against the concrete. She clutches the stick under her arm, her breaths shallow and rapid. Tentatively and painstakingly, she finds her footing on the narrow concrete stairs, hands brushing the cold stones on either side. Each step is a battle, searing pain riding through her bones. Since the accident, she hadn't set foot in the basement. "No more horses after that," George had insisted. It had broken his heart, too, when they had to say goodbye to Bernie. Always wanted the best for her. Always put her needs first. She'd tried lots of hobbies since, but none of them stuck.

*I don't like it.*

Biting at her lip, she continues her descent until, at the bottom of the steps, she lets her body rest against the coolness of the wall. Exhausted, riddled with pain, she lets out a shiver. She shouts her husband's name again and waits for a response that doesn't come.

*Come on, George. Come on!*

Her eyes scan the basement, taking in the stuffed boxes and shelves filled with items they'd likely never use. One of the large shelving units stands out, its position askew, scuff marks marring the otherwise pristine concrete. The panel behind it, too, is slightly out of place, prompting her to drive her stick down and take a step towards it.

George is at the window, eyes fixed on the earthy lid and the dark abyss it continues to unveil. He tries not to breathe and fog the glass, but that's easier said than done when the ground's opening. "Sweet Jesus." The lid looks like a perfect square, perhaps sixty-inch sides and seven inches thick. He shakes his head, blood pounding a beat.

"Can't be happening. Just can't."

Blood pounding in his ears, he remains glued to the window.

"Sweet Jesus. Oh, sweet Mary-Lou."

Angled towards the blood-red moon, the thick crust of earth stops moving.

Silence falls.

George exhales from the corner of his mouth, his eyes fixed on nature's trapdoor. Peripheral vision allows a blurry view of the advancing silhouettes, but there's a new act in town. His skin tightens as if trying to crush his bones. A cloud of mist emerges from the hole, a loud groan following.

"You've got to be fucking with me."

Every part of him wants to retreat, but he remains, watching the earth offer another smoky exhale, as though *breathing*. An accompanying deep groan feeds through the floorboards, vibrating up his bones. Afraid he'll miss something but terrified of what it might reveal, he wipes at the pane of glass.

Another groan. Another billowing stream of smoke.

A breeze wraps around the house, its moans and groans only adding to the heaviness in his chest. "Can't be happening. Can't be real." A shiver runs through him, making itself at home. Still, he stares into the darkness within, the fog in his head as thick as the clouds occasionally emerging from the earthy mouth.

*Ahhhhhhhhhhhhhhhhhhhh*

The breath is louder, more urgent.

The silhouettes are getting close, but George can't peel his eyes from the lid. Only as he sees something poke from the darkness does he begin to retreat. "No fucking way. No fucking way. No fucking—" The porch light flickers on, giving him an eyeful of the semi-skeletal hand that searches the ground in front. He opens his mouth, his throat offering a fizzy pop. "No. Uh-uh. No—" He gropes behind, his heart jumping in his mouth as the metal fire poker clatters to the ground. His fingers tighten around the knife's handle, but only to stop them from shaking.

*Ahhhhhhhhhhhhhhhhhhhhhh*

A semi-decomposed carcass begins dragging itself from the hole. Bony fingers claw small trenches in the red-tinted mud, dissecting the remaining begonias. The skull's eyeholes fix on George, deep and desolate. Threadbare straps of what looks like a dress hang loosely from shoulders that resemble post-barbeque leftovers. The moon continues bleeding, offering grey bones a tinge of pink.

"There just ain't no way," he mutters. "Ain't no way."

But although most of his days are spent confused and weary, George suddenly knows exactly what this is. His balls shrink into his chest, and his heart takes it up a notch.

"I'm sorry," he croaks. "I'm sorry."

The house creaks again, strained rasps from yesteryear carrying on the draught.

Offering another guttural moan, the skeleton emerges and unfolds. Eliminating any doubt in George's mind, bony fingers brush at a stained, tattered dress that should have rotted away many moons ago. The fog shifts, a memory playing with crystal clarity: *White sandals, the floral dress full of bright red flowers, and the summer breeze blowing wisps of hair back into her mouth.*

George begins to cry but would likely do it all over again, such were the devils in his ear at the time. And, oh, the rush it brought. "That wasn't me; I'm—I'm a different person now. A different person. I'm sorry, okay. I'm sorry!"

The skeletal figure approaches, finger raised towards him as the dirty dress and bedraggled hair catch on the breeze. Above, the moon appears even redder, as though about to burst with blood. "Different person," George croaks again but he knows the past has come for him. "Different times."

The seething rage would never let him be. Like a poker to the smouldering embers, the voices burned deep, making him do such terrible things. *Different person.* And oh, the temptation when they came looking for work on the farm. *Different times.* So young, so full of life, so goddamn gullible. No permit? That's fine; there's a place for you here. Young men and women—it didn't matter—they were there to quench hunger and help release the bile.

*George Devlin?*
*Stand-up guy. Always good for a laugh.*
*Heart of gold beneath the sarcasm.*
*Family man.*
*Loves his wife.*
*Never heard the guy even raise his voice.*
*Wouldn't hurt a fly.*
*Goddamn salt of the earth.*
"I'm sorry. I'm—"

It's at the window now, cheekbone to the glass, fingers tapping. Another skeletal figure follows closely behind—T-shirt hanging by a thread and dirty but intact jeans. George lost count of how many. Never sexual. But he did get off on the power, on the fear in their eyes, just like he expected his father did when the pubs closed. Truth be told, such ridicule only elevated the voices that were already in his head. And the thoughts that plagued him.

*Tap-tap.*

"You'll never amount to anything," his dad used to say. "Just like your useless whore of a mother."

And he was right; Maud's money bought the farm. She bankrolled them through the rough times. She made all the decisions and carried all the clout. He just wanted something for himself, his own little legacy, and the voices told him how to get it. It wasn't even about the killing for him, more about those precious moments before—when he was somebody, a rare moment of control reflecting in eyes full of fear.

*Tap-tap, tap-tap, tap-tap.*

Focussing on the figure at the window, he watches the jaw move up and down, the words on the wind colder than the cold. "When the moon turns red. When the moon turns red. When the—"

His stomach drops.

*When the moon turns red.*

In a sucker punch of clarity, he's back in the secret room in the basement, his hands around her neck, his face turned away to avoid her clawing nails. Echoing groans against the walls and the sound of shoes against the concrete provide the soundtrack.

*When*

*the*

*moon*

*turns*

*red*

Words that chilled to the bone, keeping his eyes open well past midnight. How could they have left him, he wondered? Dementia? His mind putting up barriers? Either way, his blood runs cold on their return. And as though a key to a locked door, her name falls back into his head. "Dawn," he mutters—his last victim.

A vivid scene flashes in his head—blood speckling her left eyelid and the repeated phrase leaving her almost blue lips: "When the moon turns red." Long after her breathing ceased, he could still hear the chant. *When the moon turns red. When the moon turn—*

*Tap-tap, tap-tap, tap-tap.*

Full of inexplicable fear, he'd buried her quickly. Yet even after smoothing the earth, the words continued to haunt him.

Tap-tap-tap.

"I'm sorry."

The breeze ramps up, carrying words into the house with even greater intent. "When the moon turns red. When the moon turns red. When the—"

"I'm sorry. I'm sorry. I'm sorry!"

It's why he stopped. He remembers now as if it was yesterday.

The nightmares. The times he woke up sweating, tangled in his sheets with those words in his ears. Sometimes, he would hear them carrying on the breeze when he worked the farm or sat on the porch. Sometimes, he heard them coming from his wife's mouth. Fear stopped him from moving the body; even the thought scared him more than his dreams.

*When the moon turns red. When the moon turns red. When the moon turns red.*

As his brain started failing, the visions and the words on the wind ceased. As did the voices in his head.

*When the moon turns red. When the moon turns red. When the moon—*

More than just a departing ramble.

A threat. A promise.

*Tap-tap, tap-tap, tap-tap.*

Coming from the laundry window now.

He lifts his gaze back to Dawn to see her skeletal jaw opening and closing, those dark pits for eyes offering nothing but bleakness. Behind her, others gather, ready for the show.

*Tap-tap. Tap-tap. Tap-tap.*

Everywhere now.

He glances over his shoulder at the basement door. "I'm sorry, Maud. I love you. Always did, always will." Bone scratches against the glass, causing George to wince and draw back from the window. After knocking back the last of the bourbon, he zips up his jacket, squeezes the knife in his grip, and makes for the front door. The chill wastes no time wrapping around him as he descends the porch steps, but the chorus carrying on the breeze delivers an even greater sting.

"I'm sorry."

*Dawn* snaps her head around and lifts an accusing bony finger. Bones click in and out of place as she staggers across the mud.

*George Devlin.*

*A loving husband, father and grandfather.*

*Wouldn't hurt a fly, but killed twenty-three people.*

*Buried them on his farmland under the light of the moon while his family slept.*

*Goddamn salt of the earth.*

George lifts his chin from his jacket and runs the knife across his neck. His life flashes before him, a montage of mundanity interspersed with scenes of rage and brutality. *I'm sorry.* But he isn't. Different times.

Same people. Eyes on the moon that now carries only a pinkish hue, he sinks to his knees, wavering for a while before finally crumpling. Mud and the taste of metal fill his throat as the crowd drags him towards the earthy lid, singing their sinister chorus.

In the secret basement room, Maud adjusts her position in the uncomfortable plastic chair. She stares at the box on the small wooden table. All marriages have secrets, she tells herself. Coming up to fifty years now.

*Where are you, you silly old bastard?*

Memories fill her head, most of them happy ones: family dinners, nights drinking wine on the porch, grandchildren's laughter.

*Come on, George. Come—*

The basement door clicks.

"That you, George?" She pushes herself from the plastic chair and collects her stick from the wall. "George?"

It suddenly feels about ten degrees cooler, her skin prickling as she arrives at the opening.

The door creaks.

Silence.

Maud tightens her grip on her stick.

"George?"

A shadow appears against the stone wall.

The lightbulb fizzes off... on... off... on... off.

"Geeeeeeeeeorge!"

The silhouette is nearly halfway down the steps when the light fizzes back on. Maud squeals and drops her cane.

*Click-click.*

To the sound of bones clicking in and out of place, Maud takes a small step back. And another.

The wind howls, bringing further chill and a series of distant cries. A scuffing sound fills the room.

*Click-click.*

Maud's bad leg gives, pain exploding up her thigh as she and the table come crashing down.

*Click-click-click.*

More whispers and cries fill the room.

"Geeeeeeorge!"

She lifts her head and gets to her elbows, eyeing the spilled jewellery draped across her belly. Most of it is non-descript, but the four-leaf clover earring sparks a memory of an Irish girl called Maeve, a sweet lass with a penchant for singing and cigarettes. She lifts one in the air, almost able to hear the girl's throaty tones.

*Click-click-click.*

"Where did Maeve go?" she remembered asking George on return from one of her horse-riding trips.

"You know what these travelling types are like," he'd replied. "Easy come. Easy go."

It wasn't as though she never had her suspicions, but she was brought up to believe marriage extended beyond loyalty, an institution that withstood all external influences. And George always treated her with nothing but respect. Never angry, never possessive or controlling. All those trips with her horse-riding buddies, but he always saw her off with a smile.

*For better. For worse.*

*Click-click-click.*

Sometimes, she'd wake up in the middle of the night, George's side of the bed empty. Or go downstairs in the morning, only to see his boots next to the door caked in mud, even after cleaning them for him the night before. She'd say nothing, of course. And even less to the police officers who occasionally called. "Salt of the earth, my husband," she'd say to anyone who asked. "Proper family man." Everyone agreed. And all marriages have secrets; it was just the way things were.

*To love and to cherish.*

*Click-click-click.*

Maud shuffles against the cold wall, preparing to pay for her silence. She reaches for the cane, eyes on the gap in the wall.

*Click-click.*

The light fizzes out.

*Click.*

"I'm sorry! I'm so sorry!"

*Til death do us part.*

A strong gust wraps around the house, the moans from its timber frame and Maud's final cries consolidating into a blood-curdling symphony.

*Maud Devlin.*

*Loving mother and grandma.*

*Wife to murderer, George Devlin.*

*One hell of a blind eye.*

Her head lollops against the wall, the four-leaf clover spilling from her grip.

Beyond the walls, the breeze dies, and the moon turns pale.

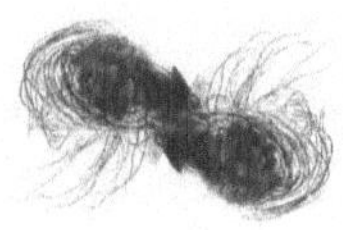

Later that year, the land sold for a bargain price. Months after that, the property boasted its most bountiful harvest yet.

The earth never forgets.

And sometimes, it bleeds before it can heal.

When

the

moon

turns

red

# Supplication

## by Richard Thomas

North of the city, past the cornfields, about two hours away from the hustle and bustle, the steel and glass, is a forest ringed with black pine trees that bend and sway, dry needles scattering across the dying land. Upon closer inspection, the dark trunks and deadened cones are not burnt, merely drained of all color. They form a perimeter around a hundred acres of deformed, swollen, twisted foliage—holly bushes with razor sharp tips housing crimson berries the size of grapes, oozing a sickly gray pus; oak trees with leaves eaten away by rot, holes punched through their faded skin, veins of purple throbbing within; tall grasses lining an archway that punches into the darkness, covered with tiny silver insects that scrabble and chitter across the bent, yellowing blades. It carries on the wind the echo of violence, the moment after a flurry of frenetic activity, consequence muffled by shock.

This entry to the forest is at the end of a long dirt road that twists and turns, past a lopsided shed full of tools and supplies, past the parking lot that lies cracked and abandoned, past the park signage that has crumpled and fallen due to neglect. To find this opening—blocked by a metal gate, by posts and chains, by barrels filled with waste, by fallen limbs and rotting wood—would be difficult. And so, it yawns in quiet contemplation and silence, no birdsong to be heard, no crickets chirping in communion, no small animals squeaking in fear, or desire. It does not appear on any maps, it does not hold a casual gaze, it does not welcome or call or lure. It is a wave of unease that rolls across a stomach clenched in knots, it is a sheen of sweat, a headache just beginning, a trembling in the hands that will not cease—an infection that is slowly spreading.

Beyond this trail head, mere footsteps into the woods, the temperature immediately drops, a chill filling the air, a pressure in the air akin to suffocation. Encased in that cool air is a moisture that would goosebump exposed skin, an electricity that would make hair rise, an ache that would cause hands to become arthritic. Farther down the path, mere steps inside the cooling shadows, the darkness contracts, pushing in, tighter and tighter, the opening fading and dimming, faster than it should. To glance back would be like peering into a telescope, but in reverse, getting smaller and smaller, the gap fading as it blurs and disappears—time, distance, and sensation warped and unsettling in its finality.

And yet, the trail continues.

It is not overgrown with branches, bushes, greenery, and vines—it is well-used, trampled into a flat dust. If it had rained recently, the muddy path might show footsteps, paw prints, hooves, and claws in a range of sizes from mouse to rabbit to wolf to bear—and beyond. Smeared and smudged, shifting in the squirming earth, deformed markings would have confused and distracted—too large, too many digits, too deep. At times, unrecognizable. But it has not rained recently, and so these markings are gone—blown and dusted, flattened and altered, hidden and erased. There is no evidence at this point in the path that anything other than man and common beast has been here.

And that would be incorrect.

To continue, is to meander up hills, and down bent paths again, ducking under a hanging vine that seems out of place, something from African jungles perhaps, a trickle of rusted water seeping across the path, a yellow sludge of slime at the edges of gray puddles, a sour smell of sulfur and decay filling the air. On the sides of the path, up into the trees and bushes, there are cracks in the earth, dried soil and rocky outcroppings, a warm, moist air pushing up out of the wounds, foul and thick, a great exhale from some dying creature, a quivering vibration shaking the woods, acorns falling, branches snapping off and crashing into the brush, before settling back into a quiet ache.

Tepid, dark waters fester down the hillside in the shape of something creek-like as creatures writhe and squirm in its tainted bath—three-eyed frogs splashing in the water before quickly turning belly up; crawfish with their deep red claws, clicking and clacking in an organized rebellion; mayflies dotting the surface with their bounty of deformed eggs before flying away, to die.

Just beyond the water, edges layered in scum and froth, there opens a brief respite to the choking darkness and thick, heavy air of the woods, in the form and shape of a field. Back out into the light, it would seem like an obvious time to find peace, fresh air, a sense of emergence, shackles shed in pursuit of normalcy.

That would be wrong.

In the field that opens—bisected by the dirt path like a zipper of teeth, like a wound stitched in haste, like a split lip that has swollen and bruised—there is a clearing, and in the center of that clearing is a cairn of bleached white bones. At first, they seem tossed in haste, a random gathering of like items, piled high and wide, in a desire to collect and separate the waste, rot, and stench. Upon closer inspection, a great design has been erected, starting with a ring of skulls, around this great pyramid of death. Tiny bird skulls, with their pointed beaks, and gaping sockets edge the perimeter before giving way to squirrels, rabbits, coyotes, wolves, and something human. Or at least, what looks human, at first. Upon closer inspection the skulls are too large, and too varied—some with extended foreheads, others with elongated teeth or tusks, and a few with horns in a range of execution, some curved, some black, some faded, and some branching off into antlers. This ring, this frame, this exterior wall to the pile of bones is locked in place in order to hold the femurs, vertebrae, humerus, sternum, and pelvis. Added to that are jawbones, rib cages, and what must have been a structure that once held massive wings together—feathers or leathery skin stretched tight, it's unclear. The details and markings on these bones are distressing—teeth marks, lines and crosshatchings, bullet holes and indentations—some severed cleanly, some snapped in a violent manner, fractured and sharp.

If it was just this sight, and nothing more, it might be tolerable, but the stench that emanates from the pile—it is a wave of oily translucence, decay, and rot in layers of sweet, sour, and bitter—in the heat of the exposed clearing only makes matters worse. A shimmer of musk and urine fills the air, suffocating as it expands, unholy waves of death, dismemberment, bloodshed, and suffering. The marrow that oozes from broken, shattered limbs collects bloated flies and iridescent beetles in a buzzing haze, pools of liquid like a festering moat, ringing the pyre with a mossy scum.

Scattered around this clearing is evidence of something else—a great quarrel, a territorial feud, an exorcism, or perhaps an evolution. There are ruts in the earth, uprooted plants and bushes, oily stains sprayed across the dirt and leaves. Flung across the foliage and stuck on thorny bushes are tufts of fur, strands of hair, and nibbled on bits of organ meat, and drying strips of flesh.

Moving away from the circle, like rays of sunshine, are exposed pathways, flattened grass, broken branches, and spilled liquids. These new trails expand in four directions, like the points of a compass: headed north, littered with feathers; headed south, where bark is scorched; headed east, leaving behind soggy moss and soft depressions; headed west, flattening everything in its path. There is no sound, only the aftermath, the furious silence of a gunshot spent, a limb snapped, a howl fading into nothingness, a scream that dies in mortal distress.

And yet, beyond this intersection, the path continues, on both sides of the structure, and then back into the forest, limping forward, deeper into the density and darkness, a welcome respite from the rolling stench. The air is sharp with pine, musty and earthy, the loam of overturned soil and wet moss a sign of struggling life—and the deeper the trail goes, the thicker it gets. There is life here, after all, spreading across the hills like a disease—seeping, growing, weeping, bleeding. It will not surrender, no matter how deformed, fractured, and splintered. It is alive in its desperation, unwilling to surrender.

As night slowly falls upon the woods, shadows spill across the trees, their leaves rising up to the sky, crowding out what bitter glow there might have been, a dampness returning with the darkness, a rustling as a stuttering wind pushes through the red maple trees, the ancient oak, the blue spruce and hickory, elm and walnut. Low foliage holds a pop of color in the encroaching dusk—the perfume of lilac in bursts of purple, the pink flowers of a redbud coloring the forest floor, a rush of magenta phlox across lush greenery, a bright layer of forsythia in a shrieking yellow. In spite of the damage and decay there is growth, after all, somehow flourishing in the otherwise dark, dank, musty, undulating land. Nature finds a way, it seems, to survive, in spite of the sickness, pollution, waste, and neglect.

As the woods descend into a heady gloom, the path pushes on—deeper, winding up and down, limping across ambling creeks, red clay seeping with infection, as the water lurches on. A humming of insects suddenly fills the air, violating the quiet with a reckless abandonment, rising and falling, the noise unbearable as winged creatures fill the air, latching onto trees, buzzing as they flitter about, tiny red beady eyes glimmering in the darkness. They have awakened after a long slumber and they are hungry, mating and falling to the ground—the deeper into the forest, the more shells are found, stuck to trees, littering the forest floor, a writhing mass of incessant droning. And then it is quiet, all at once, the silence deafening in its throbbing ache.

There is movement in the dark, bushes rustling, a crashing of tree limbs being moved, tossed, and broken. Smaller creatures dash and dance about under the greenery, a wave of swarming bodies headed into the heart of the forest, all pointed in the same direction. Above them, larger animals lumber and gamble forward, some on two legs, most on four, fur torn and stuck to thorny bushes, a yelping and barking as they amble forward. Larger still, there are other beasts that stomp and plow their way through the underbrush, clawing and swiping, fur and leathery skin, great horns stabbing the air, as they inhale and exhale. Sweeping through the grasses, unseen, other creatures slither with scales and rattles, intricate patterns woven into their hides, a hypnotic pattern glinting in the odd beam of moonlight.

A storm brews overhead, lightning splitting the sky as hail and rain pummel the forest. The clouds sweep over the dark sky as a jaundiced moon emerges, spilling weak light over the land with a trembling expansion. In a rush of wind and electricity there is a thundering boom, and a strike in the woods, turning into flame and fire, as up from the earth bubbles a crimson liquid, a glowing magma, a seeping redness that spreads across the ailing soil.

They gather in the dark, this flickering light, as one. They are legion, and they have been called. As the wind whispers, and the dying creeks babble, the darkness howls and snaps at the night. They are dispatched in waves, limping and galloping, frothing at the mouth, eyes bulging with rage. Fur and horn and claw and wing, fang and tail and talon and tentacle, in packs and herds and flocks and colonies. They rise up and disperse—defending and destroying, as the earth limps forward, waters rising, glaciers splitting, crops dying, her disease knowing only one cure.

Rebirth.

# About the Authors

# Jonathan Louis Duckworth

Jonathan Louis Duckworth (he/him) is a completely normal, entirely human person with the right number of heads and everything. He received his MFA from Florida International University and his PhD from University of North Texas. He is the author of Have You Seen the Moon Tonight? & Other Rumors (JournalStone Publishing) and his work appears in Best American Science Fiction & Fantasy, Vastarien, Pseudopod, Fantasy & Science Fiction, Beneath Ceaseless Skies, and elsewhere.

Bluesky: https://bsky.app/profile/jduckwriter.bsky.social
Twitter: https://x.com/Joduckwo
Instagram: https://www.instagram.com/jduckwriter/

# M. Edusa

M. Edusa (she/her) is a Kansas City transplant who enjoys writing in all genres, but her first great love is horror, particularly featuring queer and marginalized characters. Her professional background is in Law Enforcement and the military. She is currently writing short horror stories (and plugging away at a novel) from the Middle East, where she is stationed with the U.S. Army.

You can find her on Instagram @m.edusa.writes

# David-Jack Fletcher

David-Jack Fletcher is a gay Australian horror author and editor, specialising in work that emphasises the everydayness of LGBTQI+ individuals. His debut horror-comedy released early 2022 titled The Haunting of Harry Peck, and was an international Amazon #1 bestseller in several categories. It is now in its second edition, published through Lethe Press in February 2024. In June 2023, his debut novel, Raven's Creek became a #1 bestseller in several international Amazon categories, and subsequently won the 2023 Bookstagram Award for LGBTQ+ Novel of the Year. He has also appeared in several anthologies across the US, the UK, and Canada. He has recently released The Count, with upcoming titles including, Hell is other People (March 2025, Lethe Press), Indentured (April 2025, Truborn Press), Stowaway, and Wires in the Gut (2025).

David-Jack is also the co-founder of Slashic Horror Press, a queer indie press focused on promoting under-represented voices—and stories—in horror and dark fiction.

Facebook: https://www.facebook.com/davidjack.fletcher
Instagram: https://www.instagram.com/fletcherhorror/
Twitter: https://x.com/fletcherhorror
Threads: https://www.threads.net/@fletcherhorror
Bluesky: https://bsky.app/profile/fletcherhorror.bsky.social

# C.M. Forest

C.M. Forest, also known as Christian Laforet, is the author of the Benjamin Franklin award winning novel Infested, the novella We All Fall Before the Harvest, and the short story collection The Roots Run Deep. His short fiction has been featured in over a dozen anthologies. A self-proclaimed horror movie expert, he spent an embarrassing amount of his youth watching scary movies. He lives in Ontario, Canada with his wife, kids, three cats and a pandemic dog named Sully who has an ongoing love affair with a blanket.

Website: ChristianLaforet.com
Facebook: Author C.M. Forest
Instagram: @christianlaforet
Twitter: Bluesky: @authorcmforest.bsky.social
Exhaling slow, was ready to leave for work. Exhaling slow, was ready to leave for work. TikTok: @christian_writes_horror

# Philip Fracassi

Philip Fracassi is the author of the story collections Beneath a Pale Sky (a finalist for the Bram Stoker award), Behold the Void (named "Best Collection of the Year" by This Is Horror), and No One Is Safe!.

His novels include A Child Alone with Strangers, Gothic, and Boys in the Valley. His upcoming novels include Sarafina and The Third Rule of Time Travel.

Philip's stories have been published in numerous magazines and anthologies, including Best Horror of the Year, Nightmare, Black Static, Southwest Review, Centipede Press, and Interzone.

https://www.facebook.com/philipfracassi
https://bsky.app/profile/pfracassi.bsky.social
https://www.instagram.com/pfracassi

# Maxwell I. Gold

Maxwell I. Gold is a Jewish-American cosmic horror poet and editor, with an extensive body of work comprising over 300 poems since 2017. His writings have earned a place alongside many literary luminaries in the speculative fiction genre. His work has appeared in numerous literary journals, magazines, and anthologies. Maxwell's work has been recognized with multiple nominations including the Eric Hoffer Award, Pushcart Prize, and Bram Stoker Awards.

Find him and his work at www.thewellsoftheweird.com.
@cybergodwrites on Instagram and Threads
website: www.thewellsoftheweird.com

# Laurel Hightower

Laurel Hightower is a bourbon loving native of Lexington, Kentucky. She is the Bram Stoker-nominated author of WHISPERS IN THE DARK, CROSSROADS, BELOW, EVERY WOMAN KNOWS THIS, SILENT KEY, SPIRIT COVEN, and THE DAY OF THE DOOR, and has more than thirty short fiction stories in print.

website: www.laurelhightower.com
twitter: @hightowerlaurel
Bluesky: @laurelhightower.bsky.social
IG: @laurelhightower:

# Patrick Hurley

Patrick Hurley has had fiction published in Lightspeed, Factor Four, Abyss & Apex, Galaxy's Edge, and New Myths. A graduate of the Taos Toolbox Writer's Workshop, Patrick lives in Seattle where he works for Paizo as Managing Editor.

To read more of Patrick's stories, check out www.patrickhurleywrites.com.

# Ai Jiang

Ai Jiang is a Chinese-Canadian writer, Ignyte, Bram Stoker, and Nebula Award winner, and Hugo, Astounding, Locus, Aurora, and BFSA Award finalist from Changle, Fujian currently residing in Toronto, Ontario. She is the recipient of Odyssey Workshop's 2022 Fresh Voices Scholarship and the author of A Palace Near the Wind, Linghun, and I AM AI.

Find her at www.aijiang.ca
X: https://twitter.com/AiJiang_
Instagram: https://www.instagram.com/ai.jian.g/
Bluesky: https://bsky.app/profile/aijiang.bsky.social
Facebook: https://www.facebook.com/aijiang0/

# Jenny Kiefer

Jenny Kiefer is a Kentucky native and avid rock climber. Together with her mother, she is the owner and manager of Butcher Cabin Books, an all-horror bookstore in Louisville, Kentucky. Her debut novel, This Wretched Valley, released in January 2024.

Instagram: @_jennykiefer
TikTok: @_jennykiefer
Twitter: @_jennykiefer
Website: jennykiefer.com

# Joe Koch

Joe Koch writes literary horror and surrealist trash. Their books include The Wingspan of Severed Hands, Convulsive, Invaginies, and The Couvade, a 2019 Shirley Jackson Award finalist. His short works appear in Vastarien, Southwest Review, Nightmare Magazine, Children of the New Flesh, The Mad Butterfly's Ball, and many other anthologies and journals. Find Joe (he/they) at horrorsong.blog.

https://horrorsong.blog/
https://x.com/horrorsong
https://bsky.app/profile/horrorsong.blog

# Dexter McLeod

Dexter McLeod resides in western Kentucky, where he writes in the darker shades of Southern Gothic, folk and cosmic horror, science fiction, and the New Weird. His work has been published by or is forthcoming from Air and Nothingness Press, Chthonic Matter Quarterly, Dark Moon Books, Eerie River Publishing, The Horror Tree, KJK Publishing, Sci Phi Journal, and TDotSpec. His stories have also been performed in over a half-dozen volumes of Hawk & Cleaver's award-winning horror and science fiction podcast series, The Other Stories; in Hollow Stone Press' apocalyptic podcast series, Bleakwood; and in Dissonance Media's Gothic horror podcast series, After the Gloaming.

Visit linktr.ee/dextermcleod to connect with him online.
Bluesky: https://bsky.app/profile/dextermcleod.bsky.social
Goodreads: https://www.goodreads.com/dextermcleod
Instagram: https://instagram.com/dextermcleod
Letterboxd: https://letterboxd.com/dextermcleod/
Twitter: https://x.com/DexterMcLeod
Mastodon: https://mastodon.social/@DexterMcLeod
Pinterest: https://www.pinterest.com/dexterwmcleod/
Threads: https://www.threads.net/@dextermcleod

# Christi Nogle

Christi Nogle is the author of the Shirley Jackson Award nominated and Bram Stoker Award® winning first novel Beulah and three short fiction collections, the Stoker-nominated The Best of Our Past, the Worst of Our Future; Promise: A Collection of Weird Science Fiction; and One Eye Opened in That Other Place. Her work has also appeared in over fifty publications including PseudoPod, Three-Lobed Burning Eye, and Apex Magazine. She is co-editor with Willow Dawn Becker of the anthology Mother: Tales of Love and Terror (from Weird Little Worlds) and co-editor with Ai Jiang of Wilted Pages: An Anthology of Dark Academia.

Follow her at https://christinogle.com and on across social media @ christinogle

# Christopher O'Halloran

CHRISTOPHER O'HALLORAN (he/him) is the factory-working, Canadian, actor-turned-author of PUSHING DAISY, his upcoming debut novel from Lethe Press (2025). His shorter work has been published or is forthcoming from Uncharted, Kaleidotrope, NoSleep Podcast, Cosmic Horror Monthly, Brigid's Gate, Dark Moon Books, and others. He is editor of the anthology, Howls from the Wreckage. Visit COauthor.ca for stories, reviews, and updates on upcoming novels.

Twitter.com/ChrisOhal
https://www.tiktok.com/@burgleinfernal
https://www.instagram.com/burgleinfernal

# Em Starr

Em Starr (she/her) is an Aussie horror writer whose work has been produced by the NoSleep Podcast and has appeared in publications such as Fear of Clowns: A Horror Anthology, and Spawn 2: More Weird Horror Tales About Pregnancy, Birth and Babies. She lives in Melbourne, on Boon Wurrung land, with her husband and two dogs, Nikko and Franco (Dick-Dack and Fron Bon Jovi). She is currently writing her debut novel, a surf horror set in 1990s Australia.

www.emstarr.com.au
https://bsky.app/profile/emstarr.bsky.social

# Richard Thomas

Richard Thomas is the award-winning author of nine books: four novels—Incarnate, Breaker, Disintegration, and Transubstantiate; four collections—Spontaneous Human Combustion, Tribulations, Staring Into the Abyss, and Herniated Roots; and one novella of The Soul Standard. He has been nominated for the Bram Stoker (twice), Shirley Jackson, Thriller, and Audie awards. His over 175 stories in print include The Best Horror of the Year (Volume Eleven), Cemetery Dance (twice), Behold!: Oddities, Curiosities and Undefinable Wonders (Bram Stoker Award winner), The Hideous Book of Hidden Horrors (Shirley Jackson Award winner), Weird Fiction Review, The Seven Deadliest, Gutted: Beautiful Horror Stories, Qualia Nous (#1&2), Chiral Mad (#2-4), PRISMS, and Shivers VI. He has also edited five anthologies.

Visit www.whatdoesnotkillme.com for more information.
https://www.facebook.com/wickerkat/
https://x.com/richardgthomas3
https://www.instagram.com/richardgthomas3/

# SJ Townend

SJ Townend, an author of dark fiction, has stories published with Vastarien, Ghost Orchid Press, Gravely Unusual Magazine, Dark Matter Magazine, and Timber Ghost Press. Her first horror collection, Sick Girl Screams, is out Oct' 2024 (Brigid's Gate Press) and her second horror collection, Your Final Sunset, is coming in 2025 (Sley House Press). She also runs Bag of Bones, an indie horror press who raise money for charity and help elevate new voices.

Twitter:@SJTownend

# Mark Towse

Mark Towse is an English award-winning horror writer living in Australia. He would sell his soul to the devil or anyone buying if it meant he could write full-time. Alas, he left it very late to begin this journey, penning his first story since primary school at the ripe old age of forty-five. Since then, he's been published in over two hundred journals and anthologies, had his work made into full theatrical audio productions on shows such as The No Sleep Podcast, and has penned fifteen novellas, including Mischief Night, Nana, Poison Ivy, Gone to the Dogs, 3:33, and Crows. Chasing The Dragon, his debut novel from Eerie River Publishing, was released in March 2024.

https://www.instagram.com/towseywrites/
https://x.com/MarkTowsey12
https://www.tiktok.com/@marktowse?
https://www.facebook.com/mark.towse.75/

# Ally Wilkes

Ally's debut novel, All the White Spaces, was a Bram Stoker Award finalist, and her second novel, Where the Dead Wait, was one of Esquire's best horror books of 2023. Her short fiction has been published in numerous magazines and anthologies including Nightmare, Three Crows, FOUND: an anthology of Found Footage Horror, and Darkness Beckons.

Ally grew up in a succession of isolated—possibly haunted—country houses and boarding schools. After studying law at Oxford, she went on to spend eleven years as a criminal barrister, learning how extreme situations bring out the best (or worst) in human nature. Ally now lives in Greenwich, London, with an anatomical human skeleton, and far too many books about Polar exploration. Whatever the time of year, she's probably thinking about Halloween.

Instagram: @av_wilkes
Bluesky: @unheimlichmanvr.bsky.social
Twitter/X: @unheimlichmanvr

Holley Cornett

Cohal

Dexter McLeod

River

Em Starr

# Kickstarter Backers

A huge thank you for all your support!

Zack Fissel, Zach Anderson, Virginia Shay, Veronica V, TW Iain, Trip Space-Parasite, Toryn Todd-Rogers, Tim Woolworth, Tiffany Pedroza, The Underwoods, The Unawarewolf, The Creative Fund by BackerKit, Tanya Semmons, Talees McDonald, Susan Jessen, Stewie, steven duane allison junior, Stephen Loiaconi, Steph, Sirrah Medeiros, Shelby, Shaun Rosel, Seth Davis, Sebastian Zanker, Scott M Sidner, Scott Fedor, Scott Casey, Sarah Duck-Mayr, Roger Geis, Robert Helfst, Rob, Richard O'Shea, Ray Slakinski, Rachel, Peter Rosch, Paul, Olivia Sander, Nelson Truong, Molly, Mitch Hull, Mike Falconer, micwebs, Michael, Matthew Spinks, Lisa Para, Leanne Rodd, Lauren Kelsen, KT Wagner, KLGaffney, Kiera Carroll, Kendra Augustine, Kelly Keach, Keily Blair, Kalyn Williams, Kai Delmas, Joshua Tatum, Joshua McGinnis, Josh Buyarski, Jon Gensler, John O, John Fahey, Joe Kontor, Jessica Peter, Jessica Enfante, Jes Malitoris, Jeremy Kniola, Jennifer Rawlinson, Jenna, Jason McDonald, Jacob, Heather, H Michael Casper, Gracie Villegas, ExhaustedTech, Esa Eriksson, Erik D. Harshman, Erica, Engilbert, Eileen, Edward Abbott, Denise Mercer, Del Warren, David Thirteen, David Swisher, David Perry, Craig Brownlie, Conor Neilson, Connor Lehmann, Christopher Alden Hawkins, Chris Phillips, Chiara Cooper, Chad G, Cat Treadwell, Caroline Coriell, Candace, Bryan Holm, Bryan Cranston, Bruce Baugh, Brian Bondurant, Brandy Pastore, Beetective, Bearris, Asha Jade Goodwin, Aric S, Anthony R Cardno, Amy, Amanda Hickman, Amanda Cas, Alice Hanov, Alex, Adgee Harville, Adele.

# EERIE RIVER PUBLISHING

## NOVELS & COLLECTIONS
**After:** Horror Novel (2024)
**A Shadow Over Haven:** Nick Holleran Series (2024)
**The Roots Run Deep:** Collection of Horror by C.M. Forest (2024)
**Gulf:** Dark Walker Series Book One (2023)
**Breach:** Dark Walker Series Book Two (2024)
**Chasing The Dragon:** Horror Vigilante Novel (2023)
**The Naughty Corner:** Novella Collection (2023)
**Dead Man Walking:** Nick Holleran Series (2022)
**Devil Walks in Blood:** Nick Holleran Series (2022)
**The Darkness In The Pines:** Nick Holleran Series (2023)
**The Void:** Dark Sapphic Fiction (2023)
**They Are Cursed Like You:** Trailer Park Witches Series (2023)
**Infested:** Horror Novel (2022)
**SENTINEL:** The Bensalem Files (2021)
**NOTHUS:** The Bensalem Files (2022)
**Miracle Growth**: A Cosmic Horror Novella (2022)
**Helluland**: Urban Fantasy of Legends (2023)
**A Sword Named Sorrow**: Fantasy Novel (2022)
**Storming Area 51** Dark Science Fiction (2019)

## ANTHOLOGIES
**The Earth Bleeds At Night**
**Year of the Tarot:** Four Book Series
**AFTER:** A Post-Apocalyptic Survivor Series
**Elemental** Cycle: Four Book Series
**It Calls From Series:** Horror Anthology Series
**Blood Sins:** Linked World Anthology
**Last Stop:** Whiskey Pete
**Of Fire and Stars:** LGBTQIA+ Fantasy Anthology
**From Beyond the Threshold:** Cosmic Horror Anthology

## DRABBLE COLLECTIONS
**Forgotten Ones:** Drabbles of Myth and Legend
**Dark Magic:** Drabbles of Magic and Lore

## COMING SOON
**Seed:** Dark Walker Series Book Three
**Rotten House:** Horror Novel

# More from Eerie River

Eerie River Publishing is a leader in independent horror, dark fantasy, and dark speculative fiction. We are dedicated to publishing anthologies, collections, and novels from some of the best indie authors around the world. Our goal is to become a go-to resource for horror, dark fantasy, and dark speculative readers, and to provide a safe space for authors to share their stories.

Interested in becoming a Patreon member?

By joining our Patreon, you will be supporting our artists and authors, who work hard to produce high-quality and original content for your enjoyment. You will also get access to exclusive perks, such as early releases, behind-the-scenes updates, bonus material, and more. If you love dark fiction and want to support independent publishing, please consider becoming a patron today. Thank you for your interest and support.

www.patreon.com/EerieRiverPub

To stay up to date with all our new releases and upcoming giveaways, follow us on Facebook, Twitter, Instagram, and YouTube.

linktr.ee/eerieriver

The
Roots
Run
Deep
C.M. FOREST

THE
NAUGHTY
CORNER
THREE NOVELLAS,
INCLUDING TOWSE'S WILDEST OLD-PEOPLE HORROR YET, 'THE GENERATION GAMES.'
MARK TOWSE